MY FAMILIAR STRANGER

The Vampire Hunters

Knights of Black Swan, Book 1

by Victoria Danann

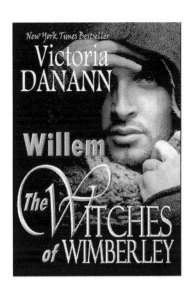

New York Times Bestseller
Victoria DANANN
Willem
The WITCHES of WIMBERLEY

JOIN MY NEWS LIST AND GET A FULL LENGTH

NOVEL FOR FREE.

http://eepurl.com/cL9TEH

PROLOGUE

"If I had a world of my own, everything would be nonsense. Nothing would be what it is, because everything would be what it isn't. And contrary wise, what is, it wouldn't be. And what it wouldn't be, it would. You see?"

—the Mad Hatter, *Alice's Adventures in Wonderland*, by Lewis Carroll

H E WAS TALKING fast and her brain couldn't process. On some level she may have known she was in shock. She'd just witnessed the murder of her family and that alone would be enough to disorient a person, but that was only the first painful trauma.

Thelonius Monq, tutor to the royal children opened a safe and produced a device that looked like a common remote control. When he pointed and clicked, a plain stone wall became a swirling vortex, a cylindrical tunnel of violet blue light that seemed to stretch to infinity.

Slowly it began to rotate like a tumbler. As it gained speed it gradually turned faster, finally creating an optical illusion of spirals going round and round that in turn created a hypnotic effect.

Elora Laiken stood staring at it, feeling numb in body, mind, and spirit. She tried to focus on what Monq was saying as he scurried around the lab, waist long, white hair swaying in time with his agitated movements. "I'm sending you off world."

In a moment of clarity she shook her head and whispered, "Off world?', then added, "No," just on the improbable chance that such a thing was possible.

If Monq heard the barely audible protest, he didn't acknowledge it. "Your destination's been calibrated to find the nearest life pattern matching my own." His gaze swept over her frozen pose and glazed eyes, but there was no time for sympathy. He grabbed her roughly and embraced her. "Look for someone like me. When you find him…" He removed the locket he always wore around his neck. "… give him this and tell him to retrieve the data."

He ripped the heavy costume away from her body, leaving her in the street clothes she wore underneath. Luckily, her black pants had a watch pocket and were tight enough to keep the locket and chain secure. He stuffed them inside.

Normally Monq would have had no chance of overpowering Elora. She was young, strong and at her athletic peak, while he was an old scientist and sometime sorcerer who spent his days puttering back and forth between lab and study. Two things were on his side: the element of surprise and the absolute trust of his favorite student. Using that advantage, he summoned what strength he could gather and pushed her through the opening.

"Be happy!"

In less than a second she had disappeared from view. He turned the device off and the portal resumed its disguise as a plain stone and mortar wall. Hearing pounding at the door, he rushed to put the handheld control in the blender he used to make smoothies and turned it on, thereby destroying any chance of assassins following her escape. There was just enough time to get to the other side of the room and wipe the hard drive before the ramming post broke through the door. He reached for a handful of peanuts then faced the intruders with a smile knowing that his life's work and prize pupil were far, far away.

———————

CHAPTER 1

THE THREE REMAINING members of B Team sat looking unhappy and feeling worse in the room known as the Chamber. The room was starkly masculine with walls of gray cement blocks accented with gas lit torches to give it an anachronistic feel. It was reminiscent of a medieval fortress, a reminder that The Order of the Black Swan was an old organization with a long and colorful history.

The occasion couldn't have been more grim. They were recounting the circumstances of Lan's death. Their teammate, Sir Landsdowne, had been far more than a coworker. Each was wondering, in his own separate head, how to properly mourn a guy who'd been at their side in so many life or death situations?

The three survivors were aware that they were being observed and evaluated by the unit's psychiatrist. He sat a few feet away on one of the bench seats, pretending to be invisible, but fooling no one.

They were near the end of the formal debriefing when there was a sudden, upward shift in temperature, like a hot sirocco wind blasting a door open. That was followed by a flash of light and a pop as something the size of a person curled into fetal position materialized a few feet above the floor. It didn't hover, but fell instantly to the stone floor, making a sickening plopping noise on impact. It appeared to be a bloody, quivering mass of scored meat partially covered by shreds of fabric that were either black, or charred, or blackened by blood.

The five men present stared at the thing. Even in their line of work, being accustomed to highly unusual phenomena, an event like that was astonishing. There they were – the scientist, the administrator, and three battle-hardened knights of The Order of the Black Swan, members of the elite B Team, frozen in indecision, a development that was foreign to men whose lives depend on quick thinking.

Being in charge and presumably wisest, Sovereign Sol was first to speak. "What the fuck?"

"What is that?" Ram asked with an Irish lilt. To punctuate his revulsion, his face was screwed up the way it might be if something smelled very, very bad. He shook his gorgeous head of hair and leaned forward just a little for a closer look with laser sharp blue eyes.

Rammel Hawking was the smallest member of B Team, or Bad Company as their peers liked to call them, at just about six feet one. He had a thick head of multi-hued blond hair that was at once a mess and a miracle. It waved, curled, stuck out in random places, and hung to just short of his shoulders.

Kay cocked his head then glanced toward Storm. "Shaped like a human."

Sol sniffed and took a step to his right as if he could learn more from a different angle. He answered for Storm. "That's not much of a recommendation. So are lots of things that aren't."

While the five continued to speculate, the blob on the floor began to move and moan softly.

Ram was slammed with an acute case of gut instinct. His solar plexus throbbed, sending off signals he couldn't begin to interpret. He didn't know whether the feeling was alarm or interest. Worse, he was disturbed by getting an autoerotic hard-on which was, at the very least disgusting, and, at the very worst, perverted. In a completely out of character moment, he went contrary to his usual impulsive, risk-taking behavior, and decided to err on the side of caution. "I have a bad feelin'. I think we should kill it. Kill it now."

Engel Storm was standing closest to it. He looked down at its face, into thin slits of eyes – greenish blue maybe. They were recessed behind gruesome protrusions of swelling that could make the most calloused warrior squeamish. It was then that the thing reached out to him. He hesitated for a heartbeat then knelt down, almost compulsively, trying to sort out the best way to gather it into a shape that he could lift and carry.

Sol stepped in. "Don't touch that! We don't know what it is. It could be anything... a machine disguised as organic matter, or a suicide mission carrying explosives, or toxic chemicals, or even a spell."

Storm ignored his boss's comments, not even bothering with the courtesy of a glance in that direction. He continued rearranging the mess as gently as possible.

Whatever the thing was, it was hurt. Badly. It groaned and whimpered in pain with every touch or movement, opening and closing its mouth in agony. It needed help. It had asked for help when it reached out to him and it was neither Storm's style nor job description to stand around debating precautions and policy when someone, or some *thing*, desperately needed assistance.

"Call the infirmary. Have them make ready for an incoming emergency." He said it calmly, but the teammates who knew him so well heard the underlying resolve.

Ram started toward the wall phone.

"Ignore that!" Sol said more forcefully. His glare and He was starting to sound exasperated and was glaring at Storm. "Are you not hearing me?" He wheeled on Ram, "Hawking, don't you move another step!"

Ram hesitated for two seconds, looking back and forth between Storm and Sol, before saying to the older man, "Sorry. You know we do no' do orders."

"I'm not joking!" Sol gaped at him. "Two minutes ago you were voting to kill it now."

Ram looked over his shoulder and shrugged as he punched in the infirmary code. "Stormy's call."

Engel Storm was six feet four with shoulders as wide as a doorway, but he still struggled to get to his feet with the thing in his arms. It was heavier than it looked. A lot heavier. Plus all the blood and oozing made it slippery. On top of that his sympathetic nature made him wince internally every time it tried to cry out in pain.

Seeing that Storm needed assistance, Kay had squatted down on the other side of it to help with the lifting. He pinned Storm with a pointed look and lowered his voice. "Might be better to have them send a gurney. You could be causing more damage." He looked down at the unidentifiable mass. "If that's possible."

Storm shook his head to get dark locks away from his eyes and turned that familiar, piercing, no nonsense gaze on his friend. "No time."

Kay nodded and tried to help lift the whatever-it-was so that Storm could get a good enough grip to carry. "Hope you know what you're doing."

Once Storm and Kay had it up and balanced in Storm's arms, the thing's head lolled onto his chest and stayed there. He walked as fast as he could. The infirmary wasn't far, but he was carrying what felt like his own weight. Fluids were leaking so fast that rivulets were running down his pants, onto his boots and under the soles, making for slick footing. A couple of times he had to jerk an upright correction to keep from going into a skid on the polished marble flooring.

He was breathing heavy, but speaking quiet assurances, words of encouragement delivered in short sentences. "Hang in there now. It'll be okay. We're almost there. Almost there."

Ram and Kay, passing him on either side, went ahead, crashing through the infirmary double doors a second before he arrived. "Where do you want us?" Ram shouted at the med staff that ran to meet them.

Within seconds the med team had taken Storm's burden and moved it onto a gurney. The team hustled toward the operating theater firing questions about the nature of the injury on the way. Then the three remaining members of B Team found themselves standing side by side staring at the blank side of a door.

Ram looked at his teammates. "What the fuck just happened?"

"I guess they're pretty good at their job. At least

they're fast," said Kay.

Ram nudged Storm on the shoulder. "Stormy. Good call. Let's go get a drink."

Kay snorted. "Is there ever a time you don't want to get a drink?"

Ram looked thoughtful as if he was trying to formulate a serious answer to that question.

Kay just shook his head, smiling: "Never mind. You can't help being Irish, but sometimes I think it's your answer to the meaning of life."

The two started away. Looking down at the front of his clothes, Kay realized he was wearing a lot of gore. "We might want to grab a shower and a change first."

After a few steps they noticed Storm hadn't moved. "You coming?" He continued to stand motionless, looking at the closed door. Kay eased back to Storm's side and spoke in hushed tones. "Hey. What's up? You've seen stranger stuff than this."

Ram had come up on the other side. "Lots stranger."

Storm blinked and looked down at the bloody mess that used to be his clothes. "These are gonna have to be burned."

"Yeah. Probably. Let's get cleaned up and grab a whiskey." Kay nodded and glanced at Ram like he was projecting telepathically. He was thinking they'd been through a lot and that it might be showing on Storm.

Storm looked at Kay and focused in. He could see that, from their point of view, this would appear to be odd behavior. Truth told, he had been trying to cover up a little depression since Lan's death. Intellectually he knew he wasn't responsible, but his heart wasn't in complete agreement.

"Thanks for the back up." He looked between Kay and Ram and even managed a little smile.

Kay raised an eyebrow that said, "I'm not buyin' it", but let it pass. He was a couple of inches taller than Storm, with sandy brown hair that streaked blond in summer and Northmen blue eyes. He was a poster child for split personality. At times such as these he was the essence of reason, the counsel you would seek if your life depended on good advice.

Then, there was the other side. Kay was a full blooded berserker from a legendary line that had immigrated to south Texas in the late nineteenth century and settled there. His name was actually Chaos Caelian. When he first landed on B Team, Ram started calling him Sir Kay, after the round table knight who was King Arthur's foster brother, thinking the play on words was pretty funny. Ram had a talent for keeping himself entertained. It caught on. Pretty soon everybody else was calling him Kay and it stuck.

Ram gave Storm a grin that showed off teeth so white and even you would swear they were veneers. But they weren't. "Anytime."

Storm had to admire Ram's ability to stay upbeat no matter what. He wasn't exactly what you'd call easy going. In fact, he was downright excitable, but he was also optimistic and fun. Sure, people got mad about the practical joking.

One time he hired a big Rottweiler from a guard dog service and left it in Geoff's pride and joy Porsche on his wedding day. Geoff wasn't especially amused about being late to the altar not to mention the poop, the claw scratches on the leather seats, or the drool marks all over the insides of his windows.

Another time Ram photo-shopped Bran's head onto a

porn shot of a guy with a fifteen inch dick and sexted it to the somewhat reserved girl Bran was wooing on Match-Me.com. The fact that the only way Bran could prove he didn't do it was to offer a nude meet-and-greet didn't help his case with the prim bachelorette.

Yeah. There were a lot of guys lying awake at night plotting payback. Somewhere in his future was a truckload of revenge coming down the road with a bead on that pretty, peaches and cream forehead. But if the world was coming to an end, Ram would find a way to make it sound like an adventure and bring his own party. Kay and Storm had decided long ago that he was worth every sweat drop of maintenance.

"I'm gonna hang out here a while and see what happens," Storm said. He looked back at the door. "You know. Curious."

Ram leaned his shoulder into the wall thinking he might as well get comfortable, but Kay surprised him by saying, "Okay. Call if you need us. We'll be close." They started away.

"Stop right there!" The door to emergency was swinging closed behind Sol as he stalked toward them.

Ram rolled his eyes. "Uh oh. Stepped in it." He looked at Sol. "Again."

Wanting to avoid making a public spectacle of disciplining knights, Sol motioned them into the waiting room that was empty at the moment.

"Look. I know you three are going through a rough patch. I've been there. Lan meant something to you. I understand that better than you think. Teammates always feel that way, but you just took it upon yourselves to make a decision that could endanger everybody in this unit."

He paused to shift his weight to a less aggressive stance and raked a hand over his nearly shaved head. "I know you've got problems with authority. Hell. That's half the reason why you're here. But you either compromise with the management – that would be me – or you're no good to this organization." He looked pointedly at all three, one at a time. "Is there any chance I'm making myself clear?" They nodded and tried to look sincere. "We have to finish the inquiry." Seeing their faces fall and shoulders slump he said, "But we can do it another day." They murmured thanks to Sol.

Kay and Ram slipped away. Storm went back to staring at the door. Sol left instructions at the nurses' station to call him as soon as they had something to tell about the new arrival. Anything at all. She responded that, based on what she'd seen as the gurney passed, it could be a very long time. Sol returned to Storm's imaginary post outside the O.T. door and suggested he go clean up and change. Storm thought that it was a small concession he could make to appease the rift he'd caused by disobeying orders and agreed.

He jogged to his apartment on the fourth level, threw the ruined clothes in a plastic bag, showered quickly, and jogged back to the infirmary. He sat down in the waiting area and began to do just that. Wait. After a couple of hours, one of the staff brought him a cup of coffee and asked if he would like anything to eat. He took the coffee gratefully, but declined the offer of food.

Six and a half hours later, the O.T. doors opened. Two doctors and three nurses emerged looking exhausted. The patient was being rolled to intensive care. Storm jumped to his feet and hurried over to the orderly bringing up the rear. "Do you know what it is? Will it be okay?"

The orderly glanced at him, but didn't miss a step. "Sir

Storm, Sol would have my job if I gave you info without clearance. You know that." They disappeared behind doors. Again.

Storm resumed his routine of alternately pacing and pretending to read "Two Wheel News". A half hour later Sol walked past the waiting room on the way to one of the doctor's offices. Storm hustled to fall into step with him. "I want to hear."

He stopped and looked at Storm. "You'll be briefed after the intel is evaluated." When he turned away he felt something pull at his starched cotton sleeve. His eyes found Storm's hand on his sleeve.

"Please." The way Storm said the word suggested it felt strange on his tongue. He let go of Sol's sleeve, but his eyes were still saying, Give me this.

Sol scowled and crossed his muscled arms while he looked at the floor. He wouldn't want it rumored that he was a soft touch. How do you keep twenty-four raucous second sons in line if they think you're easy? The answer is – you don't. You get replaced by somebody who's better able to keep his sentimental impulses in check.

Sol liked to believe that he showed no favoritism, but

Storm was one of those he had personally recruited. Storm had been a good looking fourteen-year-old, scary smart, and always in trouble. His school and his parents were out of their depth with a kid like him, but he was an ideal candidate for Black Swan. Sol told himself that he didn't feel any particular pride in Storm's record as he watched him work his way up to the Jefferson Unit B Team, the crème de la crème of Black Swan knights.

"Don't be thinking you can get around me with drippy words like 'please'. This stays between us."

Storm nodded. "Thank you."

The two of them were ushered into the office of the unit's surgeon general. They sat on the other side of the doc's desk in leather chairs, Sol with a handheld computer, Storm with twitchy hands and legs.

Storm hadn't been in a room with a window for hours. He knew how much time had passed, but there was a part of him that was still surprised to see that it had grown dark outside while he'd waited.

The door opened and the doc swept in with a rustle of white coat, wearing glasses on the crown of his silver hair, and looking exactly like the person you would hire for that role if you were casting for a movie. The clipboard he carried made a loud clack as it was half-tossed onto the desk. He sat and rolled the tufted, high back chair forward in a business-like manner while pulling the glasses down over his nose.

Rifling through the pages held by the clipboard, he said, "The patient is female, human, or close enough, though there may be some slight irregularities. One of those irregularities is the fact that she's alive. We can't understand how she survived whatever did that to her. There's not an inch of her body that is uninjured. In addition to practically being skinned alive, she has multiple broken bones and extensive internal damage. Several organs required repair. We're going to keep her soaking in an experimental ointment that Monq devised to prevent scarring, in hopes that it will help regenerate skin."

"Prognosis?" Sol asked.

"My medical opinion is that she shouldn't live to see tomorrow, but if I had to put up my own money, I'm betting she does. Don't know about the ultimate outcome or quality of life. But she has strength of will."

"I want to be kept current on any change. If she does live until tomorrow, the intensive care facility needs to undergo a little remodeling. I'm proposing a large, glass-front room facing the nurses' station so that the patient can be observed at all times. The enclosure will be designed as secure, but the integrity will partly depend upon cooperation from your personnel."

"A prison cell you mean," Storm said. The other two men looked at him like they had forgotten he was present.

Sol spoke quietly. "It would be foolhardy to do anything else until we know more about the… patient. If you were in my position, responsible for the safety of everyone in Jefferson Unit, you'd do the same thing."

Damn logic. Storm couldn't argue with that. If he was in Sol's position, that's precisely what he would do.

ELORA'S CONSCIOUSNESS WAXED and waned. During moments of fleeting awareness she registered blinding bright lights and masked people in blue milling around her body like it was an inanimate mound of flesh. She saw the remains of her clothing being cut away by one medic while another fastened a needle to her hand. When the locket was withdrawn from her watch pocket she tried to reach for it, but the protest came out as a moan so low it wasn't heard.

There was a muted, rhythmic sound of a machine beeping, keeping time with the throbbing of blood being pumped through her ruined body. Every pulse was torment. Every breath was agony.

Images of the massacre of her family, most of the clan, slid across her mind like a slide show followed by the gut wrenching memory of Monq's betrayal.

"Be happy!" was the last thing she heard as she was sucked into a giant vacuum hose. Mercifully, Monq had not seen that a layer of betrayal had been added to her stunned expression. In a matter of minutes, Elora Laiken's life, which she would have previously described as boring beyond compare, had been turned upside down and inside out. Under other circumstances her mind might have begun trying to sort through these events and make sense of them, but pain trumped processing. And there was pain.

Perhaps she was screaming. She thought she might have been, but nothing could be heard above the roar.

Over and over again she was beaten by the giant tumbler. Newly formed bruises, cuts, and abrasions became bigger bruises, cuts, and abrasions every thirty seconds until there was no part of her body that wasn't bleeding, broken, or swelling. At times she thought she might have heard a thump every time the tumbler carried her up and dropped her again, but it was probably just the brain filling in blanks. Just as she had begun begging the gods to kill her and end it, she was blinded by a bright light, felt a blast of cold air, and was slammed onto a hard surface.

After a few seconds of stillness she realized she had stopped moving. That's when the true punishment began. The pain was beyond describable, beyond mortal capacity to bear. But through the curtain of anguish, she thought she heard voices, muffled, maybe far away. The noise in the machine had left her hearing partially impaired. If she thought she would live and be whole again, she might have cared.

The only constant was pain. Relentless, excruciating pain.

She might have been in that swirling tunnel for minutes or hours or days. Trauma overrode all sense of time passage. She remembered a sudden burst of frigid air that instantly chilled her wet body and, as a parting insult, she was dropped on a cold, smooth, surface that was hard as rock.

What little wind was left in her lungs was knocked out of her on impact. At first she couldn't inhale and thought – hoped – she would expire from that. But, just when her vision was going dark, her body involuntarily dragged in an agonizing, ragged breath.

There were muffled voices. She tried to look around, but even the tiniest movement was restricted by pain, breakage, and swelling. Breathing hurt. Moving eyeballs hurt. She thought she was curled into the fetal position, but couldn't be sure. Through wet strands of hair she saw a blood-covered arm lying on the floor in front of her face. Beyond that, large boots moved into view; well worn brown leather with squared-off toes.

First, she tried raising herself on an elbow, but fell back when her wet forearm slipped out from under her. Once again her body slammed against the stone floor. She probably hadn't moved an eighth of an inch, an action that would have been imperceptible to onlookers.

The voices were saying, "…fuck. What is that?"

Next she tried to roll over onto a shoulder blade to get an idea where she was and who was speaking. Her first thought was that it must be assassins who had singled her out and were keeping her alive for ransom or torture. She opened her mouth to scream from the shooting pain of rolling over, but all that came out was a groan that sounded like it had originated somewhere else.

From the new position she could see blurred shapes. Oddly, she didn't get the sense that she was in danger or that they meant her harm, even though she thought she heard one voice say, "Kill it now". Surely she could not be the "it" to which they referred?

She reached out to a large shape in dark colors, holding her hand toward the figure until her fingers slowly began to curl under involuntarily as if all muscle control wilted away with the last of her energy. Just before losing consciousness, she remembered thinking that was very likely the last thing she would ever do and she welcomed the peaceful escape of the silent blackness.

Suddenly she felt herself being pulled and lifted roughly, aggravating her injuries, jabbing the wounds, making the pain even worse than before. In her mind she was screaming. Just let me die. Please. Just let me be still for a minute. And die.

When her body came to rest it was against a surface softer and warmer than the stone floor. She was being jostled, pressed into the upper body of someone who now carried her. She smelled aftershave, a hint of cigar, and felt the timbre of a masculine voice murmuring assurances about being okay, calmly, but breathlessly.

The recovery room nurse looked at her face, noticed she was awake and said cheerfully, in a strange accent, "Hey there. How you doin'?"

Elora tried to say, "Hurts," but through torn and swollen lips, it came out more like a hiss, "urrrrzzz".

"I know, sweetheart. We're taking care of you though. In just a minute you're going to get some really good sleep."

Now that she was lucid and responding to questions, they would grant the boon of deliverance drugs; drugs that temporarily allowed the sweet mercy of sleep. She tried to ask for the locket, but before she could make herself understood, she was claimed by a blissful wave of oblivion.

CHAPTER 2

BLACK SWAN FIELD TRAINING MANUAL

Section I: Chapter 1, #1

The plural of vampire is vampire.

T HE ORDER OF the Black Swan maintained fifteen operations facilities for paranormal investigations around the world. One of those was Jefferson Unit, located in the middle of Fort Dixon in New Jersey. There were a lot of advantages to housing an installation in a military no-fly zone with a doubly secure perimeter. It was forty-five minutes from New York by train and seven minutes by whister.

Thomas Jefferson had funded it in perpetuity with proceeds from his estate, which is why it bore his name. He'd personally experienced a paranormal event that shaped his spiritual and political perspective, and believed that the future of humanity was at risk without coming to a better understanding of mysteries that are typically denied by the collective while continuing to lurk on the edge of human consciousness.

For well over two hundred years Jefferson Unit had functioned with a series of secret government liaisons, each serving an appointment for life or until a violation of the mandatory vow of secrecy ended their… appointment.

Black Swan knights were trained to deal with several kinds of threats unknown to the general human population. One of those threats, their specialty in fact, was vampire.

Knowing where to hunt vampire was the easiest part. They liked cities that stay open late with lots of pedestrian traffic. That narrowed the hunting territory down a lot. In the Western Hemisphere, New York City was the number one qualifier.

THELONIUS C. MONQ had been teaching at M.I.T. when he was recruited by Black Swan. They offered him unlimited funds and support for research in exchange for cutting edge innovation and weaponry. He was part philosopher, part inventor, part chemist, and part magician although he would never list the last descriptor on a resume. He also had enough training in psychiatry to wear the hat of resident shrink when necessary.

The death of a knight was one of those occasions classified as 'necessary'. Surviving team members usually dealt with cross-currents of grief and confronting their own mortality, which was at risk on every rotation of duty.

That was why Monq was present in the Chamber for the debriefing when the "event" occurred. Hearing the recounting of the circumstances of death first hand meant that he'd be prepared should one or more of the team members arrive at his door one day looking for something needed, but not named.

He'd attended many such debriefings over the years, counseled many bereft friends and peers, and helped many warriors come to terms with whether or not they could or should remain on active duty. It was the only part of his job that was unpleasant.

His work at Black Swan was challenging and never dull, but nothing could rival the excitement generated by the arrival of the guest who spontaneously materialized from nothing; living, organic matter springing into being where only air and space had existed the moment before.

Nothing could rival that except for the locket he'd received after the patient was admitted to the infirmary. It was old looking, a mix of pewter and silver, decorated with a Celtic knot design. Handsome, but not particularly valuable. Certainly nothing that any adept thief would bother stealing.

What was valuable beyond his wildest dreams was the encoded data embedded in the design, an elegantly sophisticated and brilliant expression of "hide in plain sight". It took several days to discern how to extract and decrypt the data for analysis.

The locket contained a lifelong journal of scientific notation including experiments in the theory of interdimensional intercourse along with the postulational and philosophical musings of one Thelonius M., for Mallory, Monq; a name that was much too close to his own to be called a coincidence.

If the similarity of names wasn't already shaved too fine for synchronicity, his mother had once told him that he, himself, was almost named Thelonius Mallory Monq because of her appreciation for Thomas Mallory, but that she'd conceded to her husband's wish to honor his late father, Chester. If his mother had been a hair more insistent, he'd have been named Thelonius *M.* Monq, like the owner of the journal.

At the moment he was the only one who knew the locket was something more than a simple personal effect. It might have been selfish, but he wanted a little more time alone with the precious find before revealing its existence.

Like blood and tissue samples drawn from the bearer of the locket, the jewelry went through a thorough analysis. Within five days he could say with certainty that the information harvested was mind boggling even for someone such as himself, who dealt in the supernaturally improbable every day.

Knowing he couldn't continue to keep a discovery of that magnitude to himself any longer, he scheduled a private meeting with Sovereign Sol Nemamiah in his subbasement level suite of offices, labs, testing ranges, and living quarters.

Promptly at three the subbasement elevator opened. Clocks could be set by Sol's schedule. Monq welcomed him into the lab where he'd been scrutinizing his findings, dismissed his assistants, and invited Sol to make himself as comfortable as possible in a wheeled desk chair. Monq and Sol couldn't be said to be friends, but had a congenial business relationship and occasionally collaborated.

Monq began with an intriguing tidbit – the near identical match between his name and that of the locket's creator. When Monq paused to wait for a reaction, Sol emitted a small grunt as if to say, "If you're waiting for me to emote, you'll have to do better than that."

"Among my counterpart's notations was the theory of travel between dimensions and detailed schematics on a device he was building to attempt such a journey. There was no indication that it had been tested or that there were plans to do so. It seems the incident that delivered our guest to the Chamber could have been a lab accident or there may have been some catalyst. We'll know more when we can talk to the visitor."

Unsure how much technical information would interest Sol, Monq decided to give him the lecture and then dumb it down later if necessary.

"In order to explain what's happened, or I should say

my speculation, I need to tell you a story about P-Brane."
Monq's eyes darted to an erasable board. He stood, wheeled the board closer, grabbed a blue marker, and spelled out P-Brane. "It's a spatially extended mathematical concept that appears in string theory. The variable "P" refers to the number of spatial dimensions of the brane. String theory proposes eleven dimensions, but there could be multiple layers between dimensions vibrating at different rates which would make the number exponentially inconceivable."

Monq sat down. "Did you ever play a musical instrument?"

"Trumpet. High school."

"Okay then. As you know, musical scale doesn't slide from a perfect middle C to a C sharp. There is a continuum range that exists between each step in the scale. That's why piano tuners are so highly specialized. Perfect pitch means targeting a note and hitting it within its arbitrarily assigned center without wandering over or under looking for it. Most of us may not be able to distinguish all the infinitesimal changes in tone between C and C sharp, but that doesn't mean they don't exist."

Sol nodded his understanding, prompting Monq to continue.

"This event is proof that there are multiple dimensions that parallel our own in similar, but not necessarily identical ways.

"I believe our guest upstairs has come to us from another version of life as we live it. My findings indicate that the physical damage was caused, at least partly, from pushing a body designed for a different vibration, a different experience of reality, through the P-Brane. The fabric of her cells is slightly denser. Not much, but the tiniest variation would create the effect of being wedged through a giant cheese grater."

"She's human? Or essentially human?"

"Yes. Essentially human. And, as further proof of the parallel nature of her reality, she understands and speaks a dialect of Anglish, albeit with either an accent or a handicap resulting from her injuries. We won't know which until healing has progressed further."

"She'll definitely recover?"

"Physically. Yes. Actually, this slight variance in cell density is probably going to assist her recovery. The live cells I've been working with have been trying to repair themselves with uncanny speed."

Sol gave a big sigh. "Other differences?"

"We're sure to learn more as we go along, but I expect her natural temperature will burn a degree or so warmer than our typical 98.6." Monq stopped again. This time Sol made a circular motion with his hand adding a little impatience to the gesture. "Because of the increased cell density, she's heavier than you'd expect. And very likely stronger, too."

"How much stronger?"

"That would only be a guess at this point."

"Strong enough to be a security risk?"

"She featured prominently in the other Monq's journal. He was quite fond of her as a student, thought she was extraordinary in several ways. Based on reading the personal thoughts expressed in his journal, I have no reason to suspect a threat."

"But you don't know that for sure."

Monq shook his head. "You already know the answer to that."

"For all we know the journal could be part of a complex cover."

"Hard to imagine any sane being knowingly volunteering for what she's been through."

"We'll be making no assumptions."

AFTER ANOTHER HALF hour's discussion, they agreed to proceed to monitor the subject with caution and maintain a reasonable level of alert.

CHAPTER 3

A S WAS THE usual custom when a team member had been killed, B Team was given leave to go home and encouraged to spend time doing ordinary things with friends and family. The more ordinary the better. Storm decided to forego leave and stay on base. He was waiting at the main entrance to see Ram and Kay off. They'd be driven to the private landing strip on base just a couple of minutes away where Ram would hop the "company" jet to Edinburgh and transfer from there. Kay had booked a small charter to Texas.

Putting an affectionate hand on Storm's shoulder, Kay said, "You know that 'Confucius say' about being responsible for somebody if you save their life?"

"Yeah?"

"Well. It's not true."

Storm laughed good-naturedly. He was touched by

Kay's concern for his well-being. Neither of them would hesitate to die for the other, but both hoped they'd would never have to prove it.

"I'm good. It's what I want. Go home. Make home movies of you having marathon sex with your girl. Shop at the grocery store. H.E.B. isn't it? Annoy the hell out of your sisters. I'll be here when you get back."

Ram gave Storm a shoulder bump, strapped on an army issue duffle, flashed his signature killer smile and swung up into the jeep transport. That duffle caught Storm's attention. Rammel could afford the most expensive luggage in the Universe and people to carry it for him, too. But instead, he chose to throw his stuff into an unbleached canvas, surplus bag with "ARMY" stamped on the side.

Storm watched them pull away then headed back to the infirmary.

Elora looked a little better every day. In fact, her rate of improvement was remarkable. Her caregivers whispered to each other that she was beginning to look human. Scrapes and cuts turned into scabs. The swelling that had once obscured her features receded so that the structure of bone and cartilage underneath was becoming visible. The skin that had originally appeared to have been flayed from her body was restored to a random abstract of mottled blue and purple with an occasional streak of yellow or splotch of sickly green. Medical staff often developed a macabre sense of humor to cope with their jobs. One nurse joked that the patient was a work of art – a perpetually changing watercolor relief in an otherwise completely white room.

One day a nurse came in to check the I.V. and left the door open out of habit. Elora heard a masculine voice in the hallway just outside that caught her attention. He was asking questions about a patient. She couldn't place it at first, but knew the sound was familiar. And comforting.

One of the young doctors entered with the squishing sound of soft-soled shoes. On the way past the foot of Elora's bed she said to the nurse changing the I.V., "You left the door open again, Janna."

"Sorry, doctor. It's hard to remember to keep doors closed." The doctor peered over Elora with dark, almond shaped eyes and her best bedside manner. "Good morning. I'm Doctor Ivagi. Can you tell us your name?"

"Lorrr Aikei". Elora Laiken wasn't going to be possible until more of the swelling around her lips receded.

"Lor, can you tell us how you're feeling?"

"Urzzz." Pause. "Berrrr."

"It hurts, but you're doing better?"

"Hmmm."

Dr. Ivagi smiled at that. "Okay. Good girl. Now I need you to listen to this carefully. I'm putting a device with a button into your hand. Feel that? You're going to be able to control your pain meds yourself from now on. When you need more, just push the button and a measured dose will release into your I.V. Do you understand?"

"Ezzzz."

The medical community ascertained that patients would typically administer a smaller dosage of pain medication when they could self-regulate. As disabled as she was, Elora welcomed regaining even that little bit of control.

Improvement continued so rapidly that the medical staff looked forward to coming on duty so that they could marvel at the change from the day before. Everyone involved knew they were witnessing something unique, part mystery, part miracle.

One day when Monq stopped by the infirmary to check on the patient's progress, he found Engel Storm standing in the hallway looking through the glass of the newly constructed recovery room. Quietly he asked one of the nurses if Storm came by frequently. The nurse snorted at that and said he was a fixture, that the staff was so used to having him stand in that spot that they sometimes walked around it even when he wasn't there.

Gleaning a kernel of opportunity, Monq suggested to Sol that Storm be asked to assist with the discovery phase of evaluating the subject for threat risk. Storm was called into a private meeting during which Sol and Monq proposed giving him carte blanche clearance to visit within limits of medical advisability and suggested that he use the time to learn what he could. They went on to say they would provide him with a list of questions.

Storm was indignant. "I'm not a spy and, frankly, I'm surprised you'd ask this."

Sol leveled his gaze and spoke evenly. "It's not spying, Storm. It's simply gathering information so that we know the best way to proceed. We do that every day."

"You want me to pretend to befriend her for the sole purpose of gaining information and reporting what she says. Sounds like spying to me."

Sol glanced at Monq then continued. "Her name is Lor. So far she hasn't said much, but she is responding to treatment and soon we expect her to be able to talk without difficulty. We'd like her to be thinking of you as a confidante by then."

Storm shook his head, turned his back, and walked away, but stopped at the door. "It feels... wrong. It isn't what knights do." He turned around to face them. "And you both know it. Since when do we compromise principle for expediency? Or have we always done that and I'm the naïve tool who thought we were better than that?"

Monq started to interject. "Storm..."

Storm waved his hand and cut him off, turning to Sol, "I'll do it."

A moment ago Sol had been mentally digging in for what looked to be a lengthy debate. Switching gears, he nodded. "I thought you'd see things our way. You know you're one of the..."

Storm shot him a look that stopped Sol mid sentence,

but spoke softly. "Save it."

Sol's jaw tightened as it was his turn to be offended. "Remember not to disclose anything about who we are, where we are, or what we do."

"Like you need to spell that out," Storm sneered.

Sol opened his mouth to say something else, but Monq interrupted. "We have a sincere respect for you and your loyalty, Sir Storm. We know that you will always act in the best interest of The Order and the work we do to preserve the lives of innocents."

"Yeah." Storm threw one last challenging look Sol's way before he left, wondering who was looking out for the best interest of that poor thing suffering in the infirmary, who could very well be an innocent herself.

The nurse told Storm that the patient was resting quietly with eyes closed, but that she was awake and would respond if he spoke to her. Storm approached the bedside for the first time. Elora was dozing, drifting in and out of a morphine-hazed cloud, thinking she smelled aftershave and a hint of cigar.

"Hello," he said quietly. "My name is Engel Storm. People usually call me Storm. I'm the one who brought you here and, look, this is important. Before you respond I need you to know that everything you say and do is being monitored and recorded. You have no expectation of privacy... except in the bathroom... you know."

Two floors below, Sov. Sol Nemamiah, observing the exchange, rose from his chair so quickly it turned over. That was followed by spluttering a string of curses that would make a beet turn red. If Engel Storm wasn't the very essence of knighthood, Sol would personally kick his hard ass to the curb.

Monq, on the other hand, was smiling with approval. "Excellent. He told her the truth, but solicited her trust at the same time. Smart move."

Elora stared up at Storm. Did he seem a little embarrassed about mentioning the bathroom? Unquestionably handsome. And he was charming the caution right out of her – without even trying.

She would guess he was late twenties and big, almost imposing at that proximity. Locks of hair fell onto his forehead when he leaned over the bed. She was thinking that the world was full of people with dark hair and eyes and yet somehow it looked unique on him, like he was the only person who had eyes so black you couldn't distinguish pupil from iris. They reflected the light like black mirrors, giving him a look of intensity and something else, sincerity maybe.

"So your name is Lor," he continued. She shook her head no, slowly, with as little movement as possible. He looked confused. "That's what they told me."

"Elorrr," her voice rasped, but the 'ah' at the end got swallowed on an inhalation. It didn't sound like her. She realized her mouth and throat were dry. She'd been taking all her liquids through the I.V. and couldn't unclench her teeth without her face hurting. Plus, her voice hadn't been used much and may have been damaged from the screaming. "Elor?"

She knew that confirmation or denial were equally futile so she decided on blinking and staring. He smiled. From a reclining position in a hospital bed it was impossible to tell how tall he was, but he was certainly a lot taller than the nurse who had just left. The room was bigger than a typical hospital room, but he still seemed to occupy a lot of it with size and presence.

He wore jeans and a black tee shirt that showed off a

hard, athletic body kept in perfect condition. She couldn't see his footwear, but suspected he was wearing worn brown leather boots with squared off toes.

"Elor, I'm going to come see you whenever I can if that's alright with you. I know you can't say much right now, but when you can, and when you want to, I'll be here. We're all very curious about how you came to be... our guest... and about what hurt you like this..."

The nurse came in. "That's enough visiting for today." He nodded at the nurse over his shoulder without taking his eyes away from the pitiful creature in the bed. "Do you need anything? Something we may not have thought of?"

Elora stared at his face with a pained expression and spoke with effort. "Hwinnn. Doh."

Storm frowned just a little, but enough for a couple of small lines to appear between his eyebrows. A window was out of the question. They had just built this... holding cell... especially for her. And it had no windows. "We don't have a room for you with a window. I'm sorry." He seemed genuinely apologetic. "Is there something about not having a window that would retard your recovery?"

Elora shook her head almost imperceptibly and

thought Storm might have looked a little relieved. "You just like to look outside?" Tiny movement of her chin in an up down direction. "Yeah," he smiled. "Me, too. Okay. I'll be back tomorrow." He turned away then thought of something else. "You know, when you're better, maybe we can go outside sometimes. That's even better than a window."

"Thane ooh."

His smile illuminated his eyes, brilliant and beautiful as a cloudless night. "If there's anything else…"

"Ah ke."

He frowned again. "Sorry. I don't know what that is." The patient seemed to respond with agitation and he knew it wouldn't aid recovery if she was upset. "It sounds like 'ah ke' to me. Is that what you're saying?" She shook her head no almost imperceptibly. "You're not able to say the word clearly because of the swelling around your mouth?"

She sighed. "Hmmm."

"Pretty soon, maybe even tomorrow you'll be able to tell me. For now, I'll think of it as a puzzle and try to solve it."

He said he would come whenever he could. That

turned out to be every day for most of the day. Elora's speech started to improve and soon she was able to enunciate her full name and correct the misimpression.

Storm didn't ask a lot of questions nor did he reveal anything pertinent. He would make small talk about weather and ask how she was doing. Every day he asked if she needed anything and every day she answered that she wanted a window, but one day she followed that with a request for "locket".

"Locket." He looked perplexed. "You had a locket with you?"

"Yes."

"Are you sure it was with you when you came here?"

"Yes." Although she could form words at this point, it was still with great effort, so her sentences were as efficient as possible. "Saw them take."

He said he would try to find it. He asked the nursing staff about the locket, but no one was on duty who had been there when she arrived. While he was there, he made sure they understood that the bursar in the Operations Office had been instructed to release funds for whatever she wanted when she was able to ask, unless it was a weapon or something that could obviously be used as one. He anticipated the day would come when she would want some of her own clothes or toiletries and such.

Storm came back into the room to let her know he would look for the locket and asked if there was anything else before he left for the day.

"Where am I?"

"You're in a hospital unit on a military base. We don't know how you got here, but when you're better, we're hoping you'll tell us. Right now just use your energy for getting well. That's your only priority. Everything else can be sorted out later. Right?"

"Okay. And thank you. It's nice they assigned me to somebody named Angel."

"You speak German?"

"Some."

"Well, don't start setting the bar too high. It was wishful thinking on my mother's part."

SOL LOOKED UP from reading a brief when he peripherally noticed a shape standing in the open door of his office. Storm was waiting for an invitation. Sol took his feet off the desk and turned the swivel chair toward the door, motioning Storm inside. "Sir Storm. What can I do for you?"

"Sovereign." Storm replied in kind, using Sol's formal title, nodding in the way men with combat experience greet each other, as if there was an unspoken fraternal consciousness that only they shared. "It's about the patient upstairs."

Sol's mouth, held semi-permanently in a rigid line, turned up just a little at the corners. "I suspected as much."

"She says she had a locket when she arrived. Do you know where they would have put something she had on her person that was salvageable?"

Sol scrutinized Storm while contemplating whether it could do any harm to return the locket. He realized, of course, that the hesitation had already given away that he did, in fact, know something about it. The near-imperceptible release of tension in Sol's shoulders was the tell-tale signal that he had decided to give up the information.

"Go see Monq," was all he said. When Storm left

without another word, Sol called Monq and told him to expect a visitor momentarily. Then he gave Monq clearance to release the locket and brief Storm on the intelligence gathered so far.

After hearing Monq out, Storm paid a second visit to the infirmary. Elora was sleeping. So he pocketed the locket, planning to return the next day.

He decided to spend the evening researching Elora's supposed counterpart in his dimension. He grabbed a club sandwich to go from the hub diner and took it back to his quarters. When Monq had mentioned the similarity between his name and the owner of the locket, Storm had reasoned that, if Monq's hypothesis regarding near-parallel experiences held, there would be an Elora Laiken, or someone with a similar name, in their reality.

With relatively little effort the investigation revealed that there was, in fact, an Elora Laiken, born twenty-three years earlier, died at the age of twelve, daughter of a Briton royal clan. Cause of death was a freak case of pneumonia that didn't respond to any known treatment.

There was a short article written about her with a photo of her in equestrian gear, wearing a shy smile and holding a trophy with blue ribbon that was far too large for her.

The article said she had just won a steeplechase event and that she had personally trained the black, thorough-bred jumper named Crowers Keep. He noticed the photo had a video link. When he clicked it, the photo came to life.

The young Elora was telling an interviewer that the gelding, Crow, had been a gift for her ninth birthday, that he was two-years-old at the time, and that he had shown an extraordinary exuberance for running and jumping, the two skills required for steeplechase. With self-effacing humility and a relaxed and engaging style far beyond her years, she said she couldn't really take credit for training him, that she had more or less just hung on for the ride.

As if on cue the horse nudged her from behind with his forehead, forcing her to take a short step forward. She laughed, stepped to the side, looked up at him affection-ately and began to rub him between the eyes. As she talked, she took the blue ribbon and tied it to the horse's bridle behind his ear. "You should interview him," she said. "He's the one who ran the course."

The reporter asked her how she felt about winning her division.

She grinned. "Who doesn't love to win?"

She was as cute as a twelve-year-old could be with a slightly upturned nose and a scattering of freckles. It occurred to Storm that the little boys must have been crazy for her and it made him sad to know she didn't live to be someone's lover, someone's lifelong friend, someone's great-grandmother.

ELORA WAS AWAKE when Storm arrived the next day. Naturally she was happy to see him. His visits were the highlight of her day. He came through the door smiling like he had a secret, walked straight to the side of the bed and, without saying a word, pulled the locket out of his pocket. He held it by the clasp, dangled it above her heart, then slipped it into her palm and draped the chain over her hand so she didn't have to waste energy or hurt herself reaching for it. When he looked back at her face, he got all the thanks he needed from her expression.

"What else do you need?"

"Catheter. Out."

The nurses smiled at each other when he brought the request to their station. They knew that a demand for removal of a catheter was the harbinger of a patient getting well. He argued with the doctors on her behalf until they agreed that she could have the catheter out when she could walk back and forth to the bathroom by herself. She could start by trying to sit up on the side of the bed and he could help with that if he wanted.

When he returned to the room to ask if she'd like to try sitting up, he found her more than eager. Nurses stood on either side of the bed and acted as coaches.

They lowered the bed so that her feet would touch the floor, then told Storm he could gently pull her arms while she tried to maneuver her legs and turn her body. She groaned, but told him not to stop. By the time she was sitting on the side of the bed she was breathing hard. He sat down beside her carefully and she slumped over, leaning against him. The nurses praised her for making a big leap of progress and shuffled Storm off so that they could take advantage of the moment to give her a sponge bath and change the bedding.

Since she was staying awake longer at a time, they gave

her a TV remote. That's when she began her second life in a new world. She quickly realized that the tunnel Monq had pushed her through might as well have been Alice's rabbit hole. She was in a world similar to the one she'd left, but with differences that were inconsistent, surprisingly so.

She was a stranger in a strangish land.

Two days after sitting up for the first time, Elora's doctors gave approval for her to try to get out of bed and walk to the bathroom for a shower. It was a task equal to racing a triathlon. By the time she got to the bathroom with catheter and IV unit in tow, she was tired but exhilarated by the promise of feeling completely clean and having a few minutes' privacy. Her first peek at the mirror was shocking. Intellectually she knew that her face must look like the rest of her, but that didn't prepare her for the emotional upheaval. The face that stared back was a monster mask framed by flat, lifeless hair that could be road kill. They had given her some soap, shampoo, and an ugly cotton gown to change into after her shower.

The shower was adequate in size with nice water pressure and a powerful, triple shower head. Normally these are good things, but not in Elora's condition. There were no handles for starting or controlling water. In the end she had to give up and ask a nurse, who showed her that she simply needed to enter the water temperature she wanted on the keypad just inside the shower door, then press on or off. Not knowing what temperature that might be, she reasoned that she couldn't go too wrong with her own body temperature so she punched in 99.2. That felt pretty good, but she made upward adjustments a couple of times after she got used to the water. Washing her hair and body was no small accomplishment, because even the shower stream was painful.

She hurt in places she thought had no nerve endings. After she'd toweled herself off like she was made of blown glass, she tied the gown in place and thought that, without the catheter, she might feel almost human. There wasn't enough energy left to comb through her hair, but one of the nurse's aides did it while she sat on the side of the bed and tried to eat solid food for the first time.

She was still sitting up, her hair almost dry when Storm arrived. He didn't so much enter a room as conquer it. Like always he strode in like a person used to having his way – not arrogance or entitlement, just good old-fashioned self-assuredness. At least her long hair had managed a full recovery. With renewed life and volume, it shined with her true color: light brown with streaks of blond, out-of-this-world fiery red, and a hint of pink. In her dimension it was a common color usually thought boring. In this world it would only be made possible by spending many hours in the best color salon in New York and leaving many dollars behind.

"Wow." He smiled, "look at you."

The locket hung from its chain, surrounded by beautiful, thick hair that fell around her breasts, trying to separate into curls where it was dry. She still looked gruesome, but the swelling had receded around her eyes a little more. And now there was this gorgeous hair. For the first time he wondered what she was going to look like when she was well. Her speech was good. She had a beautiful voice, a pleasing accent unlike anything he'd ever heard, and a slight, but noticeable formality in her choice of words.

Doc du jour came in with a nurse while Storm was there and spoke to him as if he was a representative family member advocating for the deaf, mute patient. "Damage to organs or systems is minimal and the fractures have practically healed. No lingering evidence of concussion." The doctor glanced her way without really looking at her. "Now she's just one big bruise. Never seen anything like it really." With that he looked her way again. "Tomorrow, we need to get her up and moving around more. How would you like to help her walk up and down the hallway, big guy?"

"Sure." Storm looked happy about the prospect of having something physical to do. "Tell me what to do."

"We'll talk you through it tomorrow." He turned to leave.

"Hey, doc," Elora called. The man froze, as surprised as if she was a talking monkey. "What about the catheter? The agreement was that it shall be removed upon performance of a successful, unassisted round trip to the facilities. Isn't that right?"

With a little half smile, he capitulated and gave the order, adding that the I.V. could also be removed, since she was tolerating solid food.

The next day's trek began with the nurse bringing

traction booties. To Storm she said, "We have to get her on her feet again." After putting the booties on the patient's bare feet, they helped her to a standing position, nurse on one side, Storm on the other. "Just crook your arm like this so she has something stable to hold onto and let her lean on you for support. Let her set the pace. It will feel tortoise slow to you, but like a marathon for her. Once to the end of the hall and back today. Maximum. If she can't make it that far it's alright, but try. Okay?"

He turned to Elora. "Ready?"

Elora put one arm between Storm's powerful body and his bicep, then nestled in close. Looking at the top of her head he said, "Hey! You're tall for a girl. I hadn't noticed before."

Two inches shy of six feet does look tall on a woman.

"Uh-huh." Her equilibrium was off so looking around was risky. Plus she might be a tiny bit queasy and really didn't want to yak in the hall. That's what she thought they had called it on TV. Inching along at a snail's pace was still a big adventure, the first time she'd been out of the hospital room. It was exciting, but also so exhausting that she was practically asleep before she made it back to the bed.

The next day she was sitting up when Storm came in carrying a bag and looking very pleased with himself.

"What's that?" she asked.

He beamed. "I still can't get you a room with a window, but I've brought you the next best thing. A laptop."

A thousand images rushed across the screen of her mind. "That's a portable computer?"

"I guess that means you know what the internet is." She nodded. "How about credit cards?" She nodded again. He pulled the rolling table over, set the laptop up and plugged it in with an Ethernet cord. It had a mouse that detached from the housing for easy browsing. He pulled a plastic rectangle from his pocket and handed it to her. "Here's a credit card that you can use to get stuff on the internet. I can trust you not to buy cars, right?"

"No cars," she repeated.

"Yeah, no cars or home theatre systems. Also," he added offhandedly, "no weapons, or I'll be in more trouble than usual." He looked around the room. "You've got some space limitations. And please tell me you're not a jewelry freak." She shook her head no. "Good. You can use it to get… you know, clothes and," he looked at her hair, "hair ribbons or magazines or music and stuff. Here's the address you use for billing." He handed her a note. "And here's the address you use for delivery. They'll do overnight if you want."

"Hair ribbons?"

He cocked his head. "I guess women don't really wear hair ribbons, do they?"

"I'm, ah, hoping not."

"Well," he smiled, "you know what I mean." She nodded again and smiled back, wondering if this man was really this kind to monstrous looking clumps of bloody flesh in general, or just her. "Let's go for our stroll. You think we'll go faster today?"

"I'm positive you could. Go ahead. Save yourself."

"Elora!" He sounded surprised. "You have a sense of humor." He was looking around like he'd lost something. "So where do they keep the booties?"

She thought he had to be the cutest, most considerate person who had ever lived. Seeing this man with the shape and bearing of a warrior of old searching the room for traction booties made her throat feel tight.

"Aha!" He straightened from where he'd been opening drawers, holding up a clean pair of traction booties still sealed in a plastic wrapping. He seemed so pleased with himself, over such a small thing, that it tugged at her heart strings a little. "You know, you can order your own booties or socks or slippers or whatever."

He knelt down on the floor next to the bed and started pulling the booties onto Elora's feet like she was a child. He talked about the marvels of internet shopping while he was concentrating on making the booties conform to her feet.

"And movies! Just download them right to your own monitor. You're not going to feel like a prisoner anymore."

There was a slight break in his movement when he realized what he'd said.

She jerked her gaze from her feet to his face. "Prisoner?" She thought she saw a flicker of reaction. Was it self-recrimination or… guilt?

He looked serious all of a sudden. "I mean, being stuck in a hospital room has to make you a little stir crazy."

"Oh. Yes." Her eyes wandered over the room. "It

does."

He tried to restore the mood. She walked a little further than the day before and maybe just a little faster, although at that pace it was hard to tell. She was too exhausted to do anything but sleep when she returned to the room, but she woke in the middle of the night and wasn't sleepy. She turned on the laptop, found out that she had a lightning fast connection and that Giggle.com was the search engine of choice in this world. She tried some familiar name brands just to see what would happen. Some came up right away. Some came up as no matches. She ordered clothes that looked similar to what she would have bought in her world of origin, but a few luxury items like furry brown house shoes with moose faces and antlers, and low heeled, Ferragamo riding boots.

It might take other people longer to outfit themselves via cyberspace, but she was accustomed to shopping by internet. For a member of the royal house, actual shopping was too much of a production. Permission for such outings was rarely granted because of the expense of needing two guards to protect her from rumor rag reporters and paparazzi.

A couple of days later the nursing staff began delivering boxes as they arrived. No one was trying to hide the fact that the packages had been opened and contents inspected first. Things like skinny jeans were an optimism purchase since her body was still too swollen for her regular size. Tight pants would aggravate bruises anyway. At the moment she required nonbinding, elastic waist, loose fitting clothes. Thin knit sweats and hoodies would have to suffice.

When Storm arrived to a room crowded with shipping boxes and packing paper, he said something under his breath that sounded like, "Woden Almighty," but proceeded to help organize by ordering a rolling rack and hangers since they hadn't thought to build a closet. They also bought four stacking crates with front closures for things to be folded or rolled like in a dorm room.

She felt so much better in real clothes and it seemed to show in the speed of her progress. She was getting out of bed without assistance and walking up and down the hallway without leaning on Storm – which he missed, but couldn't begrudge. In two weeks the snail's pace had increased to a walk almost as fast as Storm's normal, long-legged gait for half an hour at a time. In a couple of days she added talking and laughing at the same time.

Sometimes they played chess in the infirmary break room with a guard posing as an orderly nearby. It was the only room that had a window. Elora loved to sit where she could see gardens and trees. Storm noticed that she would lapse into melancholy if he took too long to move. One day he sat back and asked tentatively if she was ready to talk about who she was, where she came from, and how she got here. She looked away and didn't answer, which was an answer of sorts.

Elora had grown accustomed to seeing the same faces every day. She knew everyone who worked in the infirmary, how many children they had, what kind of music they liked, what they liked to do for recreation, what had attracted them to their line of work and on and on. It was a win-win. She was curious and the staff enjoyed talking about their lives.

Designed according to the 'out of sight, out of mind' principle, the infirmary was located at a dead end, out of the way corner of the Jefferson Unit ground floor. It was a destination facility, meaning that no one went there unless it was necessary. Active duty knights endured enough uncertainty without in-your-face reminders of mortality and the fragile nature of human bodies. Situated well away from typical traffic patterns, they were not likely to casually wander by and be forced to confront the fact that The Order maintained a fully functioning hospital on the premises.

One morning Storm and Elora were playing chess in the infirmary break room while having breakfast. Storm wasn't really thinking about the game. He didn't need to. He'd always been – what did they say? – too smart for his own good. He had learned chess from a cousin in fifteen minutes when he was ten and had never lost a game since.

Elora took Storm's knight with her queen and, in the same tone one might use to inquire about the time, asked, "Why are they recording everything I say?"

He stared into those arresting turquoise eyes and realized that they had continued to get bigger and more pronounced as the swelling receded by tiny increments each day. For the first time he noticed her irises had yellow and gold flecks. Scabs had turned to ivory pink skin and it looked like there would be minimal scarring, if any. There was still swelling, but the black and purple bruising had gone through the even more gruesome green and yellow stage. What remained looked more like streaks of jaundice than anything. A nose had slowly emerged in the center of her face and was starting to look like it might be well proportioned and a little upturned like that video of the young Elora Laiken. The mouth that had once been nothing more than a gash in a hideous lump of flesh was now softening into lips formed in the shape of a bow. Her hair was pulled up in a severe ponytail, bound at the crown of her head so that all that thick, beautiful hair hung down to her collar bone, and swiveled enticingly from side to side as she moved her head.

He met her gaze head on so she would know he wasn't holding back or playing omission games with the truth. "Because you arrived here in a unique way, a way no one has ever seen or heard of, and because we don't really know anything about who you are, where you came from, or why you're here."

"I see." She sat back in her chair appraising him. "Reasonable. Understandable. Prudent."

"I don't know what happened to you, but it doesn't

take a genius to know it was awful and that you probably didn't volunteer."

Elora sighed and looked out the window. "Awful," she repeated. Her eyes seemed to be transfixed on something in the trees, glazing over as she took on that melancholy expression he had seen so often since her face had started to become more readable. Once again the whole trauma was playing across her memory in quick time.

After a beat or two she blinked and turned her attention back to Storm, hair swiveling across her shoulder to her back as the focus in her eyes took on a crystal clarity and seemed to drill through him.

"Who are you? What do you do? And what kind of place is this? Really."

It was his turn to lean back and study her. He forced himself to smile and deliberately broadcast nonchalant body language. "You want to trade answers? Question for question?"

She stared at him as though evaluating the pros and cons of the offer. "Have you ever heard of someone named Monq?"

"Is that your first question in trade?" He didn't try to

hide the fact that he was amused by the possibility of an intriguing game.

She pressed her lips together. "Your proposal is tempting. Because I do want answers. Of course you know that, don't you?" She nodded to punctuate that it was rhetorical. "But I don't want to have to tell my story more than once. I'd rather make a deal for one time. One time only."

Storm leaned forward, looking intent and serious. "I think that's fair. When you're recovered I'll set it up. You say when." He looked down at the checkered board between them, moved a piece, and she saw a fleeting hint of satisfaction flash in his eyes right before he said, "Check."

Her mouth twitched involuntarily. Yes. She was in mourning, but she was still alive and able to relate to the pleasure of winning. After all, who likes to lose? "Just tell me one thing now. Am I a prisoner?"

Storm kept his expression blank while his emotions ran the gamut. Those were the words he had been dreading. A hundred times he had rehearsed what he would say when this moment arrived and now his mind was a blank. His chest heaved with a big sigh.

"Elora, I've never deceived you and I don't want to start now. Your being here, well, you're a walking paranormal phenomenon. Oddly enough, or maybe not if you believe in synchronicity, that happens to be what we do. So this is probably a best case scenario as far as places where you might have landed. When we're reassured there's no reason to be afraid of you…"

Elora barked out a sarcastic laugh. The sound startled him, but Elora was the one who was sorry because the jarring caused some remnant abdominal zingers. "So I am being held as an enemy combatant?"

Storm looked like he was working hard at choosing his words carefully. "No. More as a phenomenon of interest."

"Hmmm. You know, in the place I come from, it is well known that befriending enemy combatants," she gestured toward the chess board, "as you have done here, is a far more effective method of extracting information than torture."

"You are in the infirmary unit of a special operations facility. No one here has either desire or plans to harm you in any way. If they did, they would have to go through me and my… associates."

"And you don't consider confinement harm?" His jaw tightened ever so slightly, but he didn't answer. "What has to happen for me to gain release?"

"Satisfy my superiors that you are not a danger."

"And how do I do that?"

He scowled at the board for a moment. "I haven't asked that. I'm not sure that's been defined. But I can find out."

"Have I met any of these superiors?"

"Not formally, but one of them was present when you... arrived."

"Why do you come here every day?"

Surprise crossed his face. That wasn't a question he was expecting. He repeated the question back to himself several times while Elora calculated what was taking so long and, more than likely, speculating as to whether or not he would lie.

"I come every day because I like to. Do you like having me come?"

She didn't hesitate to answer. "Of course," she smiled with a hint of flirtation that would have knocked him on his ass if he wasn't already sitting. "You're my angel."

She moved her queen. "Checkmate."

First, his stomach did a discomfiting, little flippy thing when she called him her angel. Second, he had to process the astounding news that he'd lost a game of chess for the first time since he was ten. Was he that distracted? Or was she that good? Either way, this was by far the best assignment he'd ever drawn.

They were almost back to Elora's room when the emergency double doors crashed open and a voice was on the P.A. urgently talking about codes. Three medics were moving fast, guiding a gurney bearing a young guy with an oxygen mask over his face. He was covered with blood. One of the nurses shouted, "Make way!"

Storm pressed Elora backward toward the wall, trying to make them as small as possible quickly, but gently keeping in mind that she was still fragile.

Three guys followed the frantic activity. Every one of them looked haunted, soberly watching that gurney roll away with grave expressions and a lot of blood on their own clothes. A couple of them looked to be bleeding from their own wounds.

In their dazed state it took a couple of minutes to register Elora's presence. When they did, their heads came up in unison as they looked from Elora to Storm and back again. Their eyes came to rest on the familiar way he had his hands on her.

Female personnel in the infirmary were common. A female patient wasn't just an oddity. It was impossible.

After their eyes had swept over Elora's still swollen and discolored body, they looked questioningly at Storm. He shook his head at them and turned Elora toward the door to her room. He knew that small, silent communication would be enough to suppress the spread of rumor, but that it was only a matter of time until everyone at Jefferson Unit was aware of her presence and wanting to know more.

Once inside she raised the back of the bed, sat, then eased onto her side trying to use as few muscles as possible. She pulled her legs up and adjusted her body so that she was half sitting and half curled into a fetal position.

"Are you going to tell me or are you going to make me ask?"

Storm closed the door. "You know this is a military base."

"So you're at war?"

"Not the conventional kind, no." He pulled a chair up beside the bed. When he sat down he was so tall that they were eye to eye. "I've promised not to say more until we've had a chance to ask you some questions."

She smirked. "You mean interrogate me."

"I mean ask questions. I've never been involved in this sort of thing so I don't know exactly what to expect, but I've spent half my life with this organization and I know their commitment to ethics. I swear you will not be treated badly. I know you have a lot of questions of your own and I'll make you a deal. You get well and I will move heaven and earth to get you out of here."

She didn't know if he had any actual power or authority, but she'd bet her booties that he meant what he was saying. Her eyes were getting too heavy to stay open.

"Okay." And just like that she was asleep, snoring lightly.

Storm pulled the covers up over her and left the room.

CHAPTER 4

BLACK SWAN FIELD TRAINING MANUAL

Chapter 6, #31

Because there is an erotic element in vampirism, female victims are the rule. Human females are usually not susceptible to the vampire virus, but survivors are rare because of massive physical damage. Consequently, the great majority of vampire are male, having contracted the virus through contact rather than bite. Ironically, the contact wounds are often received in defense of a vampire's target.

Chapter 8 #22

The paralyzing saliva of vampire takes effect within five seconds of entering the bloodstream. The saliva contains the agents of paralysis and the living virus. A victim infected with the virus, but not drained of

blood, will transition to vampire in two to three
days.

T HE WORST WAS over. The pain was quickly being relegated to memory in that merciful way the brain has of protecting us from perpetually reliving every atrocity visited upon us by life. She was completely free of medication and starting to look ahead to the possibility of getting out of the goldfish bowl where she lived. Her day to day progress was accelerating. Within another two weeks after witnessing the incident of D Team returning from assignment with a man down, all external indications of injury were gone. Her skin was flawless in color and texture. All signs of swelling were gone and Storm finally got to find out what she looked like. Beautiful.

One day on his way in to visit, he passed the glass that separated Elora's special accommodation from the hallway and stopped short so that he could watch her Tai Chi routine in progress. She was wearing Danskins, going through the movements slowly, deliberately, with the grace of a dancer and the muscle control of an athlete.

The form fitting tights revealed that she was neither too thin nor overly curvaceous. *Just right.* Because she was tall, her neck, arms and legs appeared long. Even after an extended convalescence she had retained enough muscular definition to indicate that she had been in top physical condition before the injury.

When she turned she caught Storm's shape on the other side of the window in her peripheral vision. To finish quickly, she sped up the routine to the much faster pace of Tai Chi when used as a martial art rather than an exercise or meditation regimen.

Storm was amazed. He was amazed by the swiftness of her recovery. He was amazed at the strength and beauty of the movement. And he was amazed by the woman. When she stopped, they stood facing each other, separated by a glass barrier that was almost invisible, but practically impenetrable. When he made no move to enter, she finally smiled and said, "I can't come out there. You'll have to come in here." And motioned toward the door.

He shook himself out of the spell that had him mesmerized and came through the door smiling. "Is that thing you were doing your way of saying you're ready to get out of here?"

"Yes. How about now?"

"I wish. I told you I'd get you together with the powers-that-be when you're ready. I know you want to be ready, but we need to be sure you're up for a series of questions. I'm not saying it will be brutal, but sometimes people are afraid of what they don't understand. Incredibly, that even goes for people who work here. The last thing we want is to set your progress back."

"There is only one way to find out. And I need to get out of here. Will you be there?"

"I can ask if that's what you want."

When shopping for clothes online, she hadn't thought to buy a face-the-tribunal outfit. After looking through the options several times, she pulled on charcoal gray knit pants and a black silk turtleneck, not too loose, not too tight. She tucked the pants inside her riding boots and already felt better. There was something about low heeled boots that gave her confidence, or, if not that, at least made her feel a little less vulnerable.

She stretched the walk from the infirmary by going slowly so that she could enjoy the change of scenery and the larger picture of the facility where she was being healed and held. There wasn't as much to see as she had hoped. Long expanses of hallways, white floors cleaned and polished to a gleam. They encountered a few people who were clearly curious about her presence. She supposed that meant that the medical staff knew how to keep a secret.

Storm was a little amused by the leisurely pace she was setting. He had, after all, seen her in action and knew she could move if she wanted to, but he didn't see any potential harm in allowing her to take her time.

On the 1st day of October, Elora entered the Chamber for the second time. This time she walked in on her own, accompanied by Engel Storm and an orderly who sort of doubled as a security guard.

In one quick sweep she took in the surroundings. The walls were interrupted by four equidistant doors, placed at the quarter points to balance the room energetically, and symbolically forming an equal-armed cross. The doors, made of high-polished cherry, added warmth to the room despite the intricate glyph carvings suggesting the arcane, if not occult. There were no windows other than a large, domed skylight forty feet overhead.

Everything was the same, so far as she could remember, except that the portable podium had been removed and replaced by a conference table with chairs, lamps, writing materials, and pitchers of water. Seated at the table were five senior level personnel including Sol and Monq, the exact number necessary to form a quorum for purposes of a deliberative hearing. One other guy sat off to the side at a table laden with tech equipment.

Elora's eyes went immediately to Monq. His hair was cut short and he wore a button down shirt and slacks which was an odd look for him, but it was still unmistakably Monq. For a split second she was relieved to see a familiar face, but that was quickly replaced with outrage over being betrayed and thrown into a machine that had scrambled her body inside out, then rendered her prisoner by depositing her into this strange place.

The fact that he regarded her with nothing more than a dispassionate objectivity enraged her even further. Without warning she lunged for Monq. In two explosive steps she had grabbed him by the front of his shirt with both hands and effortlessly dragged him to his feet like a rag doll so that they were face to face.

"Why?" The sound she made was somewhere between an accusation and a sob. "Why did you do this? My family trusted you. I trusted you. All my life. You were more than my tutor." Her voice broke. "I thought you were my friend."

At that point the dam that had been holding back all her unspent emotion broke open. She began to sob convulsively, at the same time she was shaking Monq back and forth. For the family she had witnessed murdered. For the agony she had endured. For the uncertainty and confusion. She continued to hold him up with her left hand while she brought her right hand back and formed a fist with every intention of striking Monq in the face.

Storm, having been captivated by the unfolding drama, like everyone else in the room, swiftly moved into action. He grabbed her by the hand she had drawn back and pulled her away and into his arms. She curled into him willingly, hugging him around the waist, and sobbing into his chest for what seemed like a very long time.

When finally she quieted and began to regain some composure, she felt humiliated by the public breakdown.

No one in the room was unaffected, not even the hard crusted Sovereign. No one in the room thought she was acting a part. Storm turned to Sol and suggested that they delay the hearing for a day.

Sol nodded. "Yes. Let the young lady have a day. Reconvening here tomorrow. Same time."

Storm called for Jim, the orderly/guard, who was waiting just outside the Chamber doors, and asked him to see Elora back to the infirmary. He leaned down and promised her that he would follow momentarily.

When she was clear of the room, Storm looked from face to face around the table. "I think there's a good chance that we know more about what's happened than she does. It was a mistake to keep her isolated and completely in the dark. It may even have been cruel.

"Surely you understand that she's the victim here. When she arrived here, in this very room, she was as good as dead. It's more than a miracle she's not. I know because I was there. If you saw what she's been through you'd know that nobody, no matter how zealous or masochistic, would willingly go through it. Give me clearance to tell her what we know."

Monq, still looking pale and shaken, slid down into his chair. "I, for one, am convinced that she doesn't understand what has transpired. I am also tending to agree with Sir Storm that it would be more productive to work together to sort this out. She needs answers as much as we do."

Sol leaned against the table. "Anybody mind if I smoke?" Sol didn't wait for an answer, but took out one of his little black cigars and lit it with an old-fashioned, ornate lighter, the kind you refill with lighter fluid.

Storm figured Sol must have listed off kilter. Smoking in the building, outside the poker room, was against the rules and Sol wasn't the sort to call a rule a guideline. He was strictly by the book.

"Dr. Monq is right. She has skin in the game." Sol winced slightly when he realized that was an unfortunate choice of phrase. "Any objections to briefing her?" Heads collectively shook from side to side. Sol surveyed the group, then nodded at Storm, giving him an implied "go ahead".

Storm judged this a good time to press further. "She wants out of that room. What does she have to do to make that happen?"

Sol took a lengthy drag on his cigar, exhaled, and said, "She just has to tell the truth. Supported by polygraphic evidence. When we're satisfied that everything is what it seems, we'll explore the possibility of alternate quarters." Sol looked down at his cigar. "That comes with a new set of problems, though.

"We can't send her out into the general population saying 'have a nice life and don't mention that you're from another dimension'. Likewise, we can't give her freedom of the building and grounds without divulging the details of who we are and what we do." He looked up at Storm again. "But I agree that we're not in the business of imprisoning innocents. If she proves by truthful statement that she is a victim, as you say, we'll figure something out."

Storm nodded again. Satisfied with that, he went straight to see how Elora was doing and tell her the news that she was about to get some well deserved answers to a whole lot of questions. He held back nothing that he considered pertinent, not even the information that there had been, in his dimension, an Elora Laiken who died young of pneumonia. He did not mention her royal heritage or equestrian hobby because he was interested to learn how closely these details would match up with the Elora Laiken who was now stranded in his world.

ON THE MORNING of October 2nd, Elora walked into the Chamber better prepared to face the assembly. Sol gestured toward a chair at one end of the table. Storm took a seat nearby on a lower bench. It was a cloudy day, still too warm for the heat of gas torches, so the light in the room cast a somber feeling.

Sol sat at the opposite end of the table. "Good morning, Ms. Laiken. Engel Storm has requested to be present at this hearing. Is that acceptable to you?"

Elora's eyes slid to Storm and back to Sol. "Yes."

"Good. We'll start by outlining the proceeding so that you know what to expect. First we'll hear your statement. You are welcome to tell your story in your own words, in your own way, but we request that you be as detailed as possible as that may eliminate the need for additional questions later. We will ask that you wear polygraph electrodes. The graph produced by the result of the test will be projected onto the wall monitor so that everyone present will be aware of the results instantly. Do you agree?"

Elora sat with her back straight and her chin up. "Yes," she said simply.

"After hearing your statement we will ask you to make yourself available to answer questions posed by the representative members of this body. That will be followed by a closed door session during which we will evaluate the product of this deposition and deliberate. Do you understand?"

"I do."

"Do you have any questions?"

"Not at this time."

"Very well. Are you ready to begin?"

"I am."

The proceeding was to be recorded by airbot, a device invented by Monq and his team of assistants for exclusive use by The Order. It was a tiny, round, audio video recorder about half the size of a pea, automatic and airborne with its own internal computer, powered by a microscopic nuclear cell. Because of its size and insignificant weight, the air propulsion system didn't require much fuel, which meant that it could power itself and record without interruption for up to half a year. Also, because of its size and steel gray color, it was practically invisible. If someone in the general population thought they caught one speeding by out of the corner of an eye, they would dismiss it as a fly, gnat, mosquito or trick of the light.

The airbot's program would be matched to a particular biological signature, also known as life pattern, and then stay with that person until recalled by the lab. It would automatically seek the best angle for maximum visibility and include people with whom the subject was communicating. Under normal circumstances, the individual being recorded could pause the recording while attending to matters of a highly personal nature by coded vocal command.

Sol nodded to the young, bespectacled man sitting behind the tech table who then came forward and attached wireless electrodes to Elora's temples. She was glad she'd pulled her hair up into a ponytail. The young man returned to the table, donned headphones, and turned on some electronic equipment, including the big screen. She knew exactly when it came on because all eyes moved upward and focused on the same place at the same time. The young man asked her to state her name.

"I am Elora Laiwynn Laiken, from the Clan of Laiwynn."

The tech guy nodded at Sol who then said to Elora, "Proceed when ready Ms. Laiken."

"Is it necessary for me to deliver my statement seated?"

"Not at all."

Elora stood and began to pace back and forth in front of the head of the table. "In the interest of detail, as requested, I'll not deliberately omit anything that might be pertinent. I'll begin with the events that precipitated the incident.

"I am, or rather was, third cousin to the king and twenty-eighth in line for the throne. As an indication of how unlikely my succession would be, they cease populating the list at thirty names. I am part of a large, extended family that is in turn part of a large and powerful clan. The royal family, including the thirty persons mentioned, live in the palace in London. The entire family, which means a large part of the clan, joins us there for certain occasions and celebrations.

"I am the oldest of six with three sisters and two brothers. We are educated on the premises, along with our higher-born cousins, according to our individual talents, interests, and the roles we are assigned to play within the family structure. Two of my younger sisters are already married.

"When it became widely accepted that the gods had left our world, we, as a society, turned to science and magick for answers. My principle tutor was an authority on these subjects. His name was Thelonius Monq." She glanced at Monq.

"In addition to the disciplines of classical studies and science which I learned under Monq's tutelage, I was trained in the martial arts of weaponless defense and also in ancient weaponry, the latter being principally about pride of heritage and custom. There was no expectation that these skills would ever be utilized in a practical sense, but cousins of the monarch have been prepared to serve as bodyguards for centuries. So we are expected to keep the tradition, in appearance if not in fact. In some ways the acquisition of these skills is curiously at odds with the somewhat prim and retiring behavior expected of royal girls.

"We were not allowed away from the palace grounds often and then only under highly supervised circumstances. I frequently argued with my parents that palace life was suffocating, that it was a gilded cage that stunted the potential of my brothers and sisters. I thought the future of the royal family would be better served by looking to more contemporary models of behavior. We were locked into a rigid formality that was out of sync with the times. Custom and a skewed sense of propriety had turned us into walking anachronisms. I knew this because we were allowed to watch some television shows and movies."

Gesturing toward a glass and pitcher she asked, "May I?"

Monq answered, "Of course," and rose to pour it for her.

She took a sip before continuing. "Our extended family was gathered together for Litha, the Feast of the Summer Solstice, called Mid Summer by some. It's always magical to see the main hall decorated for a holiday. A gathering of relatives is cause for celebration in itself since we don't often get to fraternize with people who do not live or work at the palace. Even the staff is excited on such occasions.

"On my last day at… home I had spent the afternoon in the kitchen observing preparations with my fifth cousin, Madelayne. And sampling some of the fare. We left in time to get dressed. For the Feast of Litha everyone wears costumes from the Middle Ages. I don't know why. They are hot and heavy. The younger generation wears street clothes underneath so that we can shed them after the mandatory festivities are complete and have a good time in each others' company. But that is neither here nor there.

"Dinner was just being served on tables decorated with flowers and local fruits of the season. The musicians were playing wyre instruments in a centuries-old style of madrigal. I had just joked with Monq that they were playing the hits from his secondary school years. I sat with Madelayne and some of my other cousins across the Great Hall from my parents.

"Most people had finished eating and traditional dances were about to begin. I heard shouts, then the sound of guns firing, automatic weapons. I know that because of movies. Most of us were so surprised we were… disoriented maybe. We just stood there waiting to see what would happen next."

Elora stopped, took another drink of water, visibly making an effort to retain her poise. She attempted a couple of surreptitious deep breaths.

"People wearing black and carrying guns came running into the hall. At first it seemed they were firing randomly, but it became clear their intent was to leave no survivors. There was screaming, people fleeing and falling on each other, on tables of food. There was so much blood. I looked across the room and saw…" Her eyes suddenly filled with moisture and her voice broke. She took another sip of water.

"My father had taken a decorative sword down from the wall and raised it to strike at one of the attackers. He was armed with a dull, badly weighted sword against rapid fire assault weaponry. I saw his tunic stain with circles of red that grew bigger as I watched. His face looked," she swallowed again, "so surprised."

Although she was successful at controlling the emotion in her voice, she couldn't keep the tears from over-flowing. They slipped silently from her eyes, running down her face and dropping on her chest.

"I stood there and watched. Watched them die. I didn't run. I didn't scream. I did nothing. I kept wondering when bullets would claim me. I even wondered what it would feel like. But I was not wounded.

"People around me continued to fall and I almost felt like I wasn't really there. Someone grabbed my hand and I was jerked back, almost off my feet. It was Monq." The steps of her pacing grew longer and slower. Sometimes she would get caught up in a point of the story and balance her weight on one leg as if she had forgotten she was in mid-step.

"Monq pulled me through the kitchen and into a service elevator. When we were inside and starting down, he took me by the shoulders and shook me. Hard. I felt my teeth knock together. He said I needed to make myself present in the moment if I was going to survive, but in that moment, I didn't care if I survived. The elevator delivered us to the subbasement level. When the doors opened he ordered me to run, saying that I was too big to carry. He sounded so very unlike himself. Fearful I suppose.

"I did not run. I was unresponsive. He pulled me all the way to his lab and ran to his safe. He was out of breath. I was thinking he must have lost his mind, that my family was being murdered upstairs while Monq was worried about securing his valuables. He pulled out a thing that looked like a remote control and, when he pushed a button, the wall next to where I stood opened up." Her head jerked slightly to her right as if she was reliving the moment. "Simply opened up!" She repeated it almost to herself. "And there appeared a tunnel that seemed to go on without end. It began to spin. I was entranced. I couldn't decide whether to think about how impossible it was that my family was massacred or how impossible it was that a stone wall just became a spinning hole.

"Monq was talking about a locket, something about calibrating for a life pattern match. He said, 'Look for someone very like me and give him the locket.' It made no sense." She looked at Monq. "At the time.

"When I realized that he planned to put me in that thing, I started to say no, but then he pushed me without warning. I wasn't expecting it because, well, because it was not something Monq would do. Monq is methodical. When he wants to persuade us of a point of view, he reasons with us until we see the merit of his argument and choose to agree. He does not use physical force."

She stopped for another drink of water. Sol handed her a crisp white handkerchief which she used to dab at her face. She had successfully stopped the flow and become determined to get through the rest of the proceeding without more tears.

"If you saw me when I arrived here, you can probably guess what happened. The passage from my world to yours was like being birthed through a sieve and pummeled in a giant tumbler at the same time. I believe I may have come through somewhere in here." She looked down at the floor. "And after a few moments I heard voices. One of them was yours." She looked at Sol. "And one of them was yours." She looked at Storm. "There were a couple of others. Storm carried me to the infirmary. I owe him my life. That was a little over three months ago.

"Since I've been here I've learned that your world is similar to mine, but not the same. That's the end of my story except to say that, if my family had lived, I would surely be a great disappointment. The shame I carry for my lack of action, having stood in place, having done nothing while all those around me died, is something that I will carry with me every minute for the rest of my life." She swallowed hard. "I was trained to act in defense of the king, but thought it was just another exercise in useless custom. A game of sorts. When the time came, I did not defend the king or even the people I most love. I have had many weeks to think about what happened. I have sworn to leave nothing out and want to append this vow to my statement. Should I ever again have an opportunity to act in defense of the life of another, I swear that I will not stand frozen in fear and dishonor."

She looked down at the floor for a few seconds while everyone in the room remained transfixed and statue still. Then she walked, with as much dignity as she could muster, back to the end of the table, sat on the designated chair and folded her hands in her lap in a dignified and ladylike posture.

"That is all," she said.

After a few moments, Sol cleared his throat. "Ms. Laiken, do you need a break before we continue with questions?"

"No." She had not looked at Storm because she feared seeing censorship on his face. She was sure that, after hearing her confession, there would be no more visits, No walks. No smiles. No games of chess.

One of the panel asked who might have perpetrated the attack on Elora's family, not because the answer to that question was relevant to the proceedings at hand, but because they were personally caught up in the story and wanted to know more. She gave a brief answer regarding clan politics with the disclaimer that any answer would be pure speculation; that there were rivals and that history indicated that a pattern of power shifts occurred every two hundred years or so.

Another asked what differences she had noticed between the worlds. She replied that any knowledge of differences had come from watching TV because she was not able to move about freely in their society. She said her initial impression was that their world was more advanced technologically, but lagging behind the pop culture of her world by about twenty years or so. By pop culture she meant such things as clothes, hair, makeup, music, and dance styles. She said she often had to ask about the use of certain phrases, but that she was making progress in understanding; that she listened carefully and tried to match the cadence of the Anglish dialect commonly spoken. She said there were many foods that were popular on TV that she had never heard of like fried chicken and burritos.

Another asked what sort of place she thought she had been in for the past three months. Since she was facing the wall with the giant, Black Swan banner, her eyes traveled upward and rested there for a moment before she answered. "I've been told this is a military base and that you carry out some sort of special operations. I know it must be dangerous work because you maintain a fully functional hospital complete with surgery. I witnessed the arrival of an emergency, not long ago, one that looked quite serious. The young gentleman's comrades were quite distraught and almost as bloody as was he.

"Also, I don't know the exact nature of what you do, but, even though I object to the decision my Monq made to send me through an untested device, I believe he intended to do a good thing. He thought he was saving me. The last thing he said was," she blinked rapidly, "'be happy.' I don't think his counterpart in this world would work for an organization that doesn't meet his ethical standards. People here have been kind to me."

Without thinking, Elora looked over at Storm and almost dissolved into tears again when she found nothing but admiration on his handsome features. "Storm. And the people in the infirmary. It would be difficult to believe that these people are on the wrong side of a thing."

Finally, Monq asked if she would go back if she could.

She sat looking at her hands for a long time before finally saying, "Even if I were willing to undergo the physical challenge, I don't think my world has the medical expertise to put me back together again." She looked up at Sol. "It would be a death sentence."

She sighed as she absently glanced up at the huge silk Black Swan banner, hung high at the center point of the wall facing the entrance. The background was the bright crimson of blood as it appears in the moment when it first leaves the body, before adjusting to the chemical composition of air. The rich red background was relieved by a white, equal-sided cross almost as large as the banner itself. In the center, in front of the intersection of the arms of the cross, was a large black swan. The graceful bend of its long neck was exaggerated by its bill resting on its shoulder, giving an impression of sadness or melancholy. A medieval looking script superimposed on a banner across the bottom read, *Furchtlosigkeit im Gesicht der Hilflosigkeit.*

"Perhaps that's what I deserve."

The walk back to the infirmary was slow and solemn. Storm looked at her several times, but said nothing. He stepped into the room behind her, closed the door, turned her around and, taking her by the shoulders, placed a tender kiss on her forehead. "I'm sorry for everything you've been through," was all he said. Then he left.

STORM WALKED AWAY with a newfound clarity, knowing why Elora had always lapsed into sadness and despondency whenever she was left alone for a few minutes. He realized for the first time how much courage it had taken for her to choose to survive the desolation of being the last one standing. His heart was swollen with sympathy, but also with respect and admiration. And he was determined that she wouldn't face the future without support and protection. And love.

THE HEARING HAD been both emotionally and physically taxing and she was used up. She put on her softest, warmest comfort clothes, turned out the lights, and crawled into bed where she immediately fell asleep.

When she woke three hours later, Elsbeth, one of her favorite nurses, was checking her pulse. "Hi."

"Hi, yourself," said Elsbeth. "There was a big guy around here earlier asking about you. Left you this." She picked up a worn paperback book and put it on the bed next to Elora.

As soon as she had left, Elora sat up and looked at the book. *Lord Jim.* There was a bright, lime-colored post it note sticking out so she turned to that page. It said, "Read this. – S."

Three sentences were highlighted: *I've been a so-called coward and a so-called hero and there's not the thickness of a sheet of paper between them. Maybe cowards and heroes are just ordinary men who, for a split second, do something out of the ordinary. That's all.*

CHAPTER 5

BLACK SWAN FIELD TRAINING MANUAL

Chapter 7, #7

The vampire virus does not impart extra human abilities such as shape shifting, teletransportation, transmutation, telekinesis, or dematerializing. Their bodies are subject to the rules of physics including gravity. They are not adversely affected by plants such as garlic. Their bodies will be seen in any surface that reflects images including mirrors. They do not require a ritualized special invitation to enter any premises to which they wish to gain access. The aforementioned traits are primitive folklore.

However, when excited, vampire are able to concentrate their physical abilities into bursts of power that result in extraordinary strength; not unlike that expressed under circumstances of stress by the mentally ill. In what appears to be an evolutionary survival trait, the cuspids commonly known as canine teeth, or fangs, do elongate and sharpen over time, but are retracted into the gums when not feeding. Vampire do acquire the uncanny ability to hypnotize humans as a dubious benefit of the infection. We cannot offer a satisfactory explanation for this phenomenon as of this writing. We do, however, suggest that field operatives be conditioned against vulnerability to this form of influence.

HEARING DELIBERATIONS DIDN'T last long after Elora left the Chamber. Addressing the quorum members, Monq confirmed critical parts of the story with evidence he had collected. He indicated that his other-worldly counterpart, whose handwriting, by the way, was an indistinguishable match with his own, had programmed the transportation device to search for his DNA signature. It was because Monq was located in the Chamber room of Black Swan and for that reason alone that Elora Laiken was delivered there.

Monq related his suspicions that her cell density probably translated to strength that would be super human, meaning strength greater than the strongest person, male or female. He went on to say that he suspected that, if she wanted out of her confinement, it would be hard to stop her.

"To use a pop culture expression, she is very likely 'hard to kill'. Regarding informing her as to who we are and what we do, I suggest we use the same method we apply when interviewing potential personnel. I will supervise the process myself. If the results are satisfactory, there is no reason not to allow her freedom of movement within the compound.

"However, she has sustained multiple traumas layering one on top of the other. She has witnessed the massacre of her family and all those close to her. She has undergone such massive injury to her body as defies description. And she now finds herself in a world that is slightly off center, similar, but not the same. There are some conventional points of reference for her, but, in some ways, that almost makes the differences more pronounced and confusing. Worse, she sees herself as alone. I will want to monitor her psychological rehabilitation."

Since no one voiced a dissenting view, he continued. "It cannot have escaped the notice of anyone present that there are larger implications. The method by which Ms. Laiken unintentionally pioneered inter-dimensional travel could not have been more crude or punishing, but that is not to say that other, more advanced societies may not have refined the means by which to slip through dimensional barriers heretofore thought impenetrable. Certainly we may review thousands of unsolved cases in the annals of The Order through the prism of this new information."

The ruling of the assembly was unanimous. If Elora Laiken passed the typical employee interview process, she would be given alternate quarters and freedom of the building and the courtpark. Eventually, when her emotional rehabilitation was complete, she might even choose to work for the Order in some capacity.

The next morning Elora was asked to participate in a series of tests. She was not told that her freedom depended on the outcome, but she was happy to be out of the infirmary regardless of the reason.

The Order's interview process had been developed and refined over time to a masterpiece of predictability. It consisted of a layering of psychological reactions probing the subject for predisposition to three behavioral factors: tolerance to evidence of unusual phenomena foreign to conventional or previously held beliefs, loyalty, and ability to keep confidential matters secret – long term. That portion of the interview was a three-hour process that starts slow and builds in intensity as the morning progresses. If any challenge rendered a questionable result, the subject was dismissed without ever knowing why or what they were being tested for.

Elora Laiken made it to the lunch break having matched the best score ever received by any of the Order's agent operatives including knights. After lunch, she was shown to a room with low, recessed lighting and asked to sit in an overstuffed reclining chair. After a brief wait, Monq entered and closed the door.

"Ms. Laiken, the next step in this series of testing procedures is a short session of hypnosis. Is that something you're familiar with?"

"Yes. In the sense that I know what it is, but not in the

sense that I have been hypnotized."

Monq nodded. "I see. The purpose of hypnotizing you is to determine how susceptible you are to suggestion. Do you have any objection to this?"

Elora thought about it a moment. "Well, I haven't had a chance to apologize for accosting you, but I am sorry. I hope you understand."

Monq studied her for a minute and then giggled, which could not seem more out of place on a person. Elora wondered if the oddity of that was part of the test. "No, my dear Ms. Laiken, I have no grudge or ill will toward you whatsoever. In fact, I feel our entire world owes you a debt of gratitude, because you have provided us with proof of a scientific theory that has been the subject of skeptic's ridicule for a very long time. This is the most important advance in understanding the structure of the universe since we learned to build fire. Whether intended or not, this was accomplished at great personal cost to you. And I haven't had a chance to thank you."

"You're welcome?"

He smiled. "May I proceed?"

"Sure." She shrugged.

Monq indicated that she should lie back in the recliner and find a comfortable position. An hour later, he had not successfully put her under. He called in one assistant after another, each one trained in hypnosis and hypnotherapy, to have a try. Eventually they were forced to conclude that Elora was one of those relatively rare individuals with a natural immunity to the process. She simply could not be hypnotized.

Moving on to the final portion of the process, he explained that they were part of a very old organization whose purpose was to investigate paranormal phenomena and, when necessary, protect the human population from negative supernatural events. For purposes of clarification, positive supernatural events were those deemed to be harmless such as sightings of guardian angels. Or Elvis.

"What qualifies as a negative supernatural event?" she asked.

"Vampire. For example. Which happens to be one of the specialties of this particular unit."

"You're not kidding."

Having heard that response a few times, Monq wasn't either surprised or put off. The best news was that she wasn't laughing. If she had laughed, he would have gone along and said something to the effect of, "Got 'ya. We like to hire people with a sense of humor." Then, with a pat on the back and a, "Thanks for coming in. We'll let you know in a couple of days," that would be the end of that applicant's future with The Order.

"Unfortunately no. I'm quite serious about this as has been every person who has worked for The Order for almost six hundred years. Since 1458 to be exact."

Intrigued, Elora asked, "And what happened in 1458?"

"You want the synopsis or the whole story?"

"Guess."

"Whole story." He waited for her nod and then smiled, seeming pleased with her answer. "Every time."

Monq suggested they move into his study which was a room covered with inset paneling and beautifully designed moldings. Two walls were shelves that held all manner of curious goods. He gestured toward one of two red leather chairs set at a conversational angle in front of an oversized fireplace. It was not yet cool enough for a fire, but there was a large monitor sitting in front of the hearth displaying a video of a roaring fire. She decided that this version of Monq was proving to be just as eccentric as her own Monq. The room was a treasure trove of contradictions. He poured pink sherry into two stems of very old, museum-quality crystal and sat down to retell a story he had repeated countless times and knew by heart.

"IN THE YEAR 1458 there was a Count who lived happily with his wife in the mountainous region where Germany borders Austria. Their goldenrod-colored house was as picturesque as a fairy tale, more stately than a manor, but smaller and less grand than a castle. It stood on the shore of an idyllic lake. The surface, which was usually still as glass, reflected the forest that lined its banks and changed color with the mood of the sky above.

The Countess, who was known to be both kind and generous, had not been blessed with children even though it was her fondest wish. So the affection that might have found expression in watching little ones grow was instead bestowed on other living things: her gardens and a small herd of black swans that decorated the lake named for them. Even though all the swans in the land were, by law, owned by the king, she secretly, in her heart, counted these her own pride and joy. She would never pass a window without looking toward the lake.

Every day she would walk to the water's edge with crumbs and tidbits delectable to swans and call the gorgeous bevy to draw near. They would glide effortlessly to the shore, reach upward with their graceful necks to accept her offering, bask in the light of her adoration and, though she could not know it, they returned her devotion in kind.

One day the Countess, taken ill with a fever, slept through the day until well into the night. When she woke, she saw that it was dark and that her husband was already sleeping. Her first thought was that her beautiful black swans would think she had abandoned them. Being fearful that they might be confused by her absence, she took a candle, and went to the kitchen in night dress, on bare feet. No one heard her steps as she passed through the halls. With no concern for her health, she gathered two partial loaves of bread and went out onto the wet grass, into the bright moonlight. In the ribbon of light that fell upon the lake she could see the shapes of her pets turning and gliding toward her as she whispered encouragements.

There was no warning, no moment to fear or entertain recriminations about choices badly made. Silently, in less than a breath's time, something emerged from the forest shadows and paralyzed her by sinking fangs into the nape of her neck. It dragged blood from her body in great gulps. Each time the flow began to slow from a puncture wound newly opened, the thing withdrew its fangs and struck again at another font of her body, ripping at flesh with ragged nails for no reason other than the foulest of depraved pleasures.

The Count woke with dread to the sound of strange, unearthly voices piercing the silence of night with a nightmarish song, beautiful and horrible at the same time. What he heard was the cry of swans as they rushed from the water, walking upon the land with wings spread to full span as they gave alarm. They threw themselves at the creature who tore the body of their mistress. Some were spared the monster's claws while others were struck down, swatted away without effort, but that is neither here nor there, as none escaped because, as everyone knows, a swan who sings pays the price with its life.

It was over before a single rescuer reached the door,

left standing open. There were none who could bear witness to the strange and gruesome event. What the Count and his servants found in the bright moonlight near the water's edge was the pale and lifeless form of the Countess, torn, ruined, covered with blood. And, scattered all around her were the pitiful, limp remains of black swans who had given their lives for love.

The Count, whose wife had filled his house and heart, was stricken with a soul-crushing grief and fell into a melancholy, the depths from which he could not be roused. Some years passed without improvement in his condition. Being honorable and dutiful by nature, he fulfilled the responsibilities of the office of Count, but enjoyed no personal pastime or comfort.

One rainy night, a traveler came to the kitchen door requesting shelter for the night. He was a tall man and old, at least old for the times, with gray hair beginning to show among the brown of his beard. He wore a heavy, hooded cloak over modest clothes and would have been unre-markable in every way except for a glittering spark of intelligence in gray eyes that appeared much younger than the rest of him. He seemed harmless in spite of his size, bearing, and the fact that he had a foreign accent. So the kitchen maid looked to the cook and scullery maid for their opinion as to whether shelter should be granted. Both shook their heads in a vote of nay.

Turning back to the hapless, wet pilgrim, she opened her mouth intending to turn him away, but, unaccountably, she opened the door and motioned him inside. She looked sheepishly at the cook and scullery maid, shrugging as she led the stranger to a bench by the fire. She bade him remove his cloak, sit, and warm himself dry and he did so gratefully. When the shivers of his chill subsided, the man introduced himself to the kitchen workers as Dankwart der Recke and asked the maid to humbly request an audience with her master on his behalf.

Thinking that the kindness she had shown by inviting the man in could be cause for her master's displeasure, she promptly refused. But, after lengthy and charming persuasion with assurances that the master of the house would benefit from such a dialogue, she passed the request on to a manservant whose station merited speaking directly to the Count. Because the Count no longer cared who did or did not spend time in his company, he agreed to have the traveler dine with him and speak if he must.

Count Jungbluth and Meister der Recke ate in silence except for the crackle of a fire and the raindrops hitting lead glass windows set high above their heads. Because the night was too cold to heat one of the larger rooms, they dined in a smaller room near the kitchen, at either end of a rough hewn table; the sort that might be found in an inn. The room was rectangular, as was the fashion, with stone floors and a fireplace six feet high and eight feet wide. It was comfortable and warm, intimate enough to enjoy a tankard and a tale on such a night. Above the fireplace there hung a battered, brown tournament shield, bearing a coat of arms with the image of two black goats with long spiraling horns rearing on hind legs, front hooves striking the air on either side of a noblewoman wearing a trailing green dress and holding a banderol that read *"Hab Mych als Ich Bin"*; take me as I am.

The Count scarcely glanced at his guest from supper's beginning to end. Nor did he utter a sound. He stared at the food, stared at the table, then stared at the fire. Der Recke, on the other hand, used his considerable power of observation to study his host, taking stock of his mood and character. When the meal was cleared and the servants retired from the hall, the stranger said he had heard the story of the murder of the Countess, his host's wife, and offered solemn condolences.

He said that he also had lost a wife along with a child, far from there, but in a curiously similar manner. He then began recounting tales he had collected on his travels; tales of monstrous creatures who bear a resemblance to humans, who stalk victims in the night for the purpose of desecrating their bodies and drinking their blood, creatures who are an abomination to the natural world. He said that there were many like themselves who had lost precious souls to the rampages of these demons he called vampire.

As the traveler told his stories, the Count began to listen with an interest possessed, but long forgotten. He perceived the pattern of threads that were common to all, threads that did not unravel upon examination, but formed the beginning of a tapestry.

Slowly the Count became aware of colors, textures, and sounds as if the curtain of haze that had fallen over his soul was clearing. For the first time in a very long while he was aware of the body he occupied; the sensations of breath, hands and feet, rump in chair. He grasped the tankard in front of him, appreciating the smooth feel of the pewter, and lifted it to his lips. As he leaned forward, bringing his full attention to bear so as not to miss the slightest detail, purpose rose from the ashes of his despair. Henceforth, his raison d'etre would be to learn everything that could be known about vampire and kill them. All.

That stormy night as the wind blew a gale outside, they talked and conspired. Several times the fire was stoked and logs were replenished, and an alliance was forged between strangers that transcended station and class. Dankvart der Recke had a fine mind, a Cistercian education in science, history and literature supplemented with sorcery, alchemy, and an uncanny ability to judge people truly. As a member of the First Reich College of Princes and Counts, Jungbluth had a treasure second only to that of the king.

The two formed a fraternal alliance bound by mutual heartbreak and called to the highest ambition possible; to protect the helpless and vulnerable from devils that lurk in the night. In honor of the Countess and her martyred birds, they named the organization The Order of the Black Swan. The emblem was placed upon a red background in tribute of the blood shed by innocents. That emblem formed both crest and talisman, an equal-armed cross with a swan superimposed at the center. The cross stood for the intersection of the four winds, a symbol that there is nowhere on Earth where predatory monsters may be safe from the wrath and righteous justice of the knights of The Order of the Black Swan. The swan is a memorial to love and courage, fearlessness in the face of helplessness, an elegant expression of death before dishonor.

So the two founders set about accomplishing their mission by trolling the families of the European aristocracy, which often faced the problem of two male heirs living to adulthood. As the custom was to keep family estates undivided and pass to a single male child, the quandary facing such families was what to do with second sons. The redundancy of healthy, adult second sons was both blessing and curse.

Placement in the clergy was politically expedient in terms of power and wealth. Such a position was a good match if the boy demonstrated the unusual traits of being a next-in-line who was both compliant and ambitious. Others, true to the rebellious nature typical of their place in the family hierarchy, sought out the Knights Templar and other enterprises where high-born progeny found career, adventure, and sometimes discipline as gentlemen soldiers or highly paid mercenaries.

The most exceptional of these were recruited by the Order of the Black Swan. There they found a purpose that far transcended an inheritance of wealth, power, or public recognition and, in the end, counted themselves the more fortunate between their older brothers and themselves."

ELORA HAD LISTENED with rapt attention to this tale of triumph over tragedy and every part of it resonated deep within her. "And there are no women knights?"

"No."

"There has never been a woman knight?"

"There has never been a woman knighted by The Order of The Black Swan. There have been a couple, in the sense that we bestow the title: Jeanne Hatchet, 1472, and Marie-Angélique Duchemin in 1798. Either the French are forward thinking or Jeanne d'Arc paved the way."

"And you just happened to have those facts on the tip of your tongue? Including dates?"

He shrugged. "Photographic memory." He handed her a little, soft cover book with a yellowish tan cover marbled like parchment. The title was in bold, black print. *The Order of the Black Swan Field Training Manual.* "This is available on electronic tablet of course, but I like to do some things the old fashioned way."

She opened to the first page. Near the top an italicized item caught her attention. *The plural of vampire is vampire.*

"Why have you given me this?"

"Because you have passed my test and are granted freedom of the building and grounds on a probationary basis. Since you are now able to wander the facility at will, I think it's important that you understand the nature of the work we are doing." Elora practically leaped from her chair, but he held up a hand in a gesture to 'wait'. "There is a condition." She narrowed her eyes. "I would like to monitor your psychological adjustment to your new situation with one hour sessions two times a week."

She looked at him suspiciously. "Psychotherapy?"

"Yes," he said flatly and without apology.

She looked wary. "Are you bound by confidentiality?"

"Yes."

"Agreed."

"Very well. You will be moved to one of the apartments this very day if you are ready to leave your nest at the infirmary. I know they will be sorry to see you go."

"Quite humorous," she said as she was moving toward the door. Suddenly she stopped in her tracks, the elated mood gone as quickly as it had arrived. She turned toward Monq. "Those boys I saw, in the infirmary, the ones who were covered with blood. They're vampire hunters?"

Monq rested a solemn gaze on her and nodded. "It's dangerous work."

"And Storm is one of them?"

"No. He's not one of them. He and his team are the best there is."

CHAPTER 6

NOT MUCH PACKING was required to get Elora ready to move. Almost all her clothes were already hanging on the rolling rack. Storm was able to carry the four crates all at once, which meant the two of them were able to make the move in one trip. Elora said goodbye to the staff on duty, accepted hugs and graciously thanked them for their care and patience.

Down one long hallway, turn right, and up the elevator three floors. She made a conscientious effort to remember the way. The apartment had last belonged to a knight who was no longer in service at this unit. There was a faded rectangle on the door where the name plate used to be. She didn't ask too many questions, because she didn't want to take the chance that answers might take some of the exhilaration out of the moment. Storm had made a point of saying these quarters were just temporary until they sorted out the best solution. She didn't care if she had to pitch a tent every night. She was just glad to be out of the infirmary holding pen.

The apartment had ten foot ceilings which made it feel expansive. After months of confinement in a small room, she needed all the feeling of spaciousness she could get.

The galley kitchen had a pass-through bar featuring a fully stocked wine cooler. Beyond that was a small dining area with glass top table and good view of the courtpark.

One wall of the living room was glass with double doors opening onto a balcony. Another wall featured a gas fireplace, recessed with bookcases on both sides and a big screen TV monitor.

No one would accuse the former resident of exploring his feminine side in any significant way. The décor featured minimal lines, function and efficiency with colors mostly in mahogany, black, stainless steel, and shades of green varying from forest to sage. But no expense had been spared and the result was an overall sense of quiet luxury.

The bedroom mirrored the living space and shared a chimney with the living room so that both featured a gas fireplace with everything else reversed.

The floors and walls of the bath were covered in multicolored slate to compliment the large, black, whirlpool bath at the ready to soothe the sore muscles of a tall person. The sport style shower was large enough so as not to require either a door or curtain to contain water spray. Most amazing was the generous expanse of mirror which had a TV monitor embedded within. When turned on, the TV program seemed to appear within the mirror like magic.

She opened the double doors to the balcony and stepped out into the open air. The fact that she could open her front door and walk out into the hallway anytime was a privilege she would never take for granted again. The fact that she could be alone, unobserved, was heaven.

As soon as Storm had set the crates down on the closet floor, she hustled him out, wanting to unpack and get ready for her big night out. Storm allowed her to give him the bum's rush. He helped her program a personal code into the keytouch lock, gave her a small, thin phone, showed her how his personal number had been programmed in, and promised to be back at 8:00 o'clock.

As he turned to go, a very big guy with impossibly orange hair walked up and nodded at Storm as he was punching his code into the lock on the door across the hall. Over his shoulder he said, "Hey, Storm. Somebody moving into Lan's place?" He opened his door and turned back for an answer. That was when he saw Elora in the doorway. He gave Storm a questioning look with eyes as big as golf balls.

"Not much." Storm shrugged like nothing was out of

the ordinary and walked away, leaving the guy standing there gaping at Elora. She gave him a big smile and a little wave, stepped back, and closed the door.

Ram and Kay returned to base the same day Elora Laiken moved into temporary quarters. Storm had invited her to come to dinner in the Mess, meet his teammates and celebrate her probationary freedom. He couldn't wait to show her off. They weren't going to believe what the lump of flesh had turned out to be. Not to mention what she looked like all cleaned up and put back together. Elora was thrilled about the prospect of expanding the limits of her environment, but nervous about meeting Storm's closest friends.

Thanks to the guy across the hall, Elora was no longer a secret. You would think that someone would have thought through how to spin her presence at Jefferson Unit. Sometimes the most obvious details fall through cracks. Within fifteen minutes Sol was getting calls asking about the girl in Lan's place. In turn, Sol called Storm and found out exactly what had transpired, also learning that she would be making an appearance at Mess that very night, a little after eight, in what would no doubt turn into a spectacle unless it was managed first.

Sol decided the most efficient approach would be to meet the situation head on and simply make an announcement in the Mess. So he showed up at 7:45 and demanded attention with a handheld mic. He spent less than five minutes explaining that the unit was hosting a visitor from another dimension, that she had spent the past three months recovering from wounds received as a result of pioneering a scientific exploration heretofore thought impossible, and that she would be staying for a while. He asked everyone to make her feel welcome and ended by saying they would get that opportunity soon because she was expected in the Mess in ten minutes. The knights and staff took it in stride. Truthfully, many of them had borne witness to things that seemed much less believable. As soon as Sol left, they went back to talking and eating as if nothing out of the ordinary had happened.

Elora finally decided on the black, Ferragamo boots, a silk skirt – the only one she had purchased – and the black Armani sweater with the zip front. She zipped the sweater up to just below where the locket fell between her breasts and left her hair down. When she looked in the mirror she thought the best thing about the way she looked was that she could be mistaken for an ordinary woman, out in the world without supervision or script or bodyguards or paparazzi. It wasn't all bad. Maybe.

She was standing in the kitchen watching the LED time on the microwave oven when she heard a light knock on the door. No matter how many times Storm told himself that he was an escort and not a date, he couldn't make himself believe it. He still had his hand in the air when the door opened. She was wearing the same shy smile he had seen on the twelve-year-old Elora Laiken from the internet video.

"Hi," she said with a little chest-high wave of her right hand.

"Hi. You look wonderful."

She took in his long sleeve gray tee and the black pants that he seemed to wear so often. They were made of a fabric she wasn't familiar with. It looked a little like leather, but, even without touching, it was obviously soft, draping over Storm's tight, masculine curves like silk. "So do you," she said and he laughed in that unguarded way that made him seem so genuine and comfortable in his skin.

In addition to spreading the news that Elora was across the hall, the carrot-topped guy was also responsible for letting it slip that the apartment had belonged to the recently K.I.A. member of B Team. She knew because, on the way to dinner, she asked Storm who Lan was. Storm seemed fine with the arrangement, but she didn't know how the other two would react.

The Mess at Jefferson Unit was quite elegant. It was a long rectangular room with an expanse of courtpark windows along one side. Next to the windows and along the opposite wall were rows of tables for four arranged dining car style with one end against the wall. The arm chairs were big enough to seat four large men comfortably, two on either side. Each table had a small, green shaded lamp. The effect was soft, ambient lighting; good for quiet conversation. The tables were set with herringbone white linen, heavy Waterford crystal glasses, and sterling silver. In the middle of the room, between the two long rows of tables for four were round tables that would comfortably seat six with wide aisles on both sides to allow for ease of service. The carpet was an upscale floral design with a dark green background. The walls were painted a soft shade of sage and accented by glossy white chair rail and moldings at floor and ceiling. It was relaxed luxury at its finest.

The Mess offered two meal seatings at dinner. The trainees, educators, and support staff ate at six. The knights, medical, and research staff ate at eight. There were also quick meal options in the bar and to-go meals in the hub diner and grocery.

There was no assigned seating in the Mess but knights usually sat at tables with their own team members. It was just a little like having the evening meal with family.

Even though the room full of people had taken the news that there was an inter-dimensional guest without missing a beat, everyone stopped and stared when Storm entered the room with Elora. She wasn't an introvert, but she didn't crave that sort of attention either. So she reverted to what she was trained to do – act like royalty.

Krisp, the maitre d', appeared out of nowhere, saying: "Right this way." Of course Storm knew the way to the table usually occupied by B Team, but he thought it was good of Krisp to go out of his way to make Elora feel welcome.

She swept along behind Krisp looking striking and statuesque. Storm was thinking she would have attracted stares even if she wasn't a paranormal headline. She didn't make eye contact with any of the occupants, but was able to ascertain that diners came in all manner of dress from shorts and flip-flops to leather jacket and tie.

On seeing their approach, Kay and Ram stood up for introductions as a matter of courtesy. Storm hadn't given them any details about her background thinking that was personal information; her news to tell should she choose to tell it.

As they approached the table, Elora sized them up, noting Kay's huge frame, distinctive cheek bones, square jaw, and concluded that she wouldn't want to fight this man. He immediately put her at ease with a smile and relaxed body language. He was wearing a collared shirt, brown twill pants that she thought were called khaki, and square toe boots that looked comfortably broken in. With a little twinkle in his eye he said, "Wow. You've changed a lot since the last time I saw you."

She raised her chin, giving the impression that she believed she was the same height and smiled. "Have we met then?" she teased back as she offered to shake hands.

She turned to Ram who was wearing faded jeans and an intricately patterned, black, tee shirt with a large AC DC and lightning strike symbol on the front. He took her extended hand in his, but when he said, "Hello," she jerked her hand back to her side like she'd been burned. Looking confounded and a little embarrassed he asked, "What's wrong?"

Elora pulled herself up until her presence was nothing less than commanding. Storm was fascinated, having not seen this side of her before. "Your voice is what's wrong, Mr. Hawking. It sounds very much like one I've heard before saying, 'kill it. Kill it now.'" Her tone was crisp and slightly imperious.

Ram's face fell when he realized she had both remembered and made the connection. Though feelings of intimidation were completely outside his range of emotion, he was unsettled. He looked at his feet as if trying to form a response and then glanced up to see that everybody in the room had stopped, looking at them like it was a show. His coloring deepened by a shade. "Hey! Find somethin' else to do for Paddy's sake!" He shouted a challenge at the crowd in general, then said, "Wankers," under his breath.

Knowing Rammel Hawking's somewhat unpredictable temperament, curious onlookers decided it was in the best interest of a quiet evening to pursue their own business in terms of dinner and conversation.

Satisfied with that, he turned back to Elora, leveled a steady, blue eyed gaze, and leaned in so that he could speak in a much lowered tone of voice. "Naturally I regret that, my girl. Please," without taking his eyes from hers he bent his head in a little gesture of contrition, "accept my apology."

She stared at him for a minute. He was just three inches taller at six feet one which meant that, in her Ferragamo riding boots, a stretch of posture, and a tilt of her chin, they were practically looking eye to eye. She took in the boyish features; flawless skin, full, pouty mouth, and mess of multicolored blond hair. All that came together in a perfection of creation with watercolor eyes that seem to waver between sea blue and midnight sky. She didn't know if she liked him, but her intuition said he was sincere and there was no arguing with the allure.

She took so long to respond that finally he leaned even closer, captivating her with glittering eyes that made the reflected light dance. He spoke so quietly it was almost a whisper. "Do no' be mad."

She was willing to bet that few people had ever been able to resist him when he turned on that adorable, puppy dog plea. As if he could tell the moment she relented, he smiled in a way that seemed far too intimate for a recent introduction.

"If we're goin' formal, 'tis Sir Hawking when we're on these premises, but I'd like it if you call me Ram."

He was close enough that she could smell that his breath was sweet, like a baby had just chewed spearmint, but his underlying scent was a heady mixture of musk and wild fern. She took a half step back and dropped her chin slightly. The man was dangerously disarming.

"Okay," she said simply and the wave of relief that circled the little group, still standing, was palpable.

Ram and Elora sat next to the window across from each other. Storm sat next to Elora with Kay across from him.

When they were settled in, Kay said, "So, welcome to

Jefferson Unit."

"Thank you. Until today I haven't really seen anything except the infirmary. And the Chamber room," she said as an afterthought.

"Is that the now-famous locket?" Kay nodded in the general vicinity of Elora's chest.

Storm followed his gaze and realized he didn't want Kay studying the locket too closely where it snuggled in the cleavage between her breasts. He mentally caught himself being irrationally possessive and gave himself a little internal shake.

Krisp came by and oversaw the pouring of water by a young man in a black vest and white waist apron. He rattled off chef's selections for the night. The only dish Elora recognized was chicken. She didn't understand pecan crusted, but she did like mushroom sauce so she asked for that. After everyone had ordered she admitted that she didn't really know the dish choices by name and would need to get a quick education on food. They were served a tomato soup course which she thought was delicious, but eating red soup can be worrisome when trying to make a good impression.

Kay turned to Elora, "So far what's the biggest difference between your world and ours?"

"Vampire," she said. "Plural. The plural of vampire is vampire, right?"

Kay exchanged a surprised glance with Storm, thought about it for a second and then asked, "How do you know?"

"Black Swan Field Training Manual, Section One, Chapter One, Number One."

Kay chuckled softly and shook his head. "I mean, how do you know there aren't vampire in your dimension? Only a tiny fraction of our population knows that our world is crawling with them."

Her brows drew together as she considered that. "Crawling?"

He smiled at having been called out on an exaggeration. "Okay. Maybe crawling is a bit much. I guess it just seems that way to us sometimes."

When they took the soup bowls away, Elora realized that Rammel had been staring at her the entire time. She knew that cultured persons do not initiate confrontations, but she'd had enough so she trained the full force of her attention on the man across the table. "Why are you staring like that?"

Kay looked from Elora to Ram. "Don't let him bother you. Elves are not known for manners."

Ram dragged his eyes away from Elora long enough to turn a sarcastic comment toward Kay. "Oh. And berserkers are the essence of Miss Emily Post I suppose?"

"What do you mean, elves?" she asked Kay.

Kay shifted in his seat and looked at Storm like he was trying to get a clue if he'd said the wrong thing. "You know. Elves. Pointy ears? Big feet?"

She looked at him waiting for the punch line or the clue that it was an inside joke. "You mean like in fairy tales?"

Rammel's head jerked up and his face took on a slightly pinker color as he sucked in a gasp. He had the look of a person who had just been slapped. "I am no' a fairy!" He stared at Elora with gaping indignation like she had just delivered the most profound insult in the history of effrontery.

"Um," Storm began, "elves and fae have been at war for over a thousand years. They hate each other." He glanced at Ram. "A lot."

It took a minute for Elora to realize that they were being serious. Somehow it was easier to accept the possibility of vampire than elves, maybe because of her love of fairy tales. She turned to Kay.

"Would you mind changing places with me?"

She caught a flicker of surprise, but, like a gentleman, he said, "Not at all," as he rose and surrendered the seat next to Ram.

Elora moved around to the other side of the table and sat. Turning to Ram she studied him for a moment, then lifted her right hand toward his hair and said, "May I?"

He nodded, looking completely intrigued. Gently she ran the backs of her first two fingers underneath the hair covering his left ear. *Feels like corn silk. Looks like spun gold.*

While Ram did his best to suppress a shiver, she lifted his hair up and out of the way until his entire ear was revealed. A beautiful, and, to her, quite magical, pointed ear lay close to his head. And it was her turn to gasp.

She thought she saw a firefly of silver dance across eyes gone dark blue, but dismissed it as a trick of the light. She touched the tip ever so slightly, looked from his ear to his eyes and back again, then suddenly grinned at him like he had just performed the most incredibly marvelous feat. It was the first time Storm had seen her smile turned up to the full power of radiance squared. The effect was breathtaking. She lit up the room.

Elora reluctantly pulled her hand away from Ram's hair, but continued to look at him like he was a bona fide miracle. "In your world, do you not have a collection of stories called fairy tales?"

Ram shook his head and drew his brows together slightly. "Sounds most disturbin'."

She smiled. "Well, there are some that are rather unpleasant, but most are magical and charming. These stories feature mythical creatures that do not exist in my world. Creatures like fairies, elves, dragons and ogres." She continued to stare for another minute, then, looking around the table she said, "Do you also have dragons and ogres?"

All three men looked at each other, simultaneously shaking their head and murmuring no's like they were disappointed to not be able to offer more.

Then Ram asked, "What's an ogre?"

She gave a brief summary after which Ram said, "Well, then we may have been wrong. Sounds very much like a description of Sol."

Laughing softly, without looking up from the salt and pepper he had been arranging and rearranging, Kay said, "It does raise an interesting question though." Everyone turned to Kay who stopped fiddling with the condiments and lifted his eyes to Elora. "If there are no elves in your world, then how do you know about elves?"

At that, trays arrived with the main course, which gave everyone time to consider the implications of the question. Elora stayed in Kay's chair, neither requesting nor offering to switch back. In the infirmary she had eaten what she was served without caring to ask for dish names or ingredients. Now she was more interested in the subject. She inquired about the nuts used in the chicken breast topping. Storm asked for a bite which she fed him from her fork, not realizing that the simple act, initiated innocently, can imply the sensuality of foreplay. He hummed approval and confirmed that the crust was laden with pecans.

After asking about every other entree on the table and

sampling each, she turned to Kay and said, "Are you thinking that elves lived in my dimension in our prehistoric past? That's what it would have to be, since there is no pictorial or linguistic record. Or are you thinking that there was an elfin visit to my dimension and it caused enough of a stir to become part of the race consciousness?"

"Something like that. When did elves first appear in your literature?"

"I'm not an authority on the subject, but I'm thinking between three and five hundred years ago?"

"Sounds like a visit, accidental or otherwise."

"Like in *Accidental Tourist*?"

Kay nodded. Every time Elora discovered a parallel between her world and this she relaxed a little more.

She continued, with no discernible segue. "Ummm. What's a berserker?"

All three of the men were amused by the abrupt change of subject. Storm explained that the berserker gene, which causes rage behavior, is triggered by battle circumstances or threat of violence and that the rampage fever, once engaged, is almost impossible to subjugate until the berserker perceives the threat is neutralized. They went on to explain that berserkers weren't usually candidates for Black Swan, but that Kay had more tolerance than usual for situations of extreme stress. Storm said with a tone of pride that Kay had mastered his demon.

"So you're saying berserkers go out of control?"

Ram barked out a laugh, "Out of control? Wacked up insane mother fuckers is what they are."

Elora stared at Ram, not so much because she was offended by the language, but because Ram made even the word "fucker" sound appealing somehow. Storm and Kay joined her in staring at Ram, but for different reasons.

"What?" Ram asked innocently.

"Where I am from," Elora interceded, letting him off the hook, "your accent would be typical in a place called Ireland. Is there such a place here?"

Ram looked delighted by the question. "Aye. 'Tis my home. We have had a truce with fairies for two hundred years. We do no' go to Scotia uninvited and they do no' cross the borders of Ireland or Wales. Except on preapproved business."

Elora nodded thoughtfully.

Ram took another bite, then, as an afterthought asked, "Do you like my accent?"

Her eyes slid sideways, pleased that he cared to ask. "Sure," she smiled and gave a beguiling little shake of her head. "Musical."

"I would like to hear these fairy tales," he said 'fairy' like it created a bad taste in his mouth, "but would like them all the more should they be called elf tales."

Elora laughed out loud. The joy of the sound was contagious. All three men were affected, but, after Storm had witnessed every step of this woman's metamorphosis from blob of quivering gore to the stunning creature now sitting across the table, he felt his heart swell with a longing to hear it again.

Two more times during dinner she reached over and carefully pulled Ram's hair back from his ear. Storm was starting to wonder how anyone could possibly be attracted to a pair of ugly, misshapen ears. Couldn't she see that's why he kept them covered with hair that couldn't decide what color to be or which way to go?

Throughout dinner several of the knights came by to be introduced, to Elora and Storm did the honors. She shook hands and repeated every name back in hopes that she might remember. The knights were not all as tall as Storm and Kay, but every one of them looked like athletes, well-proportioned with hard bodies and flat, muscular stomachs. Storm was trying to be patient, admonishing himself that he would be curious too, but the table was starting to feel like a receiving line. It was impossible for Storm to tell whether others were fascinated because she was an extra-dimensional alien or because she was extraordinary when held up to any lens. Of course there was always the chance they were just going out of their way to make her feel welcome because of chivalry, but he wouldn't bet on it.

When the dessert course, which was Black Forest cake with raspberry sauce, was set in front of Elora, she expressed uncertainty about the look of it. She didn't think dark brownish black was an appetizing color for sweets. That prompted a question about chocolate in general which led to an admission that chocolate did not exist in her reality, so far as she knew. In the infirmary, she had heard about it on TV, but had never seen it personally.

With all three dinner companions insisting that she

give it a try, she eventually acquiesced, picked up her Wallace silver fork and took a bite. As soon as the mixture came in contact with her taste buds, her eyelids slid closed, and she began moaning. She didn't stop moaning until every crumb of the cake was completely gone from her dessert plate. Storm and Ram both watched transfixed, with parted lips, responding to the sensual sounds of approval in ways that made them shift in their seats, repeatedly, and breathe deeper.

Kay, who had just spent a very satisfying three months never far away from the bed of his wife-to-be, observed the reactions with amusement, resting his elbow on the table with hand over his mouth, barely suppressing outright laughter.

Elora finished her piece of cake that had been portioned to satisfy a rugby player after a game, and looked at the empty saucer as if she was struggling to keep from licking the plate. Her eyes then came to rest on Storm's untouched dessert. Without a word he shoved it across the table. She beamed, politely asked, "Are you sure?" and then dived in before he had a chance to rethink the offer. In minutes the second dessert saucer was empty.

Still mesmerized, Ram asked if she would like his too, while thinking, "Great Mother of Paddy, let her say yes!" She was eyeing it longingly when she realized Storm and Kay were both chuckling. Looking around the table she got the distinct impression that she might have been overly demonstrative in showing her newfound appreciation for chocolate. Feeling her face heat and hoping she wasn't blushing visibly, she decided a new subject was in order.

As they rose from the dinner table, Storm invited Elora to join them in the lounge for a drink. She declined, on the excuse of having already experienced a long and eventful day and being eager to finish unpacking.

Storm said he would see her back to her apartment and then join his friends, but Elora insisted that she find her way alone. He said he would like very much to give her a complete tour of the building the next day and help her finish settling in with such things as groceries. He would come by at ten and their first stop would be for coffee and muffins. When they reached the lounge, Elora said good night and continued to the elevator bank.

Ram watched her walk away thinking he must certainly be the mother and father of all idiots and scolded himself silently. *Shit, Ram. You almost killed your own mate.* That funny feeling he'd had in his stomach in the Chamber that day three months ago hadn't been a harbinger of danger. Those bells and whistles clanging against his intuition and tweaking his cock had been trying to signal that the one and only had arrived to change his life forever. How was he to guess that she would show up as a pile of goo that was unrecognizable as homo sapiens?

He had misread the instinct and fucked up majorly this time. He'd left to go play for three months while Storm stuck around and spent every damn day becoming her anchor to this world. If that wasn't bad enough, it looked like he had abandoned the scene and allowed one of his two best friends in the world to fall in love with the one female who was destined to be his. What a cluster! He was more than a moron. He was self-saboteur to a degree that any masochist would envy.

But he couldn't be too concerned with that right now. He was too elated about having just met his future and finding out that she far exceeded any fantasy. She had to be the most potent wet dream ever conjured. The fates had seen fit to give him a beauty beyond compare, even if she was human; that hair that defied color description, those turquoise eyes, that gorgeous smile. And when he had leaned close to her to apologize he had smelled wild jasmine in bloom.

It was not completely unheard of for elves to mate with humans, but it was rare and not without its problems since elves mate for life and are naturally monogamous, while humans seem to struggle with fidelity. If she was elf, he could simply walk up to her, tell her she was his mate, and that would be that. This, on the other hand, would require some finesse, not one of Ram's primary attributes.

Still, he wanted to focus on his good fortune because his natural optimism wouldn't allow those details to be more than minor obstacles. He loved the fact that she was close to the same height, most beneficial for slow dancing and other romantic activities that thrive on the alignment of bodies. She was long legged, but curvy with a graceful, rolling gait that made his teeth clench with aching. He loved her contradictions. She was smart, polished, and charming, but had an appetite like a starving rugby player.

He smiled to himself remembering the way she moaned over chocolate and coveted Storm's cake. He smiled even bigger when he relived her reaction to seeing his ear. He had barely suppressed a full-on shudder when her fingers had feather brushed up his ear and touched the tip. If his pants hadn't been holding his cock down, it would have popped up at full attention. It made him wonder how his body would respond when she touched other places.

"What's so funny?" Kay asked as they walked toward the lounge.

Thinking quick on his feet Ram said, "Just thinkin' about how much cake she ate. I've never seen a body enjoy food so much."

Kay just said, "Um hum."

Storm didn't like the idea of Ram walking along thinking about what Elora said and did. He was starting to think that maybe bringing her to dinner had been a bad idea.

CHAPTER 7

BLACK SWAN FIELD TRAINING MANUAL

Section I: Chapter 13, #31

Vampire are difficult to recognize as such on sight. The vampire's coloring remains the same as it was at the time of inception if it has recently fed. If not, it will be pale by comparison to most people. That is the main reason for the myth of walking dead. The only physical characteristic that is permanently altered is the color of the iris which suffers loss of pigment. The extremely pale eyes are striking in appearance and, unfortunately, that serves to add to their allure. This feature cannot be relied upon as the only indicator as humans are occasionally born with similar coloring.

E LORA DIDN'T SLEEP much. The pleasure of privacy was too sweet. Knowing that she was not on view like an animal in a zoo, restored some dignity and gave her a more hopeful outlook about adjusting to this strange reality.

Putting her things away didn't take very long. The Operations Office had been thoughtful enough to provide bottled water, clean sheets and towels, fresh fruit and a few high protein snack bars. By far the most touching thing was a vase of calla lilies with a card reading, "Welcome Home, Thelonius C. Monq."

She knew that Thelonius M. Monq had taken a very big risk, no matter how well calculated, by sending her through an untested, purely theoretical device, but, if it had been a choice between that and certain death... The invaders were clearly determined to wipe out the Laiwynn Clan. She supposed that he did know what he was doing. If she had come through the portal anywhere but Jefferson Unit she probably wouldn't have survived or wouldn't have wanted to. Her heart softened toward Monq a little, especially since she supposed he must be dead.

She found the thermostat that controlled the temperature in the unit, turned it up a little, crawled between the sheets, and turned out the light. Lying awake in the darkness she played over and over in her head the incredible evidence that elves were real. Fairies, too, for that matter. She told herself to remember to ask Storm about fairies; if they were small, with gossamer wings. Again she thought it was odd that she received the great vampire revelation without missing a beat, but couldn't get over the real life presence of elves. Of course, the elves of fairy tales were not six feet tall, but everybody was smaller back then.

Thoughts were a jumble in her head: multiple layers of similar, if not parallel dimensions, elves, fairies, modern day knights who protect the weak from their own blissful ignorance of things that go bump in the night. When she found herself unable to settle her thoughts and sleep, she turned the bedside lamp back on, located the Black Swan Field Training Manual, got back under the covers and started to read.

She woke to a knock on the door. She hadn't thought

to set an alarm because she didn't think it would be possible to sleep later than seven. A quick look at the clock had her scrambling out of bed. She was decent in her yoga pants and cami and gods knew Storm had seen her that way many times, and worse. Much worse. So. No point in being shy.

The door flew open. Elora pulled him in and told him to make himself comfortable, that she'd just be a minute, then left him looking amused while she performed obligatory bathroom functions, splashed water in her eyes, scrubbed with the tooth brush, and untangled with the hair brush. She threw the mass of heavy hair up in a high ponytail, jumped into a pair of chocolate brown velvet leggings and donned a soft knit top.

She opened the bedroom door and said, "Ta daaaaa." She had seen that on the TV show, "Dear Diana", and hoped it meant "ready to go".

He smiled, opening the door for her. "Late night?"

"How did you know?"

"Psychic."

"Sorry to make you wait. It was exciting being out of the infirmary. I couldn't sleep and was up late reading."

She squeezed past him while he held the door. "This is a big day for me. I've been wondering about the world outside my glass front box."

When she said the word 'box', it made him wince a little. Of course he'd feel the same way in her place. That's why it had eaten at him when she had asked if he thought confinement was harm.

"Have you ever given a tour before?"

"Nope. First time, but I do accept tips." Then he added. "Of the monetary sort."

It might have been funny if she'd understood the reference, but, he knew that questioning look on her face, so he said it with her, "What's a tip?"

Knowing it was meant in a good natured way, she laughed with him.

On the rest of the walk down the hall past apartment doors, down the elevator, out into the busy junction, he explained the fine art of tipping: who gets one, when, for what service, how much, and how it should be given. She thought it was way too complicated.

He stopped to point out various places where services were available before they came to the coffee shop. The chalk board menu displayed some nice choices of hot drinks and the glass shelves showcased some giant, yummy-looking muffins. She asked for a large hot chocolate, a double chocolate muffin with chocolate chips, and a cup of mixed fresh fruit.

Storm laughed and asked if she wouldn't like some Hershey's syrup on the fruit cup.

They found a table for two in the solarium which, she was sure, would be her favorite indoor space. Storm had ordered a coffee called Americana and a thing that looked like unleavened bread stuffed with bacon and overcooked eggs. It was kind of disgusting, but she was willing to overlook a lot where Storm was concerned.

After all – suddenly she heard in her head an audio flashback of Storm's voice speaking softly, saying, "It's gonna be okay. We're almost there. Almost there." He had carried her to the infirmary in time to save her life, all the way urging her toward hope and survival. He alone made the decision to rescue her despite dissenting voices saying things like "don't touch it" and "kill it". With that inexplicable torrent of memories, she felt a wave of appreciation, affection, and admiration wash over her.

"What's in that disgusting looking thing you're about to put in your mouth?"

He chuckled and explained about breakfast burritos while chewing and insisting she take a bite. She agreed, but only on condition that she could keep her eyes closed while doing so. Her conclusion was that she wouldn't be ordering one anytime soon. She said she was old enough to know that everything can't be chocolate, but fortunately those weren't the only two choices.

It would be hard not to notice that passersby did a double take when they saw Elora. Celebrity was the last thing she wanted. It was anathema to her, the very reason why she'd lived the equivalent of captivity her entire life, mostly restricted to palace grounds.

"How long do you think it will take for people to get used to me?" she asked.

Storm looked around. He'd been so focused on every nuance of Elora's mood, every slight change of expression, that he hadn't realized she was drawing unwanted attention and feeling self-conscious.

"Oh. Yeah. I guess you're the new kid in town. People get used to change really fast around here. I'd give it twenty-four hours, which means you're more than half way to being part of the scenery."

"You can't imagine how good that sounds. So, now I think I'm ready to hear about what happened to Lan. If you're ready to talk about it."

Storm sat back and looked out the window for a minute. She was just about to withdraw the question when he turned back to her.

"We've been hunting a big nest of vampire, practically a community. They've been doing stuff that's out of character for vamps. Drugging women in bars and clubs with, ah, aphrodisiacs. Do you know what that is?" Elora nodded slowly without taking her eyes away from his. "I guess it makes it even easier to get women to leave with them quickly. No need to waste time with drinks and ploys."

He looked up at Elora to see if she found the subject objectionable, but she was looking at him steadily, with interest. "Anyway, the short version is we came across a group of them. There was a difference of opinion about who was going to live and who was going to die. We took a lot of them out. They killed Lan."

Looking down, he rotated his coffee cup a couple of turns. "One of the alarming things about this is that young vampire, under a hundred years old or so, are too blood-crazed for sophisticated operations like planning strategy. So there's organization involved. And that is very unnerving." He looked up at Elora. "The one of us hardest hit, although he doesn't let it show, is Rammel because Lan was his partner."

"And, I wouldn't like for anyone else to know I said this, but a lot of people think of B Team as being...," he paused, looking like he wasn't sure he should continue, "...elite or some such nonsense. There's a concern that it affects morale more than usual if one of us..."

Looking at this man who had spent so many hours selflessly trying to give comfort, she wished there was some way to repay that in kind. "I'm sorry."

"Enough of that." He pushed out his chair, got to his feet. "Tour bus is leaving."

Storm spent the next couple of hours showing Elora the sights.

The unit was housed in a facility built after the model of the Pentagon, not in the sense of seven sides, but in the sense that the hexagon-shaped building surrounded and enclosed a large open area. In that opening, called a "courtpark" by residents and staff, were tall trees, garden walks with fountains, and picnic facilities. In the center was a rugby field with a track around it. There were no windows breaking up the plain, tan perimeter of the 1950's style building. All windows, with the exception of the Chamber dome, faced the interior park.

The ground level featured a large circular foyer called the hub, a glass solarium, the main meeting room known as the Chamber, the infirmary, library, mail room, dining hall, a small grocery, a coffee bar, billiards room, and a country club style lounge with an oversized oak bar, card tables and plush seating set in small conversational groupings.

The media center, server rooms, offices, workout facilities, training simulators, firing ranges, classrooms, and laboratories were on lower levels. Apartments for the seventy-four personnel and trainees who lived and worked at the facility were on the higher floors. There were also two whister pads on the roof.

The building was home to twenty-four knights, twenty-four trainees, medical staff, teachers, administrators, clerical personnel, cooks, engineers, whister pilots, and maintenance crew.

Original funding for the organization had been generous, but two and a half centuries of well-invested funds had rendered a treasury that would be the envy of most small nations. Black Swan knights might live with their mortality hanging by a thread, but no luxury was spared their off duty hours.

She had seen part, but not all of Monq's facilities. The biggest surprise was finding the boys in classrooms and tutelage, the fourteen to twenty-two-year—olds who fit the physical and psychological profile and might someday develop into the sort of exceptional person who expressed the traits of Black Swan knights. The boys looked at Elora with great interest, which was to be expected. Storm would have been worried about them if they hadn't.

They stopped by the mail room so Storm could introduce their very own postmaster. "I know Henry is going to be one of your favorites because he's the one who makes sure all those packages find their way to you."

The tour would have been delightful as well as educational were it not for a brief stop near the Black Swan mascot, a one hundred twenty pound, black Alsatian male, who had been relegated to a lonely life in a basement kennel. When Storm and Elora came within a few yards of the cage, the dog began snarling and charging the chain link. Storm said he was ruined, not trainable. They didn't want to euthanize him because he was young and healthy, but he was too dangerous to let out. So they did nothing except feed him and hose out his kennel. Elora kept her opinion to herself, but was revolted by the untenable solution.

Courtpark entrances and exits were of particular interest because she had spent months longing to be outside. After stopping at the grocery to gather up supplies for her pantry and refrigerator, they returned to Elora's temporary quarters.

Storm said he was expected to spend the afternoon in a meeting, but that he would like to see her that night. She seemed a little fidgety, embarrassed almost.

Finally, she said, "I wonder if I could ask you about something of a delicate subject matter."

Storm ducked his head a little to catch and hold her

gaze. "There is nothing you can't tell me or ask me. And whatever it is will remain between us. I'm good at keeping things to myself."

"Well, do you know if anyone has given thought as to how I may earn money?"

He frowned. "I don't think that's been addressed, but the credit card I gave you will buy a lot of stuff. And you're welcome to use it. No strings attached."

"Thank you. That is most generous and I'm very grateful. The thing is that it is one thing to accept such a gift when helpless, but to continue would be – I think the term is – freeloading."

His features smoothed out and he nodded slightly. "I get it. How about this? We'll make it a loan. I'll keep a record like a running tab. When you start making your own money, you can pay it back."

Her relief was evident. "That would be wonderful. So long as I don't get too far in debt before that happens."

"So what is it you need?"

"Well, for one thing, in my world I played a musical instrument a lot like your guitar. And I miss it."

He stood there wondering how much more there was

to know. He'd probably just scratched the surface.

"Please, Elora. Get what you need. Criminently! Forget need. Get what you want. I think I could make a case that it should go on The Order's bill. They owe you big. How much is it worth to find out that some of the creatures we chase may be slipping dimensions? We'd never know that was a viable possibility if it weren't for you. You may be the key to a thousand unsolved files gone cold. If you want a Rolls Royce to use as a living room sofa, you should have it. You're important to this organization." He started to turn and then came back, again ducking his head in that charming way of his that brought them eye to eye. "And to me, too," he smiled.

"I don't want a whatever-that-Rolls-thing-is, but I would like a few more clothes, a guitar, and a good amp."

Storm's chin pulled back as he raised an eyebrow. "Electric?"

"Yes. What did you think?"

He laughed shaking his head. "I don't know. Delicate princess. Old-fashioned lyre."

"Delicate?"

He looked her up and down unapologetically. "Well,

feminine anyway." He opened the door and then stuck his head back in. "No weapons."

"No promises." Assuming she was joking he chuckled, closed the door, and strode away.

———————

CHAPTER 8

BLACK SWAN FIELD TRAINING MANUAL

Section 1: Chapter 1, #2

Soon after infection, the vampire virus begins to inhibit normal function of certain parts of the brain. Cognitive reasoning is impaired and conscience is suppressed in vampire for long periods, sometimes centuries.

ELORA THOUGHT A hot chocolate would make a perfect pairing with internet shopping. Feeling confident about navigating her way to the coffee bar and back, she decided to venture downstairs for a to-go cup.

As she stepped into the hall, she found Ram coming out of the apartment next door. He seemed surprised, but pleased.

"Good day," he offered with a radiant smile. He was

wearing faded, button down jeans again, with a grayish blue, Metallica tee shirt that made his blue eyes pop and sparkle. "Ms. Laiken."

She returned his smile while her entire essence quivered with a silent exclamation. *There's an elf living next door!*

"Call me Elora." As she pulled the door closed she remembered this had been his partner's apartment. Suddenly she felt awkward about the chance meeting and her expression changed to embarrassment. "I know this was your, uh, friend's quarters. I hope you don't mind. It's just temporary."

Ram had walked the few steps down the hall so that he stood next to her in front of the door. "Tis fine, Elora." He said her name like he was tasting ambrosia on his tongue for the first time. He glanced at the faded rectangle where Lan's name plate had been. "Tis no' like he's usin' it."

She seemed surprised. Realizing how callous that must have sounded, he hurried to say, "Lan was no' the sort who would want a memorial made of his quarters. He loved women and would relish knowin' you're the one who is sleepin' in his bed. Temporary or not."

Elora cocked her head at him and narrowed her eyes. "So. You're a silver tongued elf."

He shook his head slightly and lowered his sparkling eyes to fix on her mouth. "No. My tongue is sweet. Regular and pink. Will you come have a taste then and see if I'm true?" As he leaned in like he would kiss her she took a step back looking at him like he was daft. Noting that her expression and body language signaled wariness rather than playfulness, he laughed softly and straightened, changing tactic and topic.

"So, where are you off to?"

They started ambling toward the elevator. "The hub. Coffee bar. Only I'm not getting coffee."

"Let me guess."

She gestured as if to say, "Be my guest."

"Judgin' by the way you devoured Black Forest cake last night which, by the way, was quite somethin' to see and hear, I'm thinkin' you'll be after more chocolate."

She grinned, delighted despite herself. He was a clever elf. She added that to a growing list of attributes that included smooth talking, possibly fun to be with, and, of course, gorgeous in an ultimate sex fantasy sort of way.

His manner seemed boyish at times, but there was no mistaking the fact that he was a fully grown man in every respect that counted.

"Hot chocolate. It comes in liquid form. I discovered it at breakfast this morning and am thinking about forming a Cult of Chocolate."

"It also comes in cold liquid form as chocolate milk. Humans are addicted before they have teeth."

As they reached the elevator he pushed the down button and was suddenly serious, as he was thinking she had probably had breakfast with Storm and discovered hot chocolate without him. He wanted to be the one to see her learn everything new about his world.

Bringing him back to the moment she turned toward him and asked, "Where are you, um, headed?"

"Somethin' no' nearly so fun as chocolate." The elevator doors opened and they entered. His expression turned sober and he sighed. "A discussion about replacin' Lan with a new fourth team member."

"Oh. Storm said something about a meeting this afternoon. Sounds dreadful. For all of you."

"That about sums it up." The elevator doors opened

into the busy hub. Casually leaning his body into a brace against the opening to make sure the door held, he nailed her with that devastating smile and said, "Life goes on, right?"

She nodded, psychically agreeing to keep it light, and stepped out into the busy junction.

"I'm goin' down another floor. You know your way? How to get there and back?"

"Oh yes, I've known how to get to the hub ever since the day of my hearing." She gave him a little, chest-high wave with her right hand as she started off in the direction of the coffee bar. He paused for a couple of seconds to enjoy the saunter of her retreat, the confident stride, the flare of her hips, the sway of her body. He smiled to himself thinking he would never get tired of watching her go and never get tired of seeing her come.

Then it registered that she had said 'my hearing'. He didn't know she had been through a hearing, but made a mental note to get a copy. The Order was meticulous about video records.

On the way to the coffee bar she spotted a courtpark entrance and decided hot chocolate could wait a little longer. For three months she'd pined for the feel of unconditioned air on her skin – no ceiling, just sky above. When she opened the door and stepped onto the paved apron, a feeling of freedom and exhilaration swept through her that could only be understood by those who had similar experience with a lengthy convalescence or penal confinement. The tree leaves rustled and preened in the breeze with the brilliant colors that follow a cold winter and dry summer. Some had begun to fall. She spent an hour walking on leaves that made a pleasant crunching sound beneath her feet. She explored some of the garden walks and the open space of the track and rugby field. By the time she turned to go inside she was spiritually renewed and committed to making a go of a new life.

The table in Elora's temporary dining area did an adequate job of subbing for a desk. Enough light. Enough room. In fact it was going to be her favorite place she had ever lived. Of course that was a very short list – the first residence had been a palace in another dimension, the second a twelve by fourteen infirmary room.

There were Ethernet outlets throughout the apartment. She plugged in the laptop, got a lightning fast connection, and settled down to the consuming task of online shopping. She ordered a few items of clothing to fill in some gaps, then spent a couple of hours choosing a guitar. She was careful about return policies since she knew it might take a few tries to get the perfect fit, feel, and sound. It was lovely to learn that Marshall amps existed in this world. She knew a half stack was an extravagance and that she would blast the floor away if she ever turned it up, but Storm had said to get what she wanted. So she did.

Last she ordered an extra large face collar, a six foot, braided leather leash, and a tranq pistol with preloaded darts to be shipped separately, and specified overnight shipping for everything.

B Team had assembled in Sovereign Sol Nemamiah's office for the purpose of discussing their reentry into regular duty rotation. All three had dreaded the meeting. No one wanted to replace Lan. Just talking about it felt like a betrayal of friendship, camaraderie, and shared history. But a patrol team is four members, not three.

Breaking in a new team member is a lot like marriage. There are personality quirks that have to be negotiated to everybody's satisfaction. Which takes time. And then there's the trust issue. It's one thing to talk about having somebody's back, but security in that belief has to be earned. Which takes time and experience. Confirmation of honor and courage was a field experiment with a lifetime price tag. Literally. There was just no way around the added stress the entire team suffers from the uncertainty of not knowing for sure how the new member would perform in a moment of truth.

Ram slouched on one end of a leather couch twirling a paperclip he'd lifted from Sol's desk, looking surly and rebellious. Kay sat at the other end with an ankle crossed over his knee. Storm was feeling too restless to sit in either of the two remaining chairs so he leaned his back against the wall facing Sol's desk.

"You know I don't like this either," Sol began, "but it's on the top of the has-to-be-done file." Who could argue with that? Storm and Kay studied the high grade, commercial carpet. Ram turned his head to look out the window. "I've got a short list, but of course the three of you have final say about your fourth."

After a few beats Storm crossed his arms and jerked

his chin toward the paper sitting on Sol's desk. "Who are you thinking?"

"First is Ghost, naturally." Ram huffed and rolled his eyes. Sol pinned him with a look and continued. "Finnemore. Sanction. Blytheson."

The only sound in the room was a big sigh from Kay. Storm continued to study the carpet. Ram looked at Sol like he wanted to kill him. Like Lan's death was Sol's fault. He knew it was immature, but, once Lan was replaced, he would really have to face the truth that Lan was gone and not coming back.

Finally Storm looked up. "Let us have a day to mull it over. Sleep on it maybe."

"Sure," Sol said, maybe even more relieved than the rest of them to end the meeting. "Same time tomorrow."

The rejuvenating effects of three months off duty had been swept away in a fifteen minute meeting and the loss had slammed home again in full force. The remnants of B Team emerged from the Sovereign's office looking despondent and battle weary.

Ram started toward the elevator. Storm said, "Where you going Ram? We've got to talk about this."

Ram pushed the button for up and turned back. "I'm thinkin' we can talk just as easily with two tablespoonfuls of fine Irish Whiskey poured over ice."

They made their way to the lounge in silence. It was early in the day to be drinking, but it was a drinking sort of occasion. They had no trouble finding empty chairs in a corner where they could talk without being overheard. It was cool enough for the gas fire to be lit. They commandeered big, plump chairs then, one by one, looked out at the gloomy day thinking, perhaps subconsciously, that overcast was the correct backlighting for the mood.

After several minutes Storm said, "Okay. Let's come up with ground rules. I say that, if all three of us say no to somebody on the list, we draw a line through his name." Kay and Ram both nodded and murmured sounds of agreement. "Finnemore. Yes or no."

"Finnemore is a wanker." Ram was nothing if not colorful and succinct. If asked, he would affirm it was a gift.

Storm leveled a warning look at Ram and said evenly, like he was marshalling patience with an adolescent. "Yes or no."

Ram raised his eyebrows at Storm as if to say, "That's

as far as I would go with the attitude." He articulated every syllable of his reply with deliberate punctuation. "That. Would. Be. A. No."

Kay glanced at Ram and nodded, "I agree. It's a no. But, look. Sol's right. This is no fun for any of us. Also, it's time somebody said it out loud. Lan's death was nobody's fault. Not his. Not ours. We all wish there was somebody to blame so that we could…, but there isn't. Let's put a lid on the tempers and move on."

Storm looked at Kay for a moment and then said, "Unanimous. Finnemore is out. That leaves three."

They spent the next two hours wrangling pros and cons on three other names. In the end the only possibility left was Ghost who also was considered, theoretically, to be next in line for the job.

Gauthier Nibelung, a.k.a. Ghost, was thirty, old for a field active Black Swan knight. He was a hard core warrior with a reputation for getting it done. He also happened to be albino. Hence the nickname, Ghost. He had served Black Swan with passion and had excelled at every task.

Ram didn't like him, but couldn't, in good conscience, let that be a reason to blackball him if that was the only issue. Of the four on the list, he was the least objectionable. Not a rousing endorsement, but there was only one Lan. And he wasn't coming back.

Storm suggested they take the night to think it over individually and meet at Storm's place the next morning to be sure they were in agreement before the meeting with Sol.

Ram said something about wanting a workout before dinner and the other two thought that sounded like a plan. So they officially adjourned to the gym.

While changing into workout clothes, Storm decided to ring up Elora. She had the phone sitting next to her laptop and answered on the first ring.

"Hey, it's me. I'm going for a workout. The athletic center wasn't on yesterday's tour route, but you might want to see it. We call it The Dungeon because it's on the lowest sublevel and because it frequently feels like torture. Want to go along?"

"Sure. I just need to change into something I can work out in."

"Whoa. Hold on. I wasn't suggesting you actually work out. You're not really ready for that yet, are you?"

She snorted and immediately regretted it. *Okay. So now you know. I snort.* "I'll meet you at the hub in five minutes." She hung up before he could protest further.

She threw together something suitable for work out. Danskins can be flexible in more ways than one. She was fairly dissatisfied with this dimension's old fashioned sports bras, but whatever. It actually took ten minutes to get to the hub, but Elora thought it couldn't be all that terrible to keep a gentleman waiting five minutes. He was wearing sweats and a tank top, holding a black and purple gym bag. This was the first time she had seen his bare arms and shoulders and thought he seemed even bigger with more skin exposed. His sculpted body clearly enjoyed the benefits of rigorous, repetitive resistance training. She gave him a wave and held the elevator open.

Storm got on saying: "I still don't think you're giving yourself enough time to recover."

Her answer was a bright smile and an, "SL3. Going down," as she pushed the button.

The fitness center was huge, taking up most of sublevel three. In addition to treadmills and bikes, there was every sort of exercise machine ever conceived in multiple quantities, an Olympic size swimming pool, basketball court, a large room with a suspended floor for sparring, and a locker room with showers because it would not be gentlemanly to give offense to fellow passengers on the elevators.

As large as the facilities were, they still posted three categories of hours for usage. One set of hours was for active operatives, – which, in the case of Jefferson Unit, meant knights – one for trainees, and one for all other personnel. That being the case, a woman present during knights' workout times was unheard of. Storm gave her a tour of the facilities and then asked if she would like to maybe start slow on a bike while he went through his regular routine.

She did feel a little self-conscious being the only woman in a large facility of men trying to pretend they weren't looking at her. Finally she left the machine galley and wandered down the hall to the room with the suspended floor – which was empty.

She took off her shoes and bounced across the floor with a little giggle. It was freeing to have such a large space all to herself. She had been doing some yoga style stretches for about half an hour when several knights, including Ram, came in talking and laughing. The others stopped abruptly when they saw her, but Ram, also wearing a tank top and sweat pants, continued toward her without breaking stride.

"Hey," he said. She noted that he was less bulky than a lot of the other guys she had seen in the gym, but his arms, and the part of his chest she could see, were more cut.

"Hey," she replied in kind. Knowing that the men had come in because they planned to use the room she added, "I was just going."

"We were just goin' to spar a little. Stay and watch."

"Um. Alright. Maybe for a minute."

The men donned boxing gloves, paired up, and engaged each other in a friendly style of mixed martial arts that was, from Elora's perspective, woefully primitive. From her point of view the lack of skill was appalling and she couldn't help thinking that it was no wonder they were losing people. Finally, when she couldn't stand it any longer, she approached Ram and his partner. They paused to see what on earth might cause a woman to interrupt.

"Might I try this?"

Ram didn't have a chance to gape for long because everyone within hearing distance began laughing. Elves were hard wired by evolution to want to coddle their mates and please them in every way they can. Saying no wouldn't be impossible, just uncomfortable. He decided he could control the situation, assuring she wouldn't be hurt, if he insisted on being her partner. He took a moment to congratulate himself on his reasoning skills.

"Sure," he grinned, "but you must promise to go easy on me."

He asked his partner to give her his gloves, which turned out not to be all that big on her. Then she asked him to spell out the rules and the goal of the exercise. Naturally, everybody in the room gathered round to watch. The idea of a woman sparring with a Black Swan knight was on the far, far side of ludicrous.

Apparently the general goal was development of speed, flexibility, and reaction time. The only rules were no biting and no shots to the groin. He stressed the latter with some reference to "the boys". Easy. Simple.

Ram and Elora began to circle each other. The first clue that this was not going to go as expected was when

Elora shifted effortlessly and lightning quick into the stance and demeanor of a fighter. Whenever Ram stopped, or thought about changing position, even for a split second, Elora angled her body away, making herself the smallest possible target, keeping her defensive side to the front. She also wore on her face the single-minded concentration of someone accustomed to facing experienced opponents. For Ram, it was confusing as hell.

Storm had missed Elora and gone looking for her to make sure she wasn't overdoing. When he and Kay walked in and saw the match underway, Storm let out a string of curses that had Kay raising an eyebrow. Fortunately he kept his treatise on Ram's recklessness, immaturity, and stupidity to sub-distraction volume.

Ram thought he might give Elora a little tap on the outer bicep, not enough to hurt, but enough to scare her into calling it a day. He feinted left and charged right. In response she waited until the last millisecond, took a quick step to her right and then used his own forward momentum to catch him around the mid section and turn him end over end so that he slammed down on the mat on his back.

He hit so hard the breath was knocked out of him. Few things inspire panic quicker than not being able to breathe. Elora watched in horror as Ram's shocked face went through changes of color from pink to red to purple before his lungs were finally granted a reprieve.

A moment after he resumed breathing his brain registered that there was more wrong than just a temporary loss of air. The huge gasp of air stabbed him with a pain zinger. When he tried to sit up, he let out something between a yell and a groan. He lay there wincing for a minute, but didn't make a further move to rise. Finally he looked at Elora and said, "Bloody Paddy's Day, woman! I told you to go easy on me. I think you broke a fuckin' rib!"

The knights who witnessed the event exchanged looks that were worth a thousand words.

Elora dropped to her knees next to Ram saying, "Ram, I'm...oh, gods... I'm so sorry. This is not.... I've executed that move a thousand times and I've never injured anybody. What can I do?" She started tugging at the laces with her teeth so she could get the gloves off. Then she heard Storm's calm, take-charge voice behind her.

"Stay still Ram. Med's coming. Let them take a look

before you move."

Ram's rib hurt like hell, but it almost hurt worse to look up and see that Elora's eyes filled with big tears that were dropping on his chest. Peering into those turquoise pools brimming over, turning red around the edges, his only concern was comforting her. "Shhhh. 'Tis probably no' more than bruised ego. Stop now before you make me cry, too."

A doctor came in with an assistant close behind. He wasn't running, but he was moving pretty fast for a middle aged guy who had never heeded his own advice about diet and exercise. Injuries to knights were taken very seriously.

Storm pulled Elora up and away to make room for them. The doc knelt down and pressed around a little. At one point she knew he'd found the spot when Ram clenched his jaw, squeezed his eyes shut, and then reopened them to give the doc a look saying he was a dead man if he did that again. The diagnosis was, very likely, a broken rib, the severity of which would be confirmed by x-ray in the infirmary. They called for a wheelchair.

While they were waiting there was a murmur that rumbled through the crowd, followed by a very loud voice shouting, "What the hell happened here?" Sol stomped toward Ram lying on the mat looking miserable.

Storm intercepted him, putting his hands up as if to block Sol from moving forward. Storm reported quietly that it was merely an accident. Glancing back toward Elora, he asked Sol to step outside in the hall where they might talk more privately.

In the hallway Sol got the short version, to which he replied, "Jesus," and raked his hand over his head as if there was actually hair there. Scowling, he asked Storm if he was going to the infirmary.

"Of course. I'll wait for results and call you."

Elora watched Sol nod at Storm, look her up and down, then retreat the way he came. He was red in the face and clearly mad as a hornet. Apparently there was a "notify first" standing order to report knight injuries to Sol immediately which was what had brought him on the double.

Elora paced up and down in the waiting room of the infirmary. She would have been glad to see familiar faces, but not under these circumstances and, truthfully, she had hoped she would never see the inside of the infirmary again. She was beside herself that Ram was injured and devastated that she was the cause. In her mind she kept replaying the scene over and over trying to determine how it could have happened. She'd never given anyone anything worse than a light bruise in her life and she didn't like the feeling.

Kay came in with a coffee for Storm and a hot chocolate for Elora. She sat down and stared at the top of the cup thinking it would be wrong to enjoy hot chocolate. Storm took the seat next to her.

"This was not your fault, Elora. Monq suspected you might be stronger than people... here. Sol knew it, too. They should have told you." He looked down at his own cup. "In their defense, however, they wouldn't have thought anybody trained by this organization would be stupid enough to spar with a woman. Any woman."

"So you're mad at Ram?"

"Yes, Elora. I always suspected that he is an imbecile who managed to con his way through the program and today he provided insurmountable proof." He glanced at Kay who just shook his head a little and looked away. Elora was staring at him like she didn't approve of what he was saying. "Don't get me wrong. He's our imbecile and we take care of our own."

"How much of a freak am I?"

He regarded her with that all-is-well-because-I'm-here composure. "You're not a freak. Just…strong. We need to find out how strong. Clearly we're botching the job of hosting an inter-dimensional traveler. But that's our fault. Not yours. Tomorrow we're going to go to the fitness center together." He nodded toward Kay. "You and Kay and I. Monq can come if he wants. And we're going to find out exactly how strong you are.

"Don't worry about Ram. He's tough. He'll be fine and we'll figure this out."

Elora looked at Storm and then back down at her cup. "I was watching the sparring and all I could think about was how many mistakes they were making and about that injured boy we saw. And I was thinking that, maybe he wouldn't have been hurt like that if he was trained differently." Looking between Storm and Kay, she said, "It was hard not interrupting to say, 'No. Not like that.' Can I be honest?"

Storm looked dumbfounded, but nodded.

"I don't want to hurt anyone's feelings, but I wouldn't want you to lose people if some slight changes in style could make a difference."

Storm looked over at Kay to see his reaction. Kay just raised his eyebrows and took a sip of coffee, giving him a look that said, "You're on your own."

Yeah. Storm was a little ruffled. First, this oh so feminine fantasy took out his teammate – *his Bad Company teammate* – without breaking a nail or breathing hard. And now she was suggesting that the knights of Black Swan were pussies. The ironic thing was that he guessed he'd had it in the back of his mind that he would invite her to work out so he could show off a little. Did that ever backfire!

His pride might have a hard time digesting this, but, so far, he was doing okay with not letting indignation get the best of him. He decided to take the high road a step further and see where it led.

"Okay. Tell you what, after we do an evaluation of your physical abilities, Kay and I will let you show us a couple of moves. If you can give us a tip that makes us better, who knows?"

She pressed her lips together, nodded, and then her stomach growled. She didn't have enough experience with men to laugh it off so she blushed.

Storm just said, "Yeah. I second that. We missed dinner. When they let Ram out of here we'll all go down to the lounge and get them to make us a hamburger."

Elora perked up. "They're going to let him leave?"

"Sure. A broken rib isn't that big a deal. They'll tape it up, give him some pain meds, and he'll be good as new in a few weeks."

"A few weeks?"

"Yep. Four to six."

Elora surprised Storm by saying, "And you won't go back out until he's well?"

"By 'out', you mean on active duty?" She nodded. "No."

Elora seemed pleased about that. He was about to ask why when the doctor came in.

All three of them stood up. The physician was a man of few words. "Fracture. Six weeks off rotation. If he doesn't put any strain on the rib, he'll be practically as good as new. Get him back to his own bed. If he's hungry he can eat, but the pain meds may take the edge off his appetite and he'll be sleepy."

Storm and Kay both nodded and thanked the doc. "Can we go get him?"

"He's all yours. Two doors down." The doc's face melted into a goofy little smile. On his way out he said, "Kind of a character, isn't he?"

When Storm and Kay left the waiting room, Elora stayed behind not knowing if she was welcome. After a few seconds Storm jogged back to say, "You can come."

Ram was sitting on the side of a bed, shirtless, in just his sweat pants, with a small section of tape around his ribs.

Elora tried not to notice the intricacy of the musculature on his chest and abdomen, but sweet heavenly gods he was beautiful. He was a living graphic of what might be possible if everything happened to work in perfect concert on the design of a male body. As if she didn't already feel bad enough, now she had a second layer of guilt over ogling the person whose bone she had broken. She stood there chewing her bottom lip while Storm and Kay offered to help him up.

Ram's eyes kept coming back to Elora. He didn't seem angry, more interested in where she was and what she was doing. She hoped that didn't mean he was afraid she would lunge at him and do more damage.

When asked if he was hungry, he said, "No. Loopy. Sleepy."

They walked him to his quarters. Elora trailed behind. When they arrived, Ram punched in his code, opened the door, and all four entered.

The predominant color was forest green. The shelves were filled with a few books and a lot of music and movies. One of the things that drew Elora's eye right away was a collection of electric guitars hung on the wall, five to be exact, a medium size Ampeg tube amp, and a pedal array that had been custom built, probably by him. She wondered why Storm hadn't mentioned that Ram played. In addition to the electric guitars, there was also an acoustic and an electric mandolin.

After Ram got into bed, Kay pulled the pain meds out of his pocket, read the instructions out loud and told Ram he would leave them in the kitchen, as a precaution, so that Ram had to actually get up and think about it. His bed was decked out with white on white striped sheets and a dark, forest green, satin duvet cover which might have looked girly on some guys, but not Ram.

As they were leaving, Elora spoke up. "Don't lock the door."

"Why not?"

"Because I want to be able to come back and forth and check on him during the night. I'll make sure he gets the medicine on time and take care of it if he needs anything."

"Elora," Storm began, "that is not necessary. Ram doesn't blame you for what happened. Nobody does. And a rib fracture is not that serious. Trust me. We've all had worse. He'll probably enjoy the sheet time."

"Sheet time?"

"That's what we call recovering from an injury."

"Oh." She glanced back toward the bedroom. "Still, I'll feel better if I know he's taken care of." Storm opened his mouth to argue, but she cut him off. "Personally. I want to see to it personally. It's the absolute least I can do. And I live next door." She glanced away. "Temporarily."

He looked at Kay for a reaction. If Kay protested, for any reason at all, it would save Storm having to invent a reason why not, but Kay just shrugged while Storm thought, "Thanks a lot."

He didn't like it. He didn't like anything about it. The idea of Elora walking into Ram's bedroom in the middle of the night – alone – well, it just wasn't acceptable. Ram's reputation with women was legendary. He probably had Incubus demons scrambling to keep up. Storm was pretty sure it would take more than a broken rib to stop Ram from attempting copulation with somebody who looked like Elora.

"If it's that important to you, I'll stay." Kay looked at Storm as if to say, "What the fuck?"

"That's ridiculous. I'm doing it."

Storm had seen that same determined set of her features before when she had decided she would push through whatever pain or weakness stood between her and victory over death and frailty. He knew it would be pointless to press the issue and that doing so would make him appear to be both possessive and jealous. Something told him that a woman like Elora wouldn't respond well to either. The three of them stood there waiting for him to make up his mind.

Elora knew when he gave up because he looked a tiny bit defeated. She didn't like seeing that on him, but decided her need to make sure Ram was okay through the night outweighed Storm's need to protect her from a broken night's sleep.

Storm asked if she wanted to get something to eat with them and she agreed to come down long enough to get food to go. When she got back, she took a quick shower, leaving her hair wet to dry on its own and went next door to quietly look in on Ram. He was snoring softly, out like a light.

She closed the bedroom door without a sound. Earlier she had listened carefully to Kay's reading of the prescription instructions, but reread the label calculating the hour when he could take more medicine.

There was little chance of falling asleep before midnight, with all the events and thoughts that were clamoring around in her head, but she set the phone alarm just to be sure. She ate her club sandwich even though the wheat toast was now cold and chewy, then settled on the couch with the Field Training Manual.

At five minutes before midnight she knocked lightly

on Ram's door so that she wouldn't surprise him if he was up and wouldn't wake him if he wasn't. When there was no response, she eased into the kitchen, shook two pills out of the bottle, and got a glass of filtered water from the refrigerator door.

Again she tapped lightly on the bedroom door before entering. He was on his back, still asleep. The bottle said every six hours. After brief consideration, she decided to wake him up to take it. She set the pills and water on his bedside table and called his name. No response. She tried again without success. When she leaned over to touch his shoulder, calling his name a third time, his eyelids slid half way open.

His mouth slowly widened into a sleepy smile just before he said her name and grabbed her arms to pull her toward him. Elora was taken by surprise, her knees locked against the mattress so that there was no chance of stopping the forward momentum.

In his deep, drug induced sleep, Ram dreamed that he woke to find Elora Laiken standing beside his bed, bending over him, and calling his name. She was close enough that he could smell the jasmine and feel the vibration of her voice through the mattress where her knees were touching. It was the best kind of good dream; the kind that feels real. Naturally he reached out to grab her and pull her lush body into bed with him. Even though she gave a surprised little yelp as she was falling, his first indication that he was not dreaming came when he broke her fall with his rib cage, yelling out in pain, and coming fully awake instantly.

In his confusion he watched Elora scramble off the bed, removing the breasts that were crushed into his chest and pushing on his hipbone to right herself. She took a step back. There wasn't enough light coming from the kitchen through the open door to accurately read her expression, but he thought she might look angry.

"Rammel Hawking! Look what you've done. Probably made yourself worse."

"Look what I've done? I thought I was dreamin' because, silly me, I did no' expect to wake and find you bendin' over my bed in the middle of the night." Even in his pained and woozy state, he thought better of leaving it like that, so he added, "No' that I mind wakin' to find you bendin' over my bed in the middle of the night."

"I'm here to make sure you take the right amount of medicine at the right time. I persuaded your friends to leave the door open so I could check on you. The last thing I wanted was to make this worse. It's… very embarrassing."

Ram threw the covers back and started to sit up. He was wearing flannel, Black Watch tartan boxers that looked thick, soft and expensive. And nothing else. He was clearly not concerned about being mostly naked. He had the well-developed legs of a rugby player – with golden blond hair that matched the dusting of hair on his chest, powerful legs that filled out the thighs of a pair of jeans.

"What do you need?" she asked.

"Bathroom."

She took a step back toward the bed. "Let me help you. Take my arm." She crooked her arm at the elbow to form a brace he could use to pull up. He grabbed her arm and let her haul him up using as few muscles as possible, but gave up a whisper of a groan in spite of himself.

She waited in the living room until she heard him come back into the bedroom. Gingerly, he sat back down on the side of the bed and stared at her as she handed him first two pills and then the glass of water which he downed all at once. He set the glass on the table.

"Do you want anything before you go back to sleep? I brought an extra club sandwich. It might not be good anymore. I don't know."

He shook his head. Again she offered her arm to help him down without too much strain. When he settled back, she pulled the covers over him.

"You should sleep until morning. I'm going to lock the door on the way out." And with that she turned to go.

"Elora." She stopped at the door and looked back over her shoulder, "Do no' be mad. And do no' be embarrassed either."

"Good night," she said softly. On the way out she noticed his phone on the bar. She picked it up and punched her own name and number into 'Contacts', then locked the door behind her as promised.

———

CHAPTER 9

BLACK SWAN FIELD TRAINING MANUAL

Section 1: Chapter 15, #45

Unlike most literary misinformation regarding vampire, there is one bit of lore that is mysterious, but true. There is some chemical property, or properties, in wood that kills the vampire virus, and consequently its host, upon contact with the heart.

WHEN RAM WOKE up he was sore and hungry. He sat up with some effort and noticed the glass left by the bed. In the kitchen he found a club sandwich waiting for him on the counter. *Not a dream.* The lettuce and tomato were no longer edible so he pulled the veggies off and threw them away. The rest was good enough for breakfast. He got a carton of juice out of the refrigerator, sat down at the bar, and picked up his phone to see if he had any messages.

He thought he'd call Storm and find out if he was in small, medium, or large trouble for letting Elora spar with him. Pulling up 'Contacts' in alphabetical order and scrolling down to Engel Storm, he happened to notice Elora Laiken and backed up. Great Paddy's balls. If his rib didn't hurt so badly he'd laugh out loud.

He dialed her number.

"Hello." She answered on the first ring.

"You left your number."

"How are you? Do you need anything?"

"I need help takin' a shower."

She suppressed a giggle that was far too girlish on a woman her age. The elf was chipping away at her carefully constructed walls. "You have other friends for that, Sir Hawking. I meant do you need anything like breakfast?"

He grinned. "Had breakfast. Club sandwich sans lettuce and tomato, at least I think that's what they had once been. And thank you. For takin' good care of me."

"Please do not thank me. I feel wretched about the whole mess, but we're taking steps to make sure it doesn't happen again."

"What kind of steps?"

"Storm and Kay have arranged to close the fitness level for the next couple of hours. They're setting up a series of tests to quantify my strengths…and weaknesses, I suppose."

"And this is when?"

"Half an hour."

"I'll be there."

"No. Isn't that too much activity too soon?" It suddenly occurred to her that this was the reverse of the same exchange she'd had with Storm the day before.

"My rib is taped nice and tight and tidy. Good as a cast. I'm no' proposin' bench press, just walkin' to the elevator. Believe me, I have lived through worse than this."

"But that's a story for another time?"

"Could be, if you're a really good girl."

"I am a really good girl, but I won't be asking for *your* definition. How about a bargain? I'll walk you down if you promise to come back and be truly inactive for a reasonable time after lunch."

"Like a nap?"

"Exactly."

"Will you join me?"

"No." The elf was temptation incarnate. And relentless.

"You drive a hard bargain. Naps alone it is then."

"Hallway. Twenty Minutes?"

"Deal."

Ram emerged with wet hair wearing faded 501's, a rugby shirt with navy and green stripes and a crisp white collar. Elora decided she was a fan of 501's; something about the pucker between each button of button fly jeans drew the eye like a codpiece. Looking at his smile, it would be impossible to tell he was on the D.L. – short for Disabled List – if he wasn't moving a tad slower than usual and ever so slightly favoring his left side.

"So, how are you feeling? Really."

"No' bad. I will no' be takin' any more sleepy medicines. I can sleep when I'm dead."

Like Storm said, he was tough. Elora admired that.

"I noticed your fine collection of stringed instruments. Do you play them all or are they for collection?"

"I play." He smiled. "I come from musical people."

As do I, she thought.

When the elevators opened on sublevel three, two young men that Elora guessed were in training moved in front of the opening, holding up their hands to block exit.

"Sorry. This level is closed for the next two hours, sir," one of them said directly to Ram.

Ram spoke to them in a tone that conveyed a conviction that they suffered from idiocy. Gesturing toward Elora he said, "She's the reason this level is closed! Kindly remove your dunderheads from your little, juvie asses and stand clear." When the doors started to close, from pure reflex he shot his hand out to stop the progress, then pressed his lips together to keep from letting the pain show when the elevator door jarred his rib. The resulting expression could easily have been mistaken for out-of-patience-do-as-I-say-right-now-or-else.

The two young men glanced at each other and chose the better part of valor in obliging Sir Hawking without further delay. They dropped their hands and moved away. As Ram and Elora walked past, he instructed them not to let anyone else through. Then, just for good measure, he said, "If you two are the future of Black Swan knighthood, we're in a lot of trouble." He turned his back on them then smiled and winked at Elora.

Sol, Monq, Storm, and Kay were assembled in the weight room. They were surprised to see Ram come in with Elora, but gave him a quick briefing on the plan to catch him up to speed. It was simple and flexible meaning that they would basically make it up as they went along.

First on the agenda was weight. They agreed to eyeball Elora and guess how much she weighed in pounds. Taking into account her height, bone structure, and the fact that she had a low muscle to fat ratio, the median guess was one hundred forty pounds. After they had settled on an estimate, Elora took off her cross trainers and stepped on to the scale. It read two hundred thirty six.

Kay whistled. Ram looked her up and down with renewed interest.

Storm said, "That explains a lot."

"What do you mean?" asked Monq.

"You remember the night she arrived I had a hard time picking her up? Kay had to help me. I knew she felt really heavy, but I thought maybe it was partly because she was unconscious and partly because she was... slippery and hard to hold on to."

"And none who work the infirmary ever mentioned this?" Ram looked from Monq to Sol.

"Maybe they thought we already knew." Monq looked at Elora, waving his clipboard to emphasize his point. "Anyway, it's an indicator of cell density, but it's just a number."

"You're worried that I may be self-conscious about my weight?" Elora gave him a crooked smile and a look of disbelief. "I have more pressing issues."

"Yes. So let's get to that," said Sol. "We have less than two hours to learn what we can."

Storm suggested they go through a complete circuit of weights and machines comparing Elora's performance to what might be expected of a typical twenty-three-year-old female in top physical condition. The results were astounding. Her numbers exceeded current records of males of any age.

Ram laughed out loud and then grabbed his rib turning to Elora. "I just realized you actually *did* take it easy on me. I could have ended up squashed like a bug."

They were curious to test her for speed as well as strength. So they put her on a treadmill, but, at its fastest speed, which was twenty miles per hour, she was practically yawning. They determined they would have to test her outside on the track and then all five men proceeded to argue about the best way to do that.

After nearly two hours they seemed to be winding up when Elora reminded Storm and Kay that she was supposed to get an opportunity to critique their fight style. Storm blinked at her for a minute because he had, in fact, forgotten that he had capitulated to appease her in the moment.

Grinning ear to ear, Ram said, "Oh, this should be good."

Storm and Kay danced around a little, not wearing gloves because this was strictly exhibition. Elora stood a few feet away. Within thirty seconds she had stopped them to suggest a correction to the way Kay was distributing his weight. It took Kay three tries to make the change, but, when he got it, he was impressed with the difference a slight adjustment made in his speed and ability to deflect.

She asked them to begin again. This time, when she stopped them, she gave Storm a detailed explanation as to how he was slowing his reaction time and draining endurance by carrying extra tension in his trapezius. She showed him how to keep his hands up while releasing that tension. He could tell that small suggestion not only made him instantly faster, but also allowed him to put more force behind his strikes.

Elora declared that enough for one day, saying she liked to allow time for an adjustment to be absorbed and integrated before introducing something else.

Storm and Kay turned to talk to Sol and Ram. Both reported remarkable differences from just those few minutes of instruction, but everyone observing the demonstration was already sold. The implications were clear. If their interdimensional traveler was willing to share what she knew, she might give them all a better shot at staying alive. Sol turned around to ask if she would consider instructing. She was gone.

Storm, Kay, and Ram found her at the hub bistro looking up at a digital read out of the menu above the counter.

Ram came up behind her. "Can we join you?"

She shrugged without looking at him. "It's a free country." She stopped and thought about that and then turned to the three men behind her and asked them as a group. "Isn't it?"

All three nodded and murmured assents.

"So what will you be havin'?" Ram continued.

"Deciding between cream of mushroom soup and a hamburger."

"Get both," he said.

"That would be wasteful," she countered.

"No' at all. We'll eat whatever is left."

Elora considered that for a moment, then stepped up to the counter and ordered the soup and the hamburger. She was completely unprepared for all the questions the hamburger order prompted. How did she want the meat cooked? If she wanted cheese, what kind of cheese? Which vegetables? Which sauce? What condiments? Bread with sesame seeds or without? Seeing her lost look, Ram interjected himself into the dialogue and answered the questions to please himself. Then he turned to Elora.

"Let's start there. Before long you'll know exactly how you like it."

"Thank you."

"You're welcome," he smiled. "You want juice?"

She shook her head. "Chocolate milk."

He smiled bigger. "Excellent choice."

She smiled back.

Watching and listening to this exchange from just behind them in line, Storm was feeling like a boy whose toy had been usurped by another kid. For the hundredth time he reminisced about the days when he didn't have to share Elora with anybody else. Of course he didn't want her held prisoner... exactly. But he didn't mind being the center of her universe.

The four of them sat down at a table in the solarium. Storm and Kay went back to get the trays of food when it was ready since Ram was out of commission. She and Ram talked about food she had tried, food she hadn't tried, but would like to, and food she used to like in her world.

When Storm and Kay returned, they said they were impressed with what she had shown them and that Sol was going to ask her if she'd consider training.

Elora nodded her head without looking up from the hamburger in front of her. "Sure. This is good." She ate a potato chip and took a swig of chocolate milk through a straw like a kid. "I like hamburger, but chocolate milk is amazing. Do you think the others would be receptive?"

Ram touched his rib meaningfully. "If they know what's good for them."

Elora pressed her lips together. "I wouldn't want anybody to be forced. That's my only condition. If they want what I have to offer, it's freely given, but it must be their choice."

She reminded Ram about his promise to take a nap. He said the three of them had a meeting with Sol first, but it was sure to be a short one since he, and therefore his team, were going to be off the duty roster for another six weeks. Storm asked Elora how she was spending the rest of the day. Excusing herself, she said she had a session with Monq and was also trying to find some time for personal interests.

Back inside her apartment, she took a quick shower, changed clothes, and donned a long knit vest with deep pockets. The Black Swan Training Manual went into one of the pockets. A few chicken treats went into the other.

At sublevel two she exited the elevator without being noticed. There was no one near the part of the building where the dog was kept. People stayed far, far away from him which made Elora's heart hurt all the more. Canines are the very definition of social animals. Forcing them to live a solitary existence is a cruelty that far exceeds heat, cold, hunger, or thirst.

At home the stable master had been a man who was equally good with dogs and horses, if not people. His reputation had grown and, even though he was gruff and unfriendly, people came around with problem dogs, asking for his help. Elora had spent so much time observing that eventually the old man invited her to assist and apprentice his technique.

For today, her plan was simply to introduce herself to the unhappy dog and she did not expect to get further than that. When she turned the corner that brought her within sight of the cage, the animal leapt to all fours in one sleek movement, crouched, lowered his head, and began to growl. She responded by moving very slowly and offering verbal assurances that she meant no harm.

When she came within six feet he began to snarl in earnest and leap against the cage. She simply sat down cross legged in front of the cage, pulled out the training manual, and began to read out loud.

For the next half hour, she read while the dog snarled,

growled, barked, and charged the cage. The noise he made echoed against walls and ceiling and was deafening. She couldn't hear her voice above the noise and doubted he did.

Finally, his great chest heaving, head hanging, tongue lolling, he grew quiet for eight seconds which she carefully counted off. At the end of that respite she looked up into his eyes. Most dogs will not meet a human's gaze for more than a second, but there are a few exceptions. This dog was one of them.

Holding his stare she whispered, "Good boy."

He closed his mouth, picked up his head, and pricked his ears forward. And in that moment she saw all the potential this dog held in his great heart: the character, the courage, the intelligence. She tossed a chicken bit through the chain link so that it landed at his feet. For a second, he took his attention away from her and allowed himself to be distracted by the treat. She smiled and said to herself, "Yes, indeed, you magnificent creature. You and I are going to work this out." She put the book away and started to rise, being careful to go ever so slowly. He growled a warning deep in his throat. She backed all the way around the corner.

October 6 entry, Monq's file on Elora Laiken: The subject's emotional and psychological adjustment seems to be almost as remarkable as was her physical recovery. This is due, in part, to the fact that she has social interaction with Engel Storm and the other members of B Team with whom she seems comfortable. But, even so, she demonstrates an extraordinary degree of resiliency and buoyancy considering the body of traumatic experience.

She has agreed to work with the knights and trainees, teaching a style of weaponless martial art that is clearly more sophisticated than that currently endorsed. Her contribution will undoubtedly be advantageous to the organization. Moreover, there is no doubt that she will benefit emotionally from a sense of purpose and belonging.

As predicted, the meeting with Sol was short. Since B Team's reintroduction to duty had been postponed, so had the immediate necessity for making a decision about Lan's replacement. Sol said he was temporarily relieving the extra duty stress by bringing a team up from Brazil, but urged the three to settle on their selection of a fourth so that the replacement would be ready to go in six weeks.

As soon as Ram got back to his apartment he called the media center and told them to send someone up with a copy of the recording of Elora's hearing. They asked, "Which one?"

"There was more than one?"

"Yeah. A short one on October 1st, long one on October 2nd."

"Bring them both."

The recordings arrived twenty minutes later. Ram popped the first in and sat down to watch. The airbot, programmed by one of the media geeks, hovered chest high, recording Elora's entrance into the Chamber with Storm on one side and a big, no neck bruiser of an orderly on the other. Ram thought, "Yeah. Like that would have slowed her down if she had decided to run."

Within seconds she was holding Monq by the front of his shirt, keening pain and betrayal. Ram felt adrenaline shoot into his body as he sat helplessly watching the reenactment of his mate in anguish. His fists clenched so hard he drove the ends of his short, blunt nails into the flesh and felt his stomach roil. He let the recording play through the discussion that took place after Elora left the Chamber.

The video record of the second day was a treasure trove of information. Certainly he wished he had known that she had a lifetime of martial arts training before he'd agreed to spar with her. Like all those who had been present that day, he was captivated by the story: her background, her relationship with Monq's counterpart, the tragedy that had befallen her family, and the circumstances of her transportation to this reality.

One thing he brought away from seeing the hearings was that Elora Laiken deserved a mate who would treat her as gently as a piece of fragile art glass and never deny her anything she needed to be happy.

THEY TESTED ELORA for speed late on a cool Autumn night with a bright moon. She was clocked at just under thirty miles per hour which exceeded the record by nearly four mph.

CHAPTER 10

T HE DAYS BEGAN to shape into a routine. In the mornings she visited Blackie, her pet name for the big Alsatian in the basement, and made progress with him daily. After lunch, she spent the early part of the afternoon working with the knights and trainees. Sol told them that participation in the program was entirely by choice, but that they opted out at their own peril. Only one knight refused.

Two or three days a week she spent some time practicing in the archaic weaponry wing. Not because she anticipated a need to fight by sword or archery, but because she had devoted too much of her life to these accomplishments to let them go rusty.

Of course everything had to be relearned to some extent. All the skills that had long ago been committed to "muscle memory" had to be recalibrated to match the amount of pressure her new strength brought to each activity. When she was recovering she had thought it was a natural part of being rehabilitated to such a drastic extent and didn't realize the implications. Everything from holding a fork to opening a door required adjustment. The first time she played guitar, she popped a string so hard that it flew up and split her top lip.

In the archaic weapons section, the knights also trained with modified wooden stakes since it turned out that vampire really do succumb, permanently, to wood driven directly into the heart.

One day, when no one else was around, she picked up a stake and twirled it around a couple of times to get the feel of the weight and shape. For grins, she threw it at a straw target. Although she didn't pierce the heart the first time, she did propel the stake clear through the dummy, exploding out the other side. After a few tries she came closer to the target area and discovered that, if she eased back on force, she could embed the stake rather than turning it into a missile. But, of course, the target was stationary. She made up her mind to try again with the simulator whenever she found herself alone and unobserved.

She had fallen into the habit of spending the late after-noons watching movies with Ram which proved to be an accelerated course in the culture of this world. He had little else to do these days and she felt entirely responsible for that. Not that his company was hard to endure.

They took turns choosing films. Ram had a penchant for crude and immature humor with endless references to mammary glands, female genitalia, male genitalia, blow jobs, toilet mishaps, bestiality and non-committed couplings. The fact that she was frequently appalled by the horrendous things he found funny served only to amuse him all the more.

Elora liked romances with beautiful clothes and happy endings. Ram called these movies "talkies" because there was too much dialogue to suit him. She chose to believe he was just pretending to be bored to adhere to some sort of macho image preservation ritual. Neither one of them liked horror or excessive violence. Too close to home.

Music was something they had in common. He filled her audio library with music he thought she would like. They talked about the differences in the musical histories of their respective realities and the differences in popular music. Elora was shy about playing for Ram, but he never had to be asked twice. Heavy metal shredding wasn't her favorite expression of guitar, but she appreciated his skill, that it was a very fine form of male exhibitionism, and she loved watching his strong hands alternately manipulate and massage six strings.

Ram confessed to having watched the recordings of her hearings, saying he wanted her to know that he knew what had been said. When she responded by looking at the floor, he took that as a sign that she would prefer another subject. But he was satisfied that he'd opened a door should she ever want to discuss it. Any of it.

One day he brought her a soft cover, paper copy of a book saying he had reason to believe that she was interested in the subject. The title read *Every Thing You Always Wanted To Know About Elves, But Were Afraid To Ask.* Elora raised an eyebrow at Ram and gave him a crooked smile.

"What makes you think I'm afraid to ask?" she said.

He gave her one of his more sardonic smiles and shrugged, "Just in case."

She didn't ask questions based on the book he gave her, but did ask about his home and his family. He described his part of the world as magical and beautiful. She learned that he had an older brother and a younger sister, that, in addition to music, he loved horses and liked to spend time at a tiny, family owned hunting lodge located in the middle of a forest and wildlife preserve. When she asked why he had joined The Order he said, "Wild child, I suppose. They promised I would have adventures my brother could no' imagine and that was exactly what I wanted to hear."

Ram was just as curious about her. She told him there wasn't as much to tell as he might expect, that palace life had been restricting and suffocating and that, in many ways, she had more freedom as a prisoner of Black Swan. Ram's face tightened when she said the word prisoner. He started to protest, but stopped himself when he realized he couldn't really argue with that.

In the evenings after dinner, Storm spent time teaching Elora such civilized pursuits as billiards and five card stud. If Storm stopped by the apartment during the daytime, he always seemed irritated to find Ram there.

One day, as Ram was leaving, he opened the door to see Storm standing with his hand in the air about to knock. Without pretense of ambivalence Storm asked, "Don't you have a place of your own?"

As Ram stepped past Storm into the hallway he flashed a devilish smile in open challenge. "I like it *here*."

In an uncharacteristic display of temper, Storm was just about to throttle Ram when he caught Elora standing at the doorway in his peripheral vision and decided to take a more conciliatory attitude. Truthfully, Ram wasn't overjoyed about turning back to see Storm disappear into his mate's personal quarters. Everything about that felt very, very wrong.

"It does seem like he's here a lot," Storm grumbled.

"We take turns choosing movies. He despises my choices. I eschew his."

"Yeah. I can imagine." Storm was still pouting, but seemed somewhat relieved.

SOMETIMES SHE HAD dinner at B Team's table. One night, instead of dessert, she got a cupcake with a candle in it. Storm brought out a lighter, lit the candle, and said,

"Happy Birthday." After blowing out the candle, she cut the cupcake into quarters and insisted that each of them have a piece before asking Storm how he knew. He said he had looked for her counterpart's birthday and figured it would be the same. When Elora told Storm how touched she was that he'd gone to so much trouble, Storm soaked up her praise and then gloated at Ram.

Sometimes she ate with people she knew from the infirmary, such as Elsbeth, who was the closest thing Elora had ever had to a friend who was not also a relative.

At one such dinner, Elsbeth broached the subject of Elora's relationship with B Team, which, apparently, was an item of constant gossip within the general population of Jefferson Unit. Elsbeth regaled her with stories of the exploits of the widely celebrated Bad Company saying their prowess was unequalled and what a tragedy it had been when Sir Rathbone Landsdown had died in the line of duty.

She described Storm as team leader, even though Black Swan does not officially recognize leadership in the field, and described Ram and Kay as opposites who balanced each other out. Kay was the anchor, the walking embodiment of reason and calm under fire while Ram was thought to be a short fuse hothead.

Elsbeth went on to say that Ram was also the quintessential ladies' man; that the standing joke was that his nickname, Ram, was appropriate since he was a notorious womanizer and that women were drawn to him like a magnet for reasons that transcended his beauty. She knew that to be true because a lot of the knights were gifted with looks and allure that dripped charisma without inspiring riots.

"Riots?"

"Well, that's a little bit of an exaggeration, but not much. He's the sex version of fast food drive-through. It looks so good. It smells so good. It tastes so good. And you can get it quick. But, afterward you feel yucky and are sorry you did it."

Elora had never had fast food or been through a drive through, but Ram's movies were full of drive-through situations so she grasped the idea.

While Elora let that sink in, Elsbeth shifted the conversation to Elora's training project. Elora couldn't be sure, but she thought that Elsbeth had gone into detail about Ram's reputation as a sex-dripping satyr for her benefit, as a kindness. The question of Ram's appeal was indisputable and Elora was as susceptible as anyone else, but no one is irresistible. She made a pact with herself that she would not end up a number on a pile of used and discarded lovers. He could just keep his sexy elf trouble to himself.

As they were leaving dinner Elora couldn't hold the question that was eating away at her any longer. They stopped in the middle of the hub before going their separate ways. "Look, I know this question might be off limits, so you don't have to answer, but if you don't mind me asking, have you had experience with Ram, uh, personally?"

When Elsbeth's smile reached her eyes they sparked a little. "No admonitions about 'kiss and tell' in your world? No matter. The answer is no." She leaned in conspiratorily and lowered his voice. "Not because of purity. There's a reason why I know that drive-through sex feels bad afterward." She looked around to be sure she wasn't overheard. "I guess I'm not his type. Oh, well." She sighed dramatically.

Elora didn't want to feel relieved about that because she didn't want to have to examine the implications too closely.

Occasionally she was invited to dine with Monq in his quarters in lieu of a session. One such night the conversation turned to the little manual Monq had given her. "I'm curious about one thing regarding vampire and that's why this phenomenon would still be classified as paranormal. A hundred years ago that would have made sense, but now that it's been explained scientifically…"

"Yes. A good point." He offered to refresh her brandy. "The thing is that science and the paranormal, whether you call it that or magic or mystic or mystery, have been on a trajectory course for centuries and perhaps the intersection isn't too far into the future. I'm certain that someday all mysteries will have scientific explanations.

"For instance, until very recently, we had no way of proving that there are multiple dimensions existing simultaneously in layers, tethered to our Earth. Much less inter-dimensional travel.

"One day a lovely young lady goes splat on the floor at our feet and voila! What was theory just a moment ago is now a fact."

AFTER DINNER THINGS usually got very quiet in Jefferson Unit. Knights went out on patrol. Trainees were busy with homework and non-resident personnel went home. Elora frequently visited the infirmary after dinner and Ram went along because, as he said, he had nothing better to do.

The young man who had been admitted at the end of Elora's convalescence was slowly healing and expected to make a full recovery. He was still bedridden and eager for company. No one understood that better than she.

The first night she visited, she tried to establish what would serve him best. He said he didn't have the energy to carry on much of a conversation, much less play games, but would love it if she would just talk to him. She asked if he would like to hear stories from her world, typically told to children, but loved by everyone. He said that sounded perfect.

So she began by saying the collection of stories were called fairy tales. Ram shot her a mock dirty look. "Excuse me, I meant to say elf tales. I almost don't know where to begin."

"Start with the one you like best," Ram suggested.

"Good idea." From memory she retold Snow White, trying not to leave out the important details. After that she began writing out the stories so that she wouldn't forget anything critical in the telling.

Every night, when they left the young knight's room, Ram would look smugly amused and say, "That was a stupid story." But the next night he would be back again pretending to be bored.

One of the highlights of the week was Monday morning brunch and karaoke. With hundreds of years to iron out a system, The Order had determined that people in high pressure jobs – and vampire hunting qualified – needed to balance that with big doses of frivolity. The knights were not the least shy about their vocals or lack thereof. They sang even if they were tone deaf. One of the big hits was always a group of nurses who sang girl group songs. Neither Storm nor Kay could carry a tune and their performances were stiff, but, curiously enough, there was an entertainment factor just on the other side of awful.

The other regular star was Ram who was a mockingbird. He could do anything he wanted with his voice. He could sound like an angel or like somebody who had smoked several decades too long.

One thing that was not tolerated at Monday morning Karaoke brunch was spectators. You either participated or they showed you the door. After weeks as an onlooker, the day came when someone started a chant to get Elora to the microphone. Like everyone in her clan, she'd been singing all her life, but since she had no experience singing solo in front of others she was paralyzed with stage fright.

Seeing her blanch, Ram leaned over and whispered in her ear that it was not a test of singing, but sportsmanship. That seemed to be enough encouragement to get her out of her chair to the front of the room. She picked a song she knew from the list and proceeded to stop the show with her passionate, husky alto.

Amid whistles and shouts of approval, Kay leaned over to Ram and said, "She sings like an elf."

Ram, whose dreamy-eyed gaze was still locked on Elora said, "Aye. She does at that."

THE DAY CAME when it was time to go to the next level of

Blackie's training. He always seemed to be expecting Elora's arrival because, when she came into view, he would be standing, looking through the chain link with bright eyes, big ears standing up at attention. Today he allowed himself to emote one wag of the tail. They always began with a chicken treat tossed into the cage, but today they were going to a new level. She was going to offer the treat from her hand.

She approached the cage, closer than she had ever been before, speaking quietly, holding out the treat. He watched her intently, wanting so badly to keep his gaze focused on her face, but not being able to resist looking down at the treat.

He allowed her to stand just on the other side of the fencing. He was tense, deathly still, his body language was broadcasting unpredictability, but she believed he was worth the gamble. She put her fingers, holding the chicken treat, through the chain link, knowing he could easily snap them off if he chose. After a few tense seconds he sniffed her hand, sniffed the treat, then ever so gently withdrew it from her fingers.

She wanted to leap in the air with a victory whoop, but

forced herself to remain still and quiet so as not to startle him at this critical moment. "Good boy," she whispered. Then he surprised her with the unexpected. He looked from her face to her pocket to see if she might withdraw another treat. She chuckled. He kept his attention on the pocket and wagged his tail twice. She decided that was indeed worth another treat.

After three days thus, Elora decided it was time to get inside the cage. The key to the large padlock was kept on a lanyard hanging from a wall hook a few feet away. Blackie watched her curiously as she removed the lock. She threw a chicken treat into the back corner to get him to move away so that she could open the gate and enter without freeing him.

When he turned around, she was inside and talking to him in the same even, low tones she used to read to him every day. To further minimize any threat he might be feeling, she sat down cross legged, her back against the chain link. He sat down on his haunches. The dog was so big, that put them at eye level. Blackie regarded her with interest, clearly trying to work out the situation.

She slowly pulled out the training manual and began

to read. After a minute or so his mouth opened and his tongue came out which meant he had relaxed. She could tell by his expression that he was okay with the new arrangement and that she wasn't in any danger. After another minute he approached, lowered himself to the ground and put his head on her knee.

It was such a simple gesture, but so touching it made her heart turn over. "Good boy," she said quietly. The next day he leapt for the chicken treat in the corner, gulped it down, and turned, wagging his tail like he was expecting her to sit down. He immediately came over, cuddled up beside her and put his head on her knee. Slowly she brought her hand over to his nose. He raised his head, sniffed her hand and offered a tentative lick.

She gambled the time was right to touch so she let her fingers drift up the fur of his cheek. He stilled, looking a little wary, but allowed it. She stroked quietly and slowly behind his ears until he leaned his head into the petting, and said quietly, "Yes, you gorgeous beast. We have an understanding."

She moved her hand down his head, over his neck and shoulders. Nothing could have astonished her more than what happened next. He threw himself into a roll onto his back asking to have his tummy rubbed.

Without thinking she laughed out loud. He raised his head to peer at her curiously, but made no threatening move. "Good boy," she said out loud and gave him a nice, brisk rub on his tummy.

Unlike the black on his head and back, the coloring on his sides was a mix of tan and silver, and the down on his stomach was almost pure white.

She thought it strange, as much time as she had spent at the sublevel kennel, that she had never seen his caretakers. She knew he was fed and watered and that the kennel was hosed down, but had never seen anyone come near.

After two days of being used to feeling her hands on him, Elora carefully brought out the face collar and leash. Blackie looked at her suspiciously as she explained that he couldn't leave his cell without it. The lingual explanation wasn't for his benefit, but she might as well make sense to herself while she talked.

He sniffed the leash and sneezed his disapproval. When she began to draw the collar over his ears, he tensed and looked wary, but allowed it. Clearly the dog yearned for someone he could trust, badly enough to take a chance. She attached the leash, stood, then gently led him up and down the length of the kennel a few times so that he could get used to the pressure on his face and know that no harm would come from it.

Making liberal use of chicken treats she spent the next few days teaching him to heel, sit, and stay, using an archaic language that did not exist in this world. That insured that he would not respond to commands given by anyone else. He proved to be so smart that very little repetition and reinforcement was needed. He picked up new things quickly and was eager to please.

However, she could not take the next step, which was taking him out of the kennel without knowing how he would react in the presence of other humans. She chose Ram as the most likely candidate because she sensed that he would be reluctant to say no to her. So that day when he showed up for their regular afternoon movie, she told him she had a surprise.

"You what?" Ram seemed a little out of sorts about her revelation.

"You heard me perfectly well. I've been working with

him for weeks and we've progressed to the stage where I need to see how he will react to other people."

Ram narrowed his eyes at her. "Elora, don't try to deflect with that haughty thing 'cause we're stayin' on point and it's this. People call me reckless, but even I think this is looney. You'd have to have a death wish to go inside the cage with that dog!"

"Come see. You'll change your mind. Promise."

When Ram looked at those pleading eyes, he felt his good judgment slipping. He blinked twice trying to remember his objection until he saw her pack the tranq pistol. "You know people do no' usually need tranq's big enough to bring down a rhino when they're out for a stroll with their pet."

"Just a precaution." She angled a smiling challenge at Ram as she filled her pocket with chicken treats. "Don't be such an old woman. Come on."

Ram laughed softly. "Who would have ever thought that you would end up being a bad influence on me?"

When they reached the corner past which Blackie would be able to see as well as hear and smell what was going on, Elora stopped Ram. She gave him the tranq pistol already loaded with canisters and showed him how to use it.

"Give me a couple of minutes to say hello and prepare him. When I'm ready for you, I'll call out."

He caught her by the arm. "Elora, are you very, very sure about this?" Starting deep in her throat he heard the beginnings of an ugly noise that sounded like chicken clucking.

He scowled. "Bawk bawks?" Unbelievable. He glanced away like he was trying to gather patience. "Are you serious?" Elora's bawk, bawk, bawks were growing in volume and intensity.

"I give you a first rate education in pop culture and then you use it against me?" Bawk bawks getting louder. And she was good at it, too. There was an art to bawk bawk delivery.

"Oh for… Fine. Waitin' here."

When she disappeared around the corner, he waited for the inevitable snarling and growling, which could be quite loud coming from an Alsatian. But all he heard was the clank of cyclone fencing and the hushed tones of Elora's voice. He heard her call his name and let out the breath he didn't realize he'd been holding.

She was standing inside the kennel next to the dog, holding his leash. When Blackie saw Rammel coming toward the cage he assumed stalking stance, head lowered, nose and ears pointed forward intently.

He barked out a warning and Elora gave him a slight leash correction letting him know she didn't approve. As Ram continued to advance, she told Blackie to sit. He complied. She gave him a chicken treat, petting him, and telling him he was such a good boy. He didn't take his eyes off Ram, but didn't demonstrate signals of fear. He was becoming everything a mature, well-adjusted Alsatian male should be: proud, confident and at ease. Ram thought that he had never, in his life, seen anything more amazing. That is, until she got Blackie to lay on his back and ask for a tummy rub.

Elora asked Ram to come close enough to the chain link that she could reach through and touch him. When Ram stepped too close, Blackie eyed the tranq pistol and gave him an almost inaudible growl, but Elora corrected it immediately.

There was an opening a few inches high at the top of

the gate, just enough room to get her arm through. She reached out and petted Ram, telling Blackie that Ram was a good boy, too.

Ram was wondering how pathetic it must be that he was enjoying being petted and told he was a good boy.

Blackie had passed the test with flying colors and deserved to audition for more freedom.

Elora asked Ram to back up about twenty feet. When he was in place, she opened the gate keeping a firm hold on the leash. She exited first and then asked Blackie to heel, which he did. They walked the length of the hallway away from Ram, returned and then walked past Ram without incident. Elora showered him with praise and chicken treats. They jogged up and back a few times. She was amazed that his muscles hadn't atrophied from the confinement.

Blackie didn't want to go back into the kennel, but was eventually persuaded with enough treats.

That night she had dinner at B Team's table and shared the news with Storm and Kay. Storm was even more upset than Ram had been, but, with assurances from Ram, allowed himself to be conscripted into service along with Kay. The next day Elora repeated the exercise with three men instead of one. Blackie accepted them with Elora's encouragement and walked past them without incident.

"Which one of you three brave knights is willing to be the first to pet the dog?"

After a slight hesitation born of self-preservation, Ram handed the tranq pistol to Storm and stepped forward. Elora had Blackie sit and instructed Ram to advance slowly, holding out the back of his hand. Blackie sniffed Ram's hand, gave a tentative little lick, and allowed Ram to run his fingers over the big dog's lush coat. Like Elora, Ram loved animals and had a connection with them.

They had just put Blackie back into the kennel when he startled everyone present by suddenly snarling, baring his long, sharp, white teeth and throwing himself against the cage. A man wearing a maintenance uniform came around the corner, but stopped in his tracks, looking startled when he saw the little gathering.

"Hey. What's going on here?"

Storm looked from the man, to the dog, and back again. "I think maybe you're the one who needs to answer that question. Is that a taser on your belt?" The man narrowed his eyes and looked uncertain as to how to answer. As Storm started walking toward him he backed up. "What would maintenance personnel be doing with a taser inside Jefferson Unit?"

"It's for self defense. How would you like to have the job of feeding that monster and cleaning up after it?" He looked both defensive and guilty.

Elora gasped. "You've been using a taser on my dog?" Before the three men could form their next thought, Elora had sprung for the man, seized the taser, and zapped him with it three times. The poor devil was then writhing on the floor with Elora standing over him asking how he liked it. All three brave knights got an instant and unwelcome image of being the guy on the ground as Elora shot electrical currents through their systems. It was a side of the woman none of them wanted to engage. She was preparing to administer a fourth charge when Storm deftly took the taser out of her hand.

Kay called security and told them to take this guy and hold him until they had a chance to sort out what was going on. They checked with the personnel office and confirmed that one of his duties was taking care of the mascot. Further inquiry revealed that there was no real guideline as to how that was to be accomplished and no supervision whatsoever.

The job description talked about feeding, watering, kennel cleanliness, but did not strictly prohibit cruelty. They had to concede that, technically, the man had not done anything wrong. Sol agreed to transfer him to another facility, making certain there was a gag order in place regarding his experiences at Jefferson Unit and that any violation of that would see him and his family sent to the Siberian Unit.

Elora took over Blackie's care and feeding and was able to expand his freedoms daily. An entire hallway of sublevel two was closed off the first time she let him off leash. She brought a tennis ball for him to chase up and down and she shared the joy he experienced from being out of kennel and off leash.

They decided Blackie's debut to society would be the night that Storm, Kay, and Ram were accepting posthumous ceremonial decoration for Lan. The three members of B Team could not have looked more handsome in their black sileather pants, long sleeve, black knit shirts, and Black Watch sashes. As a precaution, earlier in the day,

Ram had deposited the tranq pistol under the bench where he would be sitting, but didn't think he would need it. They left a place for Elora to sit next to them at one end of the lower benches.

Everyone was assembled in the Chamber and the doors were about to close when Elora walked in. They had arranged for the media to make an announcement.

"We are proud to present Blackie, the Jefferson Unit mascot, in his first public appearance accompanied by his handler, Elora Laiken."

Elora wore a sleeveless black dress cinched at the waist by a wide red belt. The dress fit her body through the hips, then flared, swishing around her shins on top of her boots. That vision coupled with the sight of a huge, formerly ferocious, black Alsatian wearing a Black Watch kerchief drew a collective gasp from the crowd. When Blackie was first led into the room, he drew back at the sight of so many people gathered in one place and looked at Elora uncertainly, but he was quickly reassured by the sound of her voice and resumed his natural, easy gait.

Two members of B Team felt their hearts swell with pride. She exchanged a smile with Ram as she and Blackie sat down.

Throughout the proceeding the dog remained alert but calm; a perfect example of good Alsatian breeding. Afterward, many people came by to speak to the remaining members of B Team. It was understood that it would be in the worst of taste to congratulate these men on medals received in an incident that had cost the life of their friend. So they simply said hello and shook hands.

Some of them were brave enough to venture close to Elora. When she saw signs of acceptance from Blackie, she would encourage them to reach out slowly, allow him to sniff their hand and then pet him.

Gradually Blackie took celebrity, the crowd and all the activity in stride. This was the final test that earned him the status of roommate. That night Blackie moved in with Elora. Soon she had enough trust in his behavior to let him spend time off leash on the rugby field, fetching tennis balls and playing chase.

ONE SUCH AFTERNOON, as they were returning from a romp, Elora and Blackie found the hub cleared except for six knights escorting a man in chains crisscrossed on top of his leather duster and attached to shackles around his wrists and ankles. He had shoulder length brown hair, eyes the transparent color of icy mountain water, a model's cheek bones and the barest suggestion of a cleft in his chin. He stared at Elora as he was led past, his mouth turning up in an amused smile.

Elora might have called him handsome under other circumstances, but she had no time to think about such things. She was occupied restraining one-hundred-twenty pounds of Alsatian male fury. Blackie had a serious problem with the man in chains. She hadn't heard ferocity like that since the first day she'd seen him. Right then the only thing between his beautiful, white fangs and the chained man's throat was a braided leather leash. And it was a good thing Elora happened to be unusually strong.

She pushed the elevator button behind her and "persuaded" Blackie to back into the elevator. As soon as the doors closed establishing a solid barrier, the dog went instantly quiet and docile, looking at her as if to say, "What's next?" and wagging his tail. The person who originally conceived the expression "out of sight, out of mind" must have been a dog trainer.

That night she had dinner with B Team and told them

what had happened. The three exchanged looks as if they were trying to decide what they would and would not reveal. It seemed they came to a silent consensus that there was no reason not to divulge what they knew.

The chained man was not a man, but a vampire; a very, very old vampire named Istvan Baka. He had been captured decades ago under circumstances that some believe amounted to turning himself in. He was held prisoner with privileges by The Order at a facility in the Carpathian Mountains in exchange for consulting on matters of vampire. Kay said he had heard that, when Baka was transported, he was prepared by being deprived of sustenance until they were positive that he was weak enough to be controlled by knights, should it become necessary.

B Team agreed that, since the dog had not reacted badly to anyone since his tormentor had been transferred, they could conclude two things: that Blackie knew a vampire when he saw one and that he didn't like them at all.

CHAPTER 11

BLACK SWAN FIELD TRAINING MANUAL
Chapter 8, #23

Operatives must be inoculated against contraction of the vampire virus and receive a booster once every two years. The inoculation is one hundred percent effective (to date), but, because of the extremely high cost and limited ingredients, it will not be made available to the general public even should the general public become aware of the presence of vampire among us.

I STVAN BAKA WAS born in the eastern Carpathian Mountains of Romania in 1453 and lived there throughout his life as a human. It was not a life without substance. At the time he was infected with the vampire virus he was working for the monks of Cozio, painting murals of the history of the monastery and various other religious themes. He was proud of the fact that the few paintings on canvas are owned by the Romanian Cultural Heritage Foundation and considered national treasures.

When Istvan Baka was infected, he was practically elderly for medieval times. At thirty-six he had seen his share of death and sorrow, had lost two wives and five children. Such things were expected and accepted as part of life then.

The monks had paid him a meager wage and given him an education in science and mathematics because they liked him and it amused them to do so. One day in midwinter he was caught up in what he was doing and lit more candles as the room grew darker. When he stopped for the night, it was dark outside. He left to make his way home, but never arrived.

Istvan had pulled his coat around him. The night was still, but very cold. There was a waning moon, half bright, but it was almost impossible to see the path through the forest without a lamp. He had to go slowly or risk a misstep. He was thinking about the warmth in his cottage where his third wife would have something, perhaps lamb stew, warming on the hearth. His thoughts were thus occupied when he heard a rustle and a whimper in the woods.

After a few more steps, he decided it was an overactive imagination replaying tales of horror from childhood. The first indication otherwise was a woman's scream. He ran in the direction of the sound, but was brought to an abrupt halt by a deep gash sliced open in his neck.

He was left alone on the cold mountain to freeze to death or bleed out, but he did neither. When the sun rose the next morning his body had not died, but his humanity had. His brain had regained control of a body too weak from loss of blood to respond. With great effort and exertion of will, he slowly dragged himself to a crevice behind a rock and covered himself with branches. There he stayed for a time. Days perhaps. He did not grow stronger, but his weakness was overcome by a thirst he had not experienced before.

Baka's wife, having been told that Istvan had left the monastery three days before, was beside herself with worry and searching the mountain between the monastery and the cottage, looking for some sign of what had become of him. There were rumors that he was attacked by a wild animal, a wolf perhaps. So she looked for signs of blood or torn clothing or worse.

Distraught as she was, she had not noticed the sun was low in the sky. Being caught in winter after dark on a Romanian mountainside was dangerous by any standard as the temperature plummets when the sun sets. It was the pink moment called gloaming, when twilight turns to night, when the unfortunate woman walked close to where Istvan Baka was hiding. It was then he knew what his body craved and he was taken over by instinct.

When Baka's third wife drew near his hiding place, he marshaled his remaining strength and grabbed her ankle. She was frozen by surprise for an instant which is all it took to jerk her to the ground and sink his new fangs into the neck of a woman whom he had married, if not loved. She was instantly paralyzed, as Baka had been, but, unlike Baka, she was drained of every drop of blood until she was past pain and past the concerns of this life.

Baka felt no regret. He felt only that he was stronger than at any time in memory. The body was carried to a deep gorge nearby and thrown over. By the time it was found, if ever, people would assume she died from a fall. And so began Istvan Baka's new life as a vampire.

He traveled west, often spending his days hiding in wine cellars. If an unfortunate victim happened upon him, he simply indulged in a daytime meal.

He was not in any particular hurry. It probably took a hundred years to reach France. By chance he discovered that, like most vampire, he could hypnotize humans effortlessly, and that they could be useful in the performance of certain daytime functions, as guards, or suppliers of food, luring unsuspecting women with promises of work or pay for service. Baka had acquired money by selectively targeting victims who appeared well off and relieving them of their purses as well as their life's blood. Bodies were always left with the appearance of having been rent by wild animals so that no one would suspect anything as fantastic as vampire. In France he developed a taste for lavish living, a taste he prefers even now, and he remained in the area for several centuries.

In 1925 Istvan Baka had an entranced servant arrange for his transportation to New York by merchant vessel in a cabin without porthole. He was bored with Europe and eager to experience something different. The subway system, begun twenty years earlier, was intriguing for several reasons. When he arrived, it was being rapidly expanded. He was able to create his own maze of tunneled refuges using a system of abandoned shafts.

By the time the stock market crash heralded The Great Depression three years later, his labyrinth was in place, complete with secret entrances and exits, cleverly disguised. He had even wired the tunnels for electric lights, tapped into the Pearl Street Power Station and redistributed the signature so that the source of drain wouldn't be traced. As time went on and equipment became more sophisticated, he made sure he always had the loyalty of a CON ED employee in a position to oversee billing discrepancies.

New York provided him with an endless supply of runaways, aspiring actresses, and evicted poor. Yes. Istvan Baka had turned the city into a vampire playground and paradise. It was only a matter of time before other vampire came begging him to share his cozy set up. He accepted pledges of fealty and turned lesser vamps into minions. He never had to hunt unless he felt like it. He never had to worry about being hunted. He was king of vampire – at least in New York. But, after a time, that, too, began to lose its appeal.

The centuries had started blur, one into another, in an endless stream of monotony. Suck. Kill. Suck. Kill. Suck. Fuck. Kill. He could howl from the tedium of it all, but what would be the point? He had insulated himself so perfectly no one would hear.

His conscience, the essence of humanity, and the memories from his brief life as human, were not restored gradually, but suddenly, without warning. That restoration created a state of wretchedness without equal because he also retained the memory of his life as a vampire. Even though he had not been in control of his behavior as a vampire, the guilt was staggering.

Determined to make amends, he quietly and quickly went about killing vampire who were using the tunnel system he created. It was ridiculously easy since they never would have expected death to be wearing Istvan Baka's face.

He then sealed the entrances to the tunnels and turned himself in to The Order, volunteering to assist as a consultant or informant or in whatever other capacity would be useful. Now, having endured the passing of another century, that had become tiresome as well and he began to dream about death.

Then, one day, his atrophied interest was engaged as he passed through the central lobby of the New Angland unit of Black Swan. There, controlling a large and vicious black dog, was a provocateur; a female Swan; strong, beautiful, graceful, and very likely every bit as ruthless as the knights. What could be more intriguing?

Upon return to the tower keep cell where he was held in an ancient castle fortress in the Carpathian Mountains, Istvan Baka contacted Sovereign Sol Nememiah to say that he had considered the offer. He would agree to spy for The Order and assist in bringing an end to the current infestation in New York in exchange for a private, unbound audience with the Lady Swan.

At first, Sol didn't understand the reference, but quickly put together that he was referring to their resident alien pilgrim, Elora Laiken. He learned that Baka had seen Elora in passing and that he was, apparently, under the misimpression that she was a knight.

A meeting was called to take place in the conference room adjacent to Sol's office for B Team and Elora. They had no idea what it was about. It had already been decided that Ghost would take Lan's place in ten days when Ram was cleared from the D.L. Plus, it was curious that Elora was included. When everyone reported to the conference room except Elora, they called her phone, but didn't get an answer.

"Probably on the rugby field with her hellhound," Kay said. Sol sent one of the older trainees who worked as an assistant to find her suggesting he start at the rugby field per Kay's comment.

"So what's this about?" Storm asked.

"We'll wait until Ms. Laiken is present."

Storm, Kay, and Ram exchanged looks then decided to use the time to avail themselves of the coffee service and cookies that had been set up at one end of the conference room.

Ten minutes later Elora came in with Blackie. Her cheeks were even pinker than usual from playing with the dog in the cool Autumn air. Ram thought she looked irresistibly kissable and pictured himself rubbing his cheek against the tip of her cold nose to warm it up.

She closed the door and unsnapped Blackie's leash. The dog went straight to Ram and rested his big head on Ram's thigh. Elora sat down in the empty chair next to Ram, took a half eaten cookie out of his hand and gobbled it down without pretense of courtesy. He smiled openly, loving the easy familiarity of an unapologetic theft. When she took a sip of his coffee and scrunched up her face, he laughed, "Serves you right. Get your own."

"Shall we get down to business children?" Foregoing social pleasantries, which were not Sol's forte anyway, he relayed Baka's proposal while Elora made herself a cup of sugar and cream with a touch of coffee.

Storm and Ram answered in unison with an emphatic, "No!"

As she was reseating herself, Elora gave Sol a level look while stirring her cup. "I'm in."

Ram gaped. Storm fumed. Elora ignored them both.

She took a sip and then continued, "Any ideas why he would make his agreement conditional on talking to me?"

"I didn't ask. Anything more would be pure speculation," Sol replied.

"Elora," Ram looked flustered, "please believe me. 'Tis one thing to read about vampire in trainin' manuals and somethin' quite different to come face to face with one. And, while we're on the subject," he turned on Sol, "you can no' truly be thinkin' to turn that monster loose in New York?"

Sol stood at ease with arms crossed over his chest and answered slowly. "Seen the news lately? The numbers of missing women have become alarming and we're not getting anywhere. We've reached a point where the potential benefit outweighs the risk."

Ram threw his hands up in a gesture of frustration and immediately regretted it, reaching for his rib.

Kay said, "What does he mean by private, unbound audience?"

"It would be more accurate to say semi-private. There's a very large mirror in his room that is observation glass on the other side. You'll be able to hear and see everything that transpires."

"You'll?" Storm said.

"I think we would all feel more secure if the three of you accompany her."

Elora laughed softly. "Well, we must be certain you all feel more secure." She looked at Sol in open challenge. "I have a condition." The four men looked at her. "When we return, I want to be accorded the same freedoms as anyone else. I want to be able to go shopping or to performances of the arts or take classes or whatever. In the future, whether or not I'm 'accompanied' should be my decision."

Sol sat down at the end of the table. "I need to consult with Monq."

"Alright. Get him in here." Elora sounded imperious.

"I'd watch my tone if I were you, young lady."

Elora exploded out of the chair, startling everyone in the room. "I don't work for you, Mister Sovereign. And unless you want to change that and make my employment official, what exactly is my motivation for watching my tone? What am I to fear? Incarceration?" The last word was scalding with sarcasm. "It's simple. You need something from me. I need something from you. If such negotiating tactics work for a vampire, why not for me?"

Sol appraised her with a hard glint in his eye and a tick in his jaw. Then he reached for his phone and dialed Monq. "Can you come to my office straightaway?" He said to the group in general, "Wait here," and left the room.

Ram and Storm were both a little stunned having never seen Elora on a rip. Being short on actual relationship experience, neither understood that every woman has a Medusa side.

"No need to hold back," Kay turned to Elora, evidently enjoying himself, "just come straight out and say how you feel."

"Look," said Storm, "I know this place must feel confining." Elora snorted. "And I agree it's time to adjust your security clearance so you can move around more freely, but this audience with Baka thing... Ram is right." He glanced toward Ram. "For once. You don't just have tea with a vampire. They're danger in the first degree, tricky, lethal, and evil—regardless of what the training manual says. And this is the oldest one we know of."

Elora was unmoved. "I'm not being dismissive. I've spent enough time with the manual and the annals to know that what you're saying is true. But I'm not the girl next door." Reconsidering that, she turned to look at Ram. "Well, I am the girl next door to *you*." Returning a resolute gaze to Storm she added, "I'm strong and fast."

"And way too cocky!" Storm interrupted.

"Even if that was true, it's not your call, Sir Storm."

In the middle of the argument, Storm found himself wondering when her accent had disappeared and when her speech patterns had become so informal, the cadence so contemporary. She was close to being able to pass as a native. He couldn't decide whether he thought that was an improvement or not.

"And you're not worried about the fact that he speci-fied 'unbound'? If all he wants to do is talk, why would he care whether he's bound or not?" Storm asked.

"Good point," Ram said nodding and pointing to Storm like he was Exhibit A.

Kay said, "Putting that aside for now, there's the issue of trance." He looked around. "We had nearly a decade of training to resist it. It's not something you can pick up in a weekend workshop. If you're hypnotized, all the strength and speed in the world won't help you."

"Not a problem. I'm not hypnotizable." She looked at Ram. "Is that a word?" He just stared. She shrugged. "Ask Monq."

She looked at her fingernails nonchalantly. The three

were exchanging one of their telepathic looks when Sol and Monq walked in.

Kay dispensed with the pleasantries and pinned Monq, "Is it true she can't be hypnotized?"

"Yes. That is true. A very useful trait should she decide to proceed with the meeting."

Elora looked at Sol. "Did I mention that somebody needs to take care of my dog while I'm gone? Someone of my choosing."

Storm looked at Monq like he was a traitor. "You're going along with this madness?"

Monq turned toward Storm looking sympathetic because he wasn't even trying to disguise his feelings for Elora. "Sir Storm, this is an ideal assignment for Ms. Laiken and, so far as security clearance goes, her profile scores indicate candidacy for top level duty." He leaned toward Storm and whispered. "She outscored you!"

Storm huffed in response. "Why not just bring him here?"

"Baka has proven to be reliable to the letter of written agreement. Once a deal is made, he can be trusted to abide by it, but, he will not hesitate to take advantage of any contractual loophole, no matter how minute.

"We brought him here to assess the developing situation before it gets away from us completely, but transporting him, and striking bargains with him, well, there's always a slight chance that we didn't write a flawless contract. The facility in Romania is without equal. Until we need him out, he stays in."

Quietly, Elora turned toward Sol, "So. Do we have a deal?"

He looked her over and said, "Yes. If you take the vow of secrecy. And, by the way, since you work for me now, you will give me the deference I require."

"Yes sir," she said seriously.

"You need to go get your inoculation."

"What's involved in that?"

"You never had shots as a child?"

"You mean with needles like they use in the infirmary?"

"Yes."

"No."

"Well, they administer tiny little doses of the vampire virus combined with an antidote and it instigates an immunity in your system."

"Okay." Then she brightened and turned to the three members of B Team. "Road trip!" she said with the exuberance of a person who had spent many afternoons steeping in American "B" movie culture. "When do we leave? How long will we be gone and, most importantly, what do I wear?"

If the prospect of Elora in a room alone with that thing wasn't so horrifying, her excitement would be contagious. Storm regarded her for a moment and then coolly turned to Sol to play his trump card.

"What if the three of us refuse to go?"

"Then we'll send one of the other teams." Sol replied just as evenly and without hesitation.

Storm tightened his lips, gripped the arms of his chair, and looked at Kay who simply shrugged, opened his hands in a gesture of helplessness, and shook his head. Looking utterly disgusted with the turn of events, Ram, who had been pacing, flopped into his chair like a surly teenager, forgetting that flopping doesn't help broken ribs. He winced silently.

ONCE EVERYONE INVOLVED was resigned to the inevitable, they began making plans. First, The Operations Office arranged an identity complete with passport for Elora. Second, in Chamber, she formally gave the vow of secrecy to a triad of Sol, Monq, and the sitting government liaison, with B Team as witnesses. She pledged never to reveal anything seen, heard, or learned about The Order for so long as she lived. Amen.

Elora reported to the med center for her first inoculation in the series. The needle was bigger than she had imagined, but not as big as vamp fangs as Ram was quick to point out. She was kept for two hours for observation to confirm that there were no immediate side effects of a debilitating or pernicious nature. The first injection was apparently the best indicator of whether or not the subject would tolerate inoculation.

After being cleared to leave, she spent the afternoon with Ram glued to her laptop at the combination dining desk, getting outfitted online for a trip far afield.

It was heaven to be close enough to smell her natural jasmine scent and feel the radiance of her body heat. It was hell to be close to her and not reach out to wind that shiny hair around his fingers. Or bury his face in her neck. Or pull her close to find out if her body would mold to his the way he imagined it would. A thousand times an hour.

As she concentrated on laptop shopping, he stared at the side of her breast. Sometimes he thought she suspected what he was thinking because he had the pleasure of watching her nipples tighten and bud through a silk shirt or a lightweight knit top. His hands were mere inches away from a caress. Once he literally put his hands between his thighs and the chair and sat on them because the compulsion to reach out and touch might override his will power.

When Elora caught Ram staring at her with heavy lids, eyes darkened to navy blue and magnifying the reflection of any nearby light, it made her uncomfortable because she treasured the friendship and wanted nothing to interfere with it. And it made her uncomfortable because it was titillating, a rush of excitement that ran the length of her body like a drug always beginning and ending in a little jerk of her clit.

She didn't have much experience with boys, but she wasn't a virgin either. One of her cousins had brought a friend from prep, a cute son of a County, to a big event at the palace.

While everyone's attention was on the fireworks display, the two of them had sneaked off to sample kisses and touches. At least that was what she thought. Those kisses, those eye-opening kisses, warm and delightful, soon turned into a demand for more.

She would like to say the story went that she didn't want what happened next, but she couldn't say that honestly. She'd been curious, eager for new experiences, and acutely aware that her life didn't present a lot of opportunities for sexual experimentation. So she allowed him to lift the long, costume skirts and take her against a wall, behind an old stone column. The entire event took less than a minute, or seemed so, just enough time to lose her virginity painfully. Enough time to learn that boys could make revolting noises. Enough time to be left feeling thoroughly used without anything to show for it.

He didn't even bother to walk her back to her place in the hall. He just smirked and walked away. She knew he wouldn't go back to school and brag about deflowering one of the royals or her cousin would kill him.

As a species-old rite of passage she learned that flattering words, looks of longing, and inadvertent touches are often no more than skillfully applied means to an end. The humiliation that burned inside her caught fire and crystallized into resolve. What came from the ashes of anger and shame was a determination that she would never be used for rutting again. Ever.

So, when she thought Ram was flirting with her, she pretended to be oblivious. If his knee brushed against hers, she simply chose to ignore the contact even when her body seemed to have its own ideas.

Resisting him was easy when he was engaged in raucous laughter over some movie scene with over-the-top vulgarity or nasty bathroom humor that would make the vilest of boors regard him with disdain.

Likewise, on occasions when she thought Storm might be expressing interest in her as a woman, she preferred to take that bit of presage and set it aside for examination at some later time. Storm was attentive to her, gentlemanly to a fault, and protective. That was clear. Certainly a girl could do a lot worse than be adored by a gorgeous man with exceptional intelligence, courage, and a heart that was good through and through.

There was no doubt she owed Storm everything. He hadn't just saved her life. Throughout recovery he'd been there every day, but it hadn't stopped there. After she was physically well, he'd made every effort to support her and help her find her way in a world that was strange at best and desolately lonely at worst. If Storm wanted her, she didn't know how she would be able to say no.

"Elora?" She felt a light tap on her knee and blinked out of her reverie shaking herself internally. "Welcome back." Ram's lips curled up at the corners and his eyes sparkled with teasing. And affection.

"Sorry," she smiled in return. "Where were we?"

They made certain to shop with merchants who could ship overnight in the true sense, not in the we'll-ship-overnight-three-days-from-now sense. They bought luggage and clothes that would travel well and be tempera-ture appropriate. That was the tricky part, traveling from New York to high in the Carpathian Mountains in mid October, they could encounter a seventy degree difference. The remote Carpathians were at a high enough altitude that even snowfall was possible.

Ram explained the dress-for-warmth technology of their world which was functional, comfortable and fashionable in fabrics that absorbed color with the deep intensity of silk. What more could a girl want?

They had developed light weight layers with temperature ratings such as warms to forty, twenty, ten, zero degrees and so on. One of the best features was that synthetic fur looked and felt exactly like the real thing while being extremely light weight.

By the time they were done they had everything from lightweight sleeveless silk knits to cashmere socks.

Last, but not least, Elora wanted to prepare for her meeting with Istvan Baka by learning what she could about him.

"I'm no' exactly the end all authority, but I've heard he sits in a plush accommodation writin' vampire romance novels under a nom de plume. And that they're best sellers."

Elora blinked at Ram while waiting for the punch line. When seconds ticked by without so much as a twitch of his beautiful mouth, she ventured, "You are joking, right?"

Nodding he said, "I can see why you would think so. It

does sound fanciful and farfetched." He shrugged his shoulders, stood up, and raised his arms in a stretch that made the six pack ripple in a fascinating pattern that could be glimpsed under the thin cotton tee. She couldn't have looked away if her life had depended on it. "Probably just a rumor," he yawned.

Following her gaze to his torso, and clearly pleased that she was looking, he got a fresh infusion of energy. "Hey! Caught you checkin' out the machine. Look at this." Grinning, Ram pulled his knit shirt up to his neck and proceeded to make his stomach muscles dance in and out, side to side, like a belly dancer.

She had to admit it was an amazing performance. Cirque du Soleil offered nothing more captivating. She gaped partly because of the spectacle and partly because she couldn't believe they had actually knighted someone so common and vulgar.

With considerable effort she finally pulled her eyes away so that she could register disapproval with a re-sounding, "Ughhhh!"

She stood and closed the laptop with a resolute click. "Does it even cross your mind that this is not appropriate behavior? You could use a few months of finishing school, you know that? On second thought, make that years."

"Finishin' school?" he spluttered taking his turn at gaping. "Now that is a joke!"

"No it's not a joke! Blackie has better manners than you do, elf."

Inexplicably Ram felt offended even knowing that was ridiculous, considering how often he had mocked the conventions of "manners" and gone out of his way to rebel against them.

"Really? That bein' the case, in your book it would be better manners for me to fall on my back with big, naked balls rollin' from side to side, tongue hangin' out, askin' for a nice, tummy rub? 'Cause I can manage that. Right here and now." He pointed at a spot on the floor next to her feet. "Is this good for you?"

"And besides," she continued, ignoring his rant, "doesn't that," she pointed at his stomach, "hurt your injury?" Suddenly she did a double take and narrowed her eyes with suspicion. "Or have you been faking this whole time to get attention?"

His eyes widened at the same time his mouth fell open

even further. The term 'brain freeze' took on a whole new meaning. It was too much. The very person who'd done the damage claiming he was faking! Still trying to form a response, he caught the light in her eye half a second before her mouth twitched.

"Got cha."

He relaxed, giving her wicked smile a once-over with an entirely new appreciation. "Seems I've taught you well."

Elora chuffed and gave a throaty laugh he hadn't heard before as she reveled in his admiration.

It made him want to press his face into her chest and ask her to do it again so he could absorb the vibration while he nuzzled the locket out of the way.

He didn't know how long he was going to be able to last at this outrageous business of flirting without touching. Everything about this experience was foreign for him. He'd never had to work at seduction. Women often pressed breasts into his body and shoved panties into his hand just because he had glanced in a direction where they were in his line of sight. Elora's indifference was making him crazed and enthralling him at the same time.

It occurred to him that it had been over six weeks

since he'd last been laid. Certainly that was the first since he'd reached puberty. Even stranger was the realization that he had no desire to bed anyone else. It seemed the whole thing about elf mating was true. He wanted Elora. Just Elora. And he wanted her now.

When Blackie heard the laptop close, he stuck his head out from under the table looking hopeful that it might be time to go out for a run. Elora reached out to rub between his ears and the dog automatically leaned into her leg.

SANCTION AGREED TO take care of Blackie while Elora was away. The dog never failed to give Sanction a canine equivalent of a grin and that was a good enough character reference for her. She supposed 'Sanction' was a nickname, but didn't think it would be polite to ask. In case it wasn't.

She fastened Blackie's leash and took him with her to hunt down Monq and find out the best way to go about researching Istvan Baka.

Monq confirmed that, indeed, Baka was the successful author of a very popular series of vampire romance novels.

"…however unlikely that might seem. I believe he writes as Valerie de Stygian."

"Stygian? As in the River Styx?"

"I see my counterpart gave you a decent education in classical studies." Monq looked at her above the rims of his glasses. "I suspect Baka didn't think many of his readers would catch the tongue-in-cheek reference, but, at the same time, hoped they would."

"A vampire who is a complicated personality?"

Monq summarized what he knew about Baka's history before his capture and gave her the records of his involvement with The Order since.

"Your friends from Bad Company are worried and not entirely without justification."

Elora made a scoffing noise in response.

"There's nothing wrong with feeling competent, Ms. Laiken, but you are treading very close to the edge of disrespecting your associates. They don't make a habit of hand wringing, you know. They're experienced vampire killers who know all too well what you will be facing whereas you do not. You must not get overly confident in your abilities. Even you need to be careful around a vampire as old and strong as Baka."

On returning to her apartment, Elora downloaded

eleven books by Valerie de Stygian and started to read.

Three days later she was packed and ready to go. She said goodbye to Blackie, who whined because he sensed she was leaving.

CHAPTER 12

BLACK SWAN FIELD TRAINING MANUAL
Chapter 12, #13

Once infected by the virus, vampire cease to live as humans. They retain neither conscience nor memory of their lives before onset. So, in that sense, they might be accurately regarded as "undead". In the Dark Ages vampire were considered evil, but, in more enlightened times, we recognize that they are inherently no better or worse than the mosquito that is mindlessly driven by its nature to drink blood or die. The philosophical or theological nature of the question of evil is not relevant to our purpose which is complete extermination.

ELORA WHEELED HER rolling suitcase down the hallway toward the elevator. Her body was vibrating with a hum of exhilaration at the prospect of seeing something of the world outside Jefferson Unit. And Baka alone was responsible for the junket. Owing a vampire a debt of gratitude had to be one of Fate's more comical twists.

For the first time since arriving in this world she crossed the front door threshold of Jefferson Unit. It was a beautiful moonlit night.

Two servicemen in camouflage uniforms stood next to open air Jeeps at the end of the sidewalk. They lifted luggage into the rear compartments while Storm gestured for Elora to climb onto the back seat. He swung in beside her while Ram and Kay hopped the other Jeep. She hadn't asked how they were traveling. Until now it had seemed like the least important aspect of the experience.

The ride to the base airstrip took less than five minutes. They pulled up next to a sleek, white, unmarked Learjet, lit by spotlights, and stopped next to the stairs. She arched a brow at Storm. "Private plane?"

He put his finger to his lips in a gesture of silence, then leaned over and whispered in her ear. "Ask me on board."

The breath on her ear gave her an involuntary little

shiver. She nodded an okay.

At the top of the steps stood an exotic looking woman with black hair, black eyes, skin the color of creamed coffee and rosy cheeks, an unusual, but effective combination. Her grooming was as impeccable as a doll in a toy store window. Perfect nails. Lined lips. Helmet hair.

She regarded Elora as coolly as she gushed flirtatious warmth toward the men. Naturally, they were oblivious to the double standard of behavior.

"Good evening. I'm Minerva. I'll be your attendant for this flight."

Elora gave her a look that said, "Are we going to have a problem?" Minerva responded with a grin that was both insincere and far too artificially white.

The interior of the jet was lavish and comfortable with cushy bench seating in the forward area and ottomans on tracks. In the rear were four large arm-chairs that could swivel and lock down in any direction or recline for sleeping. Between each was a hide-a-table that could be lowered and used for cards or as a desk with monitor, satellite feed for TV or movies, and laptop friendly connectors.

Elora took a seat on one of the bench units and strapped herself in. Ram sat down beside her while Storm sat across on the other side. Kay headed straight for the rear, plopped in one of the arm-chairs, reclined, folded his arms, and closed his eyes.

While Minerva secured the door, Elora asked Storm, "So, what's up with the V.I.P. treatment?"

"The Order owns six of these. We share this one with other installations in North America, but they're shuffled as needed."

"And you're not worried about the carbon footprint?"

"What's a carbon footprint?"

"It's the ecological cost of the amount of fossil fuel being burned."

He shook his head. "We've been on nuclear for a long time."

That explains the clean air. "Okay. So how long is the flight? And where are we landing?"

"Bucharest. About eight and a half hours from now. We'll have some dinner and sleep through the trip. When you wake up, we'll be in Romania."

After hearing Minerva recite the list of available food,

Elora leaned over and whispered into Ram's hair that she would like for him to ask for an extra corned beef sandwich on rye with Dijon mustard and a Diet Coke with lime. She explained that she wouldn't care for Minerva to know which food and drink was hers. Ram laughed out loud, then placed a double order just as she had requested. Storm asked for cauliflower lasagna. Kay got a Jack Daniels.

When Elora looked at Kay questioningly, Storm said, "He doesn't like to fly."

Ram pulled his monitor out of stow position, fiddled with the angle, and began reviewing choices from the video library. Elora had no doubt he would find something suited for ill bred thirteen-year-olds.

When the food was served, Elora took one of the sandwiches, moved to the rear, and sat down in the armchair facing Kay. He glanced up from his whiskey with a quizzical look.

"Hey," she said.

"Hey?" he replied with eyebrows raised. "To what do I owe this honor?"

"The honor of my company? Sarcasm, Kay?" She removed a toothpick from one of the sandwich halves. "Seems you and I don't often have a chance to chat. I know a lot about Storm and Ram, their families, their interests, but not so much about you. So I thought I'd ask about the lucky girl and see if I could maybe finagle an invitation to the wedding. Since I plan to be a free woman soon."

"I think we can afford another plate." He drawled as he gave her that easy-going, Texas gent smile.

Elora suspected that Kay deliberately went through life moving slow and easy so as not to intimidate others, which could easily happen. If the mass of his immense, muscular body was paired with a threatening countenance, there could be cause for alarm. The fact that he was a berserker meant that his calm, logical self cohabitated in a body with a beastly side suppressed, but living just under the surface.

"You'd like her," he went on. "Everyone does." He sniffed, looked out the window at the black abyss of the Atlantic Ocean at night, chuckled to himself, then turning back to Elora added, "But I guess if they didn't like her they wouldn't tell me."

Elora laughed. "No. Probably not. So, how did you meet? What does she do? More importantly, does she know what you do?"

Normally Kay would never be accused of being verbose, but it seemed his fiancé was his favorite subject and Elora had just pushed the talk button. He said that they were childhood sweethearts, that she was an event promoter, and she thought he worked for the government in some secretive capacity – that she didn't know vampire existed, much less that her intended was a vampire hunter. He talked about how much she loved disco music and disco dancing and how cute it was.

Elora tried to picture Kay disco dancing and admitted that she was having trouble with the image.

"I might surprise you then. I'm actually fair to middlin' at it. At least enough to keep my Trina happy."

When she ran out of questions to ask about the wedding and the bride-to-be, she asked about his family. He talked about his three sisters and how they had been named after the Norns, about life in South Texas, and how he would never want to settle someplace cold.

Last, she asked what he knew about the journey.

Apparently a whister would be waiting at the airport in Bucharest to take them directly to Baka's prison. Sixty years ago The Order had purchased a 13th century castle ruin on a cliff side gorge that formed the Wallachia Transylvania border. It was restored for use as an Order installation and as a maximum security prison for Baka. They frequently improved the fortification through advancing technologies so that it was a perpetually state-of-the-art facility; impenetrable from without and inescapable from within.

"Do you know why he wants to talk to me?" she asked.

Kay shook his head. "Want my best guess?"

"Sure."

"He saw you and was gripped by the bewitchment thing you've got going on."

She looked confused.

"You know. *That* thing." He looked pointedly toward Storm and Ram, one at a time, before bringing his attention back to Elora.

On realizing what he meant, her face pinked with a full on blush that was clearly amusing to Kay.

There was no point in responding so she stood,

opened an overhead compartment to get a pillow and blanket, as she had seen Minerva do for Storm, then found a length of bench seat that would accommodate her for the night and tried to get comfortable. After everyone had finished eating, the lights were dimmed. She was thinking that she was sure she wouldn't sleep. The next thing she knew lights were coming on and Minerva was offering coffee, fresh fruit, bagels, and muffins.

She sat up feeling groggy and wishing she had put her toothbrush in the backpack she'd brought on board. She made her way to the aft lavatory and used her finger to rub cold water over her teeth. Not perfect. But better than dragon breath. She straightened her clothes, pulled her hair up in a ponytail, looked in the mirror, and assured herself she was ready for the next big adventure.

It was light when they arrived in Bucharest. As light as it was going to be. The day was overcast, rainy, with poor visibility and conditions that would keep the whister grounded for the day.

After some discussion by phone, Storm informed the group that they would travel by train to Brasov and by car from there. A van had been hired to take them to the train station.

It was colder than Elora expected so she took the opportunity, as the van was being loaded, to pull a couple of extra layers from her suitcase along with a toothbrush and toothpaste. As they drove through the streets of Bucharest Elora took everything in through a filter of raindrops on the window. The old part of the city was interesting for its antiquity, but portentous at the same time.

They had first class seats on the train, which meant a private compartment with upholstered bench seats and armrests that could be raised flush with the seat back or lowered, but the train was overdue for interior renovation. The faded blue fabric had definitely seen better days as had the linoleum flooring.

Elora sat next to a window with Ram directly across. Kay sat beside her with the interior door on his right and Storm in front of him. She thought she probably appeared as inquisitive as a child, looking out the window as if she had never travelled before. Truthfully, she hadn't travelled much. The cost of security for the extended family was too high a price for a modern monarchy.

The trip through the Danube Valley was breathtaking.

The weather was warm enough in the lowland that greens had not yet given way to fall color. The mist and light fog made the landscape all the more haunting.

Ram was staring at her. She raked her gaze over his sprawled figure. As usual, he was taking up way more than his allotted space. He was slouched down in the seat, knees slightly bent, legs stretched out in front of him, feet in her space, head resting on the back of his bench seat. The posture made it impossible not to notice that Ram was remarkably well endowed. As a result of the education she had received reading the vampire Baka's series of romances, she had learned that, in some circles, he would be called a "lefty".

Looking at his feet taking up part of her space she noticed for the first time that they might be big for the rest of him. Then she remembered what Kay had said that first night at dinner. *Pointy ears. Big feet.*

His eyelids were half closed and he was wearing an odd little, self-satisfied smile like he had a secret. A slight movement drew her eye away from his face to his hand near the end of the armrest next to the window. There was, apparently, a hole in the upholstery the size of his middle finger. That finger was disappearing into the hole and reappearing in a rhythm that she imagined would match the in and out pace of leisurely love making.

At this point enough time had been spent in Ram's company to take some of the mortification out of such inferences. She knew that a big outer reaction would give him a perverse victory. So matching the exact same cadence, she allowed her right hand to begin moving across her lap, her first two fingers mimicking the motion of scissors cutting. Eyes gleaming, head thrown back and stomach muscles rippling, Ram laughed silently, thoroughly enjoying their exchange of theater.

Watching that enjoyment she couldn't help but appreciate his ever-present, infectious lust for making each moment a good time. She found herself smiling no matter how much she may have wanted to posture indignation.

At the same time, Ram was thinking his mate was a lady in every sense of the word. She could demand respect with grace and a joke. What more could an elf want?

It was early afternoon when they arrived in Brasov. Two small cars with drivers were waiting. Storm steered Elora to the first and asked if she would mind taking the back seat. Even her legs were too long and she had to angle her body sideways to fit. Ram rode in the back seat of the other car. She didn't know how Kay was able to cram his towering figure into the compact space.

Storm asked the driver to find a place for lunch before they left town. He drove straight to the café at the Hotel Bella Muzica and indicated he and the other driver would remain with the cars close by.

In response to Storm's inquiry about something quick, the waiter brought four bowls of beef stew in tomato sauce with cabbage, mushrooms, and other less easily identifiable vegetables. She could tell Kay wanted more, but Storm rushed them away saying, "For one thing, I don't want to be out on these cursed mountain roads after dark and, for another thing, they're expecting us for dinner."

So he bought bottles of water, two loaves of bread, and supremely portable chocolate candy for dessert. While those negotiations were taking place, Elora found her way to the toilet for a potty stop and a long awaited brushing of the teeth. She wasn't looking forward to getting back into that tiny car, but wasn't going to complain about it either. At least not out loud.

The ride from Brasov to Proenia was close to four hours because of necessarily slow speeds on uneven, winding roads. Seemed Storm had been right.

The views gradually changed from the lush, verdant fields of the Danube Valley to primeval forests to the stark, highland landscape of the Transylvanian Alps. When they were within a few hundred feet of their destination, a heavy fog descended to obscure the view of the mountain peak. Intellectually Elora knew it to be a natural phenomenon, a simple function of weather. But emotionally the eerie mist elicited feelings of foreboding.

It was close to dark when they drove through the gates of the ancient, white stoned castle fortress. Both light and the warmth were quickly failing.

They pulled into the courtyard and parked close to the front entrance marked by massive wood doors. Elora thought she couldn't wait to be out of the car until she stepped out into the chill of the night. Teeth chattering, her eyes were drawn to the tower keep which rose from the rear of the building. There was a soft, yellow light coming from a rectangular window near the top and she saw a shadow move across it. She wondered if it was the vampire hard at work conceiving the next best-selling vampire romance.

A handsome couple who appeared to be in their mid fifties came out to greet them. Both spoke Anglish with a French accent. They welcomed Elora saying they were very pleased to have her as their guest. In French she replied that the pleasure was hers and that she was never so happy to be free of an automobile. They said the occasion would be celebrated with a special dinner prepared in her honor.

The four travelers were shown to their rooms, located together in one wing of the second story. The rooms had been modernized to a point with careful attention paid to retaining the medieval character of the building. One had an en suite bath which the knights of B Team gallantly, and unanimously, offered to Elora.

As Ram stepped into the room designated as his for the night, Kay followed and closed the door behind him.

"Don't think I don't see what's going on, Rammel." Ram looked past Kay to the closed door and raised an eyebrow. "I'm not choosing sides – because I love you both like the brothers I never had – but Stormy's gonna have other chances to find love. Am I right in understanding that you get just the one? That is, if you've recognized her as your mate and you're sure she's the one."

Ram blinked at Kay, surprised partly by the subject matter and partly by the fact that Kay wasn't known for volunteering unsolicited opinions, or for interfering in other people's business, or for stringing together so many words at a time.

Ram nodded, curious to see where this was going.

"And just how does that work, her being human and all?"

"Bugger if I know."

"But it has happened before?"

"Aye. But 'tis rare."

"Well, that aside. You don't have a fighting chance." Kay leaned his back against the door and crossed his arms over his abs. He knew he had Ram's attention because of the frown on his face.

"Thanks for the vote of confidence."

"Do you want to hear me out or not?"

"Go on."

"First, there's a matter I'm afraid you're not factoring

in. She thinks she owes Storm her life. And she should think that because…well, she does. If it had been up to you and me, she'd probably be dead."

Ram winced as he confronted that fact for the umpteenth time. It was even harder to hear out loud. Ram's shoulders slumped and he sunk down on the bed looking dejected. "Aye. 'Tis true."

"Did you see the record of her hearing?"

"Aye."

"Then you know she has an over-developed sense of honor. For a woman. Women are usually all about practicality – which is probably why the species has survived, but Elora's different. This isn't going to be about who's cutest. And I'm not saying I would know, by the way, so don't ask. If she thinks she owes it to Storm to be with him, she may feel like there's no other choice."

Ram let that sink in, his eyes slowly taking on a horrified expression. It really hadn't occurred to him that this was a challenge he could lose. He just thought that, given enough time, she would come to know that they belonged together and that no other outcome was possible.

"So what would you be advisin'?"

"I'm glad you asked. I saw the little episode on the train." Ram looked blank. "The finger in the upholstery?" Ram bit back a grin. "Okay. See? There's the problem right there. Elora's not going to choose a guy with porn mud flaps."

Ram looked confused. "Porn mud flaps?"

"Truck flaps with nudie silhouettes in a come-and-get-it pose? Never mind. The point is she isn't going to be won by displays of vulgarity."

"Vulgarity." Ram repeated it softly like he was just now seeing himself through her eyes.

"Yes. Vulgarity. And we both know you were raised better." Ram pressed his lips together at Kay's mention of his upbringing and shot him a glare. "Knock knock in there. Anybody home? She. Is. Human. She's not just going to wake up one morning and recognize you as her mate. You need to get yourself off autopilot and get your head in the game, or by Yuletide there may be some beautiful framed photos of you and me as best men at their wedding. Have you seen the way he looks at her? They may very well get to the altar before Trina and me."

Eyes flashing silver, Ram's notorious temper surged at

the unwelcome image of Elora in a human wedding, wearing one of those frothy white dresses, leaning up to kiss Storm in his dress uniform.

"That's no' funny, Kay!"

He said it as he was hearing her voice in his head. *That's disgusting, Ram. You're in desperate need of finishing school. Blackie has better manners.* Great Paddy's Prick. Kay was simply confirming what she'd been saying all along.

"No shit?" Kay was set to be relentless if that's what it took to get through all that mess of hair to the hard head beneath it. "Even if you get her to want you, how are you going to motivate her to choose you over her sense of duty and obligation?"

Ram hesitated. "Do you know?"

His eyebrows had drawn together in worry. On one hand he thought that, if Fate saw fit to bring him a human mate, there would have to be some mutuality. But, even if that was true, would it be enough to override the strength of will that this particular human had demonstrated when she had survived the interdimensional version of highway to hell?

"You've got to start thinking like a human." Ram recoiled a little like that prospect might be distasteful.

"Love." Kay said as if it was a whole sentence.

"What about it?"

"You need to find out what romance looks like and sounds like to Elora. What are her fantasies? Does she believe in true love? You'd best stop sitting on your hands and be finding out if she believes in forever."

How ironic that Kay would use that expression when "sitting on his hands" was exactly what Ram had to do sometimes to keep them to himself. He told himself it was just a coincidence and not a sign. Just because he was Irish didn't mean he was superstitious. Exactly.

Ill at ease didn't begin to describe the anxiety Ram was feeling about the idea of staging a romantic coup de grace. His area of expertise was more along the lines of the seventy-five minute fuck: fifteen minutes for seduction which was allotted, but never needed. Sixty minutes to find a suitable environment, do the deed, offer excuses about being short of time, and haul the hell away – the ideal being in and out with no exchange of names. Again, time allotted, but never needed.

"Great Paddy, Kay, what the fuck do I know about human romance?" He ran his hand through his hair in frustration. "When elves recognize mates, we basically walk up and say, 'Tis you and me. Let's go.' The whole thing is playful. No'…" He blew out a breath of exasperation. "…so bloody serious."

"But you do love her."

"Of course I love her. I love everythin' about her and do no' even have a choice in the matter. I mean, no' that I would change it. Fuck! I can't think straight." Suddenly he stopped fretting and jerked his head toward Kay. "But, what would you be knowin' about it anyway? You've been with the same girl since you were suckin' pacifier."

"That's true." Kay chuckled as his thoughts clearly wandered to Katrina. "Just saying that, if I were you, with so much at stake, I believe I'd find a way to figure it out. Look. It all comes down to this. How bad do you want her?"

Suddenly Ram brightened like a light bulb went on. "She does believe in forever. All those stories she likes so much end with her sayin' 'and they lived happily ever after'."

Kay smiled. "Well, there you go."

THE GRAY STONE walls of Elora's room were broken up with huge, museum quality tapestries. The floor, also gray stone, was partially covered by a large rug with a teal blue background that could have been taken from a Venetian palazzo. Somehow the juxtaposition worked and the result was sumptuous.

There was enough time before dinner for a hot bath to drive the mountain chill away. She plowed into her suitcase to retrieve the warmest clothes she'd brought and was glad for them. Dressed and ready for dinner, she came downstairs wearing a long, black, knit skirt over leggings and a rose-colored sweater with a large, mink-look-alike collar.

She followed the rise and fall of voices and the sounds of clinking glass to find the dining hall. It was a huge room that, in centuries past, had been used for eating, dancing, settling disputes in times of peace, and strategy in times of war.

Three walls featured fireplaces ten feet wide and high as her chin. Small, merry little fires were burning in each.

The fourth wall was divided into three arches that opened to the foyer. The combined illumination from the gas-lit sconces, the fires, and the candles on the tables, cast reflected light off sparkling, crystal goblets. The room could easily accommodate the fifty-odd people who lived and worked at Unit Drac, the nickname they had given this unique installation, plus guests.

In front of the fireplace at the far end of the room was a table set for eight with a centerpiece of red roses and local forest greenery.

The room grew quiet when she arrived as everyone turned to watch her entrance. She would never get used to that, but unless she dyed her hair, the unusual color was always going to draw attention. With cheeks still rosy from the heat of her bath and her angelic smile, there were at least two men in the room who thought she looked breathtaking.

Elora easily located her escorts standing near the table at the far end of the room, holding wine glasses and talking with colleagues with an easy urbanity. Their relaxed body language broadcasted the fact that the three were as at home with elegant social events as they were in their reputed role of legendary vampire slayers.

On the way to the other side of the room, several people stopped her to introduce themselves. She made gracious, but idle small talk with each before continuing. When she neared the head table, Nicole du Relacque, their hostess, came forward, saying that they didn't normally build fires this early in the year, but wanted to be sure that their guest of honor was warm enough. Elora thanked her for the consideration and assured her that, with some of the red wine the gentlemen were drinking, she would soon be warmed through and through.

Ram's chest swelled with pride when he saw firsthand what a charming guest Elora made. The fact that she didn't yet know she was his didn't change the inevitability of it in the least. He asked if she would like to sit close to the fire, walked around the table and pulled out a chair at the end. She tilted her head and smiled like he had just done something worthy of a prince. Though he didn't let it show, he was mortified to realize his manners were a surprise to her.

Just before dinner was served, a young woman took the seat at the head of the table next to where Elora was sitting with Ram next to her. At the other end of the table the du Relacques entertained Storm and Kay with the history of the castle and its reconstruction.

Elora's newly arrived dinner companion introduced herself as Zutsanna Zajac. She appeared to be early thirties. Her skin and features could easily pass for twenties, but she had that look of experience in the world – good and bad – that transcends the purely physical. Her thick Hungarian accent added exotic undertones to her conversation and somehow enhanced her attractiveness.

Elora inquired about her specific duties with Black Swan.

"Please forgive me. There is no way to say this that does not sound rude. I am working on a project that is need-to-know and cannot say more, but I would so much rather hear about you and your journey cross-dimension."

That question immediately brought up imagery and memories that made Elora tense. Apparently not enough time had passed to emotionally distance her from the feelings associated with the event. Ram noticed her shoulders subtly stiffen. As she was sorting out the best way to answer, she felt a warm, strong hand reach into her lap and grasp her hand under the tablecloth with no one the wiser. She threaded her fingers through his as if it was the most natural thing in the world, as if she was accustomed to doing so. It seemed there was an invisible cord running from Ram's grounding, comforting touch to the corners of her mouth that made her smile when he covered her hand with his.

Ram felt a momentary respite from the panic Kay's lecture had incited. The ease with which Elora had allowed the familiarity and responded to him automatically was promising.

Zutsanna Zajac's personality was pleasing and she was adept at refined dinner conversation. Elora was fascinated by the grace and femininity of her movements: everything from the way she cut meat to the way she lifted a goblet made Elora feel clumsy.

"I was wondering if the rumors that a mystical vortex exists on this very spot are true. I would think people might have trouble sleeping or concentrating."

Ms. Zajac was obviously unprepared for the question. She quickly disguised the surprise that crossed her face, but not before Elora noticed it.

"Might I ask, where did you hear this?" Zajac asked cautiously.

"GilesQuery."

"The world wide web?" Her look of incredulity was accompanied with what was probably cursing in Hungarian. "Why don't we just open the doors to the tourist industry and take tickets!"

It seemed Ms. Zajac was the whole Hungarian package complete with flare, temper and temperament included. She made a half-hearted attempt to regain her poise, saying: "Please excuse me. It was delightful to meet you, but I must get back to work," before leaving abruptly.

Dinner was memorable for its presentation, the cuisine, and the company, but before coffee was served, Elora was surreptitiously trying to hide a yawn.

Storm asked about the plans for the meeting and was told that breakfast would be served at nine the next morning. The staff was prepared to arrange the interview at whatever time would be convenient for their guests.

To Storm's consternation, Ram announced he would see Elora upstairs before anyone else knew she was leaving. Just as she opened the door to the room where she was staying, Ram pulled her close and nuzzled her ear, saying: "Would you like me to tuck you in?"

The first impulse that came to her lips was to begin forming the word "yes". The press of his body, his lowered voice and his warm breath on her ear sent a thrill coursing through her from stem to stern. It would have kept her awake and restless all through the night if she hadn't drunk too much of that rich red with the sultry winter body of an ale. Her brain was trying to form a more prudent response when she was mortified to realize she had just giggled!

"Um. No?"

"You do no' sound sure." His eyes were sparking with amusement.

She stared at the inviting curve of his lips turned into a half smile, lowered her voice two octaves, made her face very serious and said, "No," again. Then burst into giggles.

Ram laughed softly. "I like it when you imbibe. Unfortunately, you're counting on me to be a gentleman." Under his breath he said, "And I never thought anyone would accuse me of that." He pushed her door open for her. "I'll leave my room unlocked just in case you get cold in the night. 'Tis that one." He pointed to the door across the hall.

WHEN SHE WOKE during the night feeling a draft and reached to pull the down comforter up under her chin, she remembered Ram's offer and smiled in the darkness thinking how shocked he would be if he woke to find her crawling between his covers. His words came back to her. *No' that I mind wakin' to find you bendin' over my bed in the middle of the night.* She wondered how thick and soft those Black Tartan boxers would feel to her fingers as she slid them away from his beautiful body. Mulling over the possibility, she hiccupped once, and went back to sleep.

———————

CHAPTER 13

BLACK SWAN FIELD TRAINING MANUAL
Chapter 25, #64

Instances have been reported of very old vampire regaining their humanity and, theoretically, an understanding of right and wrong. In such cases the vampire appear to be human in most respects, but must continue to be nourished by blood, real or synthetic, for the duration of their existence. They also retain exceptional strength and characteristic pallor of the iris.

W AKING TO SHAFTS of light coming through an undraped glass window that was wavy due to the shifting of sand over time, Elora realized that she was eager to get the meeting over with. The warmth of the red wine had gone cold in her system during the night and she knew she was going to need another hot soak in the oversized tub to get rid of the shivers. Glancing out the window on the way to the bath, she saw that there were snowflakes in the air being carried on a horizontal breeze so that they appeared to be flying by instead of falling.

Shifting from foot to foot, she stood by the tub hugging herself, waiting impatiently for the hot water to reach the spigot. It didn't take long to warm up once she was immersed in the steamy tub. She thanked the gods for large hot water heaters.

She put on a pair of expensive tan sueded leggings that could be worn inside her boots leaving enough room for one stake in each, just as she and Ram had planned when they were putting her wardrobe together. Over that she wore the warmest thing she'd brought: a thick, ivory, Irish knit zip front sweater that fell to mid thigh. When she arrived at breakfast Storm's first impression was that she looked far too fetching for the occasion. The classic simplicity and elegance of her clothes only served to accentuate the marvel of her hair and eyes. This was a dangerous liaison. Not a date. At least she wasn't wearing red which was known to attract vampire like fly paper.

Not especially hungry, she took cranberry juice, hot chocolate, and an orange scone from the sideboard. Ram noticed the hot chocolate wasn't being enjoyed as much as usual and that she picked at the scone. He leaned over until he was close enough to talk without being overheard by the others.

"Off your chocolate this morn?"

The minute her gaze met his he knew he'd guessed right. She was nervous.

Elora was thinking that he knew her well, perhaps better than anyone had ever known her. He also had a talent for instantly establishing intimacy between them, even in a crowded room; a feeling like it would be easy to forget they were not alone. She nodded and smiled a shy little smile like she was embarrassed to be found out.

"You do no' have to do this, Elora. I'll pull the plug before you can say, 'Baka, go fuck yourself'."

She so did not want to laugh at that. But she laughed at that. He even knew her well enough to know how to get rid of the nerves. "Thanks. I'm good."

He pulled back to look at her face and try to judge for himself whether or not she was telling the truth. "No one would think less of you if you change your mind. I promise."

She shook her head. "Let's do it."

"Have you a stake in each boot?"

"I do."

"When you're ready. No' before."

Elora turned to ask the little group if there were any rules like, for instance, how long the 'audience' should last? They looked from one to another. It seemed no one had thought about it.

"Well, in that case, I propose twenty minutes. That seems fair to me. If I don't like the way things are going, I'll end it then. If I think something productive could be gained by staying longer, I will."

Ram and Storm both argued for something concrete – a set twenty minutes and no longer, but Elora never backed down from a contest of wills.

They took an elevator up to the top of the tower. There was a small observation area with a large glass window through which Baka and his entire life were on display. It reminded her of the infirmary room where she had spent over three months of her life. On the observation side, the view was broken by a series of bars that had been sunk into the concrete structure. To the left of that was a round, bulkhead-style vault door that provided walk through access.

To the right was a small panel opening, used to accept and deliver laundry and other small items, the most important being sustenance. Monq had developed the current version of synthetic blood in his labs a decade before.

Baka was standing near the back of the room, as still as a statue. He gave the impression of watching them through the glass even though Elora had been told it looked like an ordinary mirror on the other side. He was wearing an untucked navy blue silk shirt that bloused a little at the cuffs, and faded jeans.

She was thinking: "What did that commercial say? If we all want to wear blue jeans how different can we really be?"

The color of the shirt complimented the translucent, ice blue of his irises and gave them a penetrating look that was disconcerting. She'd remembered that he had arresting good looks, but hadn't remembered thinking that he was stunning. As Storm went over safety precautions one more time, even though they had been rehearsed repeatedly, she was thinking that now might be a little late to wonder what she had gotten herself into.

Ram had promised himself that he would not let Elora guess he was apprehensive. He needed her to have confidence in her ability to face the most notorious vampire in the history of Black Swan, but his hands itched to pull her into the safety of his arms, tell her that she was absolutely forbidden to ever again engage in any activity with harmful potential and kiss the feminist nonsense right out of her.

The observation room attendants were a rotation of knights who took turns guarding Baka unless the door was to be opened, in which case, at least four had to be present. The men exchanged greetings. Some had met before and renewed acquaintance last night. Naturally, they were all curious about Elora and how she came to be part of this equation, but they kept their questions to themselves.

One of the attendants explained that they would be able to hear as well as see everything and that when Elora was ready to leave, she need only raise her voice and say the word "open".

She nodded that she understood.

Baka was instructed to step all the way to the back of the room and to remain still while his guest entered.

Suddenly Elora turned to the knight who was operating the security panel. "Has he ever attempted escape?"

The panel attendant seemed to think about it for a minute. The others assigned to guard Baka looked from one to another. Storm, Kay and Ram shook their heads and shrugged at the same time, indicating they didn't have an answer either.

When no one spoke she said, "You don't know?" The panel attendant said that, in fact, he did not know. "Please call Madame du Relacques and ask her."

"Now?" asked the knight who stood over the security panel.

Elora took on her resolute I'm-not-fucking-around tone. "Yes! Now! I want the answer to that question before I go in there."

Instead of doing as she asked, he looked at Storm, Kay and Ram, which infuriated Elora. B Team indicated with facial expression and gestures that it was best to give her what she wanted while she glared at the guy and considered treating him to the sort of somersault Ram got when his rib was broken.

Madame du Relacques was reached by phone within seconds and confirmed Elora's suspicion, born purely of intuition, that Baka had never tried to escape. Elora indicated that she was ready to proceed.

While one knight operated the panel, the other three took up positions around the vault door. One of them spun the wheel and pulled it open while the others trained very large weapons on Baka.

Elora glanced at Ram, who gave her a nod and a wink even though his stomach was roiling, and she walked through the circular opening without showing any sign of trepidation.

Once the last of the locks slid into place Baka said, "Lady Laiken," with just a hint of a smile and a smaller inclination of his head. "I won't bother to introduce myself because, well, because that would be silly. So I will just say welcome to my humble home." He made a sweeping gesture in self-deprecating mocking of his one-room existence as if it was a vast expanse.

Baka's native language had been Romanian. He spoke Anglish very well, but with a slight trace of accent. It was…nice.

"Thank you." Elora continued to keep her gaze trained on him. "Had breakfast?"

Baka grinned, partly to let her know he appreciated her sense of humor, and partly to show her his fangs were retracted. "Would it make you more comfortable if I sit?"

"Somehow I don't think the word 'comfortable' works for this situation. But, yes, I would like it if you sit."

He moved slowly so as not to alarm and sat in one of two overstuffed chairs by a lively fire which was crackling, popping, and inviting.

"Join me." He gestured to the other chair. "Would you like something to drink? Wine?"

Elora stared for a minute, then quickly glanced around the room and said, "Sparkling cider."

In the observation room Ram leaned back so that he could catch Storm's eye and mouthed, "Sparkling cider?"

With a blank expression, Storm just opened his hands in front of him, palms up, as if to say, "Not a clue."

Surprise had flickered over Baka's face before it broke

into what appeared to be the real enjoyment of a genuine smile. He looked directly into the mirror and said: "Sir Ansel, a sparkling cider for my guest, if you please."

Baka's room was circular except for the wall adjacent to the observation room which cut off part of the arc. The rest was possibly twenty five feet in diameter. There was a window overlooking the sheer cliff face with the Arges River valley below. Like the room she had slept in the night before, Baka's prison cell retained the original character of the structure in the stone walls and floor, but that was where the similarity ended. The room was filled with shades of brown and deep reds, in various textures and fabrics. Masculine, but sensual and romantic. Chocolate and blood.

"Who's your decorator?"

He raised his hands, palms up, and tilted his head to indicate that he had done the interior himself.

"Hmmm," she said.

"Is that 'hmmm' you like it or 'hmmm' you don't?"

Looking directly at him for the first time she spoke distinctly. "Very. Nice." She managed to leave the impression that the sentiment could be either sincere or sarcastic.

In addition to the two chairs by the fire, there was a writing desk by the window and an easel holding a canvas with pencil sketching. Next to the easel were several canvases leaning against the wall, apparently finished paintings. The one visible was a scene of crucifixion, though the feeling was contemporary and the subject looked more like Baka than traditional images of the Jesus icon worshipped by so many in this world. She would have liked to be able to take her attention away from Baka long enough to stroll over and flip through the paintings.

Several high bookshelves, conforming to the circular shape of the room, took up about half the available wall space. Such displays were rare since the advent of down-loadable technology. The rest of the wall space was divided between a collection of stringed instruments on one side and a corner dedicated to grooming on the other.

Underneath the display of stringed instruments, a Steinway grand sat regally near the fireplace. Last, on the opposite side was a large, ornately carved mahogany bed with a deep pocket mattress and piles of pillows.

In her world, she had once read that men don't "get" pillows on beds; that it's purely a feminine thing – a complete mystery to the male psyche. Maybe they had it wrong. Maybe the pillows sprang from a need for emotional comfort. Or, in the case of the lonely, a desire to see the bed populated. The general impression of Baka's living space left little doubt that no expense had been spared, but she supposed he had nothing else on which to spend the proceeds of royalties.

"You're a musician?"

"Yes."

"And you play all these instruments."

"Yes."

Elora nodded. "And paint?"

"Yes."

"And you write vampire romances. Fiction I presume?"

He grinned. "Have you read one of my books?"

"I've read all of them, Valerie."

He raised an eyebrow, letting his grin melt into a smile that was so handsome. And so human! A lifetime of discipline kicked in when she directed herself to sit up straight and remember that he was not, in fact human, just as a voice was saying, "But, people are still people even when they are sick."

He exuded sexuality so potent that lust could almost be a scent diffused into the air.

Just as she had that thought, his nostrils widened and he inhaled deeply. "And, was that research or did you enjoy my work?" His smile was sinfully seductive, his tone full of innuendo and she realized he was alluding to the juicier passages of erotica. He made a half-hearted attempt at hiding a laugh when he noticed a little flush.

She raised her chin just enough to imply defiance. "Loved it. Can't wait for the next installment in the series. What will it be? Love Bleeds?"

"Mocking me?" His eyes twinkled. "I'm crushed."

"A sensitive vampire? That has to be an oxymoron." Elora thought she might have seen a flicker of hurt feelings, but decided she must have imagined it. "Actually, regarding your books, I did notice that there was a lot written about the joys of giving blood to irresistibly sexy, good-looking vampire, but nothing about mercilessly ripping out throats and leaving unrecognizable corpses behind."

He lifted a shoulder in a casual shrug. "I write romances. I don't like horror."

"That's very funny, Baka. You're a lover, not a fiend." After a derisive snort, she glanced at the pillows on the bed. "Are you gay?"

He was obviously startled by the question and her bluntness. When he recovered from the surprise, a second or two later, he laughed out loud and it was her turn to be startled. His laughter resonated with emotion that seemed at odds with the grim reality of his existence. It was melodic. It was gorgeous. Spell-binding even.

"Why would you think that?"

"Well, let me see. You're into the arts. All the arts. You wear silk. You write romance novels. You have long hair. You're over thirty with a flat stomach. And you have lots of pillows on your bed."

That relaxed look of amusement had returned to his face. "Well, I guess six hundred years is enough time to get in touch with one's feminine side. I am not motivated to impress others with an unrealistic, arbitrary, or fashiona-ble ideal of masculinity; a superimposed caricature of a man." The panel door opened and a priceless crystal stem appeared as if by magic, filled to the brim with sparkling cider. Baka rose to cross the room. Elora stepped back watching him warily. He retrieved the goblet and set it on the end table next to the chair opposite his, then stoked the fire with a poker before retaking his seat.

The poker he used caused Elora to look around the room assessing how many weapons were readily available and how many weapons could be made from the materials at hand. Clearly, The Order was not as afraid of Baka as they pretended to be. She suspected the entire mystique surrounding his confinement, from the transport chains to the vault door was theatre. Baka had surrendered voluntarily and remained there, in the tower prison, voluntarily.

What purpose did it serve, causing operatives of Black Swan to believe he was the equivalent of the bogeyman?

There was no arguing that he had been the baddest of the bad, claiming a thousand lives as he rampaged through Europe for centuries, but now he was simply a shadow of a reputation.

He sat with legs spread in a relaxed pose. Feeling comfortable with her conclusion, she sat in the vacant chair opposite him.

Without taking her eyes away from Baka, she raised

the goblet to her lips and took a sip, then bit back a moan that wanted to bubble up from the pleasure of the sweet taste.

"Regarding my flat stomach, six hundred years ago people such as myself didn't have access to sugar, beer, fried food, or fructose corn syrup. Thank you for noticing, by the way."

"Are these two chairs a permanent part of your furnishings?"

"Yes."

"Do you often have company?"

"Never." She raised both brows. "Even vampire have hopes and dreams. Mine are simple. I dream of having someone to talk to."

The open vulnerability of that statement would rend her heart in two if it could be trusted.

"What is it that you want with me, Baka?"

He looked at her in a predatory way that, she sensed, had nothing to do with blood. "The same thing any man who isn't blind would want from you." Elora arched a right eyebrow and took another sip of golden liquid as she waited for him to spell it out. "Your phone number."

She choked on the swallow of cider in a failed attempt at laughter. Some of it ended up on the front of her sweater and some of that may have even come out through her nose. In a couple of heartbeats the choking gave way to a ragged intake of breath.

Baka had half risen from his chair to assist her before realizing that such an advance would likely result in a seven-knight-pile-on and the abrupt extraction of Elora Laiken, her witty dialogue, and her delicious heat. He thought that if he was writing this scene in one of his novels, he would say that she brought a warmth to the room that made the fire want to die of shame. And it wouldn't be empty prose. He would mean it.

Looking at him like the last thing she expected was to enjoy his company, Elora said: "I'll bet women liked you when you were human."

Baka cocked his head a little and nodded as if pleased by her observation. "I'd like to think they still do."

"Hmmm."

"Hmmm, again?" He looked at the fire momentarily. The day was gray enough with snow that she could see dim shadows from the fire flickering over his face. "I'll tell you who doesn't like me."

"I already have a list started, but who did you have in mind?"

"Your dog. Quite an awe-inspiring beast."

She grinned. "Indeed. He'd like to see you turned into a month's supply of meaty bones."

"Gruesome image."

"So you're a vampire who is not only sensitive, but squeamish as well?"

He shook his head slightly and shrugged. "Not really."

"So, phone number aside, why did you make the consulting gig contingent on a visit with me? An unbound visit with me?"

Baka looked toward the mirror, forever aware, acutely so, that he was being watched. Before she could rein in her feelings she had felt a twinge of sympathy. The only thing worse than absolute loneliness was an absolute lack of privacy. She knew that firsthand.

Baka had been a vampire for a very, very long time when his human feelings started to return. Unfortunately he retained the memories of the things he had done as a vampire. He could tell himself that he was afflicted, possessed by something not himself, when he perpetrated heinous acts of cruelty, torture and murder. But the other voice inside him said that, if he carried the memories, then it was he who was responsible. An ever abiding, crushing guilt was never far from mind and he would do what he could to curb the spread of the infection that had claimed his life and many since.

"You know you and I are very alike," he said.

"I don't see that."

"Your freedom is restricted. If you're allowed to come and go, it's with an escort of knights. Am I right? Your chains may be invisible, but they are there."

"Why do you think that?"

"I know things." His gaze glanced off the mirror, then he gestured toward the room. "You and I are both prisoners in gilded cages." He saw a flicker of emotion cross her face on hearing the term gilded cage.

How could he have gleaned so much from a brief, one time sighting that had lasted, perhaps, ten seconds? She would have appeared to be as free as anyone else even if she was a prisoner with grounds restriction privileges.

She replied evenly: "Even if that were true, one vague

similarity would hardly make us 'very alike'."

He sighed heavily. "Very well. If you prefer, let's just say we have one vague similarity in common."

"In any case, even if your assessment is true, I'm about to be given independence. Upon my return as a matter of fact."

He smiled slowly and suggestively. "As it happens, so am I. Upon your return, as a matter of fact. We're going to work together to disinfect your little corner of the world. In addition to your phone number, I wanted the chance to get to know you a little and to let you know that you don't need to fear me."

Elora pushed out a disbelieving puff of breath. "Don't need to fear you? Baka. You can't be serious."

"The thing is, we're already there."

As an afterthought she added: "What do you mean we're going to work together? You mean you and The Order or you and me?"

"You and me. We. The two of us."

"What makes you think that?" In answer he simply shrugged. "Wait. I've got this one. You know things."

He smiled indulgently. She hadn't let her guard down

because she had promised to be prudent, but at the same time, she realized it was true. She wasn't afraid.

Without further adieu, still looking Baka in the eye, she raised her voice and said, "Open." The sadness that flickered over his face stirred her compassion yet again. "So you know me a little. If you get a phone, maybe you'll get my number. First, we need to see whether you're going to be a good vampire or not." Too late she realized that she had used the phrase "good vampire".

He offered a sad smile. "Thank you for coming, Lady Laiken. I won't forget that we shared a sparkling cider on a snowy afternoon."

"Shared?" she chided.

"Yes. You drank it." He deliberately raked his gaze up and down the length of her body. "And I enjoyed watching. If there's anything I can do for you…"

Elora tilted her head to one side thinking. "As a matter of fact, I would appreciate an article of clothing, something that hasn't been laundered since you last wore it."

He raised an eyebrow in amusement. "Should I ask?"

She shrugged. "I don't mind *sharing*." She emphasized the last word. "I plan to train my dog to track vampire."

Without doubt the man, er, vampire, had the most sensual, musical laugh she had ever heard.

On hearing the locks spinning behind her she rose from her chair. Baka did the same so that they were now standing just three feet apart. She was never going to hear the end of this from Storm because being this close to the vampire was one of the things he had so strongly cautioned against.

She was about to say goodbye when he pulled his shirt tail free of his jeans and, with his gaze locked on Elora, slowly began unbuttoning his shirt. He watched her eyes fall to where his fingers moved over the buttons. When he finally pulled the shirt back, letting it fall from his shoulders, he revealed an upper body that had been toned by a hard life and, as he had mentioned, no sugar at the time he was infected with the virus. He held the shirt out and she accepted it, barely suppressing the urge to rub the sexy-feeling silk between her fingers.

"Okay. We're even." She turned her back on him and walked away without looking back. The nonchalance of her posture and gait wasn't entirely feigned.

Baka stood by the fire, shirtless and unmoving, until

after the vault was resecured.

When she stepped over the multiple grooves of the titanium threshold, the tension in the room was so palpable she almost swayed.

Ram was sitting on a counter, breathing into a paper bag and was so angry he couldn't even look her in the face. When she had gone to sit within arm's reach of Baka, he had lunged for the door, spinning the vault wheel and screaming, "Get her out! Get her out right now!"

Kay had been forced to grip Ram in a bear hug from behind and immobilize him long enough to say: "If she hears the vault opening, it will surprise her. She'll be distracted and look away from him. We can't take that chance. You understand me? We don't have any choice but to let her play it out her way."

Ram had stilled and nodded, but, for the first time in his life, was having trouble getting breath. A nurse had arrived within four minutes with a paper bag solution. Storm and Kay had wanted him to go to the little infirmary, but a legion of demons could not have dragged him from that room before seeing her safe.

"What's the matter with him?" Elora asked looking

from Storm to Kay, nodding toward Ram.

Storm wheeled on her, booming: "He's scared to death! That's what's the matter! Every one of us could just…" He held his hands up in a clutching gesture indicating that he would like to strangle her. All the while he was visibly clenching and unclenching his teeth in a most unattractive way.

Suddenly he turned on Ram. "For every time I have ever called you reckless or psycho or accused you of having a death wish, I take it all back. She makes you look downright timid."

Ram lowered the bag from his face long enough to say: "Lay off. 'Tis done."

"Are you okay?" Elora asked Ram. He gave her a murderous glare and went back to breathing through the paper bag. "Wow. It looks like there was some serious drama on *this* side of the mirror."

"Oh! Sweet," Storm said sarcastically. "Tell me something. Do you care about us at all?"

Taken aback by that accusation, Elora's mouth fell open. "What do you mean? Of course."

"Ms. Laiken," Kay began, "emotions were running a

little high because of fear. For you. And from this side of the glass, it seemed like you were sort of asking for it."

"It? Asking for it as in getting bit?"

Kay nodded.

Elora looked around the room. "So it's *Ms. Laiken* now is it?"

She really hadn't thought she would cause this much anxiety. After all, these were people who hunted vampire every day. Going from face to face though, she saw that those who weren't downright angry were solemnly grim and she decided she should soft pedal.

"Okay. I'm sorry if I gave you cause for concern." She looked pointedly at Storm and Ram. "But I was the one in the situation and I had to follow my own instincts."

"Cause for concern?" Storm first gaped at her, then turned his face to the wall and let out a roar of frustration. He wasn't used to containing the sort of emotion that threatened to boil over into torrents of rage. He turned and took two steps in Elora's direction so that he was standing over her. "Inoculations can't save you if your jugular is sliced in two." He held his hand in front of her face, thumb and first finger twitching together. "And you were this close. Even *you* wouldn't recover from that."

Elora's own temper was beginning to crowd her composure. "That's just it, Storm. I wasn't in any danger. I'm sorry you were needlessly worried, but you're going to have to learn to trust me." He hissed out his aggravation then dropped his hands to his sides as if to say he was giving up.

"What if I had told you I was going to rehabilitate Blackie? We both know you would have forbidden me to go near him. Blackie would have been sentenced to live out his life being tormented by that sadist."

"Please tell me you are not comparing that thing," he pointed to the glass, "to an abused dog! If you're saying you have plans to domesticate Istvan Baka, then you need to double down on your therapy sessions."

She recoiled as she instantly reordered her reality. A moment ago she had thought Storm incapable of deliberately hurting her.

He knew it was harsh, but he didn't care. He wanted to shock her into sound judgment.

Elora narrowed her eyes as her fists clenched while she was deciding whether or not to punch him.

Ram might have wanted to throttle Elora himself, but his instinct to protect was stronger. He jumped down from the counter and moved in front of Storm so that he stood between them. "That's enough!" He stayed long enough to make certain Storm knew he was serious, then threw the paper bag down in disgust and stalked out of the room without looking back, taking the door to the stairs instead of the elevator, and letting it slam shut behind him.

Everyone else stood silent for a time. After a while, Storm's breathing started to slow. Kay leaned back against the control cabinet, put his hand over his mouth and shook his head.

Elora glanced toward the glass to see Baka still standing near the fire, looking at them like he was watching the entire scene play out, hearing every word.

ELORA WAS SENT to her room to pack. Even though it was snowing, the wind had died. Visibility was good enough to get a whister onto the pad for transport to the airport. She surmised that a whister was very much like the helicopters of her world except that they were faster and quieter. There were six seats including the pilot. Storm took the seat next to the pilot. Kay took a middle seat and Elora moved to the rear.

Ram followed. His expression had softened toward her. When he arrived at the rear, he reached out in a gesture of affection, smoothed back the locks of hair that had fallen toward her face in the Whister's breeze, and flopped into the seat next to her.

A few minutes after they had taken off she looked over at him and whispered, "I'm sorry."

For the first time in awhile, she reached up and pushed his hair back to reveal his beautiful pointed ear. He instantly warmed to her touch, physically and emotionally.

"Do you have a history of hyperventilation?"

He looked offended, like she had just trampled his pride. "Certainly no'."

"No offense intended. I just wondered if it was an unusual reaction for you." He faced her and looked like he was about to say something else, but his gaze locked on her lips and stayed there. For a second she held her breath, afraid he was going to lean over and try to kiss her. So she thought to head off a catastrophe and steer the conversation in another direction.

"Do you think there will be a debriefing?"

He tore his eyes away from her mouth and flashed one of his mischievous smiles. "Would like that, but I'm no' wearin' briefs. I wear boxers," he leaned in close, "as you know."

She laughed as much because of the way his eyes sparkled as because of the joke, marveling at how easily he manipulated her emotions.

Ram was finding it harder and harder to be around Elora without claiming her as his mate and this incident had only magnified those feelings. Regardless of how well his intellect was advocating the virtues of going slow, his body was starting to refuse the message. He wanted to simply lock her in a room with him and cover her body with licks and kisses and caresses until she understood that there could not possibly be a future that didn't include him as her male. Her one and only male. For all time.

In a short time they were on the Learjet headed to New Jersey, with a stop in Edinburgh to pick up some passengers. They would be dropped off at Fort Dixon while other personnel either continued on to San Francisco or found other transport. Minerva had been replaced by someone infinitely more personable.

The fellow Order travelers had already boarded the Edinburgh jet when they arrived. Elora took an empty space on one of the bench seats next to a cute guy with piercing green eyes and jet black hair. It took him less than a minute to direct the force of his considerable, and no doubt well-practiced, charm on Elora.

"Hi." His smile created a suggestion of dimples that made him look younger and deceptively less dangerous than he was.

"Hi, yourself. I'm Elora Laiken."

"Caliber Magnus. Call me Cal."

She nodded. "You're a knight?"

"Nope. Mercenary."

"Seriously?"

"Well, no," he smiled, "I'm an alchemist working temp, but I think it sounds cooler to say mercenary."

"Hey. Cool is in the eye of the beholder. So, you spin straw into gold or something like that?"

That earned her a big, husky laugh. "I wish. You going to Buenos Aires?"

"New York is the final destination."

"And what do you do for The Order?"

"Knight. On probation."

His eyes widened momentarily, then lit with amusement. "Well, well, well. I wouldn't have guessed that one in a hundred years. I suppose that makes me sexist."

"I'd like to say that it does, but, since I'm the first knight of feminine persuasion, you would have to be from the psychic department to have guessed." She couldn't tell if the look he was giving her was admiration or intrigue or both. "You're going to Buenos Aires?"

"Hmmm."

"So what's going on down there? Is it a secret?"

"Truthfully I don't know myself. I expect a briefing will await." He didn't sound excited.

"That a French accent?"

"Belgian." He deliberately shuttered his eyelids and tried out his most seductive smile. "The real language of love." Another time or place that cute smile might have made her knees weaken just a little, but if he wanted to enter a flirting contest with forces of nature like Istvan Baka and Rammel Hawking, he would have to do a lot better than that. "So where are you from, Lady Knight?"

Something about that question caused a visible shut down. Her smile dropped away and the light went out of her eyes. "Far from here."

Cal was sorry he'd asked.

Storm was still refusing to look at her, which made her think maybe she had finally uncovered two flaws: that he could pout childishly and take a long time to recycle. He was sitting in the back in one of the recliners typing on a laptop. When the guy sitting next to him got up to go to the lavatory, she asked Cal to excuse her and slipped into the vacated seat. Storm was not just aggravatingly taciturn. He didn't acknowledge her in any way.

"Storm, how long do you plan to be unhappy with me?"

He looked up and stared straight ahead for an uncomfortable time without looking at her. Finally he closed the laptop and turned in his seat so that he could face her.

"Look. I'm not going to say I've never been afraid. But I've never been afraid like that." His expression softened just a touch. "You. Really. Scared. Me." That was when she knew for certain that she was not just a get-well project to Engel Storm; that he either loved her as a man loves a woman or thought he did.

"I'm sorry."

She didn't know if she was saying she was sorry because of the scare or that she was sorry because she didn't feel the same way. She loved Storm. How could she not? Just not in a romantic way.

He searched her face like he was trying to judge the sincerity of the apology. Finally his broad chest heaved with a big sigh. "Okay. Let's call it over. Please don't do it again."

She gave him a smile which, as a perfect example of seeing-what-you-want-to-see, he took as a promise.

"Have you called home?"

He looked perplexed. "Home? Oh, you mean Jefferson Unit."

"Yeah. I guess I'm the only one who calls it home." She looked a little dejected and he was sorry he had pointed that out.

"Yes. I called."

"Did you ask about my dog?"

"No. I didn't think to ask about Blackie, but I'm sure we would have been told if there was a problem."

Satisfied with that, she grabbed a pillow and blanket, and settled down to sleep the trip away.

Ram had been sneaking glances at the exchanges between Elora and first Cal, then Storm. The best part of him wanted to insert himself into the dialogue while subtly (or not) moving her farther away from the other men. The worst part of him wanted to throw the would-be rivals from the plane and laugh as he watched them fall.

His resentment of Storm's pursuit of Elora, in particular, had been steadily growing from an annoyance to a rasp that grated on his nerves.

Instead of dialing up a frat party movie, he started an internet search with the term "romance". The first result was Masspedia which meant they told you way more than you wanted to know without offering much useful information. Following that was a site called romancingyou.com with the description: "make plans for romance with romantic ideas for date nights, anniversaries, romantic travel, and romantic getaways". Seemed like a good place to start. At least they made liberal use of the word "romantic".

When he came to the musical references he started

thinking about how enthusiastic he had been to share his love of metal with her. She had been open-minded and receptive while he had scoffed and been dismissive to the point of rudeness when it was her turn to name her favorites. Great Paddy. He really was botching this!

CHAPTER 14

THINKING THE INCIDENT might be never-ending, Elora was subjected to yet another stern lecture from Sol, but not a reprimand since her handling of the Baka interview was not a violation of any specific order and because no actual harm had been done. Causing your friends grave anxiety is not against any specific rule.

She watched the airbot playback of her conversation with Baka in Sol's office. It revealed that the sexual tension between Baka and herself crackled with energy that shot the viewer through with palpable sparks. Even when viewed through the dispassionate filter of a cold, two-dimensional screen. She'd been expecting a threat to her life, not to her sexual integrity. But there it was in glorious, living color. Perhaps she wasn't technically entranced, but she was clearly susceptible to Baka's charm and Baka was… what? Given his six hundred years of experience, she was way out of her depth in trying to figure out what game he was playing.

She learned that he would be arriving the next day to initiate his part of the cooperative effort. Monq's research team had identified the epicenter of missing persons and established that the abductions were originating at or near a club at 39th and Broadway called Notte Fuoco.

Notte Fuoco was a megaplex playground for young singles with a sprinkling of divorced, middle aged men eager to spend child support money on younger women in exchange for a night of pretending they were still young and attractive. The club was a hot spot utilizing three floors referred to as street level, club level, and Underground. The street level section was a bistro with reasonably priced, nouvelle cuisine.

The club level featured the Millennium Room serving up the latest in chic cocktails and deejay dance music with a four-four beat, heavy on the snare.

The Underground offered live music, covers, and original bands. With the generous application of special soundproofing insulation in the floors and between the walls, extravagant acoustic design in the building renovation, and two heavy glass door foyers separating the glass elevator from the venues, each of the two below-street levels could contain its own musical experience without bleeding into the other.

Making fine use of Baka's history with stringed in- struments, The Order used some special contacts to arrange for him to work as the house bass player for the Underground. The former bassist was overjoyed with an all expense paid vacation until further notice.

It was an ideal situation for Baka. His constant pres- ence wasn't just explained, but expected. And, though it was often an expression of mystique for bass players to appear bored, not much was missed from the vantage point of the stage. His only uniform consisted of gray lens glasses, light enough to see, but dark enough so that no one could follow his eyes and guess what caught his interest.

The contract stipulated that Baka would remain free while performing the duties outlined for a period of three months or until such time as The Order declared the assignment complete and recalled him, conditional upon strict adherence to a synthetic blood diet and checking in with his contact once a day. Said parole officer was to be Sovereign Sol.

After the additional dressing down by Sol, Elora was informed that probationary freedom was granted as agreed. Storm proved that he was over his mad by suggesting a trip into the city for a celebration dinner. Sol hijacked the plan, saying he might as well make it a working evening; to take the rest of B Team and scout Fuoco Notte while he was at it. Storm was deflated since he had been thinking in terms of an evening alone with Elora, but a protest would have meant a public proclamation of intent to date. Which was premature. So he agreed.

Since Elora had not experienced night life in this world, or any other for that matter, she was at a loss as to what to wear so she sought help from Elsbeth, who was the personification of party central.

They borrowed a short red skirt from a friend of Elsbeth's in the Operations Office which was even shorter on Elora because of her height. No one had high heels even close to her size, but Elsbeth insisted she could noir up the black boots with patterned stockings. Elora was doubtful about the look, but decided she had no choice but to trust the only one of the two of them who had experience with club clothes. She wore her black silk sweater that zipped up the front, but zipped it just to the top of her black lace bra.

Elsbeth had her bend over so that she could spray her hair upside down, then give it a blast of heat to keep it looking big and edgy for the duration of the night. As for makeup, she reluctantly agreed to some kohl around the eyes and blood red lipstick. The eye liner made her turquoise eyes pop like neon lights and Elora wasn't keen on attracting too much attention. Elsbeth insisted that all attention is good attention, finished, and hurried away because she had plans of her own.

Elora took a look at the results. "Hey. Who's the slut in the mirror?"

It was too late to make changes because that was Ram knocking on the door right at eight o'clock as promised. She was tempted to tell him to go away, but knew he wasn't good at doing what he was told. So she opened up and steeled herself for the laughter.

He stared for a minute, the blank look out of place on his very expressive face. "Excuse me. I'm lookin' for Elora

Laiken?"

Elora's shoulders slumped and she rolled her eyes. "Okay so I'm out of my element. Elsbeth did a club night make-over. It's all wrong, isn't it?"

Ram's mouth curled up at the edges as his gaze lowered to where curls fell gracefully between her breasts. She caught her breath when he reached in to gingerly lift a spiraling lock and rub the silky texture between his fingers. His eyes moved slowly up to her mouth. As her lips parted under his stare, his tongue peeked out to wet his bottom lip as his gaze continued upward until he locked her eyes on his. What she saw in those eyes was unmistakable hunger and she knew in that moment that no woman had a prayer of refusing Rammel Hawking if he ever got serious about down and dirty pursuit. He pressed closer and showed her what sex looks like in a smile.

"Let's stay in tonight and let me show you just how very no' wrong you look."

Elora's breath hitched as some possible scenarios played out on the screen of her mind. This was far from Ram's usual lighthearted banter and it caught her by surprise since she'd grown comfortable with their unspoken understanding of flirt, but not seriously. Or maybe they didn't really have an understanding? All she knew was that he was close enough for her to feel the heat coming from his body and his gravelly rasp made her stomach quiver.

Wanting to dial things back to a manageable level, she stepped back and said, "So. Really. This is okay?"

He slumped, leaning his shoulder into the door frame with an indulgent, but slightly disappointed smile. "Perfect. Let's go."

THEY MET STORM and Kay at the whister pad on the roof. Both did their share of staring. Storm made no comment, but Kay said, "Like the come-and-bite-me outfit."

The Order maintained four rooftop pads on the island of Manhattan. Each had a private elevator going straight to the top that could be accessed by key or palm recognition. Tonight they were going to the location at 50th and 6th and would walk the rest of the way.

The flight in was a marvelous experience for Elora because she had never seen New York, in any reality, but the skyline at night by whister was a sight she wouldn't forget.

It was practically balmy for a late fall night in New York. The walk took fifteen minutes because Elora tried to take everything in. Amidst the lights, traffic, crowds, shops, markets, and cafes, she managed not to miss the fact that many passersby did double takes when they saw her companions. She supposed that it was unusual to see three such breathtaking men out walking the streets like mortals. If B Team noticed the attention, they were skilled at ignoring it.

They stopped in at the club level long enough to look around. There were three men looking for vampire and one woman looking with wide eyes at various expressions of undress performing group bump and grind. She couldn't have been much more scandalized if it had been a full-on orgy and she was sure her face was glowing as red as an exit sign. The music was too loud for talking. So when they were ready to move on, Storm pressed his hand into her lower back and motioned toward the elevator.

The Underground was much more subdued. The band playing was performing original music that was somewhat quieter, with a style that concentrated on lyrics and heavy blues influence. Elora's gaze went straight to Baka. She judged that, of the two hundred people or so in that room, only four could conceive of a six-hundred-year-old vampire standing there looking for all the world like an exceptionally handsome thirty. There was no way to tell for sure with the gray lens glasses, but she thought he was looking her way, offering the barest hint of a smile in recognition.

Kay located a corner table. Elora listened to the music. B Team looked for intel. After a couple of hours, they were satisfied they had seen what there was to see and decided to move upstairs to street level for dinner. At the bistro, they settled into a red leather booth and ordered enough food to make the waiter raise his eyebrows and chortle, even though chortling was always risky behavior when tips were in the offing. The joke was on him when he returned to find empty plates looking like a plague of locusts had swarmed the booth on their way to a Biblical nightmare. Black Swan knights burned a lot of calories that had to be replenished often.

All that eating didn't stop them from taking a look around. Elora took note of the fact that they turned supper as stake out, no pun intended, into an art form of dining and conversing while surreptitiously sweeping the surroundings, mentally cataloging every detail.

Storm paid the bill with a platinum American Express. Just when he finished signing, Kay said, "Two and a vic. Eleven o'clock."

Ram leaned over, grasped Elora's forearm to be sure he had her attention and locked her eyes with enough intensity to convey that he meant business. "Stay here. Do. No'. Move from this table until I come back."

Trying to be as covert as the behavior she had witnessed all evening, she glanced toward the door. Two ice-eyed vampire and a young woman who looked strung out were leaving through the front door. Ram, Kay, and Storm followed. A few seconds later a third figure with impossibly pale irises was walking toward the door to exit the same way, clearly following them.

Suddenly, staying put in a snug didn't feel like the right choice. The choice was: leave or lose the vamp. She left. When she emerged onto the street, she saw that he was already half a block away. She took off after him, grateful that she was wearing the riding heel boots instead of absurd platform stilettos like those she had seen in the club.

Other diners who had emerged from the bistro were strolling away on the sidewalk, reviewing service and cuisine. One of them was using a toothpick. On impulse she reached out and grabbed it on her way by with a, "Sorry. And thank you."

She caught up with the vampire just as he turned into an alleyway. Hearing footsteps behind him, he turned, thinking that perhaps he wouldn't need to insist that the pair he was following share their meal. When he turned to see what supper looked like, he found Elora advancing in a red skirt and told himself it was his lucky day. He smiled a predatory smile.

Elora wasn't sure how hunters normally confirm that a target is vampire, but straight forward generally worked for her. So, when she was just out of arm's reach, she simply said, "Show me your fangs."

Naturally, he was initially stunned by the request, but decided there was no reason to be shy. He opened his mouth wide and proudly demonstrated the descent of two very long, sharp, white canines. That was just before he was dispatched to hell or wherever his final destination might be.

Using a combination of the precision punch she had mastered over a lifetime of martial arts training, the extra strength she had gained at the price of being cruelly sucked into this dimension, and a toothpick snatched from a random mouth, she drove all two inches of the tiny stake into his heart, killing him instantly. The force was sufficient to prevent either splintering or breaking the soft wood. The vampire's eyes and mouth went wide with shock before he succumbed and crumpled to the cracked tar pavement of the alley.

Behind her she heard peals of gorgeous laughter, unmistakable in its unique, musical resonance. That could mean only one thing. Istvan Baka was occupying the same alleyway as herself and the departed.

"You took him out with a toothpick? Oh, God in heaven, as long as I have lived, I've never seen *anything* so priceless!" He was laughing so hard she thought he might cry. "Show me your fangs!" He repeated what she had said to the unlucky vampire with added incredulity and laughed all the harder.

"What are you doing out here, Baka?" Somehow, encountering him "in the wild" made him seem more appealing instead of more frightening, which was disturbing.

"Following you of course," he said with matter of fact ease, looking down as he circled the corpse. "Although it seems there was no cause for concern, Lady Laiken."

"You're saying you followed me because you were worried? About me?"

"Hard to believe, isn't it?" His pale eyes sparkled in the dim light of the alley, still damp from a fresh shower that had magically turned the entire city into a slick surface of reflecting light. Every couple of seconds his gaze wandered back and forth between the open ends of the alley before coming back to fix on her with a concentration that made her want to squirm and press thighs together. He knew he was having that effect and was enjoying it. Thoroughly.

"I like the costume. Especially the very red, very short skirt." His gaze scanned her slowly and appreciatively, top to bottom and back again before coming to rest on her mouth. "And the lip stain. Enticing. Would you call that blood red?"

"Okay. Look. I'm kind of an amateur at this. I don't

know what they usually do about, er," she glanced down at the dead vampire, "clean up. Do you?"

"Yes. They have people who take care of it. They conceal the evidence as best they can and call for pick up." He grabbed the body by the arms, easily pulled it next to a pile of garbage bags stacked by a trio of dumpsters, and sat it upright against the brick wall so that it looked like it could have been a drunk passed out.

"Right." That sounded like a good plan. "I don't know who to call."

Baka pulled his phone out of his pocket and speed dialed a number. "One of your knights just bagged a vamp, but she didn't have the clean up number."

Baka held the phone away from his ear. Elora could hear Sol shouting curses on the other end. "She? What the great father of fuck do you mean she?"

"You didn't intend to turn the Lady Laiken loose on a poor, unsuspecting population of vampire who've been running amuck, digging in and planting roots in the community? Surprising, considering that she has to be the best weapon you've got." There was quiet on the other end of the line. He glanced up at Elora. "We're in an alley off

Broadway between 38th and 39th. The package is semi-concealed and I will stay here to make sure the scene is secure from discovery until your people arrive."

She could hear the murmur of Sol talking, no longer shouting. Baka said, "Okay," and hung up.

"He wants to see all four of you when you get back. No matter how late it is. His office. He'll be waiting." Baka tilted his head as his lips spread into a beautiful, white fangless grin. *Captivating.* Then he held his phone up, saying, "Did that qualify as being a good vampire?"

Elora studied him for a second, then reached out and took the phone from his hand as casually as if she was taking hot chocolate from The Hub barista. She programmed her number into the phone and handed it back. "Don't make me sorry."

"Cross my heart." He took the phone and slid it back into a jeans pocket.

"Oh very funny. So you're a painter, a musician, an author, an interior decorator, a vampire, a spy, a possible stalker, *and* a comedian."

With the hint of a sardonic smile he said: "At a lounge near you. Shows nightly at ten and twelve."

While Elora was trying to process this bit of cognitive dissonance, he went on. "You'd better get back to the cafe. If bits of Bad Company come back and find you missing, at least two of them will turn Manhattan into a state of chaos, bedlam, and pandemonium."

Well, what could be said to that? "Thank you for your help with the, uh, mess."

With a flourish he executed an old world bow with grace and a lack of self-consciousness that could only be managed by someone who had lived during the time when such things were in vogue. "I live to serve."

"Uh huh." She started toward the mouth of the alley then looked back to say, "By the way, that was bad ass bass tonight."

Through the darkness she could see white teeth flash. "I take requests."

She chuckled half way back to the bistro, replaying in her head Baka's dry humor, quick wit and sexy mannerisms, asking herself what she was doing semi-flirting with the most infamous vampire in the annals of The Order.

She ran into the bistro just as B Team had finished its first sweep of the place and had realized she wasn't in sight. They were wearing a range of expressions from worried to perturbed. She could see relief wash over Ram's face when he spotted her. He hurried toward where she waited just inside the door.

"What part of stay here and do no' move did you no' understand?" he demanded.

Elora grabbed the sleeve of his leather jacket and urged him toward the door. "Get them now. Let's talk outside."

Ram motioned for Storm and Kay, who followed them outside onto the sidewalk. Elora urged them into a huddle where she could talk quietly and began to explain that a vamp had left on their tail, that she didn't want them caught unaware, so she followed and killed him before he could become a problem for them.

Storm just stood there without expression, shaking his head back and forth like he was choosing to simply not accept this as part of his reality. She had the inappropriate passing thought that he reminded her of a bobble head. So she turned to Ram, whose color had left his face.

He spoke so quietly it seemed like he was talking to himself. "You went after a vamp with no back up."

"Well, somebody needed to do it!" Seeing that Ram was growing steadily paler, she became alarmed. "Do not start hyperventilating!" That admonition infuriated him, but did not rob him of air.

"Somebody needed to do it?" Kay repeated. "Elora, that was truly a dumb ass thing to say, but maybe it fits, because I'm starting to think you are one." In an exquisite moment of irony, it seemed the berserker was the only one present who was capable of controlling his emotions. "Why don't you just take us to the scene?"

Elora nodded and started walking that direction. She was explaining exactly how it happened; that she hadn't been sure how to verify beyond question that a suspect is a vamp. "So I asked to see his fangs and he showed me. Then I gave him wood."

They were just turning into the alley when she finished that sentence. Baka, still there waiting for pick up, started laughing all over again.

"Gave him wood!" He shook his head and reached up to wipe moisture from his eyes. "This just gets better and better." All three members of B Team tensed when they realized Baka was in the alley. "She killed him with a toothpick that she grabbed out of some fellow's mouth as she ran by. Did you know that?"

Ram, Kay and Storm forgot being wary of Baka and simultaneously turned to look at Elora like she was an alien which, technically, she was. But they were looking at her like they'd never seen her before. Finally, she raised her hands.

"What?"

"And did you tell them that Sol is waiting to see all of you in his office as soon as you get back? No matter how late?" Baka was thinking she was very cute when her nostrils flared.

"I hadn't gotten to that part," she said through clenched teeth while glaring at Baka like the traitor he was. "Yet," she said while giving him the finger.

Storm wheeled on Ram with seething accusation written all over him.

Ram recoiled and gaped in response to Storm's seemingly irrational behavior. "Why be glarin' at me? She's the one who gave him the bloody finger!"

"Because. Rammel. Somehow I see *yer bluidy* influence all over this." Storm was unrepentant about mocking

Ram's accent. "I don't think she even knew what a rude gesture was before she started spending time with you!"

Baka broke apart in new waves of laughter. "Better and better. I haven't had so much fun in… well… ever." He patted his shirt pocket. "I need to take notes. I'm putting this in a book."

Kay decided to intercede before things escalated. More. "Okay. Everybody settle down. Let's hitch a ride with clean up. We'll get back faster and sort this out."

"You mean ride with the, uh, body?" Elora glanced at the corpse, feeling inclined to balk at the idea.

Storm's black eyes settled on her coldly. In a mercilessly detached tone he said; "If you can kill it, you can ride with it." Then to Baka. "You're relieved."

Baka tilted his chin up at Storm in a reverse nod, said, "Fine by me," and strolled away leisurely, casting a grin back over his shoulder at Elora.

Needing to have the last word in this exchange, Elora looked over the trio and said, "By the way, you're all bloody welcome." Too exasperated to argue further, she found a place several yards away to lean against the brick wall, arms crossed in front of her, and have a miserable wait for a ride.

The van arrived in a few minutes. It took two trips in the elevator to get everyone, living and dead, up to the whister pad on the roof. They rode in silence back to the base. Elora couldn't decide whether she was more creeped out about riding with vampire remains or angry about the confusing reaction she'd gotten from her friends. She really was just trying to watch out for their well-muscled behinds. Why didn't they get that?

AS PROMISED, SOL was waiting in his office, rolling a small black cigar between his fingers, and staring straight ahead. She had never seen facial features cast in such rock hard planes. As they crowded into the office Storm opened his mouth to speak, but Sol held up a hand to stop him. "I want to hear it from the young lady."

Letting the sarcasm slide, Elora recited the events that had occurred following her companions' departure from the bistro in detail, including her rationale.

Sol then asked if anyone else had anything to add, but nothing more was forthcoming. Without further comment and without visible fluctuation in his stern attitude, Sol declared the report concluded and said that he would let them know if he had further questions. Storm and Kay went off to share a whiskey without so much as a good night. Ram half-grudgingly walked Elora to her apartment, looking at the floor and not saying a word until they reached her door.

"Will you be the death of me then?"

Elora turned and was brought up short by the sorrowful, almost haunted look on Ram's face. She had scared him. Again. "I didn't do it to worry you, Ram. I did it because I was worried *about* you."

Before she could protest, he put both hands on her waist and pressed her back into the door with his body that was so perfectly aligned with her own. He buried his face in her neck, closed his eyes and filled his lungs with the deeply intoxicating scent of night blooming jasmine. His cock filled so fast it made him jerk in response. When he felt her tense beneath his hands he straightened, resolutely pushing away from her with a soft growl of frustration. Without another word, he walked on to his own door leaving her standing there in the hallway breathless, missing the warmth of his body against hers.

Elora had tensed to strangle the moan that wanted to escape her throat. He didn't know how close she had been to giving up the tenuous hold she had on her own impulses, how close she was to letting herself go soft and pliant, molding to his shape, and parting her lips to invite a kiss. She took a hot shower, washed the spray out of her hair, creamed the blood red lipstick off her mouth, dried her hair, pulled on a tank top and flannel pajama bottoms and climbed into bed.

She had just turned off the light when her phone rang. Looking toward the bedside stand where she'd set her phone, she read the caller ID. "White Fang." As tired as she was, she couldn't help but find that funny.

"Hello?" There was no response. "Hello?" No response. "Isn't it bad enough to be a vampire? Now you want to be a heavy breathing pervert as well?"

There was a quiet rumble that could have been soft laughter under his breath. "No. Just thinking I should hang up."

"Something wrong?"

"Nothing."

"Okaaaaay. Soooooo…"

There was a deep sigh on the other end of the phone and that's when it happened – the Baka epiphany.

An epiphany is a surge of comprehension that pulls together loose ends of experience with tidbits of information and flashes of intuition, then rearranges them into a moment of perfect clarity. It only takes a heartbeat for the mind to grasp a new perspective and shift to accommodate a different way of thinking.

Something about Baka's sigh caused such an epiphany. He was her. He had reawakened to life in a strange new world. He was lost, with no family, no friends, and no clear imperative as to how to proceed. He was lonely. Who wouldn't be?

"You know I've wondered where you, ah, stay when you're not working. I know it's not here."

"Hotel. The Sherry Netherland."

"Oh. Is it nice?"

There was a little snort of amusement on the other end of the phone while Baka stifled a laugh. "Yes. It's nice." After a slight pause he said: "Maybe you could sneak out of Swanville and come visit. We could share sparkling cider, conversation, and… other things."

Having never experienced the ordinary pleasures of being pursued as a teenager, Elora was a late bloomer who had been making up for lost time in the past few weeks, with an advanced education on the nuances of flirting. Now she was learning that there is a super bonus thrill attached to late night, clandestine conversations with bad boys.

"Maybe sometime I'll say yes to the cider and conversation if we can agree that there will be no 'other things'."

"Would it sound vain if I said that would be your loss?"

She smiled. "Yes. It would sound vain. Nonetheless, I'm sure it's true. No doubt the loss is mine and shall remain so." She was fading. "It's been a long day. I'm going now."

"Good night gone wrong?"

"Yeah," she sighed. "Exactly."

"It may not make you feel better, but it was *really* good for me. Adieu, Lady Knight. Don't let bed bugs bite."

"You made a rhyme," she yawned, "add poet to the list."

Baka called every night thereafter. He said he liked

hearing her voice on the phone. Elora knew she'd be in big trouble with B Team if they discovered she was carrying on a phone flirtation with White Fang, but part of her felt sorry for him and part of her enjoyed his company, however bizarre that might seem... even to her.

_____

CHAPTER 15

BLACK SWAN TRAINING MANUAL FIELD GUIDE, Chapter 11, #4.

Silver, in contact with the vampire virus cells in the skin, is a fast-acting neutralizer and creates the effect of stunning vampire so that they may be dispatched with minimum risk to the operative. The preferred formula is silver soluble salt, $AgNO3$, dissolved in gel and delivered by splat gun.

This method has several advantages, particularly when operating in areas with dense human populations. It is harmless to humans. It is silent. Close contact with the target is not necessary as range can be calibrated accurate to thirty feet at the time of this writing. It is quickly absorbed through the pores. The drawback to this method is that vampire, being aware of the risk to themselves, leave as little skin exposed as possible.

A T ELEVEN O'CLOCK Elora heard a knock on her door. She opened to see Ram smiling, holding out a peace offering of steamy hot chocolate in a to-go cup with a sleeve. "I have news."

Eyeing the cup she asked, "Is that a big?"

His eyes lit up with a knowing smile that said, "There it is. I'm in."

Blackie pushed his head around Elora's thigh to say hello and wagged his tail at Ram. She opened the door wider and took the cup.

"You know he likes you."

"I like animals. They like me." He bent down to give Blackie a pat, but Blackie immediately flopped onto his back demanding a tummy rub instead. Ram laughed at him like they shared a joke.

"Well, there's no accounting for taste." She sat down at the dining desk. "It better be good news because that's the only kind I want to hear today."

"'Tis. Today's the day I report to the infirmary for clearance. In a couple of hours I should be officially off the D.L. Fit and ready to return to duty." Elora took a swig from her cup and looked pensive. "What's the matter? You do no' look happy."

"I have mixed feelings. After what happened last night, well, it punctuated what you've been saying, that those things are fast and strong and that they have big teeth. You lost a partner. The same thing could happen to you or Storm or Kay."

His features softened as he connected the dots. "And if that should happen you'd feel alone in this world." He sat down next to her.

She hadn't thought about it like that, exactly, but hearing him say it out loud stirred emotions she didn't even know she was suppressing. Tears welled even though she was trying to hold back. When two escaped down her face, he reached over, cupped her cheek, and used his thumb to wipe away the drops. "Ah, my darlin' girl. You truly will be the death of me."

She dried her tears. "When do you go back to work? Officially?"

"Right away. We've been slackin' long enough, makin' it hard on the others." Elora nodded. "But listen to my words and please hear me. Most knights die of old age, in comfy beds, with great-grandchildren standin' all 'round.

What happened to Lan will make us all the more careful."

Eager to lighten the mood, he invited Elora to lunch and was rewarded with the smile he loved.

AFTER TEACHING HER early afternoon class she went by Sol's office, hoping to catch him in. She knocked on the open door, but stood on the other side of the threshold waiting for permission to enter.

Sol wasn't the sort of person you barged in on, especially not when he was struggling with the duty rotations program on his computer. When he looked up and saw her standing there, he didn't seem surprised. Truthfully, surprise would have been surprising since his range of emotion seemed to run on only three speeds. Mad. Madder. Maddest.

"Got a minute?"

Without a word he motioned her inside. She stepped in and asked if she could close the door. That seemed to ratchet his interest up a notch. Sitting in front of his desk she clasped her hands in her lap and began carefully, like she was navigating a verbal minefield, anticipating that a poorly chosen word could sabotage her agenda.

"I'd like to request that you hear me out completely before you respond."

Sol was not the sort to interrupt others or to make decisions prior to reviewing all data. He indicated his agreement with a nod.

"I would like to be considered as a replacement for Sir Landsdowne. I'm the best candidate and I have several good reasons to support that claim.

"I have probationary security clearance. I'm reasonably intelligent. I'm not just trained in hand to hand, I'm the trainer. I also have experience with a variety of weapons. I'm familiar with policy and can recite most of the Field Training Manual on request. I am stronger than the strongest knight has ever been. I am faster than the fastest knight has ever been. I can't be hypnotized. I have had my inoculations. I am resourceful in finding weapons when vampire are afoot and have successfully neutralized the enemy in the field. I've established a working relationship, of sorts, with the point per... uh, vampire. I have bonded with B Team. I know them. They know me. We're comfortable together.

"Last and most important. In this world, those men

are the closest thing I have to loved ones. I can't stay behind while they go out nightly to possible mortal combat – possible fatality, knowing that I could be the lynch pin that keeps them alive. It would be cruel to ask that of me."

Sol had placed his elbows on the arms of his chair. With steepled hands he pressed his index finger to the indention above his upper lip while he examined Elora as if she was a smear on a microscope slide.

She sat, holding her breath, waiting for him to give voice to the reason why he would refuse and hoping that she had a counter argument for whatever it might be. At length he raised his chin and leaned forward.

"You make a compelling case, Ms. Laiken. I have a couple of concerns and a couple of conditions."

Elora sat up straighter. This reaction far exceeded the best outcome she had anticipated. "Please name them."

"My first concern has to do with the very memorable statement you made at the close of your hearing. You believe you have something to prove in regards to courage. People with something to prove tend to behave impetuously, precisely as you did in the case of your audience with Istvan Baka and again in your first encounter with a vampire in the field."

Elora opened her mouth to protest, but Sol raised his hand. "Undoubtedly the death by toothpick incident showed uncommon initiative, ingenuity, and mental flexibility; all being traits we prize. The question here is not whether or not you possess the assets necessary to perform the duties of a Black Swan knight, but whether or not you are willing to exercise control over your tendency toward impulsive behavior."

Elora rushed to supply a reassurance that she would do what was necessary to accomplish the mission while keeping the team safe.

"My second concern has to do with The Order's policy on 'office romance'. Since there has never been a female operative in the department of hunters, it hasn't been an issue. One of my conditions would be a formal acknowledgement that you and your teammates understand the rule and abide by it."

She nodded.

"The last condition is that at least two members of B Team must agree and one of them must be Sir Hawking as you would be replacing his partner. This is a deal breaker. I will not override their votes."

Seeing that he was rising from his chair, Elora also stood. "I understand. How shall it be put to a vote?"

"I'll call them in for a meeting one hour from now in the conference room. You may be present. I suggest you wear your thickest skin because they may not react well to your proposition. But I will tell you this, if they accept you as their fourth, you will make some enemies. There is one person who believes he is the heir apparent to Lan's spot and there are bound to be others who may not be keen on the idea of a woman as vampire slayer. Sometimes camaraderie is your biggest asset. Acceptance is important."

"I thought of that, but hopefully I've made some inroads through the training program." Sol gave no response. "Well, one step at a time then. Back in an hour. Game face on. And thank you."

"Gratitude is completely inappropriate, Ms. Laiken. When you come dragging back in here one night with your teammates ripped to shreds and a desolate feeling in the pit of your stomach that we're losing this war, you may curse me instead.

"By the way, if you put this over, your probation will begin with an informal preinduction ceremony that assumes knighthood. What would you like to be called? I assume Sir Laiken doesn't work? In modern times, when women are knighted for achievement in arts or politics they are usually called 'Dame'."

"Lady Laiken."

Sol cocked his head to one side, considering. "Isn't that what Baka called you?"

"Yes." She opened the door and looked back over her shoulder. "And I like it."

There was just enough time to take Blackie out for a quick walk to relieve himself. She returned one hour and two minutes later. B Team was already assembled in the conference room. Storm was pouring himself a cup from the coffee service. All three seemed surprised to see her and gave her openly inquisitive looks. Apparently Sol had not yet revealed the purpose of the meeting.

"Ms. Laiken is going to give a short presentation. Please give her the courtesy of hearing her out before expressing your opinions." He nodded toward Elora. "You have the floor."

Nervousness was not something she had anticipated, but anxiety rippled through her when she realized that the next few minutes would have a profound impact on her future, regardless of the result. If they all said no, she would feel betrayed by the only people she cared about. In the world. If they said yes, she would be a knight on probation. Either way it was a pivotal moment.

Standing at one end of the table she delivered basically the same speech that had proven successful with Sol. She carefully observed the changes in their facial expression as she talked. Storm went from curious to resolutely pissed. Ram went from curious to stunned. Kay went from curious to thoughtful.

On completion, she waited in silence for a verbal reaction. Sol filled that silence by repeating his concerns and conditions.

Storm was first to speak. He turned to Sol and said: "You *cannot* be serious. No. Absolutely no. And that could not be more final."

"One vote no," Sol said dispassionately.

"Wrong! That would be three votes no." Storm looked at Kay and Ram to make it unanimous.

"Hold on." Kay held up a hand. "I say it's up to Ram. Partly because he's the most senior member of B Team and partly because he's the one most affected since she would be his partner. As far as I'm concerned, everything she said is true. Plus, unlike some of the guys who were on the short list, she's actually killed a vamp. She did it by herself with no real training and no help of any kind. And another plus that she didn't add is that, from a purely tactical perspective, she offers some unique benefits, as a woman, that could be useful."

Storm's brows were drawn in so tight that deep lines had formed between them. All of a sudden he grasped Kay's inference and drew in a sharp breath. "Decoy?" He spat. "You're suggesting using Elora as bait?" He was outraged. "That's the kind of half cocked idiocy I'd expect from Ram! What is wrong with you, Kay?"

"Look. I didn't put her up to this. She volunteered. Apparently we've given her the mistaken impression that our collective asses are worth looking after. She wants to be…"

"…Wendy," Ram finished that sentence while absently looking out the window with a slightly off-focus expression.

"What?"

"Tis a character in one of her stories. A responsible, nurturin' girl who takes care of lost boys."

Storm turned on Elora like a prosecutor and hit her with that laser beam streak of intensity. "Is that true? Is this about some kind of Savior Complex?"

Elora spoke calmly and evenly. "Wanting to keep your friends alive is not a psychological aberration, Storm. How do you think I would feel if they brought one of you in on a gurney one night, with me knowing I might have prevented that? My training and abilities should be used for a worthwhile purpose. You can't really think I'm better suited to clerical work.

"I get it. You're afraid I might get hurt. Now you need to understand that I feel *exactly* the same about the three of you."

Ram still stared out the window, looking dazed, half-listening while trying to sort things out in his head.

"As I see it, the only drawback is this," Kay continued, "and I'm going to be completely honest because it's just us here in this room. Right or wrong B Team is regarded as cream risen to the top. You know that Lan's place would usually be seen as a reward for an outstanding record. The feeling might be that it isn't fair to give the spot to someone who hasn't earned it the usual way."

"I think that's a very good point," Storm concurred.

Sol turned his attention to Kay. "So, is that a vote yes or a vote no?"

Kay pressed his lips together, sighed, and said, "Yes." He turned toward Storm, knowing before he looked that his partner thought his position was a betrayal. "Sorry." He shook his head. "On balance, I think it's the best thing for the team and maybe also our best shot at dealing with this outbreak. The city's counting down to panic. So far they haven't put together that what many of the missing have in common is a club in the Times Square district, but they will. We're just running out of time for indulgent choices, my friend."

Sol looked to Ram. "Guess that means it's up to you, Hawking."

Elora looked at Ram hopefully, but didn't see assent on his face. Finally, he leaned back in his chair and heaved a big sigh.

"Goes without sayin', that if she was any other female, this would no' even be on the table. But we know how special she is. I can no' stand the idea of exposin' her to what's out there, but I do no' have reasonable grounds to deny her if this is what she wants. As she said, she is stronger, faster, and is the best of us in hand to hand. She's very likely smarter as well, at least more so than I. So far as bein' my partner, I already know I like spendin' time with her. If she's goin' to be out there, I'm glad I'll be close by."

"So that's a yes?" Sol asked for clarification.

"Aye. 'Tis."

"This is madness!" Storm thundered then let out a string of curses under his breath that weren't quite inaudible.

When he was finished, Sol said, "I think as a courtesy Gautier should be told before a general announcement is made. Right or wrong, he's expecting to be named. I will inform him of the decision, but with your permission, would like to be able to tell him he will automatically be transferred to B Team the next time there's an opening. Gods forbid. Does everyone agree?" Sol took the silence as acquiescence by abstention.

"Ms. Laiken, henceforth known as Lady Laiken, report to the personnel office in one hour and they will go over your benefits package. You will receive the same salary and benefits as any knight on probation."

"What are benefits?" she asked.

"Things like pension, holiday, and sick leave."

"I don't get sick."

"You mean you've never been sick?" She shook her head. "Ever?"

"I've never been sick. Ever."

"Interesting. Your team has one week to brief you on guidelines and bring you up to speed on weaponry. It will also give us time to make adjustments in your teaching schedule."

"Are we done?" Storm grated.

Sol looked at him. "Unless one of you has something else."

Storm walked out, let the door slam against the wall on his way and didn't look back.

Sol looked at Kay. "He may be due for a workshop on temper control."

Elora was thinking Storm was making a habit of childish displays of petulance, but she was feeling a little insecure about his reaction anyway.

Kay caught her eye. "Don't worry. He'll come round." He stood up and leaned over the table, offering his hand. "Welcome to B Team, Lady Laiken."

Elora stood and shook his hand with a grateful grin. "Thank you, Sir Caelian."

"You know there's a reason why they call us Bad Company. And it isn't because we're no fun."

She smiled. "I surmised as much and will do my best to uphold the reputation for badness."

Ram left with Elora. She could think of a dozen reasons why he might not be his jovial self, but he was clearly lost in disquietude. In addition to the danger quotient and the added worry for her safety in the field, The Order's policy on "office romance" was going to create some internal havoc for two of her new teammates.

Ram saw it as a logistics problem. An hour ago his biggest worry had been how he was going to make a human fall in love with him using romance. Now his biggest worry was how he was going to make a human fall in love with him under a handicap of "no romance".

What was worse, it seemed there were rivals all around. He had no conventions or models to draw upon since elves did not compete for love. Mates were selected by a mysterious process that matched genetic patterns and other factors – maybe astrology for all he knew – so that progeny enjoyed the maximum benefits of hybrid vigor, thereby ensuring the survival of a healthy, hardy race and parents who never fell out of love but grew continually more devoted until separated by death. Granted, in that case, there would be no progeny since an elf/human couple could not reproduce, but the principle was the same.

An errant thought flitted by and silently he asked, "Why couldn't she just be an elf?"

He looked at Elora and flushed with guilt that, in a weak and selfish moment, he had just wished away the gift of this miracle in female form.

In a general meeting of hunters, Sol relayed a report from Baka that vampire were indeed making use of the underground system. As he had suspected, there was a secret entrance from the building that currently housed Notte Fuoco although clearly not all active vampire were aware of that.

Sol didn't like the idea of patrolling space where operatives would be so vulnerable, but if they didn't get the rampage contained soon, there would be a city wide panic.

THE SPLAT DECK was immense and divided into two sections: a firing range with stationary targets and an obstacle course set up very much like those designed for recreational laser tag. On the firing range side, there were several weapons lined up on a table. Kay began going over them with Elora, concentrating on those most popular for field use.

"We developed bullets with a core made of hard wood so green it won't catch fire before reaching the target, but we like the splat guns better because they're silent and if an innocent gets in the way, they won't get hurt.

"As you might guess, one of the logistics problems is how to carry this," picking up a splat pistol, "without drawing attention. That's a lot easier to do in cold weather because you can hide a world of sins in outerwear. In warm weather we pretty much have to rely on stakes in boots.

"The silver gel only works on exposed skin. That means, if your aim isn't good enough to hit a vamp in the face, it won't do you any good. So we'll start with the fixed targets at maximum range of thirty feet. Have you ever shot a gun?"

"No."

"Okay, well, we all have our strengths and weaknesses. We know you're good at hand to hand."

"And ancient weapons," she interjected.

"Yeah, but swords and quivers are not exactly low profile. Storm's the best shot." Turning to Storm: "Why don't you show her how it's done?"

Storm, who had been standing back with his arms crossed over his chest, lips pressed together said, "You wanted her on the team. You show her."

Kay opened his mouth to say something, but he was interrupted by Ram coming to stand in front of Storm, in his face. "What's this now? A fearless leader or just a pouty lunker who turns crybaby when he does no' get his way? 'Tis done! You get that? Let me say it again carefully. 'Tis. Done! She's one of us. And if you do no' come on board, you're goin' to get us all killed." He jerked his head toward Elora. "That includes her."

Storm's eyes flashed with anger as he alternately clenched his jaw and his fists while he and Ram stared each other down. He was not in a humor to be challenged today. But slowly he began to relax as the words were absorbed and he realized there was a valid point. His breathing slowed and he looked past Ram to Kay.

"Okay. Move aside."

He showed Elora how to load the gel-filled capsules and bring them forward into the chamber.

"We deliberately designed these guns with a sound identical to loading shells in a shotgun because any advantage is a good advantage. And few things sound more ominous than hearing the sound of a shell moving into the chamber of a shotgun, especially when it's both quiet and dark. Vampire scare fairly easily and then they make fatal errors." He smiled. "We like that."

The gun he was using held three shots. He aimed and pulled the trigger in rapid succession. All three hit the target in the face.

"Whoa. Seriously?" she said.

"Told you he was good," said Kay with pride.

Storm gave the gun to Elora so that she could practice the reload. He moved behind her to make sure her form was correct. The first two shots missed altogether. One hit a target in the crotch – two targets away from where she was aiming. By the fourth round she was managing to hit *her* target… in the crotch.

Ram said, "I'm beginnin' to sense a very disturbin' pattern here."

Kay laughed.

Elora said, "Maybe you should keep it in mind, partner."

Ram grinned. Stepping behind her he placed his hands on her hips and swiveled her body so that her angle to target was slightly different. He urged her body into a different position so that her weight was redistributed. He ducked a little to line up his sight with hers, then took her arm and moved her aim upward.

"You're hittin' 'round two and a half feet south of where you're aimin'. Maybe there's more of a drop in flight than you're calculatin'. So why do you no' try aimin' just that much higher and see what happens?"

She reloaded and tried that suggestion, with the result

of hitting the target in the chest.

"I'm callin' that progress." Ram smiled proudly with prejudice and affection.

Kay took the pistol from her and said: "We'll work on it, but we're gonna make sure you have boxes of toothpicks in your pockets just to be safe."

Ram laughed. Storm was still too sullen for humor.

That night for the first time she sat at B Team's table as an actual member of B Team. The conversation scattered from details of field operations to B Team's self-reported deeds of tour de force. As an example of the latter, Kay told her to ask Ram about the time he gave Storm mouth to mouth. It would be hard to say which of them wanted to throttle Kay more for bringing that up. Their embarrassment made Kay laugh until he was red in the face. It wasn't easy to get two Bad Company knights to blush at the same time. As they glared at Kay, he explained to Elora that it had been that incident that had caused them to adopt the policy that what happens as a team, stays with the team.

She was told that she must never be separated from her partner and to avoid being cornered together as a team in a dead end or a trap like an elevator, so that each partnership could serve as back up to the other. They went over other ways to identify vampire without asking them to show fangs. They discussed the unique opportunities presented by having a female operative and how that might best be used to their advantage without excessive risk to Elora.

The question of the reported powerful aphrodisiac came up, and Elora expressed her doubts. Glancing at Storm she said: "The day you told me about what happened to Lan, you mentioned aphrodisiacs and I didn't question it at the time. I know there are differences, but in my world, aphrodisiacs were proven to be a myth."

"I, for one, would very much like to hear how that was proved." Ram sounded mildly amused.

"Um, actually, it was a TV show called 'Myth Busters'. Every episode they would take a commonly held belief and put it through a series of scientifically designed tests to determine fact or fiction. I saw the one on aphrodisiacs."

Storm looked unconvinced. "Like you said, what if it's one of those differences?"

"Could be. I'm just saying that aphrodisiacs can be a

convenient 'devil made me do it' excuse."

Storm nodded thoughtfully. "Noted."

Kay turned to Elora. "On another note entirely, I don't want to be the dead messenger, but I think you ought to do something about the hair."

Elora blinked. "Like what?"

"Like cut it off."

"What? Why?"

Having three sisters and a lifelong girlfriend, Kay knew enough about women to tread carefully with a woman's vanity. "Your hair is great, Elora, but you didn't just fight your way into a beauty contest. Your priorities have got to shift from cuteness to battle readiness.

"This must have been mentioned in your hand to hand training. If you leave all that hair down, sooner or later it will get in the way, could easily create a blind spot. Wearing it up is almost worse because it might as well be a handle; grab, jerk, pull you off balance at best, snap your neck at worst. I think I speak for all of us when I say I'd rather see you *alive* with shorter hair."

Elora looked at Ram and Storm to see their reactions. Ram said: "Well, when put like that, how can I no' agree?"

He was thinking that not a night passed without him drifting to sleep fantasizing about diving into a tangled mass of jasmine scented silky strands. Or feeling it trail down his body as she feathered kisses on his skin from chin to cock. Or having it brush against his thighs as she rode him with her head thrown back. He looked at it longingly and sighed. "I, too, prefer you alive."

Elora studied her plate for a few seconds and then said, "I'll think about it."

Thinking this might be a good time for a new subject, she remembered the mental note she had made to ask about the leadership comment from earlier in the day. "I thought I heard Sol say that teams are organized without any official leadership, but, on the splat deck, you," looking at Ram, "called Storm fearless leader."

Ram nodded and looked at Kay as if to say, "You take this one."

Kay took a minute thinking about how best to explain. "Okay. What happens when you form a unit of four guys," he caught himself, "or, people, who are all alpha personalities with a raging case of Oppositional Defiance Disorder and you add to that a tradition of not formally naming a leader? Well, curiously enough, on some basic instinct level, we know that decisions can't always be made by committee. When it's final answer time, one of the four will find the other three standing there looking at him. When Lan was our fourth, that person was Storm, but group dynamics are always in motion."

Elora then presented an idea that had been germinating. She was thinking that maybe the same contact who booked the house bass player gig for Baka could arrange jobs for the four of them. That way they could be there every night without their constant presence raising suspicion, and could keep each other in sight.

Everybody liked the idea. They argued over which jobs would best fit their purpose and which of them would be best suited for a particular position.

"Can you dance?" Kay asked Elora.

"You're talking about the cage dancers on the club level?" Kay nodded. "I'd have to get a new partner if I took that job."

"Why?"

"Because Rammel would never sleep again. There just aren't that many cold showers in a day's time."

Kay snickered. Storm pouted.

With a rakish smile, Ram said, "I'd be acceptin' that challenge, my girl."

Elora grunted as if that was drivel and turned back to Kay. "Okay. Seriously. If the vamps are coming and going from the live music level, then, shouldn't that be the center of the operation?"

"She's right." Storm said. "She should serve drinks. Right or wrong that's what patrons expect to see female employees doing. Plus it gives her a mobility that we wouldn't have as bouncers or bartenders."

"Too bad," Ram stared at Elora with a gleam in his eyes, biting his bottom lip, unabashedly, and conveying the impression that his imagination was still lingering on images of a scantily clad Elora writhing, bumping, and grinding.

She was starting to feel her cheeks heat and Ram was clearly enjoying making her squirm. She knew she had only herself to blame. She had started it. But it was a lesson learned and she made a mental note. *Do not ever challenge the sex god to a duel of sexual inference. You'll lose.*

In the end they agreed that it would make the most

sense for Ram to bar tend so that he could stay in constant contact with his partner ordering and serving drinks, while Storm and Kay worked security. That gave them the perfect excuse to stand on the sidelines and observe without looking out of place.

ELORA SPENT THE rest of the week in briefing, target practice, and finally, on the splat gun course. She also spent some time with the kitchen and bar staff consulting on the details of professional drink delivery.

She made arrangements with the Operations Office to qualify a few dog lovers for walking and exercising Blackie when Elora was on duty. He was so well-behaved that they decided he could hang out in the Operations Office at night and set up a large, comfy bed for him in a corner.

Blackie was becoming a master at 'hunt the vampire' using two halves of Baka's shirt; the one to cue the dog and the other to hide for him to find. He was a very quick study, showing remarkable aptitude for tracking. As an added bonus he liked it and thrived on solving puzzles. It was the doggie version of a Sherlock Holmes mystery and also made him feel like he was working for his keep.

One beautiful fall afternoon, after a romp in the leaves, Elora decided to alter the game a little. She got Ram to let her borrow a Black Sabbath tee shirt that he had worn recently, and had him hide somewhere in the building without telling her where, stipulating that he should start in the hub. She promised to call if it looked like Blackie couldn't find him.

She took Blackie to the hub. He had grown into the role of the mascot they had hoped he'd become when he was adopted. He liked getting affection from the people he thought were in his pack: Elora, Ram, Sanction, and a few more in Operations. For the rest, he was tolerant, but not overly engaging. When women would switch to baby talk, Elora would have to stifle a laugh at the sardonic way Blackie looked at them. If he could have arched an eyebrow and said, "What the fuck?" he would have. Elora couldn't be more proud. In every way, including temperament, he was the finest example of a mature Alsatian male.

Having just stopped by the coffee bar, Storm noticed the commotion and wandered over.

"What's up?"

"We're playing a new game today called Find Sir Hawking."

"You're trying to turn that mutt into a bloodhound?"

Elora gaped. "Who are you calling a mutt? For all we know this may be the finest Alsatian alive."

"The finest what? Elora, that dog is a German Shepherd."

She looked dubious. "Whatever. Lots of dogs are good at tracking, Storm. Not just bloodhounds. They train Beagles to look for termites. I think Blackie could do just about anything he was asked to do." She absently ran her hand behind Blackie's right ear. "You're welcome to come along if you want."

Storm was wearing that signature skeptical look, but he was amused, too. "Sure. Let's see what happens."

After a few minutes most of the people went on about their business. To the rest she said: "Sorry everybody, if you'll excuse us, Blackie's on a mission today."

People looked intrigued, but backed away as requested.

Elora took Ram's tee shirt out of her backpack and put it in front of his nose as she had done with Baka's shirt.

But instead of saying, "Find the vamp," she said, "Find Ram."

Blackie brought his head up and his ears far forward as he looked at her to make sure she'd got it right because those weren't the words that signaled the beginning of the game. With an intelligence that was superior to many people, he was saying, "I'm not sure I understand you."

She repeated: "Ram. Find Ram."

He whined and wagged his tail, so she unhooked the leash. He started sniffing in circles almost frantically. He trotted to the lounge, then backtracked, sat down in front of the elevator and looked back at Elora as if to say, "Make this thing open."

Elora knew Ram was hiding on one of the two sublevels because those were the conditions of the game. Storm, Elora and Blackie entered the elevator and pushed SL1. When the doors opened, Blackie exited and sniffed around. Elora held the doors open waiting to see what would happen. After a couple of seconds Blackie trotted back into the elevator. She pushed SL2. When the doors opened, Blackie exited, sniffed in a circle, and took off running.

Elora looked up at Storm and grinned an I-told-you-so. By the time they'd jogged the length of the first hallway, Blackie was out of sight. They turned the corner, looked down the second long hallway – also nowhere to be seen, but they could hear him barking in a tone that sounded a lot like a song of victory. When they reached the end of that hall and turned the corner they found Blackie standing outside the cage that used to be his nightmare, wagging his tail. He had one paw up on the chain link gate as if to say, "Got you."

Inside Ram was sitting cross legged, reading a book.

Elora went to her knees to smother Blackie in pets and, "Good boy's", while he licked every inch of her face.

Ram stood up and let himself out of the cage. "I'd be askin' for a hello kiss myself if you were no' wearin' so much dog drool on your face."

Storm shot Ram the obligatory nasty look for talking about kissing while looking at Elora, then congratulated her on a successful exercise.

CHAPTER 16

BLACK SWAN TRAINING MANUAL, Chapter 16, #39.

The myth that vampire may sometimes be repelled by religious symbols is the result of misidentification of cause. Religious symbols, particularly in the form of jewelry, are often made of silver or contain silver in the alloy. Vampire instinctively recognize silver as a potentially fatal substance since it can incapacitate and render the vampire helpless. It is, of course, the metal and not the symbol that creates the aversion.

THE PLAN TO work at Notte Fuoco was given the green light and jobs were arranged. Ram spent a couple of hours at the lounge bar every day being trained on bartending. He carried a handbook with him so that he could study drink recipes, and Elora quizzed him nightly. By week's end, he could pass for a bartender. What he didn't have in flashy moves he more than made up for in sex appeal.

Female wait staff at Notte Fuoco wore white tank tops with the club logo, and tight, black mid thigh skirts. Elora worked with field operations to modify the uniform to a black, mid thigh, tiered skirt with a saucy kick and knee high boots.

Male staff wore black tee shirts with the club logo, and jeans. With their size, physiques, and presence, Kay and Storm were completely believable in the role of bouncers. There was no unobtrusive way to hide a splat gun behind tee shirts and jeans so they went bare bones.

Elora, on the other hand, could easily attach a splat pistol to a garter underneath her skirt. They ordered multiple pairs of low heeled boots with enough room in the calves so that stakes could be attached to specially sewn, elastic loops.

When the duty roster was posted, B Team was in rotation for the first time in months. They had Thursdays and Sundays off since those were the slowest nights at the club.

Monday night, the first night on duty, Ram seemed as at home behind the bar as if he'd been doing it all his life and, of course, there was always a throng of women three deep slurping drinks while following every move he made with lust in their hearts and dreamy expressions on their faces. Even though he seemed oblivious to all the female attention, Elora found it irritating. The fact that she was irritated made it all the more aggravating.

Storm and Kay tried to be as inconspicuous as two very large and striking men can be. To the casual observer, they might appear to be relaxed, but they were always on duty, aware of everything going on in the room, dividing their attention between watching for developing trouble of the human variety and watching for vampire to surface, prepared to lunge into action at a millisecond's notice.

Elora, on the other hand, struggled to get her bearings. She didn't always recognize the names of the drinks being ordered and cursed herself for not studying the handbook Ram had used. Whenever she entered the far end of the bar to place an order, Ram looked up and gave her that special smile that she had come to know was for her alone. The one that said: "The sun just rose in the heavens because you've arrived."

Once an hour, management sent people from other levels down to spell Ram and Elora so they could take ten minutes. After the third hour, Ram suggested they go up and out onto the street to fill their lungs with some freshly exhaust-filled air.

Getting outside of the club did make it feel more like a real break.

They had just arrived on the street when a boisterous group of young women half stumbled out of the club. Seeing Ram, one of them approached, opening her coat with pride to display the striped, sequin tank top under- neath. She stepped in front of Elora and pressed farcically inflated, permanently pushed-up breasts into Ram's torso, while batting fake Bambi lashes that outlined eyes both shiny and red-rimmed from too much drink.

The interloper was wearing her long, straight hair in one of those silly, sideways pony tails. Acting on pure impulse, without thinking it through, Elora reached out, grabbed a fistful of sideways pony tail in her right hand and pushed the skank toward the curb, saying: "Find something else to do."

The woman had to take a couple of steps and grab on to friends to catch her balance and keep from falling. While turning the air blue, she gave Elora a look of challenge like she was thinking about coming for her.

Seeing this play out on the woman's face Ram laughed, shook his head and said: "Oh. I definitely would no' if I were you."

Deciding on the better part of valor on her behalf, her friends encouraged her to move along with them. Giving Elora one last look that could kill, she half walked, half staggered away.

Ram turned a high beam expression of delight on Elora, who was stunned by her own territorial behavior and feeling embarrassed. She looked around anxiously. "I really have no idea why I did that. It was wrong. I mean it's not as if you can't take care of yourself or decide whose fake chest you want pressed against you."

"Elora…," he began.

She started away. "I've got to visit the Ladies before time's up. I'll see you down there."

"Hold on. Partners stay together." In two long strides he caught up. "Remember?"

Shaking herself internally, she fired back. "You are not using that as an excuse to come in the women's restroom with me."

He smiled. "No? Well, then I'll wait outside for a count of one hundred."

TUESDAY NIGHT, WHEN it was time to go on duty, Elora answered Ram's knock with her hair cut to within two and a half inches all over her head and spiked up in a messy, edgy do that was appropriate for club work. Ram did a double take.

She shrugged. "Kay's right. Long hair's too easy to grab. I found that out last night."

Ram nodded and gave her a little smile. He had loved the gorgeous, many-colored mane, but her appeal didn't depend on it. She was inalterably adorable. He reached up and ran his hand over her head while she resisted the impulse to lean into it.

"Still beautiful," was all he said.

Elora hadn't realized how much his opinion mattered until she saw his reaction and heard the reassurance.

Baka took short breaks when the bands did and longer

ones when a band brought their own bass. He usually spent his free time staring at Elora and she could always feel it, like hands on her body. She knew he was aware that he made her flush and she knew he enjoyed the power he was transmitting telepathically; the very potent threat, or promise, of passion with single-minded purpose.

Wednesday night Baka made eye contact on one of his breaks. Looking around to make sure no one was watching, he gave her a beguiling, teasing smile with just the slightest peek of fang. In response she turned her right side to him, brought her foot up to rest on the seat of a chair, looked around to make sure no one was watching, then raised her skirt enough to flash the garter that held the splat pistol, all while returning his smile with a wicked twist. He retracted his fangs and laughed. And, damn, if laughter didn't look good on him.

The phrase: 'flirting with disaster' came to mind. Prudent or not, she enjoyed the heady rush she got from Baka's attention.

B Team worked for three nights without incident, falling into a routine. The fourth day was Thursday, one of their days off. On Wednesday Ram asked if she would like to spend Thursday with him. She said she had already promised the day to Storm. He had agreed to do two things on her Break Out List: go shopping at the mall and teach her how to drive.

"He's takin' you shoppin' at a suburb mall and teachin' you to drive? Okay." Ram shook his head. "Better him than me." Elora gave him a pretend punch in the bicep. "Sunday. Give me Sunday."

"Sure."

"What touches your fancy?"

"Surprise me."

"My pleasure. Ten thirty. Street clothes."

ELORA'S DRIVING LESSON was filled with the usual frustrations for both driver and teacher, but the trip to the mall went better. Storm owned a sports car that had been modified for his long legs, but suspected that Elora would need cargo space for packages, so he borrowed a large SUV. The mall shops were on three levels. They explored the map so they could narrow the choices down to a few stores. They hit Ann Taylor, lululemon, J. Crew, Shoecolate and stopped at Starbucks for a hot chocolate.

When Elora wanted to spend time at Victoria's Secret, Storm decided he would drop the purchases at the car and wait for her at the food court.

She shopped for lingerie that felt good; function plus comfort. If it also looked good, well, icing on the cake. Last, she splurged on a costly, but sublimely soft, all-purpose, angel white robe.

When she turned the corner of the food court her eyes immediately locked on Storm looking so out of place, sitting in a chair that was too small for his big body, in front of a Formica top table amid strollers, spilled pop-corn, and screaming toddlers. How surprised passersby would be to know that a real live knight, who kept their children safe at night, was sitting there looking lost in front of the Panda Express. And she liked him all the more for spending his day off doing things to please her.

She dumped the packages next to him and asked if she could get him something to eat. He looked around, sniffed in a semi-superior way, and said: "Thank you, but I'll hold out for something edible."

It seemed that Storm had gotten used to the VIP treatment The Order showered on active operatives.

Edible meant dinner reservations at a small inn with a five star restaurant. Fortunately they didn't have a coat and tie policy, but probably would have let him get by in street clothes regardless.

The food, appointments, and service were no better than the Mess where they ate every day, but this place had the advantage of dinner alone with Elora. Even if it wasn't going to end with a kiss, at least it was a night when he could have her all to himself.

They easily slipped back into the comfortable, relaxed way they had conversed with each other daily when Elora was in recovery. They talked about books they liked and why they liked them. She caught him up on gossip she'd heard from Elsbeth while he marveled that there was a whole underbelly of speculative discussion going on without him having knowledge of any of it. He said he missed their chess games and worried constantly about the danger she was in as a member of B Team, to which she said: "You just take care of yourself. I've got my back and yours, too."

Over chocolate mousse and coffee, he grew quiet and pensive. "Something wrong?"

"No. Just trying to figure out how to say this. I guess the best way is just to come out with it." He took a deep breath like he was building confidence. "I want you to know I have feelings for you, the kind that Order policy prevents me from expressing adequately. I don't want to put you in a position of violating a pledge, so I'm not expecting a response. I just need you to know that things would be different if…things were different."

The only thing about this confession that was surprising to Elora was the vocalization. She looked at Storm solemnly so he would know she took it seriously. Her only reaction was a slight nod followed by downcast eyes. He took that to mean that she agreed it was best not to talk about it, so he changed the subject.

"Got one more surprise."

"What?" She perked up.

"Sanction is on duty tonight. We have an empty seat at the Thursday night poker game if you want to play."

"You sure that's okay with the others?"

"Yep. They say they're just as happy to take your money as his."

She laughed. "Yes. Well, I wish I could say that wasn't

the probable outcome. What time is the game?"

He looked at his watch. "Matter of fact, we better get going, Princess."

The Thursday night game was held in a private room off the back of the lounge. On the way in they passed a little gathering watching a contest of darts.

"Ghost is the undisputed champion of darts. Kind of unusual for an American, but he spent a few years in Scotia. Every now and then somebody challenges him and odds get made, but you'd be crazy to bet against him."

As they were passing by, Ghost looked up and pinned her with a stare which was unnerving as his eyes had the same identical lack of color as vampire. There may have been a flicker of malice before his expression melted into an affable smile, but she wasn't sure she hadn't imagined it. She knew less about him than any other knight or trainee because he had declined training with her.

"I never asked how Ghost reacted. I mean, my taking Lan's place on the team."

Storm shrugged. "He wasn't happy, but he took it like a man." He cut a puckish smile her way when he said it.

She chuckled, more to be accommodating than because she thought it was funny. "Hysterical."

Truthfully, she wouldn't have blamed Ghost if he had taken it badly. It had to be hard, looking so ghastly and being surrounded by men who could be Polo models. She doubted he had ever had a date. Certainly the dreadful looks were unfortunate, but then there was also an undeniable creep factor.

The table in the private poker room sat eight, and six were already there. The table, itself, was a work of art, a rosewood octagon with ornately carved legs. The space was lit by an octagonal, low hanging stained glass Tiffany lamp; the ambience conveying an opulence that said: "If you need to ask how much to play, you don't belong in this game."

The room was equipped with a specially designed exhaust so that players could smoke without leaving stale smells or allowing tainted air to escape to other parts of the building.

Storm hadn't mentioned that Ram was one of the regulars. As she took the seat opposite him, he gave her a look that said, "You know that no one knows you the way I do and it's our secret."

A couple of people who regularly worked the lounge stayed late on Thursday nights for the extra tips they got serving players. There was a steady circuit of delivery of food or drink. Or aspirin in Finnemore's case.

Elora's rum and coke was served in a squat, crystal glass heavy enough to feel substantial in big, strong hands. They started a bar tab for her. Another first.

The dealer went over the customary rules and limits for her benefit. Then they all hunkered down for a night of cards. Elora had never seen Storm smoke before, but when he lit a small, thin, black cigar, like the ones Sol smoked, she remembered the faint smell of cigar that night that she was carried to the infirmary with what was left of her face pressed against his chest.

When Storm had taught her how to play poker, he had figured out quickly that her face was too expressive to expect that she wouldn't divulge her reaction to cards. So he had instructed her to go the other direction, pretending to be delighted, or smug, or confused by every hand so that no one watching would be able to discern a pattern of "tells".

Storm would never have suggested including her if he

thought she might be humiliated by her lack of experience, but he had learned while teaching her the game that she had "card sense"; an innate communion with the sacred geometry of playing cards that couldn't be either taught or developed with practice. As he predicted, she did okay using the tips, tricks, and strategies he suggested along with some slight modifications of her own. She didn't win, but she didn't lose much either.

At one point she looked around and had the amusing thought that, like tales of Arthurian legend, she found herself sitting at a round table with knights bent on chivalry.

After three hours, there were five people still playing. At one point she and Ram were the only two in for a big pot. She looked across the dimly lit table and her breath caught. Ram had his chin tucked in and was watching her with eyes that smoldered like embers in the dim lamp light, fire reflected on water, and she knew that look had nothing to do with poker. That look said: "You know that no one will ever want you more than I do. And it's our secret. For now."

CHAPTER 17

ON FRIDAY NIGHT Elora passed a note to the lead guitar and asked him to hand it off to the bassist. She turned around in time to see Baka take the note which read: "I understand you take requests. I'd like to hear 'Love Bites'." He laughed and looked up, searching the room until his gaze locked with hers. She thought smiling was a good look for him even though it never completely chased away the underlying sadness.

On Sunday morning Elora was standing at her door waiting for a knock which came at exactly ten thirty. It was an early December day on the cold side as a fresh norther had blown in from Canada overnight and wind was predicted. Ram insisted that Elora go back in for a warmer coat. He had arranged for a whister to take them into Manhattan, one of the job's better perks.

"Tell me where we're going."

"You said surprise you."

"Come on," she pleaded.

"Sightseein'," he smiled. "Today we're tourists. There's more to New York than Notte Fuoco and Times Square."

They were dropped at the 39th and 7th avenue pad and walked over to 5th Avenue. On the way by Grand Central Station they ducked in just so she had a visual for the reference, then headed up 5th toward the park. Manhattan was at her best at Yuletide the way a pretty woman was even prettier with make up on.

Elora window shopped every single store on the way. Any casual observer could have pointed her out as a tourist, because the delight of discovery was plain on her face.

They stopped at Saks to look at the decorations in the display windows and then at Rockefeller Center to see the Yule tree and the ice skaters.

"Tis a tradition to get hot chocolate when you come to see the big tree."

"I could learn to love tradition," she smiled.

He snorted at that. "Very well. Let's put that to the test and begin with women in the kitchen and knowin' their place."

She laughed and went to find a table by the rink where they could watch the skaters. Ram returned with the nectar of gods heated to perfection, set the cups down and sat next to her.

"This reminds me of Yule at home." She looked a little wistful. "We always had a big tree – well, not as big as this."

Ram went still. It was the first time she had ever made reference to her life before. "With lights and ornaments?"

She nodded. "The works. Does your family celebrate Yule?"

"Oh, aye. In a big way. They are very much into good times."

"Well," she looked at him affectionately, "that explains a lot."

Ram smiled into his cup. Before they left, he handed his phone to a passerby and asked her to take a picture of the two of them in front of the tree and ice rink. They snuggled close, smiled big, and anyone who witnessed the taking of the photo would have sworn they were a couple in love.

When they reached The Plaza, Ram stood at the intersection pointing out the southeast end of the park with the carriages, the drivers heating themselves by fires burning in barrels, and the Sherry Netherland across the street.

"Oh that's where…"

"Where what?"

"Um, I just heard nice things about it."

He laughed. "Aye. 'Tis probably the most costly hotel in this hemisphere."

Ram hailed a cab to take them the rest of the way to the Metropolitan Museum. Elora said she wanted to try it the next time.

"Try what? The Sherry Netherland?"

"Ha! You wish. No, silly. Getting a taxi."

"Oh. Aye." He loved that she could find pleasure and adventure in such simple things.

On the way up Madison Avenue he told what he knew about the museum and said that the tour might be called a "taste of New York" as one day was not enough time to see very much of "the big apple".

"Why do they call it that?"

"No idea."

"Let's ask somebody."

Elora stopped the first ten people she saw after they got out of the cab to ask if they knew why New York was called the Big Apple. Four ignored her altogether. Three shook heads as they hurried by. Three stopped long enough to say they didn't know. Ram just stood patiently with hands in pockets enjoying every minute of it.

They climbed the famous steps with the colorful banners and followed the crowd into a much overheated grand foyer where they got in line to check coats. The Met was always busy on Sunday, but everything in New York was busier in December, with kids on holiday break and tourists coming to see the decorations and the Holiday Spectacle at Rockefeller Center.

Waiting in the slow moving line, Elora got caught up in people watching. She turned to point something out to Ram only to find him shamelessly flirting with someone in line behind them. She felt an instantaneous spike of jealousy and turned around, following his gaze, expecting to find a bimbo much like the one whose hair was righteously snatched outside Notte Fuoco. Instead, she found a hazel-eyed toddler with shiny chestnut curls riding her mother's hip, alternately being coy and playing peek-a-boo with Ram. Elora watched the interaction silently and had to smile at the simple enjoyment he was getting from making the beautiful baby giggle.

Ram bought two admissions, got maps, then explained that it would take weeks to see everything in the museum. Since choices had to be made, he asked what she would like to see most on a first visit. After scanning the options, she chose arms and armor.

"O' course," he said.

They spent a couple of hours in the museum before he hurried her away, saying there was so little time, so much to do, and that he had reservations for late lunch.

"What was the most surprisin' thing?" he asked as they were leaving the museum.

"How tiny people used to be." He looked confused like he was trying to place the reference and she reminded him that the suits of armor looked like they had been made for children. One of the things about Elora that captivated him was the complete unpredictability of what she might say or do next. He thought to himself that he would never be bored with her even if he lived for millennia.

They got one of the standing cabs to take them to Serendipity, famous for frozen hot chocolate, which was sure to be a hit with Elora. Ram ordered a Bi-Sensual burger with fries. She ordered black bean soup so there would be plenty of room for dessert.

When the waiter was gone she asked, "A Bi-Sensual burger? Is that code for bisexual?"

"Certainly no'," he said with confident ease and that killer smile that never failed to send a gush to the nether region. "It means twice as sexy."

She tried to get Ram to divulge the rest of the itinerary without success. When she finished her soup, she excused herself for a visit to the lounge. On return, she found him with his back turned, engaged in some dubious activity with a table of little girls. The little ladies were laughing so uproariously they were on the verge of creating a disturbance, while the supervising mom looked mildly alarmed, uncertain as to what course of action to take.

When Ram noticed that the attention of his audience was diverted to something behind him, he turned to face Elora with two very long, limp French fries hanging out of his nostrils. He quickly pulled them out of his nose and set them aside, looking sheepish.

The behavior was immature at best and revolting at worst. She supposed she should be aghast, but wasn't. She thought charming little girls was... well... charming. She couldn't help thinking that Ram was going to make a wonderful dad someday. Wonderful *and* fun.

To Ram's relief she sat down without saying a word, studied him for a minute, then smiled. He had spent weeks researching love and finally reached the conclusion that, when it came to romance, one approach did not fit all. He didn't need to know about generic courting. He needed to learn what romance meant to Elora. So he had devised a carefully crafted plan to gain intel – one that involved frozen hot chocolate.

As expected, Elora thought frozen hot chocolate was simply the perfect food. So he plied her with questions while she was distracted by mouthfuls of cold ambrosia.

"So what's the best dinner you ever had?"

"Castle Kronberg, on the outskirts of Frankfurt."

"What are your favorite flowers?"

"Stargazer lilies with Mexican red roses and tree fern. No baby's breath or leather leaf. Ughh. And I don't like flowers to look 'arranged'. I like them to look like you just cut them in the garden, brought them in and dropped them in a vase."

"Favorite movie."

"*Willow.*"

"Why?"

"The love story, of course. And the rascal-turned-hero adventure."

"Best love song ever."

"'If' by Bread."

"Tell me about your favorite boyfriend."

She stiffened. Her demeanor changed and she set her spoon down.

"I've never had a boyfriend." She looked at him like she was daring him to ask another question. "Okay, I know what you're dying to ask so I'll tell you. I'm not a virgin, but it wasn't an experience I'm eager to repeat, either."

On the one hand Ram wanted to kick himself for ruining the mood. On the other hand, he had stumbled on information he needed to know. Someone had led Elora to believe that sex was something unpleasant, to be avoided.

He carefully kept his expression neutral while thinking he would very much like to set the bloke on fire.

"Hey," he said with the ghost of a hopeful smile. "Let's go do somethin' fun."

"Like what?" She returned his smile with a small one of her own. "Tell me now."

"Demandin'," he teased thinking there was hope of recapturing her earlier excitement. "The grand dame of modern department stores, other than Harrods in London," he amended. "You want it. They got it."

"Ooh. My kind of place."

Ram settled the bill and helped her into her coat. The walk to Bloomingdales was only a few minutes, but it was cold. The wind had come up and was gusting through the deep canyons formed by tall buildings and chilled by the rivers on either side of Manhattan. It went right to the bones. Elora sidled up close to Ram for warmth and put her arm through the crook in his elbow. He took the opportunity to draw her even closer, wishing now that they had walked all the way from the museum.

"Now I have one question for you," she said. "What do you want more than anything else in the world?"

The answer was so easy it was on the tip of his tongue even before she'd asked the question. Telling her the answer, however, was impossible so long as fucking no-office-romance idiocy was interfering with the natural order of things.

"I can no' say."

"I'm betting you plan to have a big family someday, lots of children."

He turned his face into her so that his breath momentarily warmed her cheek. "Tis no' that important, Elora."

She thought that was a strange answer, but didn't press the issue. They passed a neon palm sign on a shop that read: "Fortunes Told".

"Wait, Ram, let's do this."

"Give your future to Gypsies?"

She laughed at him. "That's the most superstitious thing I've ever heard anyone say! Don't be ridiculous. Come on. It's just for fun."

This was not a day for denying her anything she wanted. So they stepped inside.

There was no wait. They were ushered into a small, dark, curtained room equipped with every cliché you might expect of a gypsy fortune teller including a large ball – glass, not crystal – and a colorful, mismatched costume.

When they sat down in the folding chairs provided, the "gypsy" asked for fifty dollars. Ram handed her a bill which she held up to the lamp, folded twice, and put down her bra while Ram and Elora exchanged amused looks and silently pledged to laugh about it later.

Abruptly she looked up at Elora. "I know why you have come."

"You do?" Elora sounded as intrigued as a child.

Ram swallowed a laugh.

"Yes. There are three men who are in love with you."

Ram was suddenly less amused. *Wait. Three?*

"You are facing danger from a monster whose eyes are very pale, almost white."

"Aye," Ram said dryly, "we get that a lot." He pulled Elora away. "Let's go. This is no' fun."

Elora had to agree.

They rose to leave and were almost out the door when the gypsy said, "I have a message for the lady." Elora turned around. "Choose wisely and love will be new for the rest of your days."

Back on the street Elora threaded her arm through Ram's and pressed as close as possible to keep the wind from getting between them.

"Okay, so I admit it. Maybe that wasn't the best idea."

"You know I do no' care what we're doin' so long as it's with you."

She beamed. That was the perfect thing to say.

As Ram predicted, Bloomingdales turned out to be Elora's idea of an amusement park. They spent hours wandering the store. She was fascinated by everything from evening gowns to gourmet kitchen appliances, even though she had no interest in cooking. At one point they were riding an up elevator behind a curvy blond with the word "JUICY" written in capital letters across her behind.

Ram leaned over and whispered: "We should buy you a pair of those very fetchin' britches to show off your gorgeous ass."

Elora gave him a scandalized look that couldn't have delighted him more. When they arrived at the next level and put some distance between themselves and "JUICY", she said: "First, ugh! Second, as my partner, you can have my permission to put my corpse in those, but only if there will be no open casket viewing. Third," and, though she tried to conceal it, he could tell that she was working to suppress a laugh, "you do not have my permission to comment on my gorgeous ass."

Ram laughed conspiratorily. "I get it. Over your dead body. You know, scratch the surface and we find your very ladylike upbringin' still hale and hearty and ready for tea with the queen. But I would no' be wantin' anyone else to see your very shapely, juicy ass in those fine britches."

She opened her mouth to reply, but realized anything she said would just prolong the dialogue and urge him on. He could keep it up longer than she could. Inexplicably the talk about le derriere was turning her on in ways that were both surprising and awkward. And had he just said gorgeous and shapely, juicy ass? It was confusing to realize that crass observations sounded romantic coming from Ram. She decided to put that in the circular file for later reflection and turned to shopping in earnest.

After a gentle reminder that they had to carry what she bought back to the whister pad, she settled for Ugg boots, ultra cool leg warmers – which was not an oxymoron – and a winter white, silk and cashmere hat and scarf. After trying thirty hat and scarf combinations on her like she was a doll, Ram proclaimed that she looked bewitching in everything, but that winter white was most striking with her flaming hair and the high coloring she wore in her cheeks, that looked like too much blush, even though she didn't wear any.

"It reminds me of my special place in Ireland. The one I told you about."

It was dark when they stepped back out on the street and even more frigid than before, but it was worth it to see the holiday lights at night. The closest whister pad was the one where they had started. It was either a short cab ride or a long walk in the cold. So Elora got her chance to hail her first taxi.

When she'd got her breath back from the cold, she talked nonstop about the marvels of Bloomingdales. The cab driver made no attempt to hide the fact that he periodically took long looks at her in the rear view mirror. Ram didn't know if the curiosity was because she was so excited in an un-New Yorker sort of way or because she was very likely the world's most beautiful woman.

When they were back on the whister, lifting off, she leaned close to Ram.

"This was the best day of my life," she said in a low voice so the pilot wouldn't hear.

Ram's heart squeezed in his chest. What he wanted more than anything was to blurt out: "I do no' want to be a vampire hunter anymore. I just want to take you home to Ireland where I can keep you safe and love you every second for the rest of our lives. I want to kiss your freckled nose and your rosy cheeks and your beautiful mouth, worship that body that slays me and make love to you over and over until you beg me to stop." But instead, he smiled, hoping she would intuit the rest just by looking into his eyes and seeing how hard he swallowed.

His reply, in a voice huskier than usual, was simply, "Me, too."

"You know everywhere we went today, people stared at you."

"You're so very wrong, my girl." He looked at her in that way he had of making her feel like a priceless treasure. "Was you they were admirin'."

Saying goodnight to Elora at her door and going to

bed alone was even harder than usual. In his head he built a fantasy of how the day would have ended if there was not a fuck all policy interfering with the natural order of things.

During the first hour at the club on Monday, Elora got a text from Baka. "Meet me in our alley in fifteen minutes."

Our alley? She reasoned that he must mean the one where she had killed the vamp. She glanced at her watch and texted back.

"OK. Must bring partner. Rules. Behave yourself."

She had to talk into Ram's ear to be heard above the noise in the club. He looked at his watch and nodded.

It was chilly, but not as cold as it had been the night before when they had been carefree sightseers. They jogged the three blocks to the alley because they couldn't be gone long. They might be undercover, but jobs still came with demands.

Baka was waiting.

"Hey," Elora panted. "What's up? We've got five minutes before we have to start back."

"I finished remapping the underground. It's pretty much the same as it was in the twenties except that somebody has updated the lighting with low energy, storm shelter fixtures. When I reported to your Sovereign yesterday, he ordered me to take E Team on a reconnaissance tour since you had the day off. I told him I thought that was a bad idea. If we were spotted by vampire we'd lose the element of surprise when we need it.

"He said do it anyway. So I took them down for an hour yesterday afternoon. We didn't encounter vampire, but there are indications that the tunnel system is... in use."

"You mean you saw signs of remains?"

Ram ran a hand through his hair and turned away. "And why be tellin' us this then?"

Baka's brows knit together. "Because something about E Team doesn't feel right." He shook his head a little. "Hunches are the hardest sort of thing to explain."

Ram glanced at Elora. "Gotta go."

Baka looked between them. "Watch out for the entrance. It's hidden in the wall at the end of the hallway where the restrooms are."

"Show me," Elora said.

Ram went back to the bar while Baka led Elora toward the tunnel entrance. Halfway down the hall Baka saw movement and knew vampire were emerging from the tunnel, coming their way. He grabbed Elora and shoved her against the wall, covering her body with his. He whispered in her ear, giving her unwelcome and untimely shivers.

"Vampire incoming. If they look close they'll think I'm an adversary. So make this look good."

Taking hold of her waist with both hands, he jerked her up the wall to where they were at eye level and pushed her back again, holding her in place with the press of his body. Her legs wound around him in an involuntary reflex. Before she could contemplate the fact that his body heat was surprising, he brushed his lips against hers. She jerked back, bumping her head on the wall behind her, but not hard enough to do damage.

Staring at his mouth an inch away, she swallowed and said in a voice that sounded too raspy to be her own, "If you bite me, I *will* stake you."

He drew back just far enough so there would be no

mistaking his meaning. "If I bite you, I'll stake myself."

This time his mouth covered hers with demand. For a minute she forgot about everything except the way he was crushing her mouth, ferociously, with an urgency that could only be fueled by desperation. She couldn't breathe, but didn't care. He pressed closer so that she could feel the erection he was subtly rocking into her core. While she went mindless, lost in the intensity of the desire coming off of him in waves, two vampire walked behind them.

After they passed, she tore her mouth away and gasped for air.

Just before he eased back, he whispered, "So warm," still holding her up until she could regain her footing. "I don't expect you to love me, Elora."

He was still clutching her around the waist, not wanting to let her go, like he was afraid he would never be this close again.

Her voice sounded hoarse when she spoke. "We need to let the rest of my team know that we've got biters in the building."

Baka stepped back with obvious reluctance and dropped his hands without another word.

Elora went straight to the bar. Ram's eyes swept over the flush on her face and zeroed in on telltale swollen lips. His eyes flashed with anger as clear and sudden as a lightning strike. She'd never seen him really mad before.

"What the bloody hell, Elora!"

"Two vampire came in while we were in the hallway. A couple of minutes ago. We've got to find them."

B Team searched all three floors of the club, the restrooms, the kitchen, and the perimeter for three blocks, but did not find vampire. Elora waited with dread, expecting Ram to bring up the subject of what had happened in the hallway, but he had apparently decided to let it pass.

They finished their shifts, caught a whister back to the Unit and, as was their custom, stopped in the lounge to share a drink before calling it a night. E Team was sitting around the fire pit just outside on the lounge veranda. Storm suggested they join them and find out what they'd learned from their tour of the tunnels.

After a few minutes Ghost rose and started inside. "Anybody need anything while I'm up?"

Elora said, "Yeah. My Hot Butter Bacardi should be up

if you don't mind grabbing it."

"Done," he said.

Half an hour later, Elora was having trouble paying attention and starting to feel a discomfiting tingle paired with a twinge of anxiety. She tried to shake it off, but the feelings were intensifying by the minute. Finally she leaned over.

"Ram?"

"Hmmm?" Ram was distracted, noting that E Team was being a little tight-lipped about their experience in the tunnels, which was odd.

Elora leaned over, turned her face away from the group and whispered next to Ram's ear with a hint of urgency.

"I need help. You've got to get me home. Please."

She raised her voice and said to the group in general: "That's it for me. Some of us actually work for a living delivering booze to letches and drunks. Have a good night then."

"Hold on. I'm goin', too," Ram said and the others said a collective good night.

When the elevator doors closed, he looked at Elora.

"What's wrong?"

"Not sure, but I'm scared that, I think maybe… aphrodisiac."

He took her by the shoulders and turned her toward him so he could get a good look at her face and know if she was joking. He must have seen something disturbing in her eyes. "Fuck."

"Exactly."

She was becoming more unsettled, even a little afraid, like she was on the verge of losing an internal struggle.

Ram's mind was racing.

Out loud he said, "Okay. We'll figure somethin' out." *What in Paddy's name will we figure out? Shit.*

By the time they reached her door, she was breathing hard. Ram punched in her code, which he knew as well as his own, and opened the door. He looked up and down the hallway to make sure that no one saw him going into Elora's quarters this late at night, or else there would be never-ending gossip, smirking, and cat calls. Humans.

Once inside, she tore off her coat and let it fall to the floor. Ram was still trying to figure out what to do next when she grabbed the lapels of his leather jacket.

"You've got to help me."

She was searching his face with a wild-eyed look bordering on hysteria.

"What do you mean?"

Having never seen her exhibit any of these emotions before, Ram was looking alarmed himself.

She made a noise of exasperation. "Don't you dare pretend naïveté with me, Rammel Hawking. You bloody well know what I mean!"

She couldn't stop herself from touching any longer. She ran her hands over aching breasts, down her abdomen, and let a middle finger linger to massage the aching apex between her thighs.

Ram gawked, trying to ignore an unwanted, but suddenly very demanding erection.

"No." He ran his hand through his hair in frustration. "I do no' want the first time to be like this."

Elora was unraveling, quickly moving from desperation to full-blown panic. She was a bundle of need and nerve endings on fire without enough sexual experience to know what to ask for.

"Ram! Either help me or get out of the way so I can

find somebody else."

She started toward the door. He was in front of her in a flash, blocking the way and exploding.

"That's no' gonna happen!"

Blackie whined, but decided to stay out of it. He withdrew to his pallet behind the dining desk and curled up. He was a very smart dog.

Poised and preparing for a fight, Elora gave him a look that said, "Well then?"

He took her face between his hands. The conflict had to be resolved, and fast. On the one hand he had spent months suffering an obdurate lust for this woman, a craving with no respite, a relentless yearning nagging to be satisfied. On the other hand, taking advantage of his mate and dishonoring his partner were equally repelling.

Growing impatient with his indecision, Elora started to jerk out of his hands, but he held firm. Her own frustration was clawing at him.

"Shhhh. Hush now. I'm here."

Then, for the first time in his life, Rammel Hawking kissed a woman with his heart as well as his lips. The purity and sweetness of it hit such a profound note that it stunned even the drug into submission.

For a moment, she was quiet and still, absorbing the age old message that kiss was sending, that Ram loves Elora. But the second he drew back, the demand of the chemicals throbbing in her blood came bounding back with a vengeance.

She seized him like a drowning man grabs onto a floatation device, feverishly coaxing his lips into an open-mouthed kiss while pushing his jacket off his shoulders. That accomplished, she proceeded to rip the club logo tee open from neck to navel, exposing bare skin to the hands she was running down his chest and over the ridges in his abs, tracing the beckoning path of golden brown hair that disappeared below his waistband.

The violence of having Ram's clothes ripped from him was disconcerting, but compelling and powerfully erotic at the same time, combining to detonate a sexual charge that could no longer be denied. Conflict resolved. He unlocked the cage and freed his own beastly passion that had been crouching just below the surface, painfully, for far too long.

Wave after wave of desire possessed him, demanding

that he yield to his body's hunger for kisses, for caresses, for the raw sensuality of skin on skin and the ultimate fantasy of plunging inside her.

He pulled her tank top and bra strap down from her shoulder to reveal a creamy, plump breast and a rosy pink nipple that reminded him of the color of her cheeks when she came in from the cold. When he bent to lave the taut bud with a tongue that was both sweet and pink, just as he had promised that day that seemed so long ago, in the hallway outside their apartments, she clutched his shoulders, threw her head back and moaned.

Hearing that, his cock swelled against the confines of his jeans. When he straightened his back to undo the fly buttons, she reached to fondle the outline of his bulge which responded by throbbing harder as if it was trying to leap through the denim and into her hand. Hissing in a breath, he angled himself away saying: "We can no' be doin' that if there's to be anythin' left for you."

He backed her toward the bedroom, both of them tearing away clothes as they went. By the time they reached the bed, she was wearing only silk little boy undies and knee socks. In one fluid motion, he stripped back the bed covers, leaving nothing but a crisp, white bottom sheet.

He pressed her back to the bed and ran his hand up her inner thigh while resuming the tangle of his tongue with hers. There was plenty of room for fingers to slip between the loose silk crotch of the lingerie and her own silky folds. The heat and moisture he found there fueled an exigency of his own that caused his breath to hitch.

When Elora felt his fingers brush her sex for the first time, she gasped and arched up with such force that he was almost thrown back. He jerked the silky drawers down her legs and away from her body just as she began shedding tears and begging in earnest. He quickly cradled himself between her legs. Just as she sobbed the word, "Please," he thrust into her and she cried out.

Ram's body responded like it had a mind of its own, propelling him into an upward spiral, his drive matching Elora's. He was caught up in a whirlwind of frantic desire to ease his mate's need and it gave him the strength to concentrate on that instead of his own. His hips pistonned relentlessly until she came. Her muscles clenched, giving him permission to release, making him thunder her name as she milked him into oblivion.

In the brief respite of afterglow, he lay on top of her, knowing her extraordinary constitution could easily support his weight. He was so grateful he had lived long enough to understand what motivates men to write love songs and sonnets, long enough to grasp the difference between fucking and making love.

"Ah, Ram. You feel so good."

He thought that, of all the ways that words could be put together, that had to be the most perfect sentence ever conceived. For a few minutes she was satisfied and passive. He kissed the tears away from her cheeks, stroked her hair, and assured her she was, without question, the most magnificent woman to ever have lived.

Then the next surge began, signaled by low moans in the back of her throat and building in intensity. She grabbed for him. He rolled to the side and used his fingers to massage in tiny circles and thrusts, giving succor and easing her toward a release.

Over the next two hours he made love to her twice more, once with Elora on hands and knees pushing back so hard he had to struggle to stay on the bed. That was supplemented with his deft fingers, trained to manipulate guitar strings with subtlety or strength, helping her to ride out three more electrifying orgasms, each increasingly taxing her already overwrought body.

At one point he heard her phone ring in the other room, but let it go to message. *Has to be a wrong number. Who would be calling at this hour?*

He lay on his back, thinking he was so glad she had drifted off to sleep because no power on heaven or earth could stimulate another arousal. Then she started moaning in her sleep, so tired she was resisting waking, but eventually the drug won and her eyes flew open.

She rolled toward Ram and grasped his flaccid penis, inanimate velvet, but was not deterred by the lack of response.

"You truly will be the death of me."

She gave him a wicked smile he didn't know she had in her arsenal of expressions. Then, without warning, fanfare, or foreplay, bent and sucked him into the heat of her mouth where her tongue began teasing a turgid response with lazy circular motions while she cupped and fondled his testicles.

His eyes widened at the same time he gasped. His shaft bloomed to life like stop motion photography when she took him into her mouth and he laughed out loud in utter surprise.

"Where did you learn to do that?"

Her gaze locked on his she pulled her mouth away, keeping the suction strong so that her mouth made a pop on release. She smiled broadly.

"Romance novels," she said, looking very self-satisfied as she straddled him and fed the very erect reward for her effort into her very willing self. She began a leisurely glide with an air of conquest he would swear had nothing to do with aphrodisia. The frenzy had subsided. The look of panic was gone.

He watched her undulating body with hooded eyes, thinking there never had been a male so fortunate or a woman so perfect.

"Beautiful," he whispered.

He had spent the wee hours worshiping his female, ministering to every part of her body, weaving proclamations of love with murmurs of adoration and devotion. During the minutes when light was first breaking, a hint of pink and gold rising to overtake the gray, they lay on their sides facing each other. Her eyelids were heavy, trying to close, and he knew it was finally over.

Her eyes opened suddenly like she'd forgotten something. She smiled ever so slightly, and whispered, "Thank you."

"Darlin' girl," he reached over and cupped the side of her face, rubbing his thumb over the softness of her cheek one last time, "these have been the sweetest hours of my life."

WHEN RAM WOKE he was spooning with Elora, his arm thrown around her protectively, covers pushed aside because of her higher body heat. Blackie was standing on his side of the bed behind him and whining to go out. He would have liked to spend time savoring waking to a naked Elora tucked into his lap, but Blackie was growing more insistent by the second. Thinking all else had failed, Blackie gave Ram a tentative lick on a butt cheek. Dogs have no sense of propriety.

Ram jerked in surprise and turned to glower at the dog who, delighted to have gotten his message across, wagged his tail and turned in circles.

Rising carefully so as not to disturb Elora, he pulled the covers back over her, then smiled at her soft snoring and at the way his clothes had been left in a haphazard trail. He suspected that everything, good, bad, or indifferent, was going to make him smile that day.

He gathered up her clothes and arranged them neatly on a chair, turned down the flame in the gas fireplace, zipped up his leather jacket to cover what was left of his torn shirt, got Blackie's leash and headed outside.

When they returned, she was still sleeping peacefully. So he gave Blackie some kibble and kidney, refreshed his water and left a note on the bar.

"Do not be embarrassed. – R." As an afterthought, under that he wrote: "Or mad either." Then he left quietly to go next door for a shower.

When Elora woke the first thing she noticed was that the fire was going, which was odd because she didn't sleep with it on. She then realized she was naked which was even more disturbing because she'd never slept that way in her life. It was also weird that the clothes she'd worn the night before were folded – sort of – on the chair by the closet. Again, something she wouldn't do.

Looking at the time she wondered why Blackie hadn't awakened her for his regular morning outing. She pulled on her robe for modesty's sake because Ram sometimes let himself in. On the way to check on Blackie she saw the note and groaned out loud. She reasoned that she must have gotten so drunk that she didn't remember anything after stopping at the lounge. Hot Butter Bacardi indeed.

She saw that Blackie had fresh water and food and guessed Ram had taken care of him. Then, she remembered her state of undress and the clothes left on the chair and thought, "Don't be mad, huh."

A shower did nothing to take the edge off her indignation. As the bathroom grew steamier from the hot water, her anger escalated from irate to seething, first conjuring images of how the lascivious incident must have played out and then imagining what she would do to Rammel Hawking for taking advantage of her when she was inebriated.

She might have suspected Ram of perpetrating a bit of duplicitous voyeurism, but she knew he wasn't a rapist. When she noticed some vaginal soreness, she attributed it to being stuck with the spin bike on the end, the one that no one wanted because it was absolute torture on the crotch. She promised herself to forego spinning the next time no other bike was available.

After pulling on a turtleneck and lululemon go-anywhere pants, she went back in the bathroom to blow dry her hair. She sensed, more than heard, someone come in.

Poking her head out and around the corner she saw that Ram had let himself in and that he was looking freshly showered, relaxed and happy, wearing that little boy smile that would be so disarming if she wasn't utterly infuriated with him.

She put down the brush and blow dryer and stalked toward the living room.

He held out a cup toward her. "Brought you a hot chocolate."

Looking at Elora, his expression was starting to falter.

She grabbed the note and waved it in the air.

"Don't be embarrassed? Don't be mad?" He set the cup down and blinked. "How could you?"

"I, em…"

"How did I end up drunk, Ram?"

"Drunk?" He said it like he wasn't familiar with the term.

"I don't even remember having more than one drink." He blinked again. "You brought me back here, undressed me, and left me in bed naked."

"Now, wait a minute."

Ram was beginning to recover from the shock of learning that, not only did she not remember their night together, but she was accusing him of behaving like a deviant – a painful affront coming from her.

"I did no' undress you."

"No? And you didn't leave my clothes on the chair either."

"I did bring you back here last night. I did take Blackie out for his walk this mornin' because you were no' up to it. And you're welcome by the way. I did pick your clothes up where you left them on the floor and I did put them on the chair. You're welcome for that as well."

She thought she knew all of Ram's facial expressions. She didn't know how to read this one, but she was sure it wasn't shame. That could only mean she had jumped to a faulty conclusion. Her shoulders slumped as she started to feel guilty about the unjustified ambush.

"I'm sorry. I know there's nothing worse than being accused of something you didn't do. I just… I've never been drunk before. Waking up and not remembering what happened is a new thing." She glanced toward the bedroom door. "And I don't like it."

Ram thought it best not to point out that she had none of the symptoms associated with hangovers.

"Happens to the best of us."

"Well, now I am embarrassed."

He smiled. "I'll do my best to make sure it does no' happen again."

Then the reality hit him like a drive-by. He'd been so caught up in the drama. And the sex. He hadn't stopped to wonder how she'd ingested the drug, who gave it to her, or why she was a target. He couldn't confide in Storm or Kay without revealing what had happened and that would compromise Elora. So he had to figure it out by himself. And quickly.

CHAPTER 18

THE SECOND WEEK was so uneventful that B Team started to feel like serving drinks and club security were their real jobs. Friday, near midnight, Elora approached a table for drink orders and found herself looking down at three pale-eyed men with blank expressions buying drinks for a young woman who appeared agitated. The look on the girl's face was alarming to Elora for some reason that was just out of reach. In any case, she knew she needed to alert Ram without taking her attention away from them long enough to lose them.

There were too many people between her and the bar for him to see there was a problem. Likewise, the crowd prevented visually locating Storm or Kay. She waited until the three were absorbed in what they were doing, then putting a booted foot on one of the bench seats lining the back wall, she stepped up onto a table top hoping to catch

Ram's eye.

Even though she was only there for a second, he saw her head pop up and locked on to her location in the room. He swung himself over the bar, not caring if he mowed down a few casual drinkers.

He was thanking the heavens that she was tall because, after he got past the throng standing by the bar, he could see her heading for the restrooms. He ran to get there ahead of her, but she had already placed herself between the disguised tunnel entrance and the three vampire attempting to abscond with a victim.

Ram was charging toward them. *Great Paddy's balls afire. She'll be the death of us both.*

She had staked one vamp and engaged another. The third had pulled a knife, but instead of the annoying girl, he suddenly found himself facing an experienced and quite lethal Black Swan knight who had more cause than usual to be angry.

Ram would have put down the third vamp in little time with little difficulty had it not been for the two women who chose that exact moment to emerge from the Ladies' room giggling, oblivious to danger, and with the worst timing possible.

Taking full advantage of the situation, the vamp with the knife slashed one of the women across the side of her neck with gruesome results as jugular blood began to spurt in time with her accelerated heart rate like a macabre fountain synchronized to "dance" with music.

Since keeping innocents safe from harm was the over-riding mission of Black Swan, the top priority and first commandment of a knight's directive, Ram had no choice but to put himself in front of the second woman and protect her with not just his skill, but his body as well. Even though he was distracted for less than the one second it took to move into place, it gave the vampire the opening necessary. Ram deflected the descending knife so that it missed his own jugular, but it caught the side of his face and sliced open a deep gash that descended down his chest. As Ram went into shock, the vamp grabbed him and threw him back into the wall.

Elora looked around in time to see Ram's head hit the wall and his eyes roll back. She shoved the vamp she was fighting and lunged toward Ram, catching him before he fell. The two vampire disappeared, with their victim, behind the secret door as Elora lowered Ram to the ground. There was so much blood she had no way of telling how badly he was hurt.

The interest that the second woman had generated with her screaming caught the attention of the other half of B Team along with Istvan Baka.

When they arrived, Kay took off his shirt and held it against as much of the wound as he could while Storm ran to street level to call in an emergency. He had to get out on the sidewalk because there was too much noise inside the club to be heard on the phone.

Elora looked at Kay. "Stay with him. Promise me."

"What are you doing?"

"You know what I'm doing, Kay. Baka is going with me."

She looked at Baka for confirmation of that and he nodded.

Kay pressed his lips together. "Storm is going to seizure when he finds out."

She glanced down at Ram. "Keep him alive."

Kay's jaw clenched as they had a wordless conversation. With his eyes he said he would go to hell himself to bring Ram back if he had to, that he wasn't planning on losing another teammate, and that he didn't need her to tell him that.

It took a minute or two for Elora's eyes to adjust to the low light in the tunnel system. She and Baka had been running for about ten minutes, following faint sounds ahead. Suddenly she realized she was running alone. She turned to see why Baka had stopped. He had a very strange look on his face and seemed to be trying to say something. She started back toward him just before he crumpled to the dirt floor. When he went down, she saw that Ghost was standing behind him and, even in the dim light, she could see that he was wearing a hideous, vindictive gloat on his doughy face.

In the blink of an eye, she took it all in – the dart sticking out of Baka's back, no doubt silver coated – and the second dart poised for launch with her as target. She didn't know what chemical surprise it was carrying, but knew she didn't want to find out.

Thinking there was a chance she was fast enough to outrun it, she dug in to sprint the opposite direction. She'd barely sprung into the turn when she felt the sting between her shoulder blades. Instinctively she reached back to try and pull it out, but it was too well placed to reach. In a few seconds, she stumbled, slowed and went to her knees. Her next to last thought before she lost consciousness was that going back for Baka had been a big mistake. Her last thought was that Ram would blame himself for losing another partner and she didn't want that for him.

Ghost planned to secure Elora and then return to finish off Baka. He would have liked to savor the thrill of shoving a stake through the vamp's heart. He had earned a reputation for vampire slaying. Only he knew that his motivation was the exquisite rush he got from hearing the squishing sound a stake made when driven into a heart with kill force. That coupled with the sound of a last breath being expelled was satisfaction like no other. What an irony that he was decorated for the vilest impulses of depravity! A slight twist of circumstance might have resulted in infamy at the least and execution at the most. But, no, he couldn't linger to pursue personal pleasure. With her unpredictable constitution, he couldn't know how long the sedative would last on Elora.

D TEAM ARRIVED with the med van carrying a plain black bag stashed with firearms already loaded with wood core bullets. Storm and Kay turned Ram's care over to the medics and lost no more time. Two members of D Team stayed to guard the tunnel entrance while the other two went with Storm and Kay.

When they came across Baka, Storm reached down and pulled the dart free thereby releasing Baka from the paralysis of the silver.

After a minute, Baka sat up slowly and said simply, "Gautier Nibelung." As he got to his feet Storm thought he saw something more than concern on Baka's face. Fear maybe. "We won't find her by ourselves. Too many possibilities."

Storm cursed then turned back to Baka and looked at him for a minute, wrestling with the inner conflict of replacing one idea – that Baka was an abomination of the highest degree – with another idea, that Baka might be his only chance. He never thought he would live to see the day that he'd be asking a vampire for advice, but, if it would save Elora, he'd beg the vamp to drain him dry.

"Do you have a suggestion?"

Baka glanced down the empty tunnel for a minute and then returned his attention to Storm.

"I've been formulating a plan. I thought there would be time to check the details carefully, search for flaws, but this development means collapsing my time frame.

"I have been exploring the tunnel system, recreating the design in a sort of blueprint form. There are a few main intersections of tunnel and hundreds of dead ends, but there are only three entrances. If we formulate a concerted attack with forces stationed at each of the three access points, we could seal the system permanently with explosive by carbon fixation.

"Two birds with one stone. Get rid of the vampire infestation – or most of it – and render the tunnel system permanently useless."

"C4."

"Yes."

"And you think that could be done safely."

"Yes. Manhattan is rock. The right amount will seal the tunnels and, if anyone above ground feels anything at all, it would be a minor, momentary vibration."

"Okay. But right now the pressing problem is that one

of my team members is missing, likely captured, and in need of immediate assistance."

"Indeed. First things first. During my interview with Lady Laiken in Romania, she indicated that she intended to train the large, black beast to track vampire."

Immediately grasping the gist of where that line of thinking was headed, Storm started to look hopeful.

"I need to get above ground so I can call Sol."

Storm made a concise report to Sol, saying that Blackie would let Sanction handle him, that they needed the dog there right away and to bring something from Elora's clothes hamper. Something she had worn. Storm jerked when Baka came up behind him and touched his arm to get his attention.

"Just a minute." He told Sol to wait.

"Tell them to bring blood. Her type. A lot of it along with someone who knows how to do a field transfusion." Storm stared at Baka for half a beat allowing the implications to sink in. "And a few syringes of sedative. Strong."

Storm relayed that information. Sol said everyone available would be called in for the operation and that Monq would verify the safety and feasibility of Baka's plan along with providing the necessary materials.

BEING PURELY OBJECTIVE, a Black Swan knight was a valuable commodity, not just in terms of the expense and the time it takes to train one, but also the relative rarity of the ideal psychological profile. When a knight was injured in the field, they didn't send paramedics. They sent the best doctors money can buy.

When the med team reached Ram, it took only a couple of minutes to diagnose the concussion. They staunched the wounds so that they could contain the blood loss until they reached the state-of-the-edge, tricked out facilities at Jefferson Unit.

Just as they were starting an I.V. with sedative for transport, Ram regained consciousness and asked for Elora. He heard voices saying, "Just rest," which caused a momentary panic and thrashing about before he blacked out again.

GHOST HAD CAREFULLY crafted a plan to create a vacancy on B Team, a vacancy that had been promised to him and, by all rights, should have been his. He had visited Monq's offices in the middle of the night to access Laiken's files in the pursuit of information about her possible weaknesses. He had tested the aphrodisiac being utilized by vampire for its effectiveness on Elora and had reason to believe she had succumbed.

After getting a brief tour, courtesy of Baka, the system creator no less, Ghost had returned to the tunnel system armed and ready for a proper exploration. Three times he took turns that dead ended. Fifty yards into the fourth tunnel branch, he came across a detention cell complete with traditional jailhouse bars. Judging by the rings in the ceiling he guessed it had probably been used to imprison victims at one time. He opened and closed the iron door, rusty, but still strong enough to hold.

He followed the black spray can markers he had left to find his way back knowing they would blend into the surroundings and be unnoticeable unless someone knew what to look for specifically.

The next day he returned carrying two heavy duty padlocks, two lengths of heavy chain that could not be broken by an angry vampire, fifteen feet of rope, two rods with shark hooks, and two sets of titanium handcuffs, one of which had been modified in the shop in sublevel two in the early morning when everyone else was sleeping. He doubled a length of rope in two and used one of the hooks to thread it through the ceiling ring. The other was used to grasp the folded section and pull the free end clear. Next he attached the rope to one of the lengths of chain and pulled it through the ring. Once the facility was ready for use, he found a nearby indention in the tunnel wall where he could await prospective accomplices.

He had learned the skill of stationary stalking by deer hunting with his father when he was a twelve-year-old; the necessity of staying statue still for hours at a time, not moving no matter how cold it was, no matter how hungry you might be, or how much you might need to urinate. He was forced to leave empty handed in time to return to Jefferson Unit for his shift with E Team, but he came back the next two days. The third day, he hit the jackpot.

Just an hour after he arrived he heard movement and went so still he was practically holding his breath. Two vampire came his way. It was as easy as shooting ducks in a barrel. All he had to do was step out and throw two silver coated darts. The vampire were down and immobilized before they had time to realize what had happened.

Ghost pulled them into the cell and left them there, paralyzed by silver, unable to move, hunt for food, or even defend themselves from rats. He wound several feet of chain between the first rung of the gate and the gate post, then fastened one of the padlocks.

The entire time he worked he talked to the paralyzed vampire saying he was sorry to leave them so, but that he would be back before they starved with meal delivery both lovely and tasty.

One thing he hadn't taken into account was how heavy Elora was. He wished he'd read the file more carefully. She weighed twice what she should have. By the time he dragged her to the cell he was exhausted, soaked wet with sweat, and hating her even more – if that was possible.

He stripped her clothes, secured her wrists and ankles with the cuffs, then ran the chain through the loops he had welded onto the manacles for that purpose. He raised her from the ground using the angled leverage of running the chain through the wall ring and suspended her from the ceiling with her feet just ten inches from touching ground.

The second padlock was used to secure the chain connected to the wall ring.

He threw two sedative darts into the paralyzed vamps. After a couple of minutes, giving the chemicals time to work their magic, he removed the silver coated darts knowing that the two vampire would awake soon and hungry. Very, very hungry.

For the piece de resistance of sadism, he had made a special aphrodisiac-laced dart for Elora and marked it as the only one with red feathers. Unfortunately he couldn't find it. He searched the pocket of his cargo pants where he had stashed it, but it was gone. After going through every pocket and looking around the area, he decided he would have to be satisfied without the additional torture of the aphrodisiac. He removed the sedative darts which were the only evidence linking him to the carnage about to take place. Even if the scene should be discovered by The Order, he would never be implicated.

The vampire were beginning to rouse. He wished he could afford to stay to enjoy witnessing the spectacle of ripping, shredding, snarling, and screaming about to take place, but decided it was more prudent to get rid of Baka.

With one last look he walked away leaving Elora to die a death worse than a demon's nightmare.

When he was thirty yards away from where he'd left Baka, he heard voices. Spraying hissed curses into the darkness he turned back. At the next tunnel intersection he headed away from the cell where Elora was about to be devoured by hungry, angry vampire.

SANCTION ARRIVED WITH Blackie in twenty minutes. Storm told Baka to hang back since the dog had previously demonstrated an extreme intolerance for his presence and had been trained using his scent. Storm asked Sanction for the article of Elora's clothing and hoped to Woden that big German Shepherd was as smart as she thought he was.

When they entered the tunnel, Storm put Elora's tank top in front of Blackie's nose as he had seen her do the day he observed the game of Find Sir Hawking.

"Find Elora." Blackie stared up at Storm intently with ears pointed forward, looking like he was asking for clarification. Say again. Storm repeated the steps.

Blackie barked and started into the tunnel pulling on the leash. He wanted to run, but they were afraid that, if they let him off leash, he would outdistance them in the space of a few seconds leaving them as lost as they would be without him. Baka followed behind them at a distance so as not to be a distraction.

Blackie and Sanction reached the cell a few seconds before Storm and Kay. They heard Sanction's shouts up ahead and broke into a sprint for the rest of the distance. By the time they arrived, Sanction was almost sobbing and Blackie was hitting the bars of the cage, reminding them of the dog he had once been before Elora claimed him.

Kay reached for one of the pistols that held the wood core bullets, planning to put an end to these particular vampire, but Storm caught his arm and pushed upward before he fired. With a chillingly flat tone he simply said, "Splat gun." Kay didn't question the request. He simply exchanged his weapon, shot them both in the face with silver gel, then used bullets to break the lock.

It took several tries since green wood core bullets are designed to penetrate flesh and not metal. They had to close Blackie out of the cell to keep him from tearing into the paralyzed vampire. Plus, the dog had not been inoculated. They didn't know whether animals were susceptible to the virus, but couldn't take the chance.

The scene inside the cell was grisly. Elora had been bitten repeatedly, all over her thighs and abdomen. Even with all the blood, the gouges and deep scratches were evident. Her neck had been spared only because they couldn't reach it. Ghost had planned to keep her jugular out of reach partly to prolong her suffering and partly because he knew it would drive the vampire into a more fevered feeding frenzy.

Storm locked his arms around her thighs. While he held her weight up, taking the strain off her wrists, Kay shot the lock holding the chain to the side wall ring. Storm readjusted his hold as she slumped over and Kay helped him ease her to the ground.

When Baka arrived, Blackie renewed his protest, but Sanction was able to take him a few yards away and keep him under control.

As usual, Baka was wearing a long-tailed silk shirt. He came forward and knelt down. He tried to feel for her pulse, but his hands were shaking. He took the shirt off, laid it over her body, then put his ear over her heart to listen. She was alive, but white as death and unconscious.

Which was undoubtedly merciful.

Storm took note of the fact that Baka was visibly shaken and that the blood was not presenting a control issue for him.

Blackie was enraged about the vampire being so close to his mistress and raising such a ruckus it was hard to hear over him.

Baka said she could make it back to the entrance where the medic was waiting with blood for transfusion if they got her there soon. They agreed that Blackie and Sanction would run back as fast as they could and have them standing by for a transfusion during transport to base. Kay would stand guard over the vamps while Storm and Baka took turns carrying Elora. All the weapons were left with Kay.

For the second time in half a year, Storm picked up the limp, bloody body of a dying woman named Elora Laiken. This time he was even more determined that she would live. They started toward the surface world. Every few minutes he and Baka stopped and transferred the precious cargo so that they could keep moving fast.

The van that would take her to the whister pad was

waiting when they arrived. Storm told Sanction to take Blackie back to base and have the kitchen feed him the biggest, seared sirloin steak they could find. He'd earned it.

Storm took possession of the sedatives that Baka had insisted on having handy and put them in his leg pockets. The two of them watched the van doors close and Storm knew that the rest was out of his hands. Again.

He watched them pull away, then looked at Baka with a tight jaw and said, "Let's go finish this."

THREE MEMBERS OF E Team had been stationed at one of the three tunnel entrance points. They had not been able to locate Ghost when they were called in and couldn't have been more stunned to see him approaching from inside the tunnel. Ghost said he had been closest to the club entrance and decided to enter there and find them. A couple of members of E Team exchanged looks and silently questioned the details of his story, but decided they would let it pass for the moment.

ON REVIEWING BAKA'S plan, Monq agreed that the tunnels could be sealed without danger to the metropolis above or its occupants. He and Baka worked together to set the charges in their right measure and gave instructions to the teams that were standing by about twenty-five yards inside each entrance.

Storm took command of the operation once the explosives were in place and everyone had their instructions. Relays were established above ground for the purpose of synchronizing the blast on Storm's signal.

First, Storm sent D Team to replace E Team at the second access point and ordered E Team to the club entrance. At the same time he sent Baka to join Kay. Half an hour later E Team arrived. He ordered Ghost to accompany him, saying he was two members shy of a team with Ram hurt and Elora missing. He wasn't sure Ghost bought the story, but didn't especially care since he couldn't be refused. The rest of E Team was stationed at the club entrance to act as relays and control curiosity.

As the two of them walked back into the tunnel, Ghost reviewed his options and came up short of a good plan any way he ran it. So he decided the only thing he could do was play it out and hope an opening presented itself. They walked in silence until they reached Kay at the cell.

Storm turned a hard-as-stone look on Ghost and said, "We've got a problem."

Kay, who was typically underestimated because of his calm demeanor and slow Southern style, reached in lightning fast and took Ghost's weapon. Deciding retreat was the best solution after all, Ghost turned and ran smack into Baka, who was happy to show him a pair of very impressive fangs up close and personal.

Storm stabbed Ghost in the neck with one of the syringes stored in a leg pocket of his cargo pants. He knew he had a minute for confrontation before the sedative rendered Ghost useless.

"There's never been a knight in the history of Black Swan who has betrayed The Order."

"There's never been a bitch put ahead of a knight in the history of The Order," Ghost spat.

"Yeah. That's about what I thought you'd say."

With that Storm threw Ghost in the cell then administered one sedative syringe to each vampire. Next he took out a knife and cut the paralyzing silver gel away from the skin where it had made contact on the vampires' faces.

Seeing where this was going, Baka said: "Sir Storm, I

have decided that you are a god of poetic justice."

Without looking up from what he was doing and without hesitation Storm replied: "Damndest thing is that I've come to think that another place, another time, you and I might have even been friends."

Baka responded with a wistful and, perhaps, grateful smile. "Indeed."

Storm took the lengths of chain and started wrapping them around the bars. The locks couldn't be reused, but tying the chains off should keep the three monsters imprisoned together long enough for his purposes. Storm, Kay, and Baka sat down with their backs against the tunnel wall facing the cell and waited for the show.

The old vampire said to no one in particular: "This won't be over after today. Someone reopened the tunnels, renovated the lighting system, and distributed a high grade aphrodisiac to vampire. That implies some kind of organizational structure. Unless they happen to be underground today, that someone may continue to present problems in the future."

While Storm and Kay contemplated that, twenty minutes passed and Ghost's sedative wore off.

When he looked around and realized what was planned his eyes went wild. He sprang for the door, looking at the still-immobile vampire. "You can't do this to another knight!"

Storm looked bored. "Exactly what I thought."

Ghost was rapidly working himself toward hysterics. "What you're doing is against the law!"

"We make our own law. You know that."

Ghost began trying to undo the chains holding the gate closed.

Storm trained a gun on his hands and said: "Back away or you won't have hands to defend yourself with when your little friends come to."

When the vampire woke, Ghost started to scream and pull at the chains again.

Kay turned to Storm and said, "How is it possible that this miscreant was knighted? The vampire sitting next to you is more deserving."

"Thank you, Kay."

"Only my friends call me that, Baka."

"I apologize."

Kay sighed. Baka's amiable manner made him feel like

a prick. "Alright. You can call me Kay."

Storm said: "You're right. The vampire sitting next to me is more deserving. Maybe he'll take Ghost's place."

As promised, Storm shot Ghost's hands to keep him from pulling the chains free. Within a few more minutes the vampire had ripped out the captive's throat and were fighting over who would drain the lion's share of the blood from the kill. Gautier's glassy-eyed stare seemed to be directed at his audience, but not one of them felt the least remorse.

Storm stood slowly and fired twice, sending a wood core bullet straight into each vampire's heart. They decided not to allow the remotest chance that the scene might be discovered. Ever.

Baka had enough C4 left to blow the cell, but no fuse. So Storm sent the other two back up the tunnel, ignited it with a shot, and ran like hell. Fortunately he was invigorated by seeing justice served. Something about being on the side of righteousness was energizing.

When all teams, relays, and charges were confirmed ready, Baka set the synchronization and counted it off. All entrances to the tunnel system were demolished, simultaneously trapping any vampire within for all eternity. They would starve to death long before they could dig their way out.

CHAPTER 19

RAM WAS CLAWING his way back to consciousness, becoming vaguely aware that he was in a hospital bed. Someone, probably a nurse, was moving around him doing something with the equipment at his bedside and talking quietly to someone else in the room. He heard loud voices coming from the hallway outside his room and thought someone said Lady Laiken.

Hearing an accelerated monitor beep indicating Ram's heart rate speeding up, one of the two nurses in the room stepped closer and shot a dose into his I.V. line that put him back to sleep.

The next time he woke, the heart monitor went straight into overdrive. The nurse present tried to calm him while another hurried in and pressed the call button to ask for a doctor.

He fought to open his eyes more. "Elora."

When he said her name, he saw the two nurses look at each other and knew something was wrong. That was when he decided he was getting up.

Two nurses are not much of a match for a Black Swan knight, not even when he has a concussion and one hundred forty-three stitches. They were attempting to restrain him physically while begging him to stay in bed, when one of the doctors burst through the door.

Ram stopped and peered at the newcomer. "Elora," he repeated.

"Sir Hawking," she began, "your partner has been injured. She is alive and close by. We are taking very good care of her. And, just like you, she needs to rest."

"See her." He pulled the I.V. out of his hand and swung his legs over the side of the bed.

"Stop!" He ignored her. "If you don't stop, we will sedate you."

Ram froze and gave her a look she would never forget. "Try," was all he said.

Knowing it wasn't their job to battle knights who were injured or infirm, possibly doing more harm than good, the good doctor decided the best outcome was compromise. After a brief negotiation, Ram agreed to sit in a wheelchair and stay there in exchange for being taken to see Elora.

The lights were dimmed in her room and the covers were pulled up under her chin. The heart monitor beeped a steady, reassuring report and she was breathing on her own. He was so relieved he could have cried. He heard the door swish open behind him and someone came in.

"What happened?" he asked the nurse standing behind him without looking away from Elora's bed. "Do you know?"

His answer was Storm's quiet voice telling her, "We'll take it from here."

Storm and Kay convinced Ram to let them push him back to his room by arguing that sometimes patients who appeared to be unconscious later report that they heard and remembered what was said. After he got back into bed and got settled, they told him the entire story including what happened to Ghost.

Ram was quiet for a long time digesting all they had told him.

"So the biggest monster turned out to be one of us.

There must be some kind of lesson in that." He agreed to take a short nap on the condition that the wheelchair be left close enough that he could get to it on his own.

"Okay, Rammel, rest and take care of yourself," Storm said. "It's report time. Looks like you're a hero. Again. Your legend is starting to get out of hand, growing to epic proportions."

Ram's eyelids were half closed and he was sounding drowsy. "Who's takin' care of Blackie?"

"He's with Sanction. You know, if it wasn't for that dog, we wouldn't have found her in time."

"Good dog," he said and drifted off.

Storm and Kay told E Team that Ghost died in service to The Order, that he was caught in an explosion, no body remaining. That was the official report. Sol was the only other person to hear the real, off-the-record story.

One of the Jefferson Unit trainees was an impressive, twenty-one-year-old who was ready for field assignment. He would be sent to Brazil for a less intense first tour of duty, in exchange for an experienced operative ready to take Ghost's place on E Team.

The Order used their influence to keep all reports of

strange events out of media coverage. Anyone who had been at Notte Fuoco that night may have wondered why there was nothing in the news anywhere with the possible exception of conspiracy blogs, which are never taken seriously.

The next morning, with doctor's permission, Storm woke Ram up with breakfast and a report on Elora. Her condition was stable. There was no internal damage and no broken bones. Her red blood cells had been restored to normal. Her white blood cell count was high and under observation.

Some of the lacerations required stitches. Normally scarring would be expected, but, since she had already proven once that she responded very well to Monq's regenerative skin salve, they expected she would probably be good as new in a few weeks, if not sooner. Last, they were keeping her mildly sedated because they wanted her to sleep for another day.

Ram asked Kay to go to Elora's apartment and find the collection of fairy tales she had typed from memory. When he had taken possession of the stories, he wheeled over to her room and sat by her bedside reading out loud, just in case she was aware on some level. Even if she didn't follow word for word, she might hear the sound of his voice and know that someone who loved her was close by and waiting for her to get well.

A flat refusal to go back to his own room forced another confrontation with a new shift of nurses. He said the only way they would get him back in bed was if they brought his bed into Elora's room and put it next to hers. After conferring with the doctors, they concluded that there was no good reason to refuse that request.

True to his word, Ram crawled into the bed next to Elora's and read to her until he fell asleep.

The next morning he woke lying on his back. The first thing he did was turn his head to look at Elora. She was turned facing him, eyes wide open and staring back with irises the cold color of translucent ice blue. Shocking to look at and frightening in implication.

He worked to keep his face passive as the urge to panic sent the painful tingle of adrenaline pumping through his body. He was so glad he wasn't hooked up to a monitor.

His heart wanted to believe that the figure lying in the bed next to his was Elora Laiken, but the person looking back at him had the eyes of a vampire. The incongruity was confusing as hell.

She didn't appear to be gripped by the mindless blood lust common to new vampire, which was hopeful. He reasoned that, if she could converse, she was still in control even if infected.

"Hey," he said quietly.

"Hey," she whispered in a rough voice. "Are we alive?"

He was so relieved his brain sent a jolt of thrill chemicals through his system to mix with the adrenaline, creating an even more uncomfortable stinging sensation, but his only concern was for the crystalline-eyed beauty on the other bed.

"Seems we are destined to die of old age, you and I."

"What fun would that be?"

Ram opened his mouth to speak, but felt a burning behind his eyes and his vocal chords didn't respond. Finally he was able to get out, "Lots." Swinging his legs toward Elora, he sat up and slid off the bed revealing a remarkable set of male genitalia as the hospital gown stayed at his waist. But that was not what caught Elora's attention.

"Rammel. Oh, gods no, Ram! What's wrong with your face?"

He was so focused on the issues involved in possibly being mated to a vampire that it took a second to realize she was talking about his injuries.

"Well," he smiled, which hurt his face, "I guess I'm no' so pretty anymore."

Then she remembered seeing the slashing descent of a knife, the blood, his head hitting the wall, the fear of losing him. Tears overflowed Elora's eyes and ran onto the pillow.

"Let me see."

He hesitated, then decided she would imagine worse if he didn't show her. So he opened the blue cotton gown.

She stared at the damage, looking like her heart would break, transfixed by the sight of a wayward line of stitches that started at his left cheek bone and continued down his chest, close to one nipple, ending just above his waist.

When he retied the gown she said, "Yes. You are, Ram – so pretty." Her beautiful bottom lip trembled as she battled catches in her breath that sounded like a series of little sobs. "Beautiful inside and out."

He had to swallow hard to get past the lump that had formed in his throat. "Please do no' weep, Elora. Great Paddy, you will make me bawl as well."

He stepped closer to the bed so that he could cup her cheek and brush tears away with his thumb.

"I'll be right back." He shuffled his way to the door slowly, not bothering with the wheel chair, and paused once to look back before he slipped out.

The nurses were surprised to see him out of bed and on his feet without assistance. He spoke quietly, leaning over the station counter. "Get the docs on duty here right now. Be quick about it and quiet as you can be."

Accurately reading the urgency and demand in his tone, one of the nurses jumped up from her wheeled desk chair sending it careening into a cabinet as she started away.

In his peripheral vision Ram caught movement at the door to Elora's room. A nurse was going in to perform some routine task on her rounds. He flew toward her with no concern for either his stitches or the pain, grabbed her arm, and mercilessly jerked the poor woman back hard enough to cause a bruise.

"No one goes into her room until I've talked to the doctors."

The nurse rubbed her arm with wide eyes and backed away just as the doctors arrived.

"Sir Hawking, why are you out of bed? What is the emergency?" Seeing the look on the nurse's face one of the doctors said: "Now look here. You have simply got to stop terrorizing the staff."

Ram pulled them aside and indicated they should lower their voices.

"Somethin' is wrong with Lady Laiken. I want you to look at her. I think Monq should be called in as well. Her eyes have gone... pale.

"Be sure that you do no' show surprise when you see her. She does no' know anythin' is wrong. Do no' alarm her in any way." He glanced at the nurse. "And make sure that every person in this fuckin' place knows that no one else is to enter that room other than her doctors, Monq, Sir Storm, Sir Caelian, or me. Unless I say so."

While Ram waited, he used the time to call Storm from the nurses' station phone. Then he called the Operations Office and instructed them to procure the biggest bouquet of stargazer lilies, Mexican red roses, and tree fern that could be reasonably accommodated in a hospital room. He added that cost was not a consideration, but time was and that he wanted them delivered as fast as possible. "Oh, and no baby's breath."

What to put on the card? There was a pause while Ram struggled to compose himself. When he was sure he could keep his voice steady he replied. "Proud to be your partner."

When the doctors emerged, they looked grim and agreed that Monq should come up as this was a development outside their experience. Or anyone else's for that matter.

When Ram got Monq on the phone he said: "Come to the infirmary right away. Whatever you're workin' on is no' as important as this. Hurry. Please."

As Ram put the phone down one of the doctors noticed that his color was not good. A nurse was instructed to get a wheelchair quickly just as Ram started swaying on his feet. He grunted as the doc caught him around the waist to keep him from falling and tearing stitches and tried to hold him up until the chair arrived. The doctor, not used to lifting two hundred nineteen pounds of well-muscled elf, was red faced, straining and wheezing by the time someone came to his aid to help ease Ram into the chair.

Monq rushed off the elevator and was ushered directly into one of the offices where Ram was waiting. The doctors who had seen Elora reported what they did and did not know after which Monq wheeled Ram back into her room.

"Look who I found outside," Ram said, mustering as much brightness as he could.

"Good afternoon, Ms. Laiken."

"Lady Laiken," Ram corrected.

Elora opened eyes that were eerily striking, eyes that might even have been beautiful in an exotic, other worldly sort of way. If they'd belonged to someone else.

"Hi," she replied with a little smile. "You gonna tell me what happened, Monq?"

"I think that can be arranged. Let me take a look around first." He reached for her face and she slapped his hand away. "My dear, in addition to the other bullet points on my phenomenal resume, I am a medical doctor. My interest is purely clinical."

Elora looked at Ram for confirmation. He nodded, then wheeled around, saying he would wait outside. When the door closed, Monq withdrew a flashlight and shined it in each eye. Then he asked her to say "ah" as subterfuge so that she wouldn't question why he was also looking at her gums. He took a glance at the wounds on her abdomen, carefully keeping his expression blank.

"Are you experiencing any pain?" he asked.

"Uh, yeah."

"How bad is it?"

"I don't know how to answer that."

"We usually use a scale of one to ten."

Elora's brows drew together. "I still don't know how that works, Monq. My ten is slipping dimensions in an experimental device that skinned me alive and turned me into dog chow. Somebody else's ten might be a paper cut."

"Very well. Use your own words."

"I need drugs. And somebody to tell me what happened."

"Alright. I'm going to chat with your doctors on the way out. Your little elf friend will be right back in to answer your questions."

"My little elf friend?" She snorted. "I dare you to say that to his face!" Monq smiled. "So what's all the secrecy about? What are you not telling me?"

"That you're going to be back on duty in no time at all, strong and healthy as ever. I'll be back to see you tomorrow. In fact, maybe we'll have a session right here since you're practically tied down." She groaned.

Outside, Monq told Ram that he and his assistants would put everything else aside to run tests. The nurse would be in to draw blood in a minute and he would let Ram know as soon as he had something to tell.

"She needs to be kept as quiet as possible. Rest can only do her good, but she's probably not going to settle down until somebody fills in the blanks. I told her you would come back in and answer her questions."

He held the door open so Ram could wheel himself back in. After briefing her, Ram gave permission for Elora's friend, Elsbeth, to act as Elora's nurse. She came in carrying a protein drink for Ram with a pink straw and a no-nonsense insistence that he would be drinking it. For Elora, she brought an affectionate smile and some apparatus for withdrawing blood.

"What's that for?" Elora wanted to know.

"Routine tests." Elsbeth was so nonchalant that Ram concluded she was either a very good friend or a passable actress. "Are you hungry?"

"No."

"Your doctors say you can have anything you want. Hot chocolate? Brownies? Hot fudge sundae?"

"No. Thank you though."

"If you change your mind, use the call button."

"Okay."

After she pulled the door closed there were no excuses left why Elora shouldn't hear what had happened. He sat on the side of his bed facing her.

"What do you remember?" Ram asked.

"After I was sure that Kay had you and there was nothing more I could do, Baka and I started after the vamps. We were about ten minutes into the tunnel when I realized he wasn't with me anymore. I turned around. His face was frozen in the strangest expression... I started back to see what was wrong and then he fell to the ground. When he went down, Ghost was standing behind him holding a dart that was aimed at me. I thought maybe I could outrun it. There wasn't anything else to try. I knew he would pin me before I could get a stake out of my boot and the gel in the pistol wouldn't have any effect on him.

"I turned and felt the hit and went down pretty fast. I had a minute to regret going back for Baka. I remember thinking I didn't want you to have to go through losing another partner. That's it."

Ram sighed heavily. "Whatever I add is second hand because I was no' there. I'm repeatin' what was told me by Kay and Storm."

He covered Baka's plan to bury the nest and destroy the hidey holes in one stroke.

"Of course everyone's priority was you. Baka insisted that there was no' enough time for standard search procedure. He remembered that you had asked for his shirt to train Blackie for trackin' vampire. Storm thought it might be a long shot, but had Sanction bring Blackie and a shirt from your hamper. The dog, Elora – your dog – was nothin' less than amazin'. They said they could no' have found you in time without him."

Big tears starting running down her face again. "Come

now, darlin' girl, you know everythin' turned out right 'cause here you are. Alive to hear the tale.

"Anyway, Blackie led Storm, Kay, Sanction and Baka straight to you. Ghost had left you shackled and locked away for two hungry vampire. You were bitten."

Suddenly Elora dragged in a gasp and looked at Ram with wild eyes. When she could speak she whispered, "Vampire…"

She choked and tried to sit up. Ram stood, stepped to the bed and used the built in motor to quickly raise the back so that she didn't have to struggle upright, then put a box of tissues on the bed where she could reach it.

"They were touching me," she said with a shuddering breath and a look of vulnerability that leveled him, "and…" For a few seconds her face froze into a silent cry of horror. "…biting." She looked down and began frantically shoving the bed covers away so she could she what had been done to her.

"No!" Ram grabbed her wrists to restrain her, but thought better of it after a few seconds. He decided it was not in her best interest to tax her strength wrestling with him. Eventually she would have to see.

All modesty forgotten she pulled the hospital gown up and away so that she could see her legs and abdomen. Ram smothered a gasp of his own. If watching her act out her terror wasn't enough, seeing her beautiful body torn and savaged in this way pitched his emotions straight to a place past fury; that place where rage overlaps insanity.

He was irrationally angry at his teammates for killing Gautier Nibelung without him. He wanted the personal satisfaction of squeezing the foul spirit out of him with his bare hands and cursing it into the abyss from which nothing returns.

When Elora saw the red, swollen bites, gouges, and slashes covering her torso and thighs, her first thought was that she was looking at someone else's body. It took a few seconds for her mind to catch up and adjust to the idea that the grotesque flesh was hers.

She sat up, pulled the gown down, and wept. Ram reached for her, not caring that it pulled at his own stitches to do so. He angled his body so that he could sit on the side of her bed and hold her in his arms. He couldn't change what was done, but he could be her rock, the one who would always be there to give comfort.

Kay and Storm had just arrived at the infirmary as Operations was delivering the flowers to the nurses' station. Kay picked up the bouquet to carry into Elora's room. When Storm opened the door what they found was Elora with her head buried in the uninjured side of Ram's chest, sobbing like there was nothing left to lose. In truth, she had lost home, family, the world as she knew it, perhaps even her former identity and sense of self.

Storm felt like a voyeur as he watched without revealing his presence. He remembered an early October day when he had been the one to hold and comfort her while she wept. His emotions were in turmoil, struggling with the conflict between compassion for Elora and the bite of jealousy he felt from being replaced as her protector. That was Storm's job. *He* was Elora Laiken's anchor to this world. Or should be. He motioned to Kay and they backed out, quietly closing the door.

After a long time she quieted and let herself fall back on the pillow. Looking up at Ram with puffy, red rimmed eyes she said, "I guess I'm the one who's not so pretty anymore."

He looked at her in that way he had that said she was

the most precious thing in the world and said, "Darlin' girl, you could no' be more beautiful, inside and out."

"There was nothing I could do, Ram." She held tissue to her eyes for a minute. "There's nothing worse than being helpless. It got so cold. I was shivering. The cold was worse than the pain."

"T'was probably loss of blood." He ran his hand over her head. "But, 'tis over now, you know. Soon you're goin' to be good as new."

"For a person who never cried until I came here, it seems like I've been doing it a lot."

"Aye. We're goin' to be changin' that."

When the nurse came in, trying to get Ram back into his own bed, Elora joined forces with her, insisting on it. So he crawled into the bed next to hers. A few minutes later, the other half of B Team returned carrying flowers. Kay set them down on the rolling table at the end of Elora's bed and handed her the card.

Elora looked at Ram. Who else would know exactly what to put in her bouquet? "Rammel," she said softly, "it's the most beautiful bouquet in the history of flowers." She read the card and then started crying again.

Ram looked too tired to pick his head up off the pillow, but managed to sound exasperated for her benefit. After an enormous sigh, he said: "For Great Paddy's sake, woman, you can no' possibly have any more tears in there to shed. Will someone please have mercy on me and put a bit of chocolate in her pretty mouth?"

That made her laugh, which hurt, and made her laugh all the more, but it broke the tension and caused all three of her teammates to breathe a sigh of relief. Storm and Kay had dinner brought to the hospital room so that all four of them could eat together. Elora still wasn't hungry, which worried Ram, but he knew she was getting nourishment from the I.V.

Eventually she got around to asking what had happened to Ghost. They told her he died in the explosion and that, so far as E Team was concerned, he gave his life in the line of duty, a credit to The Order. She caught the glances they exchanged and read between the lines.

"And Baka?" she asked.

"No decision yet," Storm said. "I recommended some sort of new arrangement. Probation maybe. I mean, he was singlehandedly responsible for bringing the crisis to an end and, in the process, he probably took out more vampire than anyone in the history of this organization. I guess I sort of vouched for him. If you can believe that."

THE LATE NIGHT nurse came in for a round of charting vitals. Elora and Ram compared blood pressure stats. The nurse commented that Elora's temperature was half a degree higher than "normal".

Ram smiled at Elora. "Aye. To be sure she is perpetually hot and that is normal for her."

The nurse chuckled at his double entendre, then turned to Elora and said, "You're a lucky girl."

Elora didn't know if the nurse meant she was lucky because she survived or because she'd received a compliment from legendary fem magnet, Rammel the Erotic.

"Okay kids. Lights out. This is not a slumber party. You both need sleep if you want to get well." She flipped the light switch, closed the door and left the room in darkness except for the LED lights from the machine readouts.

"Ram?"

"Hmmm?"

"Thank you for telling me stories."

"You heard me."

"Yes."

"You're welcome."

"I especially liked it when the elf tied scissors to Rapunzel's hair and sent them up to the tower so she could cut her braid, tie it off and use it to climb down. I also liked it when the miller's daughter got Rumpelstiltskin in a choke hold and told him that he had a choice: he could either make her a new offer or pass out in forty seconds. Your fairy tales were wonderful."

"Elf tales," he corrected.

And she smiled in the darkness.

The next morning Ram and Elora were awakened by a flurry of activity that included doctors, nurses, and Monq looking like he hadn't been to bed.

"Good morning, Ms. Laiken." Monq seemed lively for someone who was bloodshot, rumpled and sporting Einstein hair.

"Lady Laiken," Ram corrected.

"Whatever." Monq said, turning back to Elora, "You seem to be having a little reaction to the bites you sustained. We've determined that the inoculation you received wasn't up to the task of combating the concentrated levels of virus that were introduced to your body. Even though females have a hormone based antitoxin that aids immunity, it still wasn't enough to avoid infection altogether. We're going to give you a booster and believe that it will reverse any side effect of the virus still in your system."

"Okay," she said. "Go ahead."

Monq administered the injection himself.

"What side effect might that be?"

"No matter. It's about to be irrelevant. The effect of this booster will not be instantaneous, but it is relatively fast acting. By noon you'll be good as new. I'll be back in four hours to make sure of it."

After Monq left, Elora told Elsbeth she wanted to take a shower. Instead of answering Elora directly, she looked at Ram. He knew Elora would press to know what that was about.

"Can we have a minute, please?" Ram asked Elsbeth.

"Sure," she said to Elora. "Be back in a few."

When she closed the door behind her, Ram turned to

face her. "You heard what Monq said. By lunch time you will be your perfect self."

"He said good as new."

Ram's mouth twitched at the edges. "So he did. Will you trust me in this? Please. Just wait until after lunch to take your shower."

"I feel grungy."

"And will you have whine with that?"

"Oh. And I'm not entitled to a little whine? What have you got to entertain me then?"

Ram looked around. "I could make my six pack dance. I know you like that one."

She snorted. He picked up the room phone, called Kay and asked him to grab Elora's laptop and bring it.

"How about shoppin'? All that stuff you wanted at Bloomin'dale's that we could no' carry? You can buy it and have it delivered." She smiled brightly. "See? There's nothin' like spendin' money on shite you do no' need to change your outlook."

When Kay brought the computer, he stood in the hall and talked to Ram for a little while. "You've changed, Ram. You strike me as mated and mature."

Ram grinned. "Tis cruel of you to insult me so when I can no' defend myself."

Kay laughed, started to slap him on the shoulder, and stopped his hand mid air just in time. It wasn't easy to think of Ram as fragile.

While Elora shopped online, Ram stayed in bed like a good boy, answering occasional questions about what he thought of this or that. Truthfully, he was so relieved she was alive and getting well, he was happy to be close to her no matter what she was doing.

A little after eleven he turned his head to answer a question about whether she looked better in gray or black and found himself peering into turquoise eyes with a kaleidoscope of golden and yellow flecks. *Sunlight shining on a Bahamian sea.* He would have laughed with joy, but the sight had taken his breath away.

"What?" she asked.

He reached for the call button. A female voice said, "Yes?"

"Get Monq up here now." Turning back to Elora he said, "Your eyes had temporarily lost their very fetchin' color. But, thank Paddy, you appear for all the world to be well. Take a shower when you wish."

She blinked at Ram. "I looked like a vamp?"

"Aye," he said flatly.

She processed that. "Wow. Everybody did a pretty good job of covering that up."

"Tis how much they care about you."

The nurse staff gathered some soap and shampoo for Elora's shower. Afterward, she put on a clean gown and left her hair combed out to air dry.

Monq was waiting when she returned to the room. The first thing he wanted to know was if she was hungry. She thought about it for a second and realized she was.

"Can I get the I.V. out if I eat?"

"Yes," Monq said. She sat down on the bed and pulled a blanket over her lap. "And I have more good news," Monq went on. "The Order has been actively seeking a cure for the vampire virus ever since we had enough scientific understanding to know that it is a virus. It seems this incident made you an accidental catalyst. We believe your blood will serve as the basis for an antidote."

"You can cure Baka?"

"Definite possibility and we need a test subject."

"Let me ask him. I want to do it in person. Can you arrange for him to come here?"

"Given Sir Storm's surprisingly stellar recommendation, I don't think there will be a problem with that."

"Thank you. Will somebody bring me my phone?"

Ram was aghast. "Please tell me you do no' have his bloody phone number!"

Elora looked sheepish. "He's so lonely, Ram. He's got no one."

"Great Paddy Shits in the Mornin', Elora! He's a vampire! No' a stray dog!"

"See? I knew that's how you would react, which is exactly why I didn't tell you." Ram was too agitated to respond so she added. "Do not even think about hyperventilating."

He shot her a look of pure venom.

She laughed at him, but paid for it. "Ow."

"The death of me, Elora."

Two hours later Baka arrived at Elora's hospital room, surprised to be escorted with courtesy and without chains. He suspected that her request to see him was a thinly disguised trap to get him back into custody, but he didn't really care one way or the other. His hell was having to live inside his own body. It didn't matter that much where he was.

All four members of B Team were present. He nodded at Storm and Kay as he entered then turned his attention toward Elora, but didn't move closer to the bed.

"Hi," she said. The back of her bed was raised so that she was half sitting.

"How are you feeling?"

"Better. I want to thank you for your part in this. And I have a question."

He shrugged with an elegant roll of one shoulder. "Ask."

"What do you want more than anything?"

He looked around the room at the faces fixed on him, and then back at Elora. "That's a strange question. Certainly one I never expected to be asked. What is it you're after? Just speak it plain."

"It is a strange question, but humor me please. Pretend I have a magic wand and anything is possible. Would you want to be CEO of a Fortune 500 company? A Broadway star? Professional athlete? Hugh Hefner?"

He smiled sadly and shook his head. He didn't need a lot of time to compose an answer. Abject loneliness is fertile ground for self-awareness.

"Very well. You want soul baring. Sure. What difference does it make?" He glanced at the men in the room again.

"Nothing like any of those things. What I want is just to have back what was taken from me: a wife, children, a trade I can be proud to work every day with a sense of purpose and accomplishment, a bowl of stew at night, a warm bed with a soft and willing woman who thinks she loves me, a chance at old age, and people to mourn me when I'm gone."

Elora nodded. "Baka. You don't disappoint me. Nobody was ever more deserving of having their wish come true. Monq thinks something good may have come from this." She gestured toward her body. "He thinks he has a cure for the virus and needs a test subject. We suggested you."

Baka was speechless. A couple of times he opened his mouth and then closed it. When he finally said: "Thank you," his voice broke and the men of B Team looked away, moved by the palpable depth of this vampire's longing to be nothing more than a simple man with a simple life. Once again.

Elora asked Storm and Kay to show him the way to Monq's lab and then said to Baka: "I hope you get what you want, Istvan."

He smiled. "My Lady." He inclined his head in a gesture that was a marriage of a nod and a bow.

WHEN THEY WERE alone in the room again Ram said, "So how did that feel, Gepetto?" Elora gave him a blank look. "You turned the vampire into a real boy, did you no'?"

"Why, Ram, have you become a story aficionado?"

He snorted.

CHAPTER 20

The spell is broken by a kiss.

—Snow White

WITHIN TWO WEEKS both Ram and Elora had their external stitches removed and were given clearance for leave for the holidays. Black Swan teams only get holiday leave once every four years and this was B Team's year. Even though they had recently had extended time off, it would create havoc to change the schedule. So they were to enjoy December 20th through December 30th as away time.

The first day of her release, Storm caught up with Elora as she was walking Blackie early in the morning. He said recent events had made it clear to him that he couldn't postpone speaking for her. Life was too short and too uncertain. He asked her to go home with him for the holidays and meet his family. He said he knew it was selfish to ask her to take up an occupation less perilous and be a wife instead, but he didn't care.

"Is that what you want more than anything in the world, Storm?"

"Yes." He answered without hesitation.

"Okay then."

It wasn't resounding joy, but he'd take her agreement any way he could get it and call himself lucky.

When she brought Blackie back from his walk, Ram was waiting in the hall by her door with the intention of asking her to spend the holidays with him. She invited him in and told him about her decision.

He took a step toward her, looking suddenly intense. "No. Elora, you can no' do this."

"Of course I can."

"You love him?"

"Like a brother."

"'Tis no' enough."

"Well, it will have to be."

"No." He kept shaking his head resolutely like he was prepared to dig in and battle if necessary. "You do no' understand. You're mine. My mate." He made her stop and look into his eyes. "The only one I will ever have."

"Ram." She pulled away and laughed, not taking him seriously. "Don't be ridiculous. I made up my mind a long time ago that I'm not going to end up like one of your toss-aways."

"My what?"

"I know about your slutty reputation. Elsbeth told me."

"Els…!" Ram was confounded. "Elora. You've got this wrong. I have no' so much as looked at another female since layin' eyes on you. Other women – t'was practically masturbation. Just markin' time while waitin' for you."

"Ram," she laughed disbelieving, shaking her head.

He went to her dining desk and started frantically searching for something. After a couple of minutes he found what he was looking for buried under piles of stuff. It was the book he had given her. *Everything You Ever Wanted to Know About Elves But Were Afraid To Ask.*

"Did you read this?" He held it up so she could see it.

"Sort of."

"Sort of?" He gaped and started rifling through the

book. He found the page he was looking for, grabbed a yellow highlighter from her cup of pens, outlined a passage, then handed Elora the book. "Read this!" She took it. "Out loud."

She looked at him like she didn't approve of the imperious attitude, but let it pass and started to read out loud. "As a species, elves have a strong sex drive. Male elves, in particular, are highly promiscuous until they recognize their mates. Afterward they are singularly devoted and strictly monogamous."

Her smile faded as she let that sink in. "And you believe I am your mate?"

"'Tis an instinct unerrin'. One that can no' be either changed or denied. That day in New York when you asked me what I want more than anythin', the reason I could no' say was no' because I did no' know. It was because of the fuckin' office romance idiocy. Of course I know. 'Tis you, Elora. Only you. And it always will be."

Elora looked away, shaking her head and her mouth formed a grim line. "I hope that's not so, Ram."

He moved closer. "Elora. Please. Do no' do this thing. If I recognize you as my mate, there must be a part of you that knows we fit together. We're so right. You must know it. Come home with me. Marry me."

"You know what you mean to me, Ram. I'd do anything for you. Anything but this. Storm saved my life. Twice." Ram flinched.

"That's a reason to be grateful. 'Tis no' a reason to give yourself to someone you do no' love." Ram grabbed her shoulders and searched her face. "I know you're tryin' to do the right thing. 'Tis part of who you are and I love you for it. Of course I get that. But, if you choose Storm, you'll be sentencin' all three of us to a life of unhappiness."

She shook her head, looking miserable, but resolute.

"Elora, you can no' say no to me. This can no' be right."

He pulled her closer, put his forehead against hers and said, "Kiss me."

She could feel his body heat, smell the carnality of his musk and wild fern scent, and could sense the energy of distress coming off of him in waves of vibration that were invisible, but powerful enough to be staggering.

"Kiss me," he repeated. The words were ragged, like desperation being raked over his vocal chords.

"I can't, Ram. Please. Stop. My mind is made up."

He took a step back, looked at her and seeing that she was determined – that she would not be moved – slowly a pall of sorrow washed over him, graying the light of his golden aura with shadow, and the unthinkable happened. The playful gleam that perpetually twinkled in his eyes went out.

Blackie whined. Ram stood for awhile in the silence, then turned away and left without another word, closing the door quietly.

Elora spent the evening packing, trying to keep herself occupied and distracted from thinking about the encounter with Ram. She and Storm were to catch a ride to San Francisco on one of The Order's jets the day after next.

THE FOLLOWING MORNING she answered a knock at the door. Ram stood there in a pea coat with a duffle slung over his shoulder. He was handsome as ever, but looked very different with unanimated expressions.

"I'm goin'."

"Now?"

He handed her a wrapped package. "Happy Yule. If

you change your mind, or if you need me, this is how to find me." He handed her a handwritten note.

She hesitated for half a second before throwing her arms around him. He shut his eyes tightly and hugged her back. Though he fought it, he could not help turning into her hair for just an instant to take in the scent of jasmine one last time.

She put her lips next to his ear and whispered, "Don't be mad."

"I'm no' mad, Elora," he said into her hair. "Can no' be mad at you. You're my darlin' girl."

He jerked away quickly, hiding his face. And then he was gone.

When Elora closed the door, a fissure of loneliness opened in her solar plexus and began to spread outward, working its way to every extremity, until she was permeated with a sadness heavier than any she had known before, even when she grieved for her family. As the hours went by that fissure grew into a chasm.

She spent the rest of the day packing and unpacking and trying not to think. She didn't see Storm, as he was busy tying up loose ends.

Late in the day Kay knocked on her door to say good-bye. "Are you absolutely sure you've made the right choice?"

He was sure he saw doubt flutter across Elora's face. "I think maybe none of us can be *absolutely* sure we made the right choices until we're looking back from our last breath. You know, you can't connect the dots going forward or something like that."

"You're wrong about that, Elora. Every cell in every fiber of my being knows Katrina is the one for me. Absolutely. If you don't feel that way about Storm – please – back up and think this over again."

"Ram says I'm condemning all three of us to unhappy lives."

"Please don't make me say, 'Ram is right,' out loud."

She smiled. "You know, Kay, you're the best mother hen in all of Black Swan. I'm sure of it."

"Somebody has to be the grown up."

She gave him a hug. "Have the very best holiday ever. Ram told me once that most knights die of old age in their beds with great-grandchildren standing around. I swear I see that for you."

"Be happy," he said and walked away.

Suddenly she remembered that was the last thing her Monq had said before she left her world to be reborn into a new life. She had teased Kay about mothering, but respected him immensely and, if asked, would say he was without doubt the wisest of them. Perhaps the best of them, too.

His question surely gave her pause and even more un-certainty than she was already experiencing. It forced her to ask herself if she was sure that "doing the right thing" was always the "right thing to do". When it was time to meet Storm at the front entrance where they would catch a ride to the airstrip, she still wasn't sure she had answered that question satisfactorily.

Their ride let them out at the hangar, set their luggage on the tarmac, and said the plane was just landing. Elora was thinking that her commitment to Storm felt more like a business transaction than she had expected, almost like an arranged marriage. She was sure of Storm's devotion, but…

Just then, as if he heard her thoughts, Storm turned to Elora and smiled. "We're going to have a wonderful life", he said as he leaned down to kiss her for the first time.

She tilted her face up to receive his kiss. The touch of his lips on hers was electrifying – but not in a good way. The instant they came in contact she jerked like she'd received a heavy duty jolt of electrical shock.

In the blink of an eye, in the mysterious dreamlike space in the brain where time moves differently, she saw a rapid fire series of images. Ram's delight on discovering that she lived next door. Ram reaching for her hand under a white linen tablecloth. Ram hyperventilating because of fear for her. Ram sitting in Blackie's cell waiting to be found. Ram looking up from bartending to smile at her like the sun had just risen. Ram looking at her across a poker table with embers smoldering behind his eyes. Ram flirting with a toddler in the coat check line. Ram with French fries hanging from his nostrils.

Then, in a tsunami of recall that almost made her knees buckle, she remembered everything that had happened the night she was drugged: his conflict between wanting to give her the relief she demanded from him and not wanting to take advantage.

He had been her lover and her physician. She relived

every word, every touch, every sensation. *These have been the sweetest hours of my life.* She saw him rising above her, skin flushed, eyes shining, a faint sheen of sweat on his body. The spicy smell of aroused musk, and wild tree fern. Last, she saw the look of desolation that had claimed his beautiful face when she told him she was going with Storm. *You'll be sentencing three people to a life of unhappiness.*

As she jerked back from the kiss, she gasped and, for a moment, struggled to get her breath. She knew what she had to do and also knew that she would rather reach into her chest, pull her heart out, and set it on fire.

"What's wrong? Please tell me my kissing isn't that bad."

She looked up at Storm, eyes starting to tear. "I'm so sorry, Storm. I don't expect you to forgive me so I won't ask."

He straightened and dropped his hands to his sides. "Ram," was all he said.

"I owe you my life – two times over. And I do love you. But not this way. If it was just the two of us…," she trailed off and paused to wipe tears away with the back of her hand. "I wanted it to be you. Please believe that."

Storm looked out at the plane taxiing and gave a slight nod. "I do believe you, Elora. It'd be dishonest if I said I was completely surprised. I guess you'd have to be blind not to see that the two of you are in love."

He turned and looked at the plane coming to a stop on the tarmac and fingered the photo he carried in his breast pocket – the photo of the pink Italianate villa in the middle of the Sonoma Coast vineyard he constantly fantasized about, the one he had hoped to show her and maybe share with her someday soon. "Sometimes hope and denial go hand in hand."

He turned back to Elora. "I'd like to hate him. But I can't. I loved him first. I'd like to blame him for wanting you, but I can't really do that either, can I?" He ran the backs of his fingers down her cheek. "Are you sure this is what you want? I've known Ram a long time. He's a mixed bag."

"It's not a choice, Storm. I thought it was, but it's not." She circled her arms around his waist and squeezed tight. "I won't forget how much I owe you. I swear it."

He pulled back a little and did that thing where he

ducked down to look eye to eye with her. "You don't owe me a thing, Princess. I did what I did and I wouldn't change it."

He pressed a tender kiss to her forehead and gave her a smile that didn't make it all the way to his eyes. Then, looking just a little older, he picked up his bag and walked to the plane without once looking back.

She stayed long enough to watch him board. *That's what character looks like.* And she knew why three other dominants would turn to him in a crisis situation, when a final decision had to be made. He was that guy.

Luckily the driver had stopped in the hangar for coffee and was still there to give her a ride back.

She tried calling Ram from the jeep, but got a "no service" response. After running to her apartment carrying her suitcase because it turned out those little wheels aren't made to go fast, she raced to the dining desk and located the note.

It said, "Go to the southern gates of New Forest in the north of Ireland. Closest airport is Derry. You can get a car to the town of Black-On-Tarry. Ask for Liam O'Torvall. Dress warm."

Note in hand, she ran to the Operations Office and read the directions, everything except who to ask for and to dress warm. Ms. Farnsworth jotted notes, smiling, and looking through the top half of bifocals, said: "We're familiar with how to arrange this trip. We've done it for Sir Hawking many times."

"Oh! Good. How soon can you get me there?"

"That will depend on when we have a jet going to Edinburgh." She pulled up a screen on one of her several monitors. "Could you be ready to go at five this evening?"

"Absolutely!"

"From Edinburgh you must take a small charter to Derry and you'll have to pay for that leg at your own expense."

Elora frowned. "Do I have enough money for that?"

Ms. Farnsworth suppressed a snort and smiled indulgently. "Yes. You do. Likewise, we can arrange to have a car there to take you on to Black-On-Tarry, but you'll have to..."

"...pay for it at my own expense. Just get me there as soon as possible except that I need a freshen-up stop en route – some place to take a shower, dry my hair, change clothes, you know."

"Indeed I do."

Elora started away, but came right back. "What about… I mean, do I need some, ah, money? And I don't know how much is on the credit card I was issued?"

"I will arrange for you to have Irish money on hand and your credit card is not likely to be declined for any reason. Be back here at four. I'll have the documents ready and don't forget your passport."

Elora gave her a big smile. "Ms. Farnsworth. If you will open this little half door thingy, I will come in there and give you a big kiss."

"That's quite alright, Lady Laiken. The light in your eyes is thanks enough."

She had five hours to pack clothes that fit the direction to dress warm. She dumped the contents of her rolling suitcase on the bed, then remembered Ram's Yule present and tore into it. Inside pink tissue paper was a pair of soft gray sweat pants with big, pink letters across the rear end reading JUICY. She laughed out loud and teared up at the same time in a war of emotions, wondering how she could have ever thought she could live without him. "Very fetchin' britches," she said to herself. The pants went in the bag first.

She kept out the hat and scarf they'd bought together at Bloomingdales to go in her backpack. He liked her in winter white.

Most of her warm clothes had been bought with Ram's help before they went to Romania. She packed them all. Next went in her prettiest lingerie which, all of a sudden, seemed way too heavy on function and way too light on sexy. Oh, well. Last was toiletries, hair dryer, and make-up. Three hours left. She ran downstairs again. When she arrived, Ms. Farnsworth looked up and said, "You're early."

"I'm not ready. I need to get to a drug store for some, uh, things."

Without looking away, Ms. Farnsworth snapped her fingers and a young man appeared as if by magic. "Take Lady Laiken to the closest pharmacy, Daniel, and make sure she is back here well before three o'clock."

"Yes, ma'am."

"I didn't bring my credit card down with me. Give me a minute."

Ms. Farnsworth rolled her eyes, reached in a drawer and handed over three one hundred dollar bills. "That should be sufficient."

Elora took the money. She'd never worked anywhere else, but she was pretty sure this job had great perquisites. "Thank you."

"No thanks are necessary. It will be deducted from your monthly statement."

"I get a monthly statement?"

"Yes." Ms. Farnsworth blinked as she appeared to be summoning patience. "Do you have time to discuss that now?"

Elora grinned and shook her head no.

She returned from the drugstore errand with just enough time to throw on her travel clothes and load the backpack with the magazines she'd just bought, toiletries, and a change so she could make a grooming stop when she was closer to New Forest.

The butterflies that had taken up residence in her stomach were working overtime. Once the decision had been made, she couldn't wait to get to Ram.

She tried his phone again. No service.

CHAPTER 21

THE NEW FOREST Preserve is surrounded by a combination of hedges and rock fences. The village of Black-On-Tarry, which is part of the Preserve, is protected, or isolated, by a large wall.

Entrance by a huge wooden door was granted by special invitation only.

Elora asked the driver to wait. She pulled a large, knotted rope connected to a rusty bell. After a couple of minutes passed, she was about to ring the bell again when a panel slid open.

"Yes?"

"I'm Elora Laiken. I'm here to see, um, Liam O'Torvall."

"Wait here."

Ten minutes later the gate opened.

"Lady Laiken, welcome. I'm Liam O'Torvall. Please to

call me Liam." A plump man in a heavy, brown boiled wool tunic came out, smiling and offering to take her luggage. She paid the driver and followed Mr. O'Torvall beyond the gate. "If we start right away, we shall be there by mid day."

"How do you do. Liam? Is this not my destination?"

"Oh no. We must take a cart. 'Tis some distance to the huntin' cottage."

"A cart?"

"Yes. This way then."

Looking around she realized that the village was medieval in every way, not a sign of modernity anywhere. It could have been a movie set, an amusement park, or one of those historical tourist attractions. In any case she found herself thinking what a good job they had done recreating a scene from centuries past. Doors and doorways were decorated with festive greenery and red ribbons to commemorate the season.

The people, or rather elves, were curious and stared as she passed, but smiled warmly if she made eye contact. Most of them had their hair pulled back behind pointed ears which, in her view, added to the charm. Illustrations from a book of fairy tales.

"Aye, lass. Travel by cart is the only way to get to the huntin' cottage besides walkin' or ridin' and either of those would be tricky with your very fine bag with the little wheels. If you were walkin', you would also need to be wearin' your wellies on a day such as today. If you were ridin' you would need a different sort of cloak, would you no'?"

"I suppose all of that is true."

"If you be peckish, we may find a repast to your likin' before we start away."

"No. I'm not hungry. Just eager."

He looked back at her and chuckled at that. She followed him to a stable where a large, golden draft horse, perhaps the biggest horse she had ever seen, was harnessed to an actual cart with two wooden wheels. There was a simple bench seat in front and space in the cargo area for suitcases.

While she waited, Liam disappeared into the stable for a few minutes and returned leading a very fine, young bay gelding by a halter which he tied to the rear. The horse was wearing a tan wool blanket to keep his coat sleek, shiny, and free of extra winter hair. She climbed up, sat next to Liam, and they drove away from the tiny town onto a road that might better be described as a well-worn path.

She was glad Ram had added the "dress warm" post-script and was especially glad for the cashmere socks he had once insisted she buy. Her toes were feeling the extra crisp bite of the air even through the leather of her boots.

The ground was covered with a light dusting of snow and the tree branches were dripping ice. It was beautiful, but cold. The cart would have been short on comfort under any circumstances, but even more so when winter made the ground harder. The wooden wheels navigating an uneven dirt road made her grateful for a generous flare of hips that cushioned her spine.

Liam talked incessantly as they continued deep into the woods.

"Why, may I ask, are we leading the pretty gelding?"

"Oh. I would not leave you with just one horse! This three-year-old belongs to your host. Sleek and strong, but good-natured and very gentle. He'll be givin' you no trouble at all." Elora smiled to herself that Liam assumed she would require a novice's ride. "And a very fine horseman he is, too."

"Ram?"

"The same."

"So there are no cars here?"

"No cars, electronics, or anythin' powered by somethin' other than human or beast. Rammel's great-grandfather was responsible. He was a visionary who saw the future of the world and caused these lands to be set aside to preserve the old ways. Those of us who live here have chosen to forego the excitement and convenience of electricity for the serenity of peace and the beauty of nature. Life is good and we have him to thank."

She looked around. *No phone, no lights, no motor cars. Not a single luxury. Like Robinson Crusoe, it's primitive as can be.*

"I see. You sound like a philosopher."

"Oh, no. Truly. A simpler man may no' be found on the green earth. The young prince has always preferred the woods to palace life. Wild child he was." Liam chuckled with fondness.

"Wild child. Ram once called *himself* that."

"Aye. The young prince may have been only ten the

first time he ran away and came here. After three times his father settled a charge on me to watch after the boy when he showed up at the cottage. 'Tis why my wife and I have such a deep and abidin' fondness for the lad."

"But that's not the same hunting cottage we're going to. Is it?"

Liam looked confused. "Aye, the very same."

"So Ram has the prince's permission to use his hunting cottage?"

He grew very quiet. For Liam. Which seemed disturbing. "Em. I hope I have no' spoke out of turn."

"What do you mean?"

"I mean His Highness," he glanced sideways and then said pointedly, "Rammel Hawking, speaks very highly of you. Calls you a most uncommon lass. And here we are."

Just ahead Elora saw a storybook cottage, white plaster on stone with a thick thatched roof. It could not have looked more inviting. Her first impression was that it was no wonder he loved it there! With snow on the ground it blended into its surroundings so well that it could almost have been overlooked. There was an outbuilding to the rear side that she supposed was a small barn or stable.

Liam stopped a few yards away and started to get down, but Elora grabbed his forearm.

"You're saying that Ram is this young prince."

Liam looked at her like she might be slow. "That he is. And the finest ever born should you ask me."

For a plump man in his fifties, Liam jumped down with remarkable ease and pulled her suitcase from the cart. Elora was still frozen in place by the shocking revelation.

Liam held out his hand to help her. "Come down. I will help you." He obviously hadn't been told about her athletic gifts so she graciously took his hand before jumping to the ground.

"If he is no' here, I'll build you a nice fire afore I go." When there was no response to his knock or call, Liam let himself in through the unlocked door.

Elora stepped inside and surveyed the interior. The cottage was basically one large room. Clean and tidy as could be. She smiled at the neatness. Everything in its place. One might even have called it immaculate. She could see that the discipline they gave the young trainees paid off. Next to the front door were two pairs of boots, wellies and riding. Next to the boots was a metal sculpture of a bare-limbed tree formed to serve a dual purpose as coat rack.

One wall featured a fireplace and raised hearth. On the opposite wall was a large, carved mahogany bed with a moss green, velvet coverlet and a faux sable blanket that looked and felt like the real thing, almost decadent in its invitation to sensuality.

Above the bed hung a tapestry that looked very old, faded in places, threads going bare in others. The background was a tartan very similar to Black Watch but with gold threads woven into the plaid. In the center was a crest that featured a profile view of a golden lion rearing on hind legs, showing claws and fangs, juxtaposed with a lyre leaning against a banner pole at his feet. Around the emblem were the words *"i lár na Cruinne"*.

She flashed on the image of Ram battling a vampire seconds before making a decision to sacrifice himself for people he didn't know and would never meet. She saw the resemblance between his blonde hair and the lion's mane. Accompanying that fanciful association was the thought that an electric guitar was simply a modern day lyre. *True Irish royalty.*

Against the foot of the bed was a worn leather sofa the color of wine. Near the fire sat a matching chair and ottoman showing even more wear. In front of the sofa was a table fashioned from a large tree trunk, the top polished smooth and waxed with rings in irregular patterns representing nature's own art. The floor was made of dark, wide planks – also worn to a perfection that said, "Boots have walked these floors many thousands of days."

At the far end of the cottage, opposite the front door, was a kitchen with an extra large wooden hutch to the right of the sink and a waist high butcher block that served as a precursor to modern day kitchen islands. There was a large copper bathtub in the left corner. It appeared to be serviced by a pump with a stationary arm. Next to that was another pump on a hinged arm that could swing either to the sink or the tub. Over the copper sink a small window with thick, wavy glass opened to a view of the dense forest beyond. It was winged with heavy shutters to close in the event of extreme cold or leave open to allow more light.

Between the tub and the sink was a small fireplace, waist high, with a cast iron pot hung on a swinging arm. Underneath the stone hearth, was a two foot indentation with an outside hatch at the rear, providing convenient access to restock firewood. On the other side of the hutch, in the corner opposite the tub, there was a cabinet designed for storing perishables. It had some sort of filtered vent on the back for adjusting the temperature, cold enough to keep milk fresh, but not frozen in winter. *Ingenious.*

The butcher block was picturesque enough to photograph. Strawberry and blackberry preserves in glass jars beckoned the beholder to ladle some sweet goodness on a chunk of the half loaf of uncut bread. Or to slice a bit of cheese kept fresh under a glass dome, and wash it down with a hardy, red ale from a pewter pitcher with hinged top. It was as appetizing as any feast she had ever seen. A still life ready to be painted.

The overall impression of the hunting cottage in the woods was comfortable elegance. Rusticity and luxury do not marry easily, but this was the lair of a decidedly masculine personality who understood quality and treasured nice things even more after they began to show age and wear.

Liam built a cheerful fire and replenished the stack of

firewood by the hearth. He told Elora to make herself at home and then let himself out, saying it had been a pleasure to meet her.

Through the window she watched Liam untie the gelding and lead him away. After some time he returned, boarded the cart, and drove away whistling.

Left alone, Elora continued to stand in the middle of the cottage for a time, feeling like an intruder and second guessing her decision to come unannounced. When the room grew warmer, she removed her coat along with the gloves, hat and scarf and gravitated toward the kitchen, where she poured herself a little of the red ale to help drive the chill away from her bones. If it could also help with the unease she was feeling, all the better.

Alone in the cottage she walked around slowly, taking inventory of what was precious enough to Ram to keep in the place he called "home". She read titles of books, then picked up the acoustic guitar and smiled to see that it was in perfect tune, which meant he had probably played that very morning. She had never heard him play acoustic which meant there were probably many things about him she didn't know. Like that he was an Irish prince.

Only two items would qualify as artwork or pictorial features: the tapestry and a single picture on the massive mantel. It was an enlarged, framed photo of the two of them in front of the tree at Rockefeller Center snuggled close, looking happy and so right for each other.

There was only one thing left unsnooped – a large, antique armoire that held the clothes he kept on hand. When she opened the doors, without thinking, her hand immediately, impulsively, reached for a hanging sleeve and brought it to her nose. She supposed that impulse meant she had even missed his smell and thought, "What madness made me think I could make a life without him?"

She tried to cozy up in a corner of the sofa and get comfortable. But as the day wore on, alone in the cottage that was silent except for the crackles and pops of the fire, the phrase "palace life" began looping through her mind over and over, growing in volume to match her anxiety.

After a couple of hours had passed, the threat of being returned to a life of oppressing restriction simmered to a boil. No matter how well appointed, a locked tower is still locked. And her fear of that, even though irrational, was so consuming that it overcame both love and logic. She concluded that it had been a mistake to come.

The cup of ale was returned to the kitchen, emptied and placed in the sink. She pulled her black coat over the white cashmere sweater she had worn because she knew Ram liked seeing her in winter whites. The scarf and hat were thrown on hastily as she was heading for the door, planning to follow the cart path back to the village, footwear be damned. Luggage be damned. Near panic, she had to flee and couldn't even wait to get her gloves on.

As she passed the window she caught movement out of the corner of her eye. She froze, took one step backward, and looked out. Across the clear running creek a fantasy come to life was emerging from the shadows on the edge of the forest. There she saw a striking blonde elf with hair pulled back behind his ears and tied at the nape of his neck, wearing a long black coat split up the back seam for ease of movement and a generous length of wool, Black Watch tartan with gold thread weave gathered around his neck and shoulders, held in place by a kilt pin with the same crest as that in the tapestry and the thick leather strap of a quiver. The long bow he carried was so beautifully curved and crafted that she could recognize its quality even from that distance.

She knew the instant he realized that something was unexpected. The smoke coming from his chimney caused him to go statue still like a freeze frame, exactly like a wild animal does when it senses something amiss. Snow had begun coming down; huge, fluffy flakes were hanging in the air, defying the laws of physics, taking their time in falling as if enjoying the downward glide.

After a moment he proceeded toward the cottage with purpose, jumping the stream with the grace of a dancer, then resuming the powerful, athletic stride that she would recognize anywhere. Having become unsettled by an over active imagination run amuck, she was not thinking clearly, or she would have known that Ram would not simply let her say hello and dash away unaccompanied.

Just as he reached the door, she opened it. And there, on the other side of the threshold, stood an elf whose features formed harsh planes, whose face was a mask of utter stillness with eyes the image of unfathomable emptiness. He was barely recognizable. Without changing expression or taking his vacant eyes from her, he slowly set the bow on its end, leaning it against the door's casement.

Seeming to be considering whether she was real or illusion, he pulled the strap of his quiver over his head and set it next to the bow.

After she had recovered from the initial shock of seeing her Ram so changed, so unanimated, so decimated, she mustered a bright smile and effervescent tone for her greeting even if she didn't have the authenticity of cheerful emotion to put behind it. She was offering a silent prayer to the gods: "Please don't let me have destroyed what I most treasure."

"Hi." She gave a little, chest high wave with her gloved right hand.

His head turned toward the hand she had just waved. His eyes lingered there for a few heartbeats, fixated, before returning to her face. She could tell the moment he decided she was not a hallucination. Elora was there! In the flesh. In his cottage. Come halfway round the world. And that could mean only one thing. She was his.

The visual transformation that followed that realization was miraculous. Like the explosion of fire that follows putting a match to a pilot light when a surplus of gas has first escaped, the flame leaped back into his eyes. His face regained its familiar fluidity as it spread into a smile that was half proprietary and half predatory.

Elora's heart kept time with the transformation as she watched Ram's true essence reclaim his body, settle in and take up residence. Not too late.

As he advanced slowly, he backed her into the cabin and shut the door behind him, never taking his eyes away from her face. His natural scent of musk and wild tree fern filled the space between them. She had forgotten that it could be sensually overpowering when encountered in person, easily causing someone such as herself to forget everything else.

"Um, nice place." Suddenly nervous, she was talking faster than usual. "I just dropped by to say Happy Holidays and was on my way out. Liam brought me. Very nice man. Talks a lot. We came in a cart drawn by the biggest horse I ever saw. He built the fire and brought in more wood." She gestured toward the hearth. "I had some of your ale to help warm up after the ride through the woods. I hope you don't mind. It was very good."

While she was talking, he pulled the knit hat away and ran his hand slowly over her head, wondering how he could have already forgotten just what a marvel was the color of that hair. He was thinking she looked bewitching in the winter whites they had bought on their day in New York.

"Where are you going in such a hurry?" he said with a wolfish smile and a quiet tone that dripped honey.

"I, ah, want to be back in the village before dark. Great to see you. Gotta go."

He was slowly unwinding the scarf from around her neck and blocking her path to the door. "There's plenty of time and you've come such a very long way. Why do you no' stay for tea? And tell me the true reason for your visit? After that I will take you to the village if you still want to go."

He had started undoing the buttons on her coat, deliberately allowing the backs of his fingers to leisurely brush the cleavage beneath. She shivered in response to his touch and the look of pure masculine smugness he was wearing; the look some men got when they were certain they were about to enjoy a memorable coupling. "And did I mention how very glad I am to see you?"

He pushed her coat back from her shoulders and

draped it over a bare limb of the sculptured tree, coat rack that stood by the door. He was staring at her partially bare clavicle as he reached up and took the prim collar of her white, angora sweater to rub gently between his fingers. "Soft," he said, raising his eyes to lock with hers in unmistakable sexual innuendo.

She felt her breath becoming shallow and her resolve unraveling. Maybe she could stand being locked in a tower if it was with this elf. She gave herself a sound inward shake and forced herself to sound unaffected.

"I can't stay for tea unless you make tea, Rammel."

He dropped his hand resuming his wolfish smile, and started removing his own outerwear. When he was done, he was left in boots, black sileather pants, and a soft, teal blue, knit pullover that did dazzling things to the color of his eyes in that light. He poked the fire, making room to add a log, turned to make sure she was still there, and went to the kitchen to make tea. He noticed Elora was standing exactly where he'd left her by the door, now having gone from uncharacteristically chatty to uncharacteristically quiet.

Doing his best to disarm her, he motioned to the

couch: "Sit down. Please. Tea standin' up is no' nearly as good."

She looked at the couch like it was a trap. In her mind, deciding where and how to sit became an equation to be solved.

"How long have you been here?"

"I don't know. Couple of hours?" she said absently, still studying the couch like a puzzle.

Ram pumped water into a tea kettle and brought it to the hearth where he hung it on a large iron hinge which swung to suspend over the open flames.

"How was the trip?"

"It was… liberating, the first time I've traveled without people I know. It made me feel… free. Independent. Even though the details were skillfully worked out by Ms. Farnsworth."

He saw that Elora was still trying to decide where to sit. "Are you cold?"

When she looked up and saw his expectant expression she felt butterflies stirring in her stomach all over again and scolded herself for behaving like a timid schoolgirl. She silently repeated the mantra: "I am a fearless knight of

The Order of The Black Swan. Even if I am on probation."
She shook her head no and smiled.

Ram returned to the kitchen to assemble a tea service.

Every second he was gone amplified her anxiety. She forced herself to sit and decided to calm herself with conversation.

"So, partner, in all the time we spent together, you never got around to telling me you're a royal? A prince even? Liam was worried about having 'spoke out of turn'."

Ram had his back to her, but the question made his head come up and he momentarily froze in place before returning to the task of assembling tea.

"As far as I'm concerned, I'm Sir Hawking, no' Prince Hawking. I've earned my knighthood a dozen times over. I did nothin' to become a prince except have the dubious fortune to be born royal. I never wanted people I work with to think of me as different, probably for the same reason you do no' like it when Storm calls you Princess."

"How did you know I don't like it? I never said."

He looked over his shoulder and smiled. "Tis my job to pay attention to you, Elora."

"Do Storm and Kay know? About your, uh, family?"

"Aye. We spend a lot of time together. 'Tis little we do no' know about each other." After a short pause he added, "Probably."

He hastily finished putting cups, cream, sugar, and spoons on an old, wood tray in need of refinishing and carried them back to the main room. Setting the tray on the tree stump table, he had no trouble deciding where to sit. Elora had finally chosen a perch at the end of the sofa nearest the door. He pulled the ottoman over and sat facing her, close enough that his knees were almost touching hers.

"The water will be hot in a minute or so."

She looked at the kettle hanging above the fire. Something about the proximity and calm confidence of Ram's voice suddenly caused a sense of peace to wash over Elora, a feeling that everything about the moment was right; the utter quiet of a cold, gray, snowy day in a land without noise, the serenity of an ancient cottage with a happy fire in the middle of a medieval forest, and the sweet, sweet intimacy of having Rammel Hawking there, all to herself.

How strange it was to be in a place she'd never seen before, and feel so at home. That's when she realized it wasn't the place that made her feel like she'd come home. It was the elf. How she had missed him!

At some point during her reverie he had moved closer and lightly rested his hands on her knees. One thumb was absently drawing little circles on the inside of her lower thigh as he studied her face. He always left her alone when he saw her eyes glaze over and knew she was away on some private, inner journey where she sorted things out. She was so caught up in her own thoughts that she jumped when the tea kettle began to whistle. To be fair, it was as loud as a train. Ram laughed in that open, unguarded way she loved.

"Welcome back," he teased as he rose to fetch the kettle. He named the various kinds of tea he had on hand adding that he had also stocked a very fine hot chocolate just in case she should be there someday.

"Yes, indeed," she smiled. "I would like some of your very fine hot chocolate, Sir Hawking. 'Twould be grand in fact."

"Your wish is my pleasure, Lady Laiken," he said as he carefully poured hot water over her chocolate and stirred before handing her the cup. "I also have biscuits." He motioned to the plate of baked goodies.

"Those are cookies, Ram."

"No' here. Here, they are biscuits."

He began to steep some Irish Breakfast Tea for himself, then turned toward her again. "And now you will tell me the details of how my good fortune has blessed me with the privilege of servin' you chocolate on this fine winter day."

She took a sip of liquid bliss then returned her cup and saucer to the tray.

"I was actually on the tarmac, ready to leave with Storm. The jet had landed and was taxiing." He grew solemn, but nodded encouragement for her to continue. "He kissed me. For the first time."

She noticed Ram's shoulders tense and his fingers curled under even though his expression remained the same. "And what happened was strange. I have no explanation and probably never will. It gave me a jolt – like an electrical jolt – that felt real and physically painful. In the space of a couple of seconds I saw this parade of images, all memories of you, including the night we, um, found out that aphrodisiacs are not a myth."

Ram worked at keeping his face blank. He was too interested in hearing the rest of this to interrupt.

She let out a big sigh. "I couldn't go with Storm. You were right. It wouldn't be fair to him because I don't know how to be happy without you." Looking at Ram, she was momentarily mesmerized by the illumination of his face by firelight and the way he searched her eyes. "And it wouldn't be fair to you because…"

In one motion he rose, pulling her up with him, took her in his arms and held on like the salvation she was. As he leaned forward to crush a kiss to her mouth, she arched her body toward his, holding back nothing, and nothing had ever felt so natural, like such a perfect fit. It was as if they had been cast in a mold as a pair, then separated, and were now reunited. Suddenly she broke the kiss and pulled away.

"There's a reason why I was leaving, Ram, why I was going to be gone before you got back. Because I can't do palace life. No matter how I feel about you, I can never go back to that. It swallows me up. It smothers me. And it's possible you could be king someday."

"Elora," Ram gently pulled her back against him, "you

must have faith that we're well matched. I'll no' ask you to do anythin' you do no' want. Ever. If you ne'er want to set foot in my brother's house, then we will no'. If circumstances put kingship in my path and you asked me to pass on the crown, I'd be glad for it."

Elora tilted her head to the side. "You have that choice?" She studied his face. "Liam told me you used to run away."

"Aye. Understand this. The only person who can force me to do anythin' is you."

"Really?"

He thought perhaps she sounded a bit too intrigued by the possibilities. But no matter. There was nothing he would deny her.

As she stepped back into the haven of his body, he enveloped her in his arms. It made her feel sexy and beautiful, but, oddly, even though she knew she was physically stronger, it made her feel safe and protected. She buried her face in his neck where she could drag in even more of his erotic smell.

He chuckled in response. "So you will no' be needin' a ride to the town then."

It was not a question, but she raised her face and opened her mouth to reply. Whatever she intended to say was muffled by a kiss ever so much more potent than memory had served. As her tongue tangled with his and her breath came faster, she purred sounds of approval followed by a gasp as a warm hand reached beneath her sweater to cover a breast and run a thumb over one of the taut nipples that was begging to be touched.

She drew back. "Just a minute." She leaned away and bent to retrieve her backpack, fumbled around inside for a minute, then, with a flourish, she triumphantly withdrew three long strips, each containing a dozen condoms of neon yellow, orange, and pink. She waved them in the air. "Heart Throbs. Guaranteed feminine satisfaction." She seemed so pleased with herself.

Ram first looked confused, then offended. "And you do no' think I can guarantee feminine satisfaction?"

She laughed. "I know you can, but we need protection. I mean, I guess we got lucky last time, but…" Ram looked down at the ridiculously colorful circles trailing from her hand, indulged in a moment of pride when he noticed that she had bought extra large. *She does remember that night.*

Then the gravity of the situation returned and he let out a big sigh.

She looked deflated. "What is it, Ram?"

"Elves and humans mate rarely. When they do, there is no procreation."

She searched his face. "We won't have children?"

He solemnly shook his head no. Elora's knees felt a little slushy. Sinking down on the couch, she hadn't realized she really wanted children until she was told there wouldn't be any. Ram sat on the ottoman in front of her as she did a replay in her head.

"So that's why you said having children wasn't important."

His brows drew together for a moment as he looked away, trying to place the reference. Then he remembered.

"Our day in Manhattan. Aye. I said 'tis no' important. And I meant it."

"You're not disappointed?"

"Disappointed! My darlin' girl, I'm the farthest thing from that. I consider myself to be the luckiest elf in the world." She reached out with her intuition and knew he was telling the truth. He took her hand in his, raised her knuckles to his lips and kissed them. "Besides, there are little ones who are left alone in the world through no fault of their own. We could be their mum and da. Make them ours."

Her heart melted into a pile of mush and she blinked a little mist from her eyes. She reached up and traced the scar running down the side of his face that would forever be a graphic testament to extraordinary courage and selflessness, the very essence of Black Swan. *Ram isn't just heroic. He's epic.*

She smiled. "Adopt."

"Aye. Adopt."

"There's really nothing about you that isn't wonderful, is there?"

He grinned. "No. There's no'." He pulled her to her feet again, pressed her close, and grew serious. "We'll be happy, Elora. I swear it."

It was an oath she knew would be kept. There would be no power that could stop him from finding the way to their happiness once he made it his quest.

"And there's another benefit to bein' elf and human."

"What is it?"

"I do no' think I could remain erect while wearing tart pink or fiery orange."

"But lime yellow works for you?" She laughed. "Well, I guess that gives us some time to get to know each other, just the two of us."

"All the better to have my way with you, my dear." He smiled his wolfish smile and nuzzled her neck.

"The night I was drugged, you said you wanted the first time to be... not like that."

"Aye. I did say that." He was studiously playing with the pearl buttons on her sweater.

"So show me what you had in mind."

"Can no'."

"Why no'?" She teased mimicking his accent.

"Because, all those nights I was lyin' in my bed alone thinkin' about bein' with you, what I pictured was a slow burn savorin' of every inch of your heavenly body. But these past days, I thought you were lost to me... was like years in hell. I do no' think I'm good for anythin' right now but hard and fast." He bit his bottom lip. "I need you to wrap yourself around me and hold on tight while I pound into you, balls flyin', both of us knowin' beyond question that you're mine."

Elora's eyes widened as she processed that image. Her lips parted as her gaze transfixed on his mouth which was suddenly spellbinding. "That," she swallowed, "sounds good, too."

In less than a minute they were free of clothes, falling onto the bed together.

Skin to skin, their bodies had minds of their own, desperate for each other. Elora arched and bucked involuntarily with every sensual touch. He took her in one savage thrust with a ferocity that stopped just short of ravishing and she reveled in the intensity of his need. Without warning he withdrew.

She opened her mouth to protest, but the sound was drowned by a strangled cry when he found her sensitive, swollen nub and began stirring tiny circles with his finger. Just as she started to come, he drove back into her so that they would peak together. He roared his release like a tribute to the Fates who had brought his mate back to him, then collapsed, feeling foolish for having to control the urge to sob in gratitude and relief.

After some time he raised his head and gloried in the

love he saw shining back at him through half closed turquoise eyes. *Sunshine on a Bahamian sea.* Then he asked out loud what he needed to know.

"Are you mine then?"

"Completely." She answered with a half smile and not the slightest hesitation.

As the short northern day gave way to darkness, Ram rose and closed the shutters. He stoked the coals and added more logs, then rekindled a second, small fire in the kitchen. As she watched him move around the cottage, she thought that she had not known it was possible for a person to be so utterly unselfconscious about nudity, but supposed it must be one of the derivative benefits of owning physical perfection.

Ram took the cushions from the sofa and put them in front of the fire, then brought half a roast chicken, bread, cheese, and ale on a tray. Elora joined him with the sable throw drawn around her, partly for warmth and partly to hide blemished skin that was not completely healed. They ate by firelight, without utensils, and wiped their hands on linen dish towels while Ram entertained her with stories of his adventures when he had sometimes lived alone in the woods as a child. Occasionally Ram fed her something by hand, which was curiously arousing.

When they had finished eating, he pulled the sable throw away, noting that her hands immediately flew to cover the red marks where her wounds had not faded. Seeing that she felt shame about her body made his heart seize like it was pinched in a vice grip. He spread the fur over the makeshift bed he'd fashioned from cushions.

"Now let's see about the savorin'."

Ram was meticulously thorough, painstaking in his mission to savor lovemaking with Elora. No erogenous nerve ending was left unexplored. True to his promise, it was slow. And just as true to his promise, it burned, igniting new emotions in Elora that were untried feelings so raw they made her ache for something she could not call by any name other than "more". Every sensation was stretched to its limit, every emotion intensified as they delighted in the sweet intoxication of mating.

He lingered on each and every sign of trauma with single minded devotion as if he could kiss the wounds better. She felt tears burn as she watched him lovingly minister to her defaced body. Now and then he would pause and look at her face with an expression that could only be compared to reverence.

Likewise, Elora traced the length of his scar with her tongue, end to end, wanting him to know that he was all the more attractive for what it represented. She sucked the lobe of his ear into her mouth, then licked her way around the exquisitely curved point as he alternately shivered and laughed. She said she'd been wanting to do that ever since the night she first encountered her elf with the beautiful ears.

He drove her wild with light, little, teasing kisses and nuzzles to the sensitive area underneath her pelvic curls that were, to his delight, the same improbable, multihued color as the hair on her gorgeous head. When finally he rose above her she thought he had taken mercy, but merely ratcheted her excitement higher by repeatedly drawing his engorged shaft along her channel, teasing until, out of sheer desperation, she stopped begging and dug nails into the flexing cheeks of his perfectly formed buttocks.

He chuffed with surprise and amusement and submitted to her demand by sinking into her, but continued the divine torture – moving in and out so slowly and deliberately that pleasure became a wanting tinged with painful need.

As Elora became less inhibited and more wanton, her vocalizations grew in volume and intensity. Later, he joked that "they probably heard your screamin' in the village". But he loved it. His male ego was gratified beyond measure. Every squeal, giggle, gasp, cry, shout, growl, moan, murmur, and purr served as confirmation that he had, in fact, 'guaranteed feminine satisfaction'. Though he cherished every noise she made, what he craved hearing most, was, "Ah, Ram, you feel so good!"

And she told him often.

When he stood to poke the fire and add logs, he noticed she shivered when the night chill, beginning to set in, made contact with the moisture on her skin. He urged her to climb back in bed and get warm under the covers. More accustomed to the cold, when he came to bed, he flopped on his back with the covers kicked away, the firelight making a visual ecstasy of his body.

At length he said to the ceiling, "I've no' had a woman in my bed before. Ever. Just wanted you to know."

"You mean this bed?"

"I mean any bed designated as mine whether permanent or temporary. No' hotel or tent or Romanian fortress." He put his hands behind his head and lolled on the mattress next to her. Elora threw the bed clothes away from her shoulders so that she could lean up on one elbow and rest her head in her hand.

"Was there someone in a Romanian fortress who wanted to crawl in bed with you?"

He tilted his head at an angle and gave her a playful leer. "You tell me."

"You'll never know," she said playfully as she reached down and lightly ran her fingertips up his thigh until she cupped his sack. That earned her a surprised, hissed intake of air. Emboldened by that reaction, she continued upward until she could grasp and partially encircle the base of his erection. She began caressing with alternating pressures, massaging the underside of velvet on steel with sophisticated strokes. He barked out a laugh as he jerked into an involuntary half sit up.

"And just where did you learn that, Little Miss Innocence?"

"On the plane to Edinburgh. *Vogue Magazine.* 'The Lost Art of the Handjob.'" She smiled wickedly. "Like it?"

"Astoundin'." He found it very amusing until she changed stroke techniques. Suddenly his gaze shuttered, the merriment ceased, and he got very serious about intense orgasms that make semen shoot like a water pistol. Watching wide eyed, greedily learning about sexual power and the marvels of ejaculations, Elora found that display so spectacular that she couldn't wait to see it again.

He laughed. "I will be happy to oblige with a repeat performance, but my balls need a little break to manufacture more juice for your viewin' pleasure."

"Well, hurry up then! Consider it a Command Performance."

It seemed like a lifetime ago that he had told Kay he had no choice but to love everything about her, but those were just words he'd been taught since childhood, words he repeated by rote. The reality of mating went far beyond the mundane limits of description. It was perfection. Pure joie de vivre.

He loved that she was so responsive to his touch, so demanding when excited, so receptive to new experiences, affectionate to a fault. He was contented as an elf can be.

During the night he rose to put logs on the fire. He supposed the instincts of provide and protect must include a make-comfortable impulse as well. The bed that had been so cold all his life felt downright toasty with Elora's body heat working like a generator. Her temperature was always a little warm and she slept even hotter. His eyelids grew heavy listening to the sweet, rhythmic lullaby of her breathing and he drifted into sleep again smiling.

The next time he roused he knew without opening his eyes that it was light outside. He ran his hand over the sheet next to him, eyes still closed, but found no extra warm body. That spiked a momentary fear that he had just imagined that the Lady Laiken had found her way across the sea to his bed in the New Forest cottage.

Hearing something behind him, he rolled over to face the kitchen, his eyes immediately coming to rest on the sight of Elora bending over looking in a lower cabinet. The word JUICY was proudly displayed across her exquisite derriere. He suppressed a delighted chuckle, wanting to remain still and simply enjoy the experience of waking to see Elora exploring the cottage kitchen. Yesterday had begun in a dark pit of despair, a place in the heart with no room for anything lighter than hopelessness. But it had ended in rapture.

"I knew those very fine pants would look amazin' on your gorgeous ass."

She turned her head. "You said 'very fetchin' britches'. And I said you don't have permission to talk about my gorgeous ass. But thank you for the present. Happy Yule."

He smiled. "What are you lookin' for?"

She stood and turned around. In addition to the JUICY pants, she was wearing a white, long sleeve tee with no bra and fuzzy brown slippers with moose heads and antlers. He was positive that it would not be possible for a person to be cuter.

"Breakfast. I found peanut butter. Which looks and smells really good right now, but it has to be an import. I'm sure they used fuel powered machinery to make it so it must be contraband." She narrowed her eyes. "Have you been bad?"

"I have been bad, but no' with peanut butter. 'Tis legal. Will there be enough left for me?"

"Can't say. We'll have to wait and see."

He got out of bed and strode toward the kitchen allowing the sweep of her gaze to fully appreciate the grand sight of a healthy, young elf first thing in the morning. Her voluptuous stare made his erection distend even further. So he and it headed straight for her.

She laughed and moved to the other side of the butcher block island, putting it between them.

"Oh. No sir. I'm hungry. Keep that very fine penis away from me unless it's covered in peanut butter."

He grinned. When she saw the look on his face, she immediately grasped the implication of what had been said guilelessly and could see that he was choosing to accept the statement more as an offer than a joke.

Without missing a beat he went straight to the jar of peanut butter, dipped two fingers inside, withdrew a huge dollop, and, with a roguish gleam, began smearing it over, under, and around his cock, being careful not to miss one centimeter. His pelvic curls were a gold much darker than his hair, but very close in color to the peanut butter.

The sight of Ram handling himself was a turn on that Elora was unprepared for. It had her breathing faster and pressing thighs together. When he was satisfied that nothing of importance had been left uncovered, he stood there with his proud challenge and devilish smile, sucking the remainder from his fingers with relish.

He held his arms out. "Well?"

"Diabolical," she said.

He wiggled his eyebrows. "Love spelled backward is evol."

She laughed, but watching him lick the clingy ambrosia away, her body moved toward him without conscious direction from her brain. Her tongue involuntarily peeked out to wet her bottom lip in readiness and his eyes locked on the movement like a target-seeking missile.

With exaggerated grace and ladylike dignity she lowered herself to her knees without taking her eyes off the prize. Ram seemed to be holding his breath with anticipation. When her tongue tentatively reached out to touch the tip, the peanut butter covered treat jumped of its own accord. The movement sent a spike of thrill racing through her own body, ending in a puddle of welcome at the entrance to her sex.

One of his hands reached down to hold his cock in place, while the other rested gently on the side of her head.

When she took more of him into her mouth, he made a primeval sound akin to a growl. Which was sexy as hell, ramping her interest even higher.

Having read all of Istvan Baka's steamy romances, she wasn't completely without information on the subject. Encouraged by the shine in Ram's eyes and the sounds he continued to make – something between a growl and a hum – she began to lap more enthusiastically. By the time the sweet coating was licked clean, Elora had decided she liked fellatio and the intense pleasure her elf took from it.

He pulled her to her feet and kissed her, tasting himself and the residue of the gooey mixture on her tongue, then turned her around, pulling her back against him. While he cupped her braless breasts through the white tee shirt, teasing nipples, he nuzzled warm breath in her ear until she began to shudder and pant.

Feeling his erection pressing from behind, she squeezed her cheeks together reflexively. Ram moaned and gently urged her forward over the butcher block island. When he slipped his hand inside the JUICY pants over the smooth skin underneath, he bent over and said in her ear: "This was my fantasy when I gave you these lovely britches."

He entered her so slowly that she lost patience and pushed back which drove him all the way into the glove of her body, but also threatened to topple him.

"Easy," he laughed. "You're strong, remember. You'll throw me across the room."

She stilled. He bent over her, covering her outstretched arms with his and began a torturously slow bump and grind that confirmed how carnally fulfilling that position could be, while he talked dirty in her ear. That was when she discovered that laughing during coitus renders unique rewards that can both feel sublime and drive a male to frenzy.

"So this was really a Yule present for yourself. That means you owe me a present."

"Anythin' you want." The words burst out as he was nearing climax. He suddenly straightened and thrust into her so hard she saw the edge of oblivion.

She gasped. "Don't stop! Please don't stop."

"Ne'er."

He reached in front of her and began to massage her clit which, he decided, must be directly connected to her vocal cords. When he felt her walls clenching and rippling around him, he finally let go and collapsed over her, his hips continuing to rock while he spent.

THEY BROKE FAST with more peanut butter, fresh baked bread, and a cup of hot mulled wine while Ram explained the finer points of the cottage's plumbing. He looked supremely self-satisfied in the way males can when they think their sexual performance is media worthy. Elora had no trouble with stroking his ego. Or anything else for that matter.

The tub had a French drain running underneath so that water could drain through a pipe under the cottage and down the hill away from the water supply. The stationary pump was piped directly to an underground hot spring while the pump with the swinging arm brought cold well water that could be used to regulate the temperature.

He filled the tub with hot water while she used the privy, which was a closet close to the same temperature as the outdoors, with a wooden bench toilet over a hole dug so deep that there wasn't an issue with odors, at least not in winter. It was the least desirable thing about their love nest, but she thought it was a small price to pay.

In the low light of a gray winter day and a small kitchen fire, Ram rested against the back of the copper tub while Elora lay back against him, taking comfort from the throb of his strong heartbeat and the feel of his hard body supporting hers. The hot spring water was soft, steamy and divine and she was thinking there was nowhere she'd rather be.

"So you were hunting yesterday?"

"Oh, no. The creatures in the New Forest are under the protection of the king. My brother owns everythin' here."

"You were carrying a bow."

"For self defense. Some of the creatures in the wood have no' got the memo that this is a more civilized time."

She splashed a little water and fiddled with the linen cloth covering her abdomen. "I've decided you're officially an enigma; an elf who shreds metal, worships Metallica, and chooses to retreat to a society that bans electricity."

"An enigma, hmmm? Well, I'm hopin' that will keep you interested for a long, long time."

He felt Elora tense at that. "What do you mean? I thought mates are forever."

"Aye, in elfdom that is true. But I have observed that humans are no' always so…committed. Seems that, for humans, ever after is hard to come by."

"My people don't divorce. We choose. Then marry and stay together. I'll never leave you, Ram. No matter what."

"My darlin' girl, you ease the fear in my heart."

"Please don't let there be uncertainty between us. You're my charming prince."

He smiled at that. "Agreed. Please do no' let there be shame between us either."

"Shame?"

He paused for a minute.

"Elora, first, I love that my woman is the first female knight in the history of Black Swan. It honors me more than I can say. I hate that you went into that tunnel without your team, but I love and admire you for it, too. Please do no' hide from me. The sight of your body, as it is this very hour, could no' excite me more. If you bear these marks forever, you will still be the most beautiful female in the world to me. What can I do to convince you 'tis so?"

They lay relaxing in the pleasure of each other's company for some time, mulling over every word, reliving every caress, stowing them away in their hearts to keep as a foundation for forever, through good times and bad.

At length Elora took the cloth away, wrung it out and set it aside. Ram pulled her head back onto his shoulder and kissed her temple in approval, loving that she trusted him.

"What will we do about Black Swan?"

Not really wanting to think about the world outside the copper tub, he sighed. "How did you leave things with Storm?"

"He said he wasn't surprised, that anyone could see we were in love, and that he doesn't have regrets about anything."

"When we get back we'll go to Sol and explain that we'll marry." He paused. "You do plan to marry me?"

She hesitated. Just when he was beginning to wonder if he should be worried, she said: "As proposals go, that may not be the worst ever, but I think you could do better."

He smiled. "How's this then? Tell me your dreams so I can make them come true."

"Much better. And, yes, I plan to marry you."

AFTER THEY WERE dressed, Ram asked Elora if she would like to try riding. He kept a nice stable a few yards from the cottage, tight against the wind, stocked with fall's harvest of green hay and oats. Planning a little mischief at the expense of his assumption that she didn't ride, she asked for the gray mare. Ram tried to dissuade her, explaining that the mare was temperamental and accustomed to experienced riders. Elora insisted and ultimately prevailed using the selling point that she wouldn't be hurt even if she was thrown.

Ram wasn't happy about it, but he switched saddles, muttering something about stubborn women.

He helped her up, gave her a few verbal pointers, and then mounted the pretty, bay gelding. Elora couldn't remember having so much fun as pretending not to know how to ride and then giving Ram a merry chase through the woods. On his own horse no less! She laughed until her eyes watered.

Later they made a stew of chicken and vegetables and cooked it in a pot hanging over the open flame fire in the kitchen.

Ram gave her his highest compliment, saying she could ride as well as an elf. She told him some of her own stories of training and competing in equestrian events before she was even in her teens.

The next few days were lived like a honeymoon, rich in the earthy, elemental pleasures of fire, snow, and mulled wine. Indulging in languorous conversation and vigorous copulation, they thrived, each basking in the glow of the other's adoration and celebrating the pleasures of learning each other's secrets in the most intimate ways.

On the day they were to leave, Elora stood in the middle of the cottage, packed, wearing her coat, hat and scarf, replaying in her mind every precious moment, wishing she could simply restart the week and live it again without changing a thing.

As if he could read her mind, Ram came up behind her, put his arms around her waist and said next to her ear, "We'll be back."

"Promise?"

"Oh, aye. 'Tis part of happily ever after."

The fact that she shared his love for the little cottage in the New Forest was just one more thing on a long list that confirmed his certainty that he'd been paired with the perfect mate.

———————

CHAPTER 22

RAM AND ELORA deliberately returned to Jefferson Unit a day ahead of Storm and Kay so that they would have a chance to talk to Sol. They stood together in front of his desk holding hands as they explained their situation. They requested transfer to some duty suitable for a married couple. Sol said that he had already agreed to loan B Team to Edinburgh for a temporary assignment and asked that they stay on for one more mission before a major change was made.

Ram was aghast that he had been assigned to a tour in "Fairyland" which is what he called Scotia.

Sol turned his attention to Elora. "You seem reserved. Where's the enthusiasm?"

"It's not about the assignment. I don't really care where I go as long as he's there." She glanced at Ram and he beamed. "It's Blackie. I understand that, technically, he belongs to Jefferson Unit, but I think he'd be happier with me."

Sol briefly steepled his fingers and then smiled. "Consider him a wedding present from Jefferson Unit. We'll make sure the usual quarantines are lifted. Be ready to leave in four days."

While chanting thank you's, Elora ran around the desk and gave Sol a big kiss on the cheek which made him blush and left him off balance. People don't rush up to Sol with kisses. Ever.

The following morning Ram took Blackie out for a walk and stopped on the way back up for a to-go coffee and a hot chocolate. When he returned to the apartment he found Elora kneeling on the bathroom floor, vomiting into the toilet, the color of her complexion somewhere between pale and green.

He knelt beside her and pulled her hair back from her face. "What in Paddy's name, Elora?"

Frustrated by the question and the first illness of her life, Elora was feeling pitiful and snarky, never a good combination.

"I'm sick! Duh!"

"You said you ne'er get sick."

"I don't!" she shouted. Then threw up again.

As soon as her stomach seemed emptied, Ram insisted they go to the infirmary. He walked around the waiting room cracking his knuckles while she was examined. After half an hour he was told he could go in. She was sitting on the side of the hospital bed glaring at him.

"You said humans and elves don't procreate."

Of all the things he was prepared to hear, that was not among them.

"They do no'."

"Yes. They. Do. I'm pregnant!"

She watched the parade of emotions cross his face, knowing him well enough to read every nuance. Confusion was replaced by anger which was overcome by love and finally resolved in resignation, as he determined that he was keeping this woman and this baby no matter who the father was. He may as well have said it all out loud.

"Ram! Of course you are the father. This is bad enough without you thinking I would lie to you."

"I... Well, makes no difference. You're mine. You always will be. No matter what."

Elora was infuriated. "Get. Me. Monq."

"Why?"

She struggled to get her emotions under control. In an effort to overcome the impulse to scream at him, she spoke distinctly and deliberately.

"Because. Rammel. There is a perfectly logical explanation for this, and when it comes to solving mysteries, Monq is our go-to guy. Right?"

Concluding that humoring her was the best course of action, Ram called Monq and asked if he could please come up to the infirmary right away. Again.

Monq arrived ten minutes later. "Ms. Laiken."

"Shut the door," Elora ordered Monq without greeting or further pleasantries.

He did.

"I'm pregnant. Ram's the father. He doesn't believe it."

Monq looked between them, then said, "Well, first, congratulations. And, second," turning to Ram, "you don't believe she's pregnant or you don't believe you're the father?"

"I did no' say that."

Elora huffed. "He doesn't believe he's the father."

To Ram, Monq asked, "Why not?"

"Why no' what?"

"Why do you not believe you're the father?"

"Because elves and humans can no' procreate." As an afterthought, in the interest of clarity, he added: "With each other. 'Tis a biological fact no' up to interpretation. The chromosomes do no' line up."

Monq barked out a laugh that clearly offended Ram.

"And what could you be findin' amusin' about this... situation?"

"She's an elf, you idiot! Her DNA is 99.9% the same as yours. The .01% difference is that her ears are not pointed."

While Ram stood there with his mouth open, trying to absorb that astonishing news, Elora turned to Monq with a hint of menace.

"And you didn't think this was information you should pass along?"

"First, is it my job to keep up on gossip and know that the two of you are an item? No. Second, aren't elves supposed to recognize each other as mates? That didn't happen in your case?"

Slowly a grin spread over his face. "Aye. 'Tis exactly what *did* happen. Great Paddy! We're havin' a baby. I need to call my mother."

He looked at Elora's face, expecting to see a mirror of the elation bubbling up in him. What he saw instead was hurt and betrayal battling with anger for emotional supremacy. That was when he realized he had dug himself into a bottomless pit of excrement with his own stupidity, lack of faith, and very big Irish mouth. *Great Paddy if Storm wasn't right. I am an imbecile.*

"Elora," he started, "I'm sorry I reacted badly. I…"

She stopped him cold with a look, slid off the bed, and walked out without turning back. When he let himself into her apartment a little later, she simply said, "Get out." And slammed the bedroom door closed.

After twenty-four hours of refusing to talk to him, Ram went to Kay and pleaded with him to intercede.

"She'll listen to you. She always has."

With time and finesse Kay did successfully mediate a treaty between the two, stipulating that Elora would forgive Ram conditionally on the promise that he would never doubt anything she said again, no matter how unlikely or improbable it might seem on the surface. He gladly made that vow and she knew he would keep it because, with all his faults, he was an elf of honor.

That settled, Elora allowed herself to relax between bouts of morning sickness. Steeping in the glow of Ram's delight she began to find it contagious.

He could not have been happier. There was to be a little one on the way, a miracle whose mother was strong, brave, smart, beautiful... and his.

As an added benefit, there was to be no more worry about the fickle nature of humans. In hindsight he wondered how he had missed the signs that had been there all along. She was elf. His other half. They were rightly and truly mated and no obstacle could ever be formidable enough to threaten the happily ever after that was his now his life's mission.

———

ALSO BY VICTORIA DANANN

THE KNIGHTS OF BLACK SWAN

Knights of Black Swan 1. My Familiar Stranger

Knights of Black Swan 2. The Witch's Dream

Knights of Black Swan 3. A Summoner's Tale

Knights of Black Swan 4. Moonlight

Knights of Black Swan 5. Gathering Storm

Knights of Black Swan 6. A Tale of Two Kingdoms

Knights of Black Swan 7. Solomon's Sieve

An Order of the Black Swan Novel Prince of Demons

Knights of Black Swan 8. Vampire Hunter

Knights of Black Swan 9. Journey Man

Knights of Black Swan 10. Finngarick

BLACK SWAN, NEXT GENERATION

KBS, Next Generation 1. FALCON

KBS, Next Generation 2. JAX

KBS, Next Generation 3. BATISTE: Reliance

BLACK SWAN D.I.T. (Dept. of Interdimensional Trespass)

D.I.T. 1. *The Wild Hunt*

THE HYBRIDS

Exiled 1. CARNAL

Exiled 2. CRAVE

Exiled 3. CHARMING

THE WEREWOLVES

New Scotia Pack 1. Shield Wolf: Liulf

New Scotia Pack 2. Wolf Lover: Konochur

New Scotia Pack 3. Fire Wolf: Cinaed

CONTEMPORARY ROMANCE

Sons of Sanctuary MC, Book 1. Two Princes

Sons of Sanctuary MC, Book 2. The Biker's Brother

Sons of Sanctuary MC, Book 3. Nomad

TEEN & YOUNG ADULT FANTASY

R. Caine High School, Book 1. The Game Begins: An
   Introduction

R. Caine High School, Book 2. The Knight.

Links to all Victoria's books can be found here...

www.VictoriaDanann.com

I sincerely hope you enjoyed reading

My Familiar Stranger.

Reviews are enormously helpful to me. Please follow take
the time to follow a link back to the book you've just read
and post your thoughts. A few words is often as powerful
as many.

Victoria Danann

NEW YORK TIMES and USA TODAY BESTSELLING AUTHOR

SUBSCRIBE TO MY MAIL LIST Be first to know…:

http://eepurl.com/wRE3T

Victoria's Website:

www.victoriadanann.com

Victoria's Facebook Page:

facebook.com/victoriadanannbooks

Twitter:

twitter.com/vdanann

Pinterest:

pinterest.com/vdanann

Co-host ROMANCE BETWEEN THE PAGES Podcast

www.RomanceCast.com

On Itunes

http://apple.co/2fhRrOE

JOIN MY NEWS LIST AND GET THE SECOND BOOK

IN THE SERIES FOR FREE.

http://eepurl.com/cL9TEH

I send email only for new release announcements.